Library of Congress Number: 83-083075

International Standard Book Number: 0-932966-51-9

Manufactured in the United States of America

THE PERMANENT PRESS
RD 2 Noyac Road, Sag Harbor, N.Y. 11963

Sections of this novel, in considerably different form, have
appeared in two issues of *Response* and in *Junction*.

*To my parents, for
my first words, and
to Jonathan Baumbach,
for these words.*

There are four sources of all damage; they are the ox, the pit, tooth, and fire.

(Mishnah: First Gate)

I

Four are haughty, the foremost the ox . . .

(Talmud)

1.

Father felt shortchanged by winter. He loved the long, dark, Friday evenings when the enforced idleness of the Sabbath enabled him to spread the awkward pages of the *New York Times* fully open on the kitchen table and read them slowly, without interruption from ringing phones or doorbells. But he hated to pay for this leisure with the shortness of the afternoon. Though he worked nearby, at *Landau Clothes* on Nostrand Avenue, he would rush into the house barely ahead of candle lighting, head straight for the bathroom, wash in cold water, and walk out fully dressed in the clothes my mother had prepared inside. By the time he would emerge, brushing away with toilet paper water spots from shoes I had shined, my mother and I would be standing as if awaiting inspection. She, with her hair bound, though I had memories of her with her hair loose, and I: suited, necktied, hatted, especially hatted, the brim extending to the tip of my nose, a complete little man, in uniform for prayer.

After my mother's arms would usher in the Sabbath, Father would nod. When he and I would return from evening prayers at the synagogue of the Rabbi from Debrecen (transplanted to Crown Heights all the way from Hungary), he would bless the wine, wash his hands, bless the bread, sing the songs, and give his thanks. And after all that was done and his displeasure with the hurly-burly of Friday had abated, he would finally speak to me directly. "And what did you learn in school this week, Yaakov?"

"The sacrifices."

"All right. Which parts are burned?"

"The head, the fat, the stomach, and the knees."

"Of which animals?"

7

"Of all except the fowl."

"And the first act of the priest?"

"Sprays the blood around the altar?"

But no, that was not the answer. He looked at me, reached out, put a hand on my head. I shivered with pleasure though I missed the cushion of my recently cut hair. Again he asked.

"The first act of the priest?"

"Slaughters the animal?"

The hand on my head squeezed. And I finally understood that the hand was offering a hint, not love.

"The priest places the hand of the one bringing the offering on the head of the animal."

That was it. The grip relaxed. He waved his hand and released me from the table. And if I gave the wrong answer, more laying on of hands, the punishment of the priest heavy on the head and shoulders of the sinner. That has been the way since I was nine, when Father stopped going on the road, went to work for Mr. Landau (now 3L Clothiers), gave me a baldie haircut with his own hands, and sent me to my first *yeshiva*. My days filled suddenly with a teacher we called *Rebbie*, who had a flowing untrimmed beard that seemed to grow out of his cheekbones and who strode up and down the classroom with a broken chair leg in hand, chanting phrases we fearfully repeated. Our Saturdays began to conform to Orthodox regulations, and the Sabbath table became the altar where each Friday night I would be a sin-offering, or a guilt-offering, or a peace offering.

Not much had changed in fifteen years. On the night of Rachel's housewarming, all my preparations were for Father's Sabbath, not Rachel's party. Back from synagogue, I waited for Father to make the blessing over the wine. Clear plastic protected the tablecloth from spills. The only light was from the long white candles in the five branched silver candelabra, each candle a light for life: one each for the happily wedded mother and father, one for the single offspring, and one more for each of them, to commemorate the miraculous event in their lives—their survival of the years 1944 and 1945—my mother living through Bergen-Belsen and Father the hazards of a forced labor gang that built roads and delivered bread to the Hungarian Army on the Eastern Front.

Neatly arranged on the table were the twisted loaves, the salt, the wine, the tiny basin for the washing of hands before grace.

Also neatly put together, my mother. I was not insensible to her Friday night appearances. From severely tied kerchiefs at the beginning of Father's return home, she had over the years progressed to a stylish short wig close enough to her own hair in color so that she could comb the two together and make them blend perfectly. Her skin dark, her blouse white, she glowed in the candles' light. It had disappointed me, over the years, seeing her gradually surrender to the festivity of Father's Sabbath. I tried reassuring myself that there were still remnants of rebellion in the blunt ankle socks she filched from my drawer and wore to the Sabbath table on long winter nights, but knew her to be cold in the feet, could reluctantly even remember her instep being rubbed by Father's supple fingers on those Friday nights when it was his rare presence rather than the Sabbath that we used to welcome to the house.

While Father recited the blessing over the wine, I lounged against the wall, unobtrusively showing rebellion with hands in pocket. Done, amen, he sat and drank, deftly slurping from the full-bellied cup. He handed it to my mother who poured some of the wine into my water glass, then drank from Father's cup directly.

Father watched me. "It's not poisoned just because I drank from it."

My mother answered him. "I have a cold."

When he has a cold, he doesn't pour wine off for my mother or me before drinking. Her libation to me irks him. He would not mind her not drinking. He minds only her protectiveness.

In order, we lined up at the kitchen sink for the ritual washing. Quickly Father was back at the table, impatiently tapping at the Sabbath loaves with the ceremonial knife while my mother was still drying her hands and I was just filling the big-eared silver cup. Though I was as anxious to proceed as he, I could not resist forcing him to wait. I let the water rise to the brim and poured three times left and three times right, precisely as prescribed, but avoided the water and my mother's fingers when I took the towel from her. The phantom washing was another little victory. Towel in hand, I

9

caught my lips moving in silent prayer, a *yeshiva* boy's reflex. Walking slowly back into the room, I kept Father from saying the blessing a moment longer.

Across town, eyes bright, Rachel hums a welcome song, dims lights, piles food high, showers, stretches, smiles, lights short, fat, perfumed candles, blesses the night.

Spooning his soup, Father joked. "This isn't soup with noodles, this is noodles with soup. It's a good thing you found another Hungarian. A *Polisher* would have divorced your soup a long time ago." He had said this before, but I no longer formulated lines my mother should have spoken to him. As if sensing my impending rush from the house and the loss of sympathetic listener, she said, "The way you are eating, it is clear you have made a happy marriage." And turning to me, "You look handsome tonight, Jason."

I wanted to pull my head into my collar and probably would have managed without the constraining necktie. But even if I had managed to hide, my little skullcap would have stuck out on top and remained as the lightning rod between Father's thunder and my mother's flashes of electricity. "At least at the Sabbath table call him Yaakov," Father said, keeping his eyes on his plate but keeping his target clearly in sight.

"The way you are eating, it is clearly in honor of the Sabbath rather than for your own pleasure. Your eagerness to please God is admirable but he prefers his sacrifices be offered with more patience and less passion."

My mother reached across the table and touched my sleeve. "It might go down the wrong pipe."

"Carelessness," Father said, "is the disease of the young. Older people are more sensible. They look before they cross. They're not in such a big hurry. They chew more slowly. That's how they survive."

He wiped his lips daintily with a blue paper napkin, leaving the white cloth napkin untouched on his lap. There are as many years between my mother and father as there are between my mother and me. Everything that is mine should have come to me by way of her. She should have been filter and transformer. In the dim light of the candles I could concentrate on his thinning beard and hair, his big, black skullcap, the whisper of Europe in his voice. I could deny any part of him in my thick hair, neat sideburns, and small, knitted skullcap. But how to avoid the insistence at other times of the blueness of my eyes, my fallen arches, and the crease lines faint in my cheeks that correspond to the places on his face where flesh has been creviced? My brown-eyed mother seemed to have transmitted on to me Father's characteristics without leavening them.

Gathering the plates, my mother said, "Mrs. Hartstein is in the hospital, don't forget to ask her husband in *shul* tomorrow how she is."

"She choked," I said.

Father stared. "What are you talking about? A heart attack, no?"

"Yes," my mother said.

"Well, she is not so young but she doesn't take care of herself." Reassured, he leaned back. "You should know, the ones who survived in the labor gangs were not the strong ones and not the wiseguys. They were the ones who paid attention to little details, like clean fingernails, and brushing their teeth, and keeping dirt from between their toes. So that afterwards, instead of saying 'Thank God I made it,' they would wake up in the morning and kiss their own hand and say 'Thank you, sir, you did it.' "

My mother placed the large plate of cooked chicken and beef in front of us, the fatty piece Father preferred within his easy reach.

"Everyone needs a hand to kiss afterwards, if not his own, someone else's," my mother said.

"Your son," Father said heavily, "has not kissed my hand in fifteen years, even though I know very well that his friend Dov, not to mention that other one, still does so after his father blesses him."

"You don't bless him," my mother said.

"He runs away. I get home too late. Anyway, with that dime-sized cap on his head, what's the point?"

I wanted to urge them on with the meal. I told myself that if the patient being dissected walked away from the table, perhaps the operation would end, but knew that the scalpels would be turned on each other, more directly, more accurately, but perhaps more quietly. No need for the whole street to hear arguments in a foreign language. Eager for time with Rachel, I decided to please and began to chant the songs of the evening. Unbidden, I alternated tunes that Father had once taught me with melodies my mother used to hum. I sang "Peace and Happiness," followed it by "God the Ruler," closed with "This Day for the Israelites," quieting them both into the silence that passes for peace in my house. Final Grace was thus a swift, soft affair. Pacing my excitement, I cleared the table and swept it clear of crumbs. It was nearing ten when I was done. I still had an hour's secret trip ahead of me.

In the darkness of my room (the only lights on the Sabbath come from the candles and the kitchen light plugged into a time clock), I prepared to leave by slowly transforming myself from an observant, religious boy to a sinner and transgressor, a violator of the Sabbath laws that prescribe an absolute day of rest, forbidding the clicking of lights, the riding in cars, the carrying of items, the doing of anything remotely resembling work. But determined, I folded a five dollar bill smoothly inside my underwear, wondering where a wearer of boxer shorts hides his pieces of silver. Then I rid myself of the last vestiges of the Sabbath by shucking my necktie and my suit jacket and opening the collar of my shirt. A blind swipe at my hair with a brush (combs are forbidden), and I was ready for Rachel, though my skullcap had to stay on for a while, to serve as my passport through Orthodox territory.

Back in the kitchen, way station to the front door and back bedroom, I found them both waiting. Though the props were in place—Father was holding his *Times* and my mother a dishtowel—it was clear that the mellowness my singing had induced had dissipated.

"Tell him," Father said, "that I am locking the front door at twelve."

"If he takes the tie clip," my mother said, "it won't matter what you do. Let him meet his friends in peace."

"Of course, of course, naturally, and why not? He needs his peace. Isn't there a war on after all? Let him go with all the other fine gentlemen and scholars from the best *yeshivas* in town that cost their fathers more than an arm and a leg, let him go to Eastern Parkway and watch the girls. Why not? He is past eighteen, isn't he?"

12

"Take the clip," my mother said.

"Put a tie on," Father ordered, "or you can't take it."

From the shelf above the sink I took the family Sabbath key. It consisted of a key soldered onto the clasp of a tie clip. The key by itself may not be carried outside the house on the Sabbath. But fastened to the clasp and attached to the necktie, it becomes a piece of jewelry and hence permissible to wear even on the Sabbath. Decorating my tie, the house key becomes mobile, the perfect combination of Orthodox necessity and Yankee ingenuity. But I did have to put my necktie back on.

Leaving the room, I could hear my mother say, "I suppose at his age you sat at the feet of the Rebbe Friday night and prayed."

"At his age," Father grumbled, his newspaper rustling, "I was looking to make a good *shiduch*."

"Maybe," my mother said, always sensitive to my expectations, "he's looking for a wife too."

I had a long way to go and I was late. Their exchanges were familiar, just another of the many Friday night rituals. I was looking to get away from such ceremonies. A large part of my journey had to be on foot, pioneer style, through hostile Orthodox Crown Heights, where I had to remain on my best religious behavior. Worse, it was Friday night, the most dangerous night of the week to be abroad, an evening bedeviled by demons celebrating their own birth, an unhealthy night, when God allows the rains to fall, expecting all observant Jews to be indoors, a holy night also known as *mitzvah* night, when the righteous Jewish husband and wife join God in creation. But it was the night when I would be out.

My mother came after me to the door. "Have a nice time," she whispered and suddenly kissed me. Then she offered me her cheek, but when I bent close, turned it into a bit of lips, a quick chink of warmth, one kiss, lightly. Then I was outside in the furry night, envisioning the route to Rachel's house.

2.

I had met Rachel wanting to meet her friend Sheila. On a mild Saturday night in April after the end of Passover, I was on 56th Street in Boro Park. It was a section I didn't know well, accessible from Crown Heights, my home territory, only by car. A sign stapled to the bulletin board outside the English Department offices at NYU had invited all graduate and law students to a Herzl House party. The open invitation was narrowed by the postscript: party begins two hours after the Sabbath's end. That was the subtle call of one of the Orthodox house plans at Brooklyn College.

That Saturday night after the long Passover holiday was filled with expectation. There was a sense of release in packing away the special dishes we had been using just for that week and in returning to the eating of yeast-puffed, crusty bread after the dryness of unleavened baking. Grass was beginning to sprout around the city's trees, surrounding even the saplings set in concrete squares. The Jewish calendar insists that this is a mourning period and many Orthodox Jews had already taken short haircuts to mark the time, but even with those white rings of scalp all around, hope was in the air. New smells were everywhere, daylight was beginning to stretch, the city felt ready to be delivered toward summer. It was that irresistible attraction to warmth that had me in front of one of the newer houses on the block, a flat-faced, low, brick box, its tiny garden surrounded by a chain link fence.

I had just gotten out of my car, pleased to find a spot directly in front, when I noticed Sheila walking up the narrow row of steps toward the door. From the back, she looked exceptional. Her back straight, her ass high slung, her walk carefully erect, all of her so slender and firm that I stood still,

14

cleansed of desire. Rachel was her friend at the top of the stairs. She should have been noticeable too. Even in the dim light of the streetlamp a few houses away her hair gleamed, its blackness so sleek, so rich, it seemed glazed. I should have been aware of her too because of the rough edges of that hair, obviously cut in anger and straightened indifferently, a defiant gesture by a determined girl. However, with Sheila in the foreground, Rachel and her statement were beyond my notice.

"Hey," I said softly to Jonesey, "drink deep but don't breathe," forgetting how sound and prayer carry on quiet streets on Saturday nights.

But just as I had not seen Sheila's friend, Sheila did not see Jonesey's friend. As she turned, it was Jonesey she saw and Jonesey whom she acknowledged. Behind both Jonesey and the car, I was doubly hidden.

After she went inside, Jonesey stretched his hand toward me, across the car. "Give me the keys." When I hesitated, he banged his knuckles on the metal impatiently, the noise hollow. "Come on." He looked away from me, up toward the door of the house. "Pick it up at the station tomorrow. I'll give it an oil change and nothing will be out of place. Give."

Detaching first my housekeys, I slid the ring across to him.

Come, let us learn about Jonesey Kellerman; know his freckled face, his deep laugh, the personal grease stains on the inside of his fingers, a mark of his job at the American Station near the Prospect Park tennis courts. Observe in him the confidence typical of large athletes, a strut that passes for grace and enables him to move as smoothly on the hardwood dance floors at Harlow's as he does on the cement basketball courts of Lefferts Junior High, where he is the regular Friday afternoon star.

Having met Jonesey, meet his friend, Jason Kole. For many long years this youth, this chosen one, this scholar, was known as Baldie Kole, fastest kid on President Street. Since then, through additional *yeshiva* years, he has been summoned to the Scroll and to the learning bench as Yaakov, Yaankev, Yanki, Yankele, even Yaki, and who, during Brooklyn College BA and NYU Doctor of Philosophy courses, was a.k.a. Jase and Jake. Now, disguised in trim blue double breasted sports jacket and dazzling white turtle neck, hair grown long and defiant, he fights a never ending battle with his skullcap. Having recently retired it from its prominent position on his head to an obscure backseat in his pants pocket, bareheaded Kole has declared himself ready: to ride in a car on the Sabbath, to taste forbidden foods, to move out come summer, and, finally, to get it, anytime he wants it, from Jean, the whore his buddy knows on Thirty-eighth Street. And yet, only days after this same Kole has sworn never to take the fearsome trip into Manhattan or make the perilous journey through Washington Square Park with the identifying dot of a skullcap on his head, here he is at Herzl House, wearing it. Instead of taking giant steps away from Orthodox territory, he is about to intrude on sanctified grounds, his cold-turkey withdrawal from religion more difficult than expected. That is why we can see, friends, right there on his head, making a brief return engagement by popular demand, his *yarmukah*. There are alternative spellings and explanations, but he prefers this: *yar* = fear, *mu* = from, *kah* = God.

So, the big team advancing toward Herzl House consisted of Kellerman and Kole, the third member, Dov Laufer, being unavailable, though he too has made his reservations to move out for the summer. But Dov was off in genuine Rabbi school in Boston, busy reconciling Torah spoken with Torah written, intuitive revelations with textual analysis, medieval scholars with modern critics.

I was reluctant to charge up the stairs after Sheila, and in my slowness, anticipated how I would crawl out of my house later on that summer and, like a snail, carry my home with me. With much forethought and little foreknowledge I walked blindly into a reserved Rachel.

But before stumbling in, one more bit of preparation. "Hold it," I called to Jonesey and handed him an extra skullcap from the glove compartment we called the pickle jar. "See what a hot shot you can be wearing this." Jonesey, accepting it, laughed. "The Orthodox bag. Guaranteed against pregnancy, venereal disease and contamination by *goyim*. Don't worry, I can handle the handicap. Let's move it."

At the top of the stairs, he turned. "Remind me again,

16

Rabbi-Doctor, are there any restrictions I should know about? I mean extra-ordinary ones."

"Just the usual, Yossel," I told him, "remember, these are religious girls."

"Meaning?"

"Meaning you're striking out tonight, big guy. With these girl, it's all talk. You can go out with them but you can't get in."

He knew as well as I did, having kept Dov and me company in *yeshivas* for seventeen years, the quaint concept of *negeeah*, the notion of uncleanliness and hence "touch-me-not" that begins with the first womanly flow and remains in effect all through maidenhood, until the ritual cleansing of the wedding day. But he liked to pretend he was a Know-Nothing, a boor, just plain irreligious folks. The truth was that Yossel did not look very Jewish, must less Orthodox. The skullcap lay loosely on his stiff hair, obviously an infrequent and unwelcome visitor. He had a calm, even heart that didn't scare at night or go pitter-patter to discover that some movie star's real name ended in *man*, *ski* or *witz*. That he was a mechanic and had red hair both argued against his having any kind of Jewish smarts. If he hadn't worn a Star of David, there would have been no external signs of his affiliation. Except of course when I was around to call him Yossel and to hand him a bobby pin to keep the skullcap in place.

"Now you look perfect."

"Completely *kosher*," he agreed, "fit for the most Orthodox consumption." Extending his arms and spreading his fingers above my head in the manner of priests performing benedictions, he said, "I now pronounce us religious. Let's go and multiply."

Thus blessed, I stepped inside, into unexpected brightness. Where the clear light of faith is dominant there are few dark corners, I thought, seeing the marks of religion everywhere. The living room and dining room, set aside for the restrained revelry of Herzl House, still carried traces of the recently departed Day of Rest. An embroidered *challah* cover lay forgotten on the sideboard, the positions of the silver napkin holder and goblet were disturbed in the china closet, and a decorative bowl of fruit, the typical centerpiece of the Sabbath afternoon table, had somehow remained to grace the party spread. There it sat, two knives gleaming like horns, surrounded by Wise potato chips and Educator pretzels, both acceptable by virtue of the rabbinical u on their packages. And through the arch of the kitchen I could see the flickering of the solitary *havdalah* candle, the flame that separates the holy day from the ordinary days of the week.

While I catalogued these signs of observance, singleminded Jonesey, a sexual survivor, had already located the two girls. He must have kept his eyes closed as we walked in; he had the wits of a man eager to find a seat in the sudden dark of a movie theatre and had avoided the blindness that had caught me. With the expertise of a sheepdog he split the two girls, turning the one I had not noticed toward me. "Meet my friend Jason," he said. "He's dying to know whether you're Orthodox, Conservative, Reform, or other."

"Whatever you are, I'm the other," she said, but smiled slightly, more amused, I think, by Jonesey's maneuvers than words.

"Are you?" I asked. I wanted to indicate my eagerness yet maintain a physical distance at the same time, operating under the limitations of my upbringing, which had taught me to be cautious, and my experience, which had shown me that sudden movements in the proximity of religious girls were ill-advised. So she just shrugged and stood there, and I stood there, the two of us unwillingly isolated. And maybe because we were at a religious party and in a religious household and because she looked religious with her high necked dress and ruffles at the breast, her modest earrings and careless hair, I assumed she too was religious and was determined to be insulting. "Rachel," I said to her, reading her gold name plate, "a nice, Jewish name, but why isn't it in Hebrew letters?"

"You find it confusing?"

"No. Too clear. Anyone can read it. If you come to meet *yeshiva* boys, you have to show them you're exclusive property."

I began to imagine her future, seeing a boy named Yitzchok or Zelig, or Yitzchok Zelig, a nice Jewish boy wearing a black hat and the prescribed fringes, whether he goes to the pool or the bedroom; a neat chinned boy, a believer, his face untouched by razor, his sidecurls carefully folded behind his ears. A young man, chosen for her by her father; an upstanding youth who has been carefully hoarding his well-behaved Orthodox sperm, a breeder with a good pedigree—a rabbi or two on the family tree, no intermarriage, no insanity—who would fill her with neat chinned little babies year after year, for the greater glory of God and Israel, amen. I saw her hair even shorter and hidden under a kerchief. I could not see her man kissing those full breasts hidden by the ruffles, could not even imagine him looking at them, not openly anyway, perhaps a quick peek before he crouches in the dark, his purpose (like Father's) never punctuated by play or laughter. An Orthodox fuck is very serious, I wanted to warn her.

But I was misunderstood. She thought I was flaunting religion instead of rebellion. "Then it's perfect," she said. "I wore it just to make sure I wouldn't meet such exclusive people."

"Hey," I said, "good for you! I'm not a fanatic either," and reached to touch her sleeve, understanding finally she would not jump away.

"Good for *you*," she said, "I'll keep your secret," and quickly walked away, leaving my hand hanging. As she walked into the kitchen I heard Jonesey's girl call after her. "Rae," I thought it was, but that call didn't bring her back either. She walked through the kitchen and out a back door.

By the time I turned back to Jonesey, he was gone, the girl with the high-slung ass missing with him. Outside, I found my car gone too, and as I stood there, empty in that evening filled with spring smells, I imagined him flush in her, in my car. Still not having seen her face, he had by now pulled her panties softly down (Yossel smooth as silk in the clutch), and somehow circumventing all precedents and traditions of Orthodox girls, he was managing his own moon landing, months ahead of the NASA schedule.

I walked down to Thirteenth Avenue for a kosher pizza and from there took a taxi home. Once back inside the silence of my house (everyone asleep, the Sabbath tiring the whole family), I made myself promise to call Rae or Rachel, even if I had to depend on Jonesey's generosity to establish the first connection.

3.

Why the big excitement, right? Just a girl, after all, and a self-contained one at that. So why the determination?

Simple. If Portnoy had grown up Orthodox, he would never have yearned after Gentile women. In the great chain of desire that has icy midwestern blondes at the pinnacle, *yeshiva* boys resting on dark metal benches in the house of study breathe after the lower delights of *yeshiva* girls. Above those girls (and beyond the reach of most *yeshiva* boys), are the wonders of the irreligious Jewish girls. Beyond them, I cannot even imagine. For us, the season used to open on the first day of Passover. *Yeshiva* boys all, we would parade down Eastern Parkway in our new suits and admire *Yeshiva* girls, on display in light summer dresses, shivering in the cool April air, as goose pimples ran up their thighs to exotic and far away places.

I remember the stately, silent courtships of those early days. On one bench, girls. On the other, boys. Backs to each other, careless attitudes. Within our own camp there was much discussion. "Did you know that Helen Feldman has started going out for serious?" Dov says, his mandatory hat pushed off his forehead to reveal a chunk of hair, his side curls dipping modestly behind his ears.

We were real throwbacks, we were nobles, we were the knights of the post-Holocaust generation. We adored from afar and did not touch. From across the wide length of Eastern Parkway we worshipped the virgins in white graduation dresses and speculated darkly about the young marrieds entering the ground floor Lubavitcher Synagogue.

"You think the Chassidim have it better?" I ask Dov as we follow Malkie Kalman nèe Rabinowitz swirling down Kings-

20

ton Avenue after an audience with the Lubavitcher Rebbie, the same Malkie who used to fry our brains with her lightly blown dress but who, on Passover Day One, newly wedded and bedded, hatted husband in respectful attendance, has switched into an insanely tight brown outfit and a styled blonde wig and who, concealed somewhere on her precious body, carries the full blessings of the Rebbe, aye, even to the laying on of hands.

So, from beyond the wooden park benches that lined the Parkway, we flashed our meager charms. We were armored in sharkskin suits and snappy hats, and made eligible by virtue of our *yeshiva* background. Oh, the names of those places. The Place of Woven Spices. The Gates of Righteousness. The Seekers of the Law. Where the Lion Cub Rests. We wore our hats pushed back from our foreheads, bought stovepipe pants, wore our irridescent suits with flair, and wooed the ladies from The House of Jacob, The House of Rivka, The House of Leah, The Esther Schoenfeld School for Young Women. But we wanted no more than a smile or a greeting while we were on Eastern Parkway. A five minute talk in the public eye suggests an engagement, an hour's conversation assures a match.

Away from the Parkway we managed occasional dates with those Promenade Parkway girls, managed without the machinations of that old Merlin of a Lubavitcher Rebbie. But there were so many difficulties in the way. Paper and pencil were *muktzah*, consigned to weekday use, the phone itself unusable, even the very idea of asking someone for a date on Eastern Parkway, on Passover, in daylight, seemed somehow indecorous and perhaps in violation of the day's holiness. The associations wrecked the dates. The magic circle of inviolability continued to protect the girls.

There were occasional successes, even with those girls. The trick was to use the wonderful logic of the religious education that we shared. Persuade them to make the first transgression, stressing how meaningless it is, then having seduced them into the first breach, convince them of its enormity, make clear that all was now lost, the imperfection permanent, further infraction immaterial, so great the punishment for the first. And the first sin was the decision to touch. Once the Orthodox girl has permitted the very first touch, kiss, caress,

21

the only other boundary is the loss of virginity. But between those perimeters, ah, within those borders, the Paradise of the semi-Righteous. What one can accomplish without the cherry in the center of the chocolate! My triumphs then, within the unknown territory of slightly tarnished *yeshiva* girls: Monica Schwartz, nipple freak, lying against the front seat of the car (Jonesey wrestling in the back), and letting me touch anywhere I wanted to but with no more than two fingers and only from unusual angles; Sarah, accepting by way of ultimate giving the pressure of her fully dressed torso painfully against unzipped mine; and finally, Hand Job Haddie, the fastest wrist in town, most supple fingers, most angelic smile, who had an intriguing combination of strength, frequency, and sound, and who could often be found, her wrists puffy with frothy sleeves, taking on all comers in the locked section of the Student Center, alternating left hand and right without loss of tensile grip or time, oh girl of ambidextrous delights.

But one more encounter, at once the most elaborate and the most limited, a perfect instance of the wide valley of availability within the mountains of Orthodox constraint. I had been dating Tamar Jurowitz for weeks of Saturday nights, progressing from tight-lipped good night kisses to open mouthed samplings, but seemed to have settled in and around Tamar's pliant lips, leaving our hands and bodies under-utilized, not unreasonably, I thought, since her face and hair were her glory while the rest of her was not only off limits but also invisible, her breasts so tiny they would get lost in the slightest wrinkle of her blouse. Further down than that was not even an issue; where her legs came together under her skirt might as well have been the moon. But when I called her one night, she asked me over for the next afternoon, a work day. She would be staying home, she explained. Just a slight cold. Would I want to risk catching it? I would. My preparations for her were frenzied yet controlled. I made sure to wear clean underwear but did not bother with anything like prophylactics. You see, while I could not know beforehand exactly what we would be doing (or where), I could rest assured about what we would not be doing. Not with Tamar. Not with a *yeshiva* girl. TJ was in P.J.'s when I arrived, her hair freshly washed, allowed to dry loose but brushed shiny in thick brown sheaves. I followed her to her parents' bedroom, where she got under the covers, pulling them up to her chin. "We have an hour," she said, all brown eyes and hair and anticipation, "I want to try things, just remember you can't, you know." I undressed in a hurry—it was one of those fall afternoons before the heat is turned on—and got in next to her, making sure both hands and body were under the covers. We began to kiss, TJ sucking at my tongue and burrowing against my teeth, so I squirmed quickly between her legs and reached under her pajama top to slide upwards. She parted her legs but grabbed my arms and said, "You can't touch there, Jason, you can't, promise me you won't." I abandoned her breasts, why not, there was firm skin elsewhere, and reversed direction, where I discovered the route clear and posted, finding such slickness and openness that I leaped with both hands. At which point she stopped me again and said, "No, no, we'll stain the sheets," but by way of apology, remembered her hands were under the blankets and reaching inside my shorts, began to yank and rub wildly. But this is the delight of restriction; every other place is available. In a moment of inspiration, I stayed inside her pajama bottoms but reached around her and under her, cupping the moistness seeping down her thighs and making her frothy all over, but safely against the doubleweave absorbency of our clothing. But when I moved upward and grabbed her ass, I startled a gasp out of her, a tune beyond my ken, and to the background of the Beach Boys' "Let's Do It Again," she thrust mindlessly while I came and came and came, leaving us both sticky, hot, and exhausted, but fully triumphant, having maintained our virginity even while exploring hitherto unattempted territories.

Although very pleased with one another and grateful, there was also the awareness between us that the areas we had charted with fingers would not be surveyed by our mouths, at least not with each other, and that her tiny breasts above and source of liquification below would be preserved for still another, in a recurring state of purity. Such is the way of the modern, slightly-lapsed, slightly-breached Orthodox girl, waiting for her Chosen: the natural resources not yet mined but the boundaries clearly marked.

That is why the possibility of a girl like Rachel justified the excitement. Because a girl without the pathways of Eastern Parkway in her past, a girl with perhaps her own place, her own bed, her own hours, her own very good time, is a girl unknown. That was why the next day, postponing *yeshiva*, I was at Jonesey's service station. "I want her friend's number," I demanded, stalling his recital of adventures.

He smiled. "Hey, hey, Kole." I had interrupted him at work on my car. I asked no questions and he pretended I had already given him instructions for repairs. He moved to flip the hood of the Lancer up and I moved out of the way, unwilling to soil my crisp and clean shirt and slacks, the uniform of the *yeshiva* boy. Because I had started out in the morning heading for seminary school, I still had my skullcap though it was folded in my back pocket. Not entirely comfortable with the freedom of my hair, I looked around often, on the watch for familiar faces. The gas station was not that far out of Crown Heights. I could have had that beanie on my head faster than Superman his wide-rimmed glasses, the shade of my palm serving in a pinch for a phone booth's disguise.

He put his head under the hood. The morning sun jumped off the car's blunted nose. "I changed the oil like I promised and threw in a filter. The Yossel delivers."

I didn't thank him. It was his payment for the use of the car, the flattened seat in the back my punishment for accepting payment although no one could ever accuse me of usury. He came around and began pumping gas. "The extra *yammie* is back in the pickle jar. Did your old man grab you when you came in?"

"Everybody was sleeping."

He grinned at me. "I wasn't."

"Give me Sheila's number," I finally said, watching the meter roll.

"She's busy."

"That's all right. I just want her for her friend's number."

He whisked away the hose without dripping on the car, replaced the tank cap with a flourish. Then he came to stand in front of me. "You're sure?" I nodded. He took a piece of paper from his pocket. "Here." I felt myself flush taking it from him. "Call late," he said, "she works at Berkey's. Art pictures."

Looking at the paper I saw the name "Rachel," and a phone

number. "The Yossel delivers," Jonesey said, hugging himself. "And listen. Some people call her Rachel and others call her Rae but her parents only call her long distance, from Florida." Clapping me on the back, he sent me on my way. "I got the one with the ass but you, boychick, you got the one with the apartment."

I should explain that my devotion to the Rabbi's Academy is circumstantial. While I was an undergraduate at Brooklyn College, that Yale of Flatbush Avenue, that educator of the future diamond merchants of 47th Street, I was a full-time student and thus exempt from the draft. But, ever cautious after hearing Father's stories of eighteen year olds in the Old Country who lopped fingers off rather than be drafted into military service, I decided that double protection was safer and registered in a DD Yeshiva. Interpret that as either Doctor of Divinity or Draft Dodger. So, when I got a graduate fellowship to NYU, the Jewish Columbia, but lost my student deferment, there was good old Yeshiva of the Fellowship of Learners, the sanitary prophylactic that kept the diseased love of my local Draft Board at a safe distance.

Williamsburg, location of *Chassidic* yeshivas, had been abandoned by the more enlightened and wealthier Jews and left to the poorer Chassidim. Rabbi Baumel, an unaffiliated disciple, had left Williamsburg and converted the basement and first floor of his attached row house on Empire Boulevard into a training school for Rabbis. Unfortunately for him, instead of attracting *iluim* or geniuses from other schools, he was approached by indifferent scholars interested in the protection of the Sacred Word not its exegesis. Adapting adroitly, he raised tuitions and arranged flexible hours to accommodate the grad students, the businessmen, the accountants and the commercial artists, anyone whose eligibility to the Draft had brought about a sudden yearning for religious revelation.

Windowless on both sides, the long rooms like a tunnel, obscured by an apartment house in the back, Rabbi Baumel's Emporium provided fifteen hours of assorted courses a week for Sammy Schneider junior accountant at Harmon and Seligman, Chinky Chatrowitz apprentice printer, four part-time undergrads at City College who worked in their fathers'

25

stores during the day, five more from Brooklyn College's night school who did not work for their fathers, and a sprinkling of grad students from NYU and City Colleges, including one in political science, one in American Literature, two in Industrial Psychology and one, Simcha Weiss, the only student with a goatee, who was in Fine Arts at the New School but had refused to disclose whether he was sculpting, painting, tracing or carving, though we checked carefully his fingernails and unfashionable pants' cuffs for any clues.

Each semester, after registering for courses at NYU, I would sit down with Rabbi Baumel in his second floor dinette area and arrange my hours for *yeshiva*. The only real area of disagreement was about legal and local holidays. Jewish holidays, of course, meant school was closed but Rabbi Baumel, more and more elegant with each term, the tails of his gray Prince Albert coat peeping through the back of his kitchen chair, argued for make-up days on Columbus Day, Memorial Day, Martin Luther King's birthday, Brooklyn Day, Flag Day, Labor Day, Election Day.

We lost out on Brooklyn Day and Flag Day, won on Martin Luther King by appealing to common cause. Since it was April and close to Shakespeare's birthdate, I felt entitled to an unscheduled holiday. True, I was in American Lit, not British, but homage must be paid. Anyway, with Hawthorne born on July 4th, I was losing out on a celebration. In any case, to appease the spirit of the Yeshiva, I promised myself I would observe the Fast Day of the obscure Gedalia, come new year.

In the front room, Rabbi Baumel's cousin, a Latvian refugee with a literary Yiddish vocabulary, was teaching the *Tractate Sanhedrin*. The Fine Arts major was there along with one of the accountants and all of the Brooklyn College undergraduates. I waved to Chinky the printer who had offered me a discount if I wanted printed announcements of my flight from Orthodoxy. "A ripped yammie in a field of flowered panties, surrounded by a simple black border."

I headed for the second room that corresponded to the dining room area of the apartment one floor above. Unlike college classrooms that are modeled after the neat pews of a church, the seating plan here was haphazard. Slanted study

26

benches were scattered around the room, their arrangement vaguely reminiscent of the circular seating around the lectern unearthed in the synagogues of the Jews of Spain and Morocco. It was in there that Rabbi Baumel delivered lectures from different and off-center places.

Ten people were there by the time I arrived, a half hour late. I slipped into a seat under the outsized painting of the Wailing Wall, between Arnie Moskowitz, a computer technician who attended only once a week and paid twice as much tuition as everyone else, and Mickey Wiener, an Accounting major at Brooklyn. Mickey winked, pulled a deck of cards halfway out of his pocket. I nodded. I saw him getting Arnie's attention. Across the room Rabbi Baumel's idiot nephew was taking notes. Mickey claimed it was on us but I doubted it.

"The Jew was first known as the Hebrew, which in the Holy Tongue is *Ivri*. How *Ivri*? From the word *ayver,* or side. From which we learn that the Jew must be prepared to stand alone, *on one side,* because the rest of the world stands on the other."

Lazily Mickey raised his hand. "Is that all Jews, Rabbi Baumel, or is there a special spot in the corner for Reform Jews?"

"A Jew is a Jew because those that are not Jews say he is. Is that satisfactory, Mr. Wiener?"

"OK by me," Mickey shrugged.

During the break, Jewish History ended, Code of Laws next, Arnie, Mickey and I pulled our seats together and played poker, Arnie keeping score. Mickey, shuffling, was filled with news.

"Baumel has a new secretary."

"So?"

"So? I dated her once. My sister fixed me up."

"Esther Schoenfeld girl?"

"Yeah. The East Side crowd. She gives."

"What?"

"Dry humps. What do you think? She won't even let you open your zipper and it hurts like hell, but you know, she lets you come."

"No shit."

"Yeah. I think Baumel gooses her in the office."

27

Arnie, an occasional visitor but a frequent winner, showed a full house. "Boat," he announced, carefully putting plus and minus numbers on his scorecard. "You guys aren't concentrating. You know about the dog that had the train run over his tail?"

We waited. Arnie grinned. "He turned to look and the train chopped his head off. The moral of the story is, you follow tail and you lose your head."

Mickey dealt the cards. "Weitzman party Saturday night. You going?" I shook my head. I had three aces. "What about Yossel?" I told him he was booked. Mickey was ready to abandon the game. "Action?" I told him I would let him know and raised. Mickey dropped and Arnie won with a flush. Rabbi Baumel came back in and helped his nephew distribute copies of the Code of Laws. "First verse. Laws of mixing. The ass and the cow."

These, then, were the pillars of my Temple and the fence-posts of my sanctuary. While Jonesey remains safe, draft exempt by a cyst he delights to describe as "a pain in the ass," I prick myself sore on the thorns and thistles of Torah, forced into its unwilling embrace by that unbeatable combo, Father God and Uncle Sam. A blessed family portrait. Though not interested in Gentile converts, the Law allows Jews that have lapsed to be returned kicking and screaming, even beaten until they holler, "I want! I want!"

I went to phone from my room, hoping for the good omen of Rachel responding to the first ring.

Though using the extension, I was also hoping for privacy. My room was in the back of the house, far away from the kitchen and living room where my parents spent their evenings. The two windows faced the blank wall of Ernie's Automative on New York Avenue. The back porch opened from my room, but because of Ernie's brick curtain, my room was always in a cozy semi-darkness. On cloudy days I would lose any sense of time, until reminded of it by the piercing bell of the Elementary School on Montgomery Street. My desk was behind the door, keeping it from opening fully and setting up both a barrier and an early warning system for visitors. I had arranged my trundle bed with its drab olive cover alongside the desk in the rectangular room so that I could spin right off the squeaky plastic seat of the second-hand swivel chair and flop on the bed. The metal bookcases would vibrate to the sound of the Nostrand Avenue bus heading toward Williamsburg but the paperbacks on the shelves and faded gold carpeting left behind by the previous owners did their best to absorb the noises I would make inside the room. I kept the hinges of the door well oiled so that it would click closed at my lightest touch.

The Levins upstairs in the two family house made no sounds in their old, slippered feet. Even their visiting grandchildren had to take their shoes off as soon as they arrived. On mild evenings my parents would sit on the curved porch in the front, as far away from me as possible. Below me, the basement was silent, left unfurnished because Father refused to surround himself as in a sandwich with tenants above and below. All it had was a dusty ping pong table on which Father and the Levins kept their boxes of Passover dishes. Eventually, perhaps when he retired, Father planned to set up a workroom down there and buy a factory sewing machine instead of the portable one upstairs.

Although I left the door to my room slightly ajar to forestall Father's fury with closed doors, I could not avoid interruption. I had made myself comfortable on my couch-bed and found his face in ascendence above me. The unusual position enabled me to find a calm center in the midst of his anger. I could see him from below in new ways: his veined neck, the ineffectual beard that never thickened, the pale blue eyes I have inherited. I had the vision of those light blue genes of his hunting down the recessive blue hidden beneath my mother's browns.

"You were not in *shul* this morning."

"I was in a rush. Did I miss anything?"

"Tomorrow," he said heavily, "don't rush. I want you to learn for my father. It doesn't matter what as long as it's a Jewish word. Even if you do it in English." And unnecessarily added, "It's his *yahrzeit*."

The word means "time of year," or anniversary, specifically, of a death. The weeks after Passover are filled with such commemorations. In addition to the days of the Omer which mark the progress of the plague among the disciples of Rabbi Akiba, there are dates that have been set aside in

29

memory of the concentration camp deaths, particularly the uncharted, hectic cremation during the final days. The tiny bulbs in the memorial tablets set ablaze synagogue walls, while homes are filled with the flicker of the 24 hour candles in their thick glass. My grandfather disappeared during the First War. Though his death was never confirmed, Father eventually began to say Kaddish for him. The four glasses burning in the kitchen combined my grandfather's memorium with the vanishing Jews' memories. Bergen-Belsen, Bor, Buchenwald, Grandfather. I don't know who else my mother and Father recall. They are silent on the score though they maintain a silent vigil at the scoreboard. Studying in the name of the dead adds the sound of prayer to the sight.

"Are you sure you want me to learn? You never thought my dedication to studies was very genuine. Or deep."

Suddenly my mother was in the room, her apron swirling, as if she would shoo him from the room. "Please, Mordecai, the meal is ready. Go wash, please."

Sensing collusion, Father laughed a harsh noise. " 'Send away the mother before you remove the fledgling, so that you may lengthen your days on this earth,' " he quoted. "Study the passage, my learned son, understand it."

He knew well enough that I was protected by my mother no less than by my attendance in Yeshiva. I could work toward the office of Rabbi and never hope to reach it, but by studying for it, kept the Army from clothing me in green. And as long as I remained at home, my mother would help camouflage me in the leaf and vine of her presence.

"I'll learn," I said, and they left. Pushing the door three-quarters close, a small gesture of assertion that still allowed words to be heard if they wanted to listen in, I gathered myself to call. This one for you, Rachel, girl with my mother's name, girl of many spices and fragrances, girl with ruffled breasts, above all, girl with her own apartment. A prayer for you. As I dialed, I could hear Father's voice float in. "Good. Even the prayers of someone like you will be heard above."

She picked the phone up on the fourth ring. Having grown

up in apartments never more than three rings large, I would have hung up but I knew nothing about this one and waited out the fourth ring. I tried to speak very calmly.

"This is the guy from the party. Jason. No one introduced us. I couldn't apologize while I was still a stranger. Remember me?"

"Sure," she said, "the token *anti-semitnik* at every Herzl party."

"Oh," I said, surprised at the word, "if you've been talking to Father I know it's hopeless."

"It's hopeless and I don't even know your father."

It wasn't going well but she hadn't hung up. "Listen," I said, "can't we pretend the party never happened? It's a blind date. Your friend gave your number to my friend. She told him you're fantastic, he told her I'm brilliant, neither of us believes the other but we're going to give it a shot for their sake, because they're such wonderful kids and just starting out and we don't want to do anything to mess it up for them since it may be the start of something big. For them, OK? We won't think of ourselves. We're going to be unselfish. What do you say?"

I would find out that Rachel thought quickly but silently. Not knowing it, I simply waited, disappointed but unwilling to break the connection though the phone was barely breathing. "I've got references," I said, then stopped altogether.

"Actually," she finally said, her voice calm, "your buddy already gave me references. Only he seemed to be putting himself up for grabs, not you."

"Jonesey?" I said, recalling vividly Sheila walking up the stairs, "I don't think so."

"I could have been wrong."

"Would you have?" I couldn't resist.

"Freckles like his bring on this uncontrollable urge in me to connect them with a felt tip pen. Anyway, Sheila saw him first and it was her houseplan, so she gets him. Those are the rules. Thank goodness."

"In that case," I suggested carefully, "why not consider a guy without any freckles in the family, going back three generations."

"You?"

31

"Sure."

"All right," she said decisively, "let's meet. Are you in the mood?"

The boldness of liberated Jewish girls is boundless. What was the point of all those years with the Talmud, of finding my way between the intricacies of those battling knights— Shamai and Hillel, Rav and Shmuel, Abbaye and Ravi—if she was going to be this direct? What waste all these years of treading softly and listening carefully. "Of course I'm in the mood. Do you want me to come over?"

"You sound like your buddy," she laughed. "Meet me in front of my building. I'm at Ocean and Foster. We'll walk."

"Will you recognize me?"

"How could I not recognize a *yeshiva boy*," she said, getting even.

"I won't be wearing a *yarmukah*."

"It's not that," she said lightly. "It's that earnest look you all have. You just know they're too serious to just fool around."

"You *have* been talking to Father," I said.

"Don't rush it," she laughed. "See you in a half hour."

I ran to brush my teeth. Moving through the kitchen on the way out I ran the gauntlet of Father's stare. "Important engagement?"

"Nothing that serious."

I half expected him to declare closing time for the front door but he said nothing. My mother put down the pillow cover she was embroidering and came to close the door behind me. Before I walked through the door she brushed my hair straight, her hand lingering.

On the way over I was too busy feeling the anticipation to realize that I might have trouble recognizing her. I knew the idea of her much better than her face, the lie of the land where her name plate rested better than her stance or height. It was as if I had known her for a long time and she had become so familiar that I could no longer see her but needed another person's discovery to recognize her. Maybe that is why my mother could continue with Father through his changes. She has stopped seeing him, knows him by his voice and mannerism, might not even have noticed the beard he had grown. Yet when I saw Rachel, I knew her at once, saw her while I was still a block away.

She was leaning against one of the posts guarding the building. Above her, the number of the house, dusty and unclear. I leaned over and rolled the window down on her side.

"Park it and let's walk," she said, "in this neighborhood you don't waste a spot."

She was smiling, surprising me. I had expected her to be more cautious. Apparently I had already been forgiven on the phone. I was taken again by her almost jagged hair, wished somehow it would be less rigid and more willing to lie softly and just lap around her neck. No ruffles at her breasts, she wore a light blue, belted dress and sandals.

"Stop staring," she said.

"I've never seen a girl without a pocketbook," I said.

When I finally stood next to her she held both her hands out and took mine. I wanted to thank her for making it easy but could only blurt out, "You don't shake hands like an Orthodox Jewish girl shakes hands."

"How do they shake?" she said, still holding mine.

"They don't," I said, making her laugh. Daringly, I touched the tip of her nose. "You don't look like one either."

"Not seeing a pocketbook has really knocked you over," she said. "Let's walk."

We walked, trying to match fingers and palms. "Listen," I said, "what exactly did Jonesey say to you?"

"He said Sheila sent him, with a letter of recommendation. He told Sheila you wanted to double with them, that's why she gave him my number."

"What did you tell him?"

"You're more persistent than he was. I told him I had to do my laundry. And press some grapes. And grow some hair."

"Really?"

"Actually, I told him you had already called."

I marveled. "You knew I would call to apologize?"

"I knew you couldn't resist the lure of a name like Rae. Listen, I'm having a housewarming party Friday night. Why don't you come?"

That "Friday" made it clear. Final proof of her lapsed state. Unquestionably an irreligious girl. Having violated the Sabbath, she has officially placed herself beyond the outer

33

boundaries of Jewhood. At least according to Father and my Rabbis. Transgress the Sabbath and bite into bacon and better be prepared to enter through the gates of the Gentile heaven.

That she lived alone was indication enough, of course, that her Jewishness was suspect and would not withstand Father's scrutiny. Suspect too were her ancestors, even unto the fourth sinful generation in the past. No self respecting Orthodox parents would have retired to Florida the way Rachel's had. Bad enough to have a daughter live beyond eighteen and be unmarried. To be unmarried and alone knocked the bottom out of the *shiduch* market altogether. The Orthodox Marriage Exchange of Brooklyn, namely the seats from Crown Heights, Boro Park, and Flatbush, would be very bearish on Rachel's chances for a fitting match. Her lack of chaperone and immodesty of dress have so depressed her stock that she would have had to settle for second rate merchandise, perhaps a lame, deaf, or blind bridegroom; the only possible partner for someone with her moral and spiritual imperfections!

And if in the bargain she also screwed, forgot even the cripple. Instead of a good Jewish boy, a circle in hell for her, not to mention the parents who have abandoned her. Better for those parents to have risked their health in New York City's unacceptable air quality than to move to Florida and expose their daughter to slander. Better for them to have perished in the service of their daughter's maiden reputation than to live retired in Florida and have the innocent child be the subject matter of whispers during pauses between prayers on the High Holy Days. Better to have taken her with them than to live to see her go into Hazel's Fashions on Crown Street and have her shop for jeans when every decent person in Crown Heights is shaking the trees for the one unique outfit to wear while promenading down Eastern Parkway. For shame, for shame, yet how fortunate for the dear girl to have located amidst the teeming millions of Brooklyn such a fine, upstanding, semi-religious boy as Jason Kole to help her fend for herself. Non-observant parents hardly deserved such luck.

"Aren't you being just a little bit of a snob? We had two sets of dishes, you know."

"Meat and dairy?"

"Actually, kosher and Chinese. But we never brought ham into the house. We had standards."

What flavor to our courtship! Instead of exchanging favorite books and movies, determining life goals, or debating the moral issues of the Viet Nam War, we were exchanging our parents' eating habits and, eventually, sleeping arrangements. (My parents on twin beds, of course, in strict adherence to the laws of family purity; Rachel's on a single bed, one headboard, one sheet, one cover, the bed of her conception. Her parents not having observed the laws of separation and ritual cleansing, made her, in the eyes of the ancient Rabbi Akiba, a *momser*, in a word, a bastard.)

For this girl, then, my long hair, my nonchalant drag on borrowed cigarettes, the pressure of my skullcap in odd pockets, the decision to move out, at least for the summer. For her I renounce all claims to Eastern Parkway belles, abandon the flesh market of Whitehead Cafeteria at Brooklyn College, forget the exhibition halls of religious house plan parties, surrender my black suit and collection of fine knitted *yarmukahs*. In exchange, Rachel, teach me to take my religion seriously. Demonstrate the validity of its long list of no-nos. Show me what makes all the forbidden acts so popular. I am not interested in sorority girls. I yearn for no *shiksa*. No cross bearer for me. My late night desires consist of spiritual thirsts. Give me, pretty please, daddy's God, a Jewish girl, just don't let her be too nice. Give me Rachel who has blown a cooling breath at the burning bush eternal and somehow survived.

But Rachel came very dear. Her price was beyond the price of pearls. She wanted my Friday night. The yammie in the pickle jar, the unused bag of phylacteries, eating dairy after meat without waiting the prescribed six hours, those were fine but private things. But asking me to avoid the Friday Evening Meal, to be AWOL from the Sabbath altar, that was asking me to say NO, in thunder. She was asking me to shout out loud and leap immediately after, but that wasn't me. That was Jonesey's style. I don't plunge into anything. I avoid bumping into people on the street, apologizing even if I had only violated their air space. I tip-toe in and out of sleeping rooms. I consider all sides of an issue and will struggle to untwist the roots of thorny questions even if they begin to grow while I reach for them. In short, born Jewish, raised

Orthodox, *Yeshiva* taught, I was bound by temperament, environment and education to be courageously cautious. I was not prepared to live by my own rules. At best I needed rules to push against.

"We don't get home from *shul* until after eight or so. And with all the songs and blessings the meal won't be done till almost ten. Then I'll have to walk until I'm out of Crown Heights. Would it be OK if I get to you after eleven?"

By then we were squatting on the hood of my car, ugly little Lancer bought with money I had earned waiting on tables at the Sea Breeze Hotel. Not a regular waiter's job for me because that would have involved working on Saturdays. Instead, I worked the special occasions—weddings, *bar mitzvahs*, *bat mitzvahs*, anniversaries—and stayed home for the Holidays when the big money could be made. The metal of the hood was still warm.

"You don't have to ask for permission to go to the bathroom, do you?"

"I am loved to excess, what can I tell you." I touched her chopped off hair deliberately, sensing that she was uncomfortable with its shortness. "Don't you get enough allowance to go to a professional?"

"Too much love made me move out. How come you're still at home?"

I dropped my hand from her hair. "*Yeshiva* boys don't move out unless they're getting married. You're not proposing, are you?"

"First," she laughed, poking at my banlon polo shirt, "I have to find out how come you don't have the build of a *yeshiva* boy. Your shoulders should be more rounded and your ass should be much wider. All those years bent over the books."

"I'm an imperfect *yeshiva* boy."

"Ah, possibilities. But what's the explanation?"

"I keep in shape running from the draft."

She got off the car, smoothing herself. "Try jogging toward Ocean and Foster next time."

I watched her carefully. "Does that mean there are possibilities even if I can't show Friday night?"

"Try," she said, and patting my cheek, went inside her building.

5.

I drove home imagining her saying good-bye to someone
else, someone without a skullcap reflex (mine already back on
my head), someone unconcerned with Fathers and Friday
nights. Inside the hall I took my *yarmukah* off and smoothed
it carefully before putting it back on. Father was not to be
fooled with. I found him waiting for me, smiled to see his
eyes go toward the back of my head. Looking away from me
quickly and into a squared copy of the *New York Times*, he
told me to wait.

"Don't rush to your room right away. The whole house is
yours. Enjoy it."

"Thanks."

"Any time. In return for such bounty and don't pretend
you have no privileges, I need fifteen minutes of your time."

"Right now?"

"Can you spare only the time it takes to stand on one foot,
like Hillel's skeptic? But no, not right now. Thursday will be
perfect."

"Just me or also the car?"

"The car, it so happens, will be useful but it is your company I am looking forward to."

"What's the problem?"

"Is six a convenient time for you?"

"Come on, *Abba*."

"Well, since you have offered, I would like you to drive me
to the liquor store where I will buy enough wine at once to
make it unnecessary for you to extend yourself until next
Passover, at least."

"What's the big deal? I'll pick it up."

37

"No. I prefer to be there."

Father's sense of sin is uncanny. Could it be, master tailor that he is, that he has figured out that I smoothe my *yarmukah* out?

"Are you trying to tell me you don't want me to handle the wine?"

"I was thinking of making you promise not to look at it."

"Are you serious?"

Unexpectedly, he smiled, patted my back. "No. You would tell your Father, wouldn't you?"

"Geez, *Abba,* sure. It's sacramental wine, after all. I wouldn't want to trick you."

"I believe you. Make sure you're ready to drive me by six." I left him to his tea and newspaper in the kitchen.

Wednesday night, two more to Friday, I had begun my own countdown for shooting for the moon; the phone rang. I looked up to see my mother in my room, in a high necked kimono over her pajamas, her face gleaming, her voice wondering. "It's for you. A girl."

From the kitchen I could hear Father. "It's after ten. Tell her never to call here again. There are people living here." I would have risked his anger and closed the door tightly but my mother still stood there.

"Hi."

"It's Rachel."

"Who else could it be? The last girl who called was selling magazines and they only work nine to five."

"Did you buy?"

"I'm a sucker for female voices over the phone. I have a lifetime subscription to *Humpty Dumpty.*"

My mother had still not gone. I covered the mouthpiece partially. "It's for me, Mom."

"Who is it?" she mouthed. I uncovered the mouthpiece altogether, put the hand over my heart and rolled my eyes to heaven. My mother might have blushed but she walked out softly, pulling the door closed. I could still hear Father. "Is he still on? Tell him I am not paying for the extension starting right this minute. Let him take his scholarship and buy his own phone with soft music for conversations late at night."

"I'm back."

"I think I've just had my homesickness for my parents nicely cured."

"Mine is cured too. And will be again tomorrow and tomorrow and the day after."

"You've just slipped neatly past my Friday night."

"Ah."

"Right. Anyway. Come at twelve. Come at one. But come."

"Always got room for a religious boy?"

"Didn't say always. But certainly once. Will you come?"

"I'll try."

"Blessed be the Sabbath bride."

"Sunday school?"

"Hebrew school. I can also bake *chalah* and recite the blessing for the candles."

"Did you ask for Yaakov or Jason?"

"Jason. Your father seemed to know who that was. Why do names worry you so?"

"They're magic. If my grandfather had been named Saul I would be in vaudeville."

"Come as anybody you want. Hey. Didn't you feel like kissing me?"

"Sure."

"O.K. Then don't forget you owe me one."

Because I sensed something more here than I was prepared for, the words the words of encounter but the sound the sound of relationship, I ripped a page from my Modern American Poetry notebook and wrote myself a reminder in block letters, STAY COOL, KOLE, pinning it above my calendar of Sabbath candle lighting times across the nation.

Thursday noon, time for lunch before the flight into Manhattan for NYU—also Friday minus one and still counting though all systems are not fully go—I stepped into sunshine on Empire Boulevard and a headlock. "Cut it out, Jonesey," I said to the smell of gasoline and grease. He let go but not before giving my neck an extra squeeze, a reminder of old bonds and traditions. Adolescence never ends in the presence of high school friends.

39

In the car I pickled my *yammie*. Jonesey said nothing, his restraint visible. "I need the car," he said. I handed him the keys. "Don't you want to know for what?"

"I'm not interested in cunt stories."

"Thanks for the compliment but I can't get lucky every day of the week. I'm supposed to sign for the place in Rockaway today, remember?"

"Oh, yeah."

"Well, do we go halves or thirds?"

"Dov is in on this."

"Did you get it in writing from the little Jew?"

"I'll lay the money out."

"Whatever. How does he like it in Boston, anyway?"

"OK, I guess."

"Lots of loose cunt in Boston. Twat even you would like. You know, educated. Seminary boy get any?"

"I need the car by six. I have to take my old man somewhere."

"Tired of carrying him around on your back?"

"Six o'clock, Jonesey."

"Gottcha."

Not trusting him, I took the *yarmukah* back out of the glove compartment and folding it neatly, smoothed it into my back pocket. I got out of the car and he slid behind the wheel. I started walking across the street, resigned to missing lunch and taking train and bus to NYU. He called after me.

"Not gonna tell me about Rachel?"

I went back, close to him. "If the fucking car isn't back by six I'm going to have your ass."

"Relax, Jake. I was just doing you a favor, you know. Warming her up so your little *boychick* approach doesn't flop altogether." He made me lean over. "I have it on good authority, man. She kisses, she feels, maybe she even fucks. Play it cool, Kole, play it cool."

Hunched over the wheel, cramped, he drove off, looking as if he were in the grip of a giant tugging at his groin.

In the midst of the vision—a young boy dances in the air above London rooftops—Professor Greene's "Modern English Novel Before 1900" was interrupted by chanting. From fifth floor Waverly there was a clear view of a small circle of marchers, of the DO NOT CROSS POLICE LINE saw-horses and of a dozen uniforms. PEACE. NOW. PEACE. NOW. AG-NEW, FUCK-YOU. WHAT DO WE WANT? PEACE. WHEN DO WE WANT IT? NOW. HO HO HO CHI MINH.

Downstairs, from inside Waverly, I watched a girl sweating bravely against her blue jersey, her breasts flattening as she raised her END THE WAR placard. Two of the cops closest to her looked younger than the students. A kid from my Linguistics class, an accelerated undergraduate taking grad courses, was distributing wrapped sandwiches bought at Gristede's across the street. "Ham here," he was yelling and others changed it into "pig meat here." Someone opened a red flag. From one of the upper floors painted peace signs floated halfway down, then were swirled away in the updraft between the tall buildings. EAT PIG. EAT PIG. EAT PIG. The chants got louder. Moving to open the door, maybe to join, I saw the cops force the circle into a tighter arc, into a hive, into a flat line spilling into the gutter. There was shouting and much trouble. I left by way of interconnecting Main Building, took the D train and caught the connecting Tompkins Avenue, bus at Prospect Park, entered the house with my *yarmukah* a perfectly smooth dome on my head, bobby pin glinting, at a quarter to six.

At six o'clock, Father waiting grimly and no Jonesey with car, I raised helpless hands in apology.

"*Abba*, I'm really sorry. You know Jonesey."

"Spare me. I'll have it delivered. If I had to depend on you, it would be like begging for mother's milk to make *Kiddush* with Friday night."

Oh, yes, Pop. What to do with Friday night.

6.

A right out of the house to Empire Boulevard. Another right. My skullcap crouches, waits. By Rogers Avenue there are no Jews anywhere. Just to be sure, I wait until I am past Bedford Avenue and can see only black faces before I whisk the skullcap from my head. A prudent move, removing the conspicuous mark of religion and reducing the obviousness of my white face.

But I cannot shake my fear of Friday night.

When Jonesey began his Friday night transgressions, rambling to the Village, to 42nd Street, to 2nd Avenue bars, and, occasionally, to an innocent night game at Yankee Stadium, he would ask me along. I had followed Kellerman to many places since our days at *Eitz Chaim Elementary*, but I would not tempt Friday night's dangers on frivolous adventures. I could not shake a persistent fantasy that I would be crushed to death somewhere in a Friday night accident, perhaps have the right field stands collapse under me at the Stadium, and then lie unclaimed on a slab in the morgue because it would never occur to Father to look for me anywhere beyond walking distance from the house on the Sabbath. He would not imagine me violating the precepts of the day that forbid any mechanical means of transportation. Jonesey offered to take the train but would not indulge my caution and walk to a safe distance beyond Orthodox boundaries before getting on. And I would not lend him the car because I refused to park it in the war zone or some no man's land beyond Eastern Parkway or Bedford Avenue.

But I survived the area past Bedford, and having reached the D train at the Prospect Park station, began to relax. Once on the train, anticipating, I began to enjoy the switch in

42

identities, all those years of Superman comics obviously not having gone to waste. By the time the train passed Parkside Avenue, I was a lone crusader, braving nighttime danger, a secret Jew, a man in quest, fully aware that I was now past succor. In case of danger, even if I tried to summon help with some ancient cry, there would be no shareholder in Orthodoxy to come to my rescue. I was out alone, an adventurer. At the end of my adventure, a castle waited. In the castle, a maiden. In the maiden, well, that was the adventure.

I got out at Foster Avenue, walked to Ocean, entered her building, stripped myself of tie, clip and cap, and packing them neatly, hid them for my eventual retrieval behind the cool, dusty radiators in the hall. I also remembered to remove the folded bill from my underwear. Ready, I suddenly realized I had neither Rachel's last name nor her apartment number. I went to stare at the directory above the double row of mail slots, weighing Rae or Rachel and not finding either to balance with Finkelstein, Gestetner, Lustig or Moskowitz. Then I heard the elevator door slide open and saw Rachel laughing.

"I've been checking down here every ten minutes since eleven. Are you sure you wanted to find me?"

"Just so I never forget again, what's your last name?"

"Ramsess," she said, "I'm descended from the pharaohs." Linking her arm in mine, she led me upstairs.

Dimmed by the hall, Rachel burst into light as she softly opened the door to her apartment. She wore glistening silk, a bloody red tunic that left only her neck and chopped-off hair open to air. I stared. "Look at the others," she whispered. "We're all wearing our assignments tonight."

I managed to focus on a bearded guy, about my age, wearing denim over-alls, playing the guitar and singing "Suzanne" but I could not see much else in that dazzling room. There was fabric everywhere, an abundance of cloth that would have pleased Father's expert eyes. Fabric covered the pillows on the floor and draped the cartons or crates that served for low tables. Even on the walls, swatches of material, some thumbtacked but others—a checkerboard, a cool Mondrian pattern, a Peter Max rendition of the Beatles in *Yellow Submarine*—were framed.

The song was winding down. Suzanne was busy looking among the garbage, flowers and seaweed, and preparing to touch someone else's perfect body with her mind. The singer, clearly my enemy, did not look up and neither did a couple holding tightly to each other's hands and with eyes closed, rocking in unison. We sat down on the floor of the brightly lit room (there were no candles or dim lights), between another shimmering girl in sequined gauze and one in plain blouse and jeans. Rachel began to whisper introductions in my ear, her hand resting on mine, as the song started from the top again, apparently at the insistence of the rocking couple.

"The one with the guitar is Gondo. I used to go with him in high school but we're just friends now. Those two in the boat are Cindy and Andreas, from my class at F.I.T. She just moved out from here to move in with him. Because he is lefty and she's a righty they can sit in class and hold hands while they're taking notes. His khaki of many shades is more appropriate for a casual, midday occasion. She is wearing an After-Five Favorite. The material is kettle cloth, the design an interlocking pattern of prints and solids."

I let my hand rest under hers although my wrist was taking too much of my weight. Her moist whispering continued. "That beauty in the challis print is modeling a Back-To-Nature ensemble. Her name is Jeri with an *i*. She is here to hit it off with Gondo but he's got the hots for Lizzie who works with me at Berkey Photos and usually handles the confidential *art exposures*. I think Gondo is all turned on by the idea of her turning on to those pictures."

I thought it more likely that modestly dressed Gondo was attracted to the only other simply clothed person there. I half-wished I had come in the splendor of my full Sabbath regalia, including my perky little hat with the short feathers.

When the song was finally done Gondo came to shake my hand. His grip was gentle, without any animosity. It lacked the hardness of a rival's touch. Rachel moved away to put a record on and while she was away, Gondo leaned close. "Watch out for those Fashion Institute designers. They snip and snip until they get what they want but that doesn't mean they've made something wearable."

"I know," I reassured him, pleased by his concern, "my father is a sample maker. He has to ignore the designer all the time if he wants the dress to fit the model." I watched Rachel's hair and the excessive tightness of her face.

"Rachel says you used to be a *Hasid*," Lizzie said.

"Not really."

"What did you used to be?"

"Hungarian Orthodox."

"That's like Greek Orthodox," Gondo told Lizzie with a grin.

"Listen," Jeri said, "Is it true that Orthodox people in Williamsburg make love through holes in the sheet?"

A warm smell rose from her and she looked flushed, angered by her disappointment in love.

"Who told you that one?"

"Sheila, Rachel's religious friend. She collects them. Haven't you met her?"

"I almost did."

"Well?"

"Well," I started, not unwilling to account for all those years on the study bench, "it's like this." I could almost sense the sing-song of learning in my voice. "Technically, the instant the bride has been deflowered she is taboo and the groom must remove himself from physical contact until after the days of purity have been observed and she has gone to the ritual bath. But only an inept bridegroom would think of assuring purity by placing a sheet between him and his bride. According to the Rabbis, it is the responsibility of the groom to be both adept and considerate at such a delicate moment."

Across the room Cindy and Andreas shared a smile. The others seemed to be trying to visualize a woman covered with a sheet.

"That's it?" Lizzie finally asked. "Right after the first time you have to stop?" She might have blushed but there was no room for more colors in the room and she assumed her clean, white features quickly.

"Makes for a short honeymoon," Jeri said, somehow angry with the obscure procedures that would never affect her.

"Takes the incentive out of being a virgin," Gondo laughed, sending brief color into Lizzie again. "You learn this in your religious school?" she asked, "like under Health Ed. or something?"

"When I was sixteen," I began, looking around for Rachel, wanting her to hear my explanation, "I was studying the *Tractate Gitin*, the laws of divorce. The following year we studied *Kidushin*, Sanctifications, the laws of marriage. The standard joke is that you are given the cure before you contract the disease."

A Peter, Paul and Mary tune announced Rachel's success at the stereo. She came back and took my hand, trying to fit unfamiliar whorls and ridges of fingers and palms together. "Leave the oracle alone," she said, "if you don't watch it, he'll have you at the study bench. It's in the blood."

She tugged me away. "Private lessons, Rachel?" But she only wanted to show me the rest of her place, leaving untapped my years of erudition and Talmudic sophistication. Aware of my disappointment, I could not help but think how Father would have laughed, how he would have enjoyed my little lecture, how he would have approved both the sing-song and the superior tone of voice. Wasn't it just like a son of his to see himself bringing civilization to the savages? Here he is, in his Friday night disguise as *goy*, when he suddenly reveals himself to be the *Answerman, yeshiva boy*, through and through. How I would have gone on and on if Rachel had not stopped me! How well I knew that special portion of responsibility and honor that is due the Orthodox. Thirty-six of them, mysterious, modest, and remote sages, by virtue of their absolute adherence to the Law, insure the safety of the world. We are the elite among the chosen, the cream of the cream, the cherry on the dessert, the last hoop on the barrel containing chaos, the only real Jews. Others of our faith who have withdrawn from the Covenant we call *goyim*, not differentiating between them and Gentiles. While I remain among the privileged, forced by Father to wear identifying marks on my head, my tie, my lap. In an age when circumcision is an automatic procedure—a squirt to clear baby's nostril, a snip to round the foreskin—Father's rules point me boldly out.

Rachel could help. She would be the only one who could. Behind the beads that separated front room from back, I seized the offer of her lips, surprising her.

Gondo left with Lizzie but Jeri stayed, sleeping in the bedroom. Rachel and I lay amid the splendor of those expensive fabrics and kissed each other's lips raw.

Let me say this about kissing: once you accept its possibilities, it can please, terribly. As a kisser, I should say, I am a Grand Master. Though I had on occasion wandered elsewhere, I know best the vineyards of the face and neck, and in my home territory I have no equal. I am a connoisseur of lips, a discriminating sampler of tongues, an expert tantalizer of skin. I love the flight from the dark cave. I can, with just lips and tongue, perhaps the lightest fingertip control, rouse the smell of warmth so that you could almost see it rise like white steam on crisp, cold mornings.

So when I say we kissed I am saying that I was doing something with fervor, not substituting for something else. Enough of the streetlight's shine filtered through the shades for us to see each other's faces but little enough to allow us to pretend blindness and resort to touch. Earlier, when we had touched lips behind her beaded curtain, I had stiffened instantly, perhaps even before the kiss, just in its anticipation, but because I had maintained space between us, she had not known of the power of her touch. Lying next to her, tasting the raspberry of a donut she had eaten, I could not hide my hardness. I tried to back away. Father had always taught me to admit nothing. But she held her hands stubbornly locked behind me and I had nowhere to go when she drew nearer. Fitting herself tightly against me, her work done, she rested.

"Comfortable?"

"Uh, uh."

"So am I."

"Actually, my glasses are killing me."

"Take them off."

"There is no place to put them."

"Flip them. They can't break. But don't move. Throw with your wrist."

"I can't see you now."

"I'm here."

She was. Perfectly relaxed and controlled from the neck down, above we could not stop. I kept on chewing on her lips, could see them swell as though bruised by insects, could feel my own lips smeared all over my face.

"Didn't know a religious boy could taste this good."

"Try many before?"

"Just one. Bit him in Sunday school. He tasted of chopped liver."

"You did right in waiting. We're very delectable now. Tenderized and purified over the years. No toughness of skin, juicy with learning. Delicious."

I tried to see my watch. I did sums in my head. If each kiss takes five seconds and we've kissed eighty-seven times, that means I don't have that much time before Father locks the door. We also ate donuts in the dark, voracious with bodily restraint.

"Why did you chop your hair like that?"

"Someone called me a very precise person. I did it to show how uneven I could be. And how sloppily spontaneous."

"Oh."

"You don't like it?"

"How long was it before?"

"All right, I'll grow it back for you. All you had to do was ask."

We listened for Jeri to stir. Squinting, I tried to look under the drawn shades to see if morning light was making the streetlamp dim. "What a disappointment for Jeri," Rachel whispered. "So few guys at the Fashion Institute and to be ignored by one of the straight ones. I really didn't expect her to stay over."

"It's all right," I whispered back, respecting Jeri's difficulties, "I really have to go." She was nearly asleep.

"I have to go to synagogue in the morning."

That woke her up. "Really?"

"Yeah."

"Your father would understand."

"I don't think so."

"Anyway, it's early."

"Only for the morning. It's very late at night."

She leaned over me and nicked my lips. I could feel her breasts resting on me but there was no use searching for them within the great folds of that class project she was wearing. I jumped at a sound. "It's a factory whistle."

"Saturday morning? No, it was a car, a burglar alarm, a car alarm."

Fine eared like a dog, I could hear the Sabbath eve dissolving into Sabbath Day. If Father locked the door I would have to climb in through a basement window and still be spruced for prayers. It was definitely time to go.

48

A late cruising taxi, a fellow Jew according to his hack permit, picked me up, reassured perhaps by my light shirt and clamped tie. Having noticed a tinge of light in the sky, I told him to drop me off at Empire, corner of New York Avenue. That seemed the safest place, bound on all four sides—funeral parlor, gas station, public school and 71st Precinct House—by indifferent Christian establishments.

In the tiny hall before the kitchen (the front door had been unlocked), I stripped down to my underwear. Barefoot, trumpets in my ears, I was fully in the kitchen when Father walked bleary eyed out of the bedroom, nightcap on his head.

"Pajamas won't kill you," he said, "don't flush."

He went to splash seltzer into a glass, a tiny night light warming the kitchen, the refrigerator light turned off for the Sabbath. The next day, in synagogue, sitting near the East Wall, within the curtain of the black and white prayer shawls, through the sound of Father clearly enunciating each syllable of the prayers, I could think only of Rachel's breasts resting against me and ached all day with a fathomless desire for sweets.

7.

Everyone became bearable for once, Father, Jonesey, even absent but insistent Dov, writing his rabbinical admonishments, because after that abbreviated Friday night, I saw only Rachel. I saw her in daylight, particularly during early afternoons when I would rush over to wait on her doorstep (key not asked for, nor volunteered.) Fresh from *yeshiva*, I was a *kli kodesh*, a holy vessel, brimming. Sharing in my need, Rachel would appear, cutting class or avoiding work, pretend to be surprised with my presence, quickly open her door to my rush. Once inside, I saw much of her, often.

The days were turning into heat and everything was wilting. Rabbi Baumel, concerned by rumors of a draft lottery that might liberate his unwilling students, had difficulties lifting his head and often overlooked our listless attendance. In the Modern Poetry course at NYU we were reading too much about rainfalls that were expected but not forthcoming. The Yankees were losing. There were no job openings at the Board of Education. The Lubavitcher Rebbie issued a circular, urging Orthodox Jews to remain in Crown Heights and resist the exodus to Boro Park. Even Agnew's crisp, white collars began wilting.

The only compensation seemed to be that Father, his anger sapped, was content to wake me for morning prayers more gently than before, doing nothing more than rapping on my door with the needle-toughened tips of his fingers. And he decided to respect my threshhold, limiting his show of displeasure at Rachel's frequent calls by staring angrily through the open doorway.

His decision to restrain himself was a good thing because without my being aware of it, my mother was exhausted by the heat and would have lacked the energy to keep Father from me. A faint sheen of sweat seemed to gleam on her even in the dimness after sundown and she sometimes wandered through the house needlessly straightening the needlepoints on the wall and the doilies on the arms of the chairs and couch. I noticed her one day in my doorway, a slack look on her face. I was on the phone and had just exclaimed, "Oh, come on, Rachel," with the teasing voice of lovers. It must have been the tone if not the name that drew her. "Jason," she said softly, but Rachel was also saying something and I assumed my mother was just calling me to dinner and so I only raised my hand for silence with an abrupt gesture that made her fade back into the darkness of the living room.

But I was insensible to everyone except Rachel and intrigued by nothing except the gradual yearning of my body toward her touch. There were calls for my attention outside of myself. Each evening at the synagogue we continued to count the days of the Omer. My hair, obeying the stricture against cutting, grew vigorously long. Still, the occasional weekend's work as a waiter at the Sea Breeze Hotel allowed me to shave, with Father agreeing to the dispensation. But I was too full of Rachel to pay much attention.

What I enjoyed most was our leisure. I decided to ration my *yeshiva* attendance, gambling higher tuition rates for a late lottery draft number. Now I had continuous hours with her instead of hurried touchings while rushing from *Yeshiva* to University. Diminishing my devotion to American Literature allowed me to take her to the Village and have our portraits painted, although we ended up discarding them into a bottom drawer of that wonderfully mirrored dresser of Rachel's, because her hair stood out on her picture and I wore no *yammie* for mine and could not show it to anyone I knew anyway. She took me to *Thursday's*, new bareheaded and long haired me, and pulled me into the middle of the polished floor where I closed my eyes and shuffled my feet and kept my hands out toward her, yearning for support though there was no contact permitted for the dance.

"Lessons or practice?" I asked jealously.

"Many hours in front of American Bandstand," she reassured me.

I helped her choose a hair piece, quaintly called a "fall,"

that made her eyes look larger and her face thinner, confirming my determination to know her in the future when her hair would be back. Trying to reconstruct and rewrite our pasts, even if certain details had to be concealed, we went to see each other's favorite movies, first seen with other loves. On one day, four and a half hours of *Camelot* (she had seen it with someone with blue eyes, like Franco Nero's) and four hours of *West Side Story* (Mindy Kornbluth, second girl on the left on the first bench near Brooklyn Avenue, sitting with her friends in Row J while Jason and his friends sit in Row K, sniffing Mindy's savory hair). Going further back, Rachel pointed out the window of the room where she was born at New Caledonian and I showed her my foreseeable future reflected in the windows of Rabbi Baumel's Yeshiva for Artful Dodgers. I threw my arm wide and offered her my entire world: a thin wafer of Brooklyn, a sprinkling of Manhattan. What a time I had, setting aside the two hundred years required to adore each breast, and preparing to spend the required time on all the rest. Rachel, at first luxuriating in my attentive tongue, lips, and hands, would stretch and ask for my evenings, more curious than demanding when I resisted.

"Why can't you stay overnight?"

"Too complicated."

"Tell them you're with Jonesey."

"It would be safer to say I was with you."

"Then say that."

"They'll think I'm covering up being with Jonesey."

I managed to distract her by doubling and redoubling my giving. I tried to be the lord of kisses and the prince of touch. I did not even withhold intimations of love, although I did heed Father's warning in another context never to put anything into writing. I told her she was overwhelming me with her abundance. The tightness of her face had not prepared me for the generosity of her wide mouth, her smells, her oils. I said I was a greedy kid, licking the spoon, the edge of the glass, the whipped cream, the biscuit, smearing syrup all over myself, wanting the sundae to last forever. But as many students of literature, I went too far with words. Already puzzled by my flights home in the night, she tried to understand my contrived abstinence, no doubt wondering whether my careful avoidance of screwing was the result of infirmity or disinterest, concerned that the one part of me that was unquestionably Jewish was the one Jewish part I was withholding.

"I'm in my season now, Jason, this is when you should be making love to me."

It was not the time to tell her that cleavings among the Orthodox are so difficult because there are no transitions. We have no prescribed Grand Tour, no experimentation, no alternative life styles. At thirteen declared a man, at eighteen fit for marriage, at thirty-five ripe for the mysteries of the Kabbalah, but in between there is only the Law to ease our way. Other people have grandparents. We Orthodox immigrants, we "Greeners," we lost our grandparents and thus lost the intermediaries who could have absorbed all our curses and resentments with God and traditions. If only I had a toothless but understanding grandmother who ran the family in a foreign tongue or a grandfather on whose kindly knees I could have listened to heroic tales. I could have made love to Rachel if I had had grandparents to teach me the sweetness of ceremony and the strength in acceptance. But the people who could have smoothed my transition from God to Father and from Father to Rachel have been killed off. And so I take on the words of God directly. Call him my remote grandfather.

As long as we were in bed, I didn't have to talk. But I was at Rachel's mostly during late afternoons when the heat eventually drove us into the kitchen for a drink. We were making iced tea there one Tuesday, the anniversary, Rachel thought, of the day we met in front of her house.

On her shelves were tins of imported Twining Teas—Earl Grey, Darjeeling, Orange Pekoe, Formosa Oolang, Russian Caravan—as well as packets of herbals, but Rachel was using pre-mixed Lipton. These were the truths about her I needed time to understand and accept. She insisted on her ordinariness and I wanted to disbelieve her, because as long as she was exotic and extraordinary, I didn't have to take her seriously. But next to those packets and tins of cosmopolitan teas were boxes of Nabisco crackers and chocolate jelly rings. I had expected wheat germ, soy bean, natural honey, organic kelp. I looked for a mattress on the floor, a New Guinea ceremonial mask on the wall, sandals, granny dresses, clear soap, an elaborate collection of Acid Rock, a pet cat, a roommate, pills. But there was only tea, because she liked it and because it had always been part of her family's Sabbath ritual. But as for the rest, she decorated as would any student at the Fashion Institute of Technology, working her way comfortably around the remnants from her parents: the French Provincial bed and matching dresser, the portable Zenith, the plastic-backed kitchen chairs and formica table.

"You're basically a very domesticated person," I told her. "Your independence has been forced on you. Your heart isn't in it."

"My good heart and my domesticity," she sang. "Long after my exotic charms have faded, they will keep me desirable."

In the kitchen directly from the bedroom, I wore both pants and shirt, not only sensitive about my hairless chest but also paranoid about a sudden knock on the door. Proprieties had to be observed. Rachel wore a long, modest shirt, mostly buttoned, but flipped its tail at me to let me know she was indulging my desires for both modesty and secret intimacy. She was the color of late summer leaves. Her hair, crinkling, had turned itself into a precise style.

"I wrote to my parents about you."

"Who did you say I was?"

"Didn't talk about the past."

"Who I am?"

"Who you're becoming."

But that was exactly what was not so simple, why I held myself back from her.

"I hope you told them I'm becoming a tea drinker."

"And a lover. Of soft fabrics, of silky hair, of odd places on my body I can't even see with double mirrors."

"You told them I was an adventurer!"

"And a donut freak. They wanted to know what your father does."

"Father is a lover too, of soft fabrics, of simple patterns, of perfectly cut material."

"I told them you're studying in seminary."

"Were they impressed?"

"My mother started crying. She thought I was dating a priest."

"Didn't you tell them my name?"

"My father said there were no Koles where he came from. Wasn't totally convinced you were Jewish. I told him it was probably changed during the Inquisition. Or at Ellis Island. But it was the Jason part he was really having trouble with."

"Obviously the name of an adventurer."

"That's what he thought. He reminded me about my trust fund."

We observed rules, you see, on what we could talk about. Playing with time was our least guarded activity. We could expand it ("I feel I've always known you, I want to ask you if you remember things we did in kindergarten.") or we could contract it ("I remember the way you stood the first time I saw you, where you looked before you looked at me."). We didn't dare discuss our real pasts though. I was afraid to ask because the knowledge in her hands as we lay in her French Provincial contained information I did not want to hear spoken out loud. She tried asking with those hands but I stopped their inquisitiveness and twisted away, and so didn't ask in any other way either. That left us our immediate past, a very brief history, to review.

"What was the point of the name business, anyway?"

"Yaakov or Jason? Rae or Rachel? Names are everything. The quickest way to assess race, religion, spiritual commitment, how far a girl will go."

"The less Jewish the name, the better the chance for scoring?"

"Exactly. It points to less traditional, more liberal parents. Also to their reading habits during pregnancy. I've always wanted to meet a Desireè."

"What about your name?"

"Hungarians have their own system."

"And my name? What did it tell you?"

"Purity itself. My mother's name."

I gulped greedily at the iced tea, splashing it on my shirt. She parted it and licked at the droplets. "A bare chest has many tastes, a hairy one only its own. I like yours much better."

Withholding my questions, I followed her to the bedroom and held back again. But then I was hoarding everything about myself in those days. I was feeling strong and feeling full with myself, could sense my nostrils somehow widening

55

with the effort of deeper breaths. At NYU, in the 19th Century American course, Miss Gordon from two aisles over touched me on the arm after class. "We're starting a study group for the Comprehensives this summer. We wanted to ask you." And she twinkled toward Miss Goldman who smiled back at us. I had thought them to be lovers, identical girls with straight blond hair and a habit of wetting their pinkies and smoothing their eyebrows during lectures. "You're the first one we're asking," Miss Gordon said, "You'd be our Hawthorne man." It occurred to me that as a Jewish scholar I was destined to be called a *bochur*, a boy, until the day I was married, while as a scholar of literature I could be dubbed "man" by two Jewish princesses merely on the basis of my comments in class and a new confidence in my voice. Oh, I was feeling my strength. The two of them had no mysteries for me. I could have traced either of them from head to shiny toes, even with my eyes closed, and identified each and every part, the tiniest wrinkle, the most subtle smell. And so I told them "No," I could not join, I would be away for the summer, and watched them circle and envelop Jim Lang, a Melville man, without feeling any regrets. Even Dov's letters from Boston, tentative about the summer and concerned about my guarded descriptions of changes, failed to weaken me, although I found myself explaining to him in a dream why I stopped writing, showing him a handless wrist, bandaged but still bleeding a bit.

But as we counted down the days toward *Shevuoth*, The Festival of the Early Harvest, Rachel again came up against my guarded borders. I called her early in the week, not wanting to surprise her with new restrictions. Unlike previous Friday nights when sooner or later I would be at the BRIGHTON ARMS, Apartment C3, risking the dangers of the route, the complications of the encounter, and the possibilities of a discovered return home, this Friday was consecrated to God. On Thursday evening the holiday begins, and for the next two days my hands if not my heart belonged to Daddy. That first evening, after dinner, the Faithful return to the synagogue. Munching on small cakes, chickpeas, and shelled sunflower seeds, they begin to read the Five Books of Moses. A relay team of readers stands at the rolled Scrolls, racing the pages until dawn. With morning light comes morning prayer, the reading of the Daily Portion, Thanksgiving, the Added Prayer, Benediction of the Priests, until, late morning approaching, we go home to sleep.

One is allowed a break during the long night's journey, particularly around midnight. At that moment, legend says, there is a brief rending of the skies, a split in the heavens, a brief scent and glimpse of the Garden of Eden. In that eye-blink prayers arrive posthaste and even base wishes will be granted. A flight on Pentecostal Midnight over Brooklyn would find fifty thousand Jewish faces turned expectantly upward, intent and open.

The sleep that began at midday lasts until the afternoon and does not suffice. Barely awake by four, Father and I yawn through afternoon and evening prayer, eat a light, dairy meal, tumble into early sleep by nine-thirty, leaving my mother to guard the silent house. Leaving the house on such a Friday night was unheard of.

"You run for home on holidays like a married man to his wife."

"I'm working out a separation. And a divorce."

"The waiting period," Rachel said glumly, "is two years in New York."

"I'll use my influence with the ecclesiastical powers."

"Why don't you just say no instead. Try it. N.O. Look your father straight in the face and say it."

Only it was not Father this time, it was my mother. "We decorate the house together, Rachel." I slice branches from the fragrant evergreens in the back, while she buys carnations and wild flowers. "We drape the house with summer." Branches lean over the reproduction of the Matriarch's Tomb, pine needles fall to the carpet from the shelves, flowers cover the radio, brighten the stove, peep from within the interlocking cut glass of the chandelier, sit in unused key-holes of doors. "My mother and I have always done this together." This scattering of green, this decorating, this preparation. By the time we were done placing and talking, I would be so softened, so sensitive, so filled with smells, that I would feel weak, ready for any suggestion, even conversion. Even I would look expectantly at the sky. Such obligations were joys. "Do you understand?"

She understood well enough that it would be a night for communion, a long pause, a slow movement, a waiting out, done elsewhere, not with her. She said nothing. It was the first time I had pleaded other loves with her.

Shevuot evening, just before candlelighting, my house a forest, I saw my mother near the living room window that looked out at the apartment house on New York Avenue, joined by Father. "In '44," I heard her say, "in May, apple blossoms fell and fell and fell, covering the ground. When they came to take us, from the upstairs window I thought they were walking through snow."

Crossing his arms, he looked where she was looking. "On *Shevuoth*, on the Russian side of the Karpathians, dandelion seeds floated like feathers. We slapped at them, thinking they were mosquitos."

They stood silently. Scents filled the house. I dialed Rachel's number. "Will you be all right?" Her voice floated, detached. "I'll fry my brains out on the beach. I don't want to think. Tell me when you'll be thinking of me."

"At midnight," I whispered, "as the heavens part."

"I'll try to be up."

On my desk I found a letter. Jonesey's handwriting. Inside was a cartoon, raggedly clipped from some glossy magazine. It showed a baby chick, just breaking out of an egg. The caption read, "Getting laid has opened up a whole new world for me."

8.

Warmth loosens religion. Slightly. During the two days of the holiday, the laws of custom, at least their Crown Heights version, briefly dissolved. The Rabbi of Debrecen did not fuss when the young men left the synagogue during the Reading and Father did not object when I made ready to go to the Parkway without jacket, tie, or hat. Of course, when he went for a walk, he wore a hat, refusing to permit himself the pinned *yarmukah* he had allowed me. Still, he exchanged his soft black hat for a sedate but surprising straw hat and took his walk with my mother amidst the stately single family houses on President Street. Each day I waited until they left, then muffling the phone in case neighbors were listening, I dialed Rachel's number. She was not in the house either day. Greatly relieved, I slept Friday afternoon and, later, sat with Mickey Wiener and a *yarmukah*-bedecked Jonesey on the corner bench near Brooklyn Avenue, head back, sun on face, peace in my heart.

Saturday evening, Holiday at end, three stars glistening in the sky, I drove to Rachel's apartment. She opened the door deadly calm in white top and shorts, her bare hands, legs, and face startingly cool compared to her deepened color.

"Nice sun," I said, putting my face against hers.

"You didn't shave," she brushed at my holiday bristles. "When did you get a haircut?"

"Thursday. Every Jew in Crown Heights was in barbershops."

"Your ears show."

Determined to make her share my spirit, I ignored her edge. "Do you have a shaver I can use?"

"A blade."

"I'm not used to it."

Surprising me, she said, "I'll do it. Come with me."

I followed her to the bathroom, watched her gather towel, razor, and Palmolive Natural Scent shaving cream.

"You're serious about this."

"I used to be a candy striper. I've shaved helpless patients before."

From her tea cabinet she took one of her curved mugs, its shape and texture suggesting a stone age Venus, and filled it with hot water.

"Come on and lie down," she said, walking ahead of me into the bedroom, carrying her barbering paraphernalia easily.

"The floor or the bed?"

"Might as well be the patient all the way."

"Should I take my shirt off?"

"For a guy raised modestly you're ready to throw your shirt off at the slightest excuse."

"You told me I had a boyish chest."

"Lie down."

The hedge against all sins is truth, my Rabbis used to explain. They meant for a son, living at home. If he is faithful to truth, he will never eat forbidden foods or do forbidden things because he knows he must answer truthfully to the gentle questioning of his mother, that appointed guardian of faith. The hedge against sexual misconduct is the *tzitzis*, the fringed garment to be worn under the shirt. When all resolve is lost and clothes begin to be scattered in anticipation of physical touch, the garment must be pulled over the head. Its shade and caress will remind the anxious lover of other loves, more pure. And will put a doubt into the potential partner's eyes, for what is a stranger to make of a lover's hidden fringes? But Rachel is not responsible for my abandoning these at least. I stopped wearing my *tzitzis* after graduating from high school, on another warm day, refusing to let it interfere with a basketball game.

I lay back on Rachel's parental bed, propped up on pillows. She brought in a kitchen chair for herself, put the mug on the night table, tucked a towel under my chin. "Ready?" Before

60

sitting down, she looked me over, her back very straight, the posture of both designers and models at FIT. It is an attitude of remoteness, the position of a technician surveying her work, but it was only a pose. She was trying to convince me of that but I was used to artfulness, of dissembling before parents and neighbors. I found her lack of pretense disconcerting, considered her open expression of interest in me simply a ploy to keep me off balance.

"I will try," she said, razor loose in her hand, "not to make sadistic jokes while you're a helpless victim. I would not take unfair advantage of you, especially since you haven't of me."

My angle of repose on her bedding of tiny lilac flowers was much the same as the lean of my pillows when I read to fall asleep. When she began to pat water on my face I could feel it become sensitive to the lightest breeze. Trusting her touch, I looked away from it.

"The light is in my eyes."

"I can't operate in the dark."

"Mind if I close them?"

"Your mouth too. Let me concentrate on the pattern."

Before I closed my eyes I watched her shake the can of foam with a few precise pumps of the arm, then squeeze a small amount of cream on two fingers.

"When they advertise the stuff, the model dumps a handful of cream on his face. Actually, you need very little."

The foam went on with firm strokes. Lemon scented. I lifted my head to make the neck more accessible, risking the dangers of that forbidden blade.

"You look serious even with paint on your face. Was there ever an Orthodox clown? It's as if you had taken the glasses off your eyes and put them on the rest of your face." With my eyes closed, I heard the clicks as she adjusted the razor. "I'm giving you a clean blade. Intimacy and cleanliness sometimes work against each other but here it's no problem.

"Think of your face as being in four parts, in quadrants, like the division of a page in the encyclopedia. Most people shave one cheek, then the other, then move to the neck on the first side. It's a matter of habit, an unconscious sense of order. Men are so fearful of seeing themselves halved. They follow the pattern. You have one too, even with an electric

61

shaver. Knowing you, it's probably prescribed. You have to shave upward or downward, maybe like Hebrew script from right to left."

The blade scraped. her voice went lower, softer. She was shaving me straight down, from face to neck on the same side.

"Now I happen to be an up and down person. Straight lines are my strength in design class. When I get up in the morning, still in my nightgown, I put my socks on. I fold them up to my knees. I smooth them. Then I take my nightgown off in one smooth movement, straight over my head. Before getting dressed, I look carefully into the mirror, waiting to see in me that clear, straight, hard line. It's the way I know myself in the morning. Who I am. Because before waking, I am empty. I curl. But waking, I stretch. And if that edge is there, I dress slowly, building myself from the bottom up, reaching upward to the tip of that hard line.

"Now you, my love, you should be just toppling over, but instead, you chop, from the top down. You unpack yourself, flat layer by flat layer, like a stacking toy. First that little skull cap of yours, like a little circle dotting the i, so neat, so pretentious. Then that little knot of your tie, that shirt button at the collar, that ready shirt. But the downward direction stops. You take off your undershirt. You fluff your hair. You shave. On Avenue J, on Saturday mornings, I see Jewish men on their way home from synagogue, black twisted ropes around their middle. They separate. Upper and lower development is individual, not continuous. There you are. You jump and remove your shoes and socks. And wait. And I wait. I met you while you were busy becoming. I know you have in you that clean, clear, bright line."

I woke up to the darkness of the room. I knew it could not have been a deep or long sleep. Although mug and razor were gone, Rachel stood as if someone else had removed them from her hand so that her watchful pose would not be disturbed. I reached out and pulled her on top of me, insistent against her reluctance, slipped both hands under her top and held her breasts resting in my palms, her weight pushing her down on my palms, my hands holding them despite their position of self-protection.

Had she not stirred, had she remained still, perhaps I

62

would have fallen back into a dream with her. But restless, she moved and moving, released the eager little creatures that wait only to devour us. All flesh is flesh; even eaters of grass spring from the actions of little carnivorous beasts. She moved and moving, moved me. Her top came clean with one swift gesture. When I saw the white band of untanned skin like a slash across the lower part of her breasts, when I saw, instead of the roundness of breasts just a white-hot line, when I saw the dark center of that line ridge reluctantly toward me, I lost control. I became voracious. I attacked her wherever I could get at skin but especially at those startling pale bands, the borders of her holiday in the sun. Though she had managed to protect herself from the sun's burn she could not guard against mine. And yet, impenetrable that I was, I felt that she too was made of hard, uncuttable little diamonds at each point of contact so that I had to beware of bouncing off, had to shift to find space between those diamond-hard edges.

I remember both of us unclothed, finally, kneeling on the bed. I held her for a moment, then placed her into the position where I had been lying while I had been in her hands. And poised over her I saw her face give just a bit and her eyes begin to look away somewhere so I leaned forward and kissed each eyelid, to fold them back into this world, then leaning lower, brushed open her legs, parting with as tender a touch as I would have used to wipe a teardrop off her lashes, unclasping them as I would the pages of a precious, rare manuscript, eagerly but with loving respect.

I was ready then and she was too but I had brought her back too well because at the last possible moment she said *no, you can't, we can't, I don't have anything,* and twisted away from me so that I fell against the swath of her flanks, dissolving in their moistness, breathing. And though she quickly turned back to me, generous as before with her moisture, started kissing my face, eyes, mouth, saying, "Just wait a minute, that's all that it's going to take for me to put the diaphragm in, I just didn't think, not tonight," it was too late for me, I had also come back.

We put our clothes back on, Rachel looking at me thoughtfully. "If only the spirit were willing," she said.

"Have you had the diaphragm long?"

"Let me hear you say you love me."

I said it. "Was that very hard to say?" she wanted to know. "No," I said, quickly, because it had been very easy, the words trembling like water droplets on a flower's edge and falling of their own weight, needing no outside push.

"Then why is everything else so difficult? Why can't it all be simple, and natural and as easy as falling asleep or slipping into a warm bath?"

"Because nothing is," I said, "not now, not yet." I gestured vaguely, an explanation of hands to the photographs of her parents and of her youthful selves on the wall. "It would be just too much now, with everything."

She touched my cheek with one finger, the breasts I had just tasted moving under her top. "You silly boy. Are you afraid I would be insisting that you marry me?"

Caught, I said nothing, knowing she had named a circle of obligations I could not enter while I was busy trying to side-step other slithering hoops of responsibility constantly being cast at my feet.

"Well, I did say I was an old fashioned girl, I suppose," Rachel said. "Tell me, sweets, is this the little fling religious boys want to have? I mean are you allowed to go further or do you have to stop?"

"It's not that."

"No?"

"I love you," I said, and turning to the photographs on the wall, I said, "And I am sorry to you, sir, for not having debauched your daughter."

"Talk to my mother. My father almost never comes to my room," she said.

I reached out to touch her but she stepped back. "Please, Rachel," I said, "I want to."

"Always an honest person," she jeered, yet I was sincere, there was no deception in me.

"I just don't want to be confused," I finally said. "I want to know it's you because it's you and not because of something else."

"You know something," she said, "I believe you. I'm not kidding. I believe you. Only you're not quite clear about yourself. You're not quite sure the little public school girl with the hots is quite the thing for you but you're afraid of yourself, what you would do if you actually made love to me, right?"

She wouldn't let me interrupt. "So in the meantime, like little kids in the bathtub, we play with each other?"

"No," I said.

She smiled suddenly. "It's all right. It really is. You're nothing if not serious." She came back, within reaching distance. "I should tell you what I wanted to tell you when you showed up tonight."

I felt a gathering in my belly, a shapeless fear.

"Don't look so scared. I decided to go visit my parents as soon as school is done instead of waiting. And then, the way we had planned it, Sheila and I are going to Mexico." She was watching me carefully. "Sheila's big education. She barely got permission to stay at my parents' house. She had to swear to eat nothing but dairy dishes."

Rachel away, I thought. After I had considered exchanging Rockaway for time with Rachel, for motor boating, Shakespeare in the Park, Broadway shows on reduced tickets, her salty taste on the beach, above all, endless summer days and nights in her apartment, lip to neck, hands to breasts, thighs to thighs, finally beginning. Instead, Rachel away.

"With Sheila?"

"I would have asked you but I didn't think you would come."

"Well," I said, "I guess it's the Rockaways for me." She nodded. I waited.

"We'll write," she said. "And after the summer, who knows?"

"Yeah," I said. "Who knows."

She suddenly kissed me full on the lips. "Think of it as waiting for the days of purity."

I should say this before giving the final scene of this false beginning: while wholly innocent I am not without blame. True, I had been a *yeshiva* boy too long. My commitments of the heart are too easily overcome by weakness in the structure of my spine. I have sat too long curved over a study bench, I have bent my neck too often to the yoke of Torah, I have leaned over to hear Father's deadly voice too much. Acquiescence is in my blood; I have been trained to wait for the Messiah. To this day, before drinking a glass of water, with the glass at my lips, I pause and move my mouth silently. A blessing? No. Merely the imitation of the blessing, in case someone is watching. Like the phantom washing of the hands and the pretended benediction, my reflex actions are innumerable. Where everyone else is content to let sphincter muscles open and close, knees to jerk, teeth to root, arms to stretch and mouths to suck, I offer arguments for and against, test the revelations from Sinai against the utterances of the Early and Late Scholars, wait for the Lubavitcher Rebbie's weekly interpretation on the portion of the week, wonder about the taste of the final remnant on the plate of the Rabbi of Satmar. Involuntary, uncontrolled, impulsive my learned responses; by foreknowledge foresworn my desires. He raiseth some of our sons to be prophets and others of the young men to be Nazirites. What a prissy virgin, what a hoarder of precious gifts, what a frightened scatterer of seeds I am. Fine to be consecrated twice to God but why the same strip of skin both times? And yet, when that same acquiescent blood rushed to the spot, why did I resist its headstrong way?

Rachel and I said our good-byes in front of Gate 7. Off to one side Jonesey was saying his. His body hid the movement of his hand but the reflection in the giant plate glass windows betrayed the whisper of his palm against Sheila's ass. I watched the scene, feeling nostalgic, held Rachel's hand in a familiar grip.

"You'll write?"

"Of course."

"I'll miss you."

"I've been missing you for a month."

"It'll be better for us after. You'll see."

"See the world in far off Rockaway, land of a thousand miniature golf courses."

"With Jason, Jonesey, and the mysterious and invisible Dov. I can't believe the three of you went to the same school."

"Jonesey wasn't there often enough to count."

"I'll write to you too."

"I should have given you pre-addressed postcards, like my mother used to give me for camp."

"You never gave me the Rockaway address."

"Write to me at home."

"I'll make sure it passes the censor."

Then the hands of the airport clock came together and snipped the remaining time. I held Rachel for one long moment. She stretched to place cheek against cheek and rubbed. I squeezed the back of her hair. Then she and Sheila were walking up the ramp. She turned once to wave but I could see that she could not pick me out among the other well wishers. Perversely I wished I had been wearing a *yarmukah*, if for nothing but purposes of identification.

After the plane left, Jonesey and I talked about the summer. Dov had still not committed himself. Jonesey wanted me to pay for two-thirds of the rental if Dov didn't show up. I couldn't speak for Dov, his seminary classes were running late into June, but as for me, I was determined to be out of the house.

"I'd rather have Sheila for a roomie anyway," Jonesey said. "I was ready to make her a better offer than she was getting from Rachel."

"Like what?"

"Like grabbing her ass and letting my fingers do the talking."

"Right, Yossel."

He held his hand out, shuffling his fingers. "Want a whiff?" I jerked my head back and he laughed, bile making him chuckle deeply. A drop of blood falls off the heart, the Talmud says, with each hiccup.

These then the sights, sounds, smell and wisdom of the first few moments after Rachel.

II

Behold, this dreamer cometh . . . let us . . . cast him into one
of the pits . . . and we shall see what will become of his
dreams.

(Genesis 37:19, 20)

9.

Milk, spilled accidentally into meat, renders it unfit for the Orthodox table. But if the meat is sixty times the quantity of the milk, the droplet is made harmless. Such negation in numbers appeals to me. I would leave home when my departure would be absorbed in the frantic stirrings of other travelers. I would leave home early in the summer, when the wives and children of the Observant journey to the Catskills' bungalow colonies. Unnoticed amidst the preparations for the pilgrimage to Swan Lake, I can unpeg my own tent. Though my intentions are sacreligious, I cannot spoil the ritual. I become simply another Jewish wanderer, my participation in the march perhaps the most religious act I have performed recently.

Just in case, I did try to enlist my mother's help in dealing with Father.

"Tell him it would be like a vacation for the two of you, you know, the brat away from the house."

"Don't be silly. You're not in the way."

"Thanks, but tell him anyway."

"Are you sure you're going?"

"I'm sure."

"You will look nice with some color in your face."

Her face had color too, but it was bit feverish, an artificial brightness. She was not eager for me to go, yet seemed to want it for me if I did. And because I had been so much with Rachel, away from her, I am sure she welcomed our conspiratorial togetherness.

"Will you be near the beach?"

"On the first block off it."

"Maybe I can tell him we can both go out there sometime, maybe for a Sunday afternoon."

"There are no shady trees for him."

"And he doesn't like Yossel very much."

"I'm not all that crazy about him myself."

"All right, Jason, I'll talk to him. But how about your old mother? Can she come out for an afternoon sometimes?"

"Whenever you like, Mom."

"I wouldn't come empty-handed. I can be an old fashioned mother, you know, even if I'm too skinny. I'll bring you coffee cake. I found a new bakery."

"Kosher, I hope."

"Of course."

I kissed, bending only slightly. "You don't have to bring anything. Just talk to him."

"Well," she said, "I'll try, but you know your father."

I had to be satisfied with that because she, like me, had walked too long the prescribed four paces behind Father. And yet there had been a time once when she had been stronger. Stronger than Father certainly because she was responsible for his being on the road, she the one who forced him to dissipate his love and anger in the countryside, she who made him a stranger and a visitor to the house. His face used to be less familiar than that of Dov's father who used to come and claim his son after occasional weekends, his voice more mysterious than my grade school teacher's, the weight of his hand lighter than my mother's breath when she would return late and resume her guardianship with the sitter's departure.

I grew up bereft of stories. The war against the Jews killed off the storytellers. The time before the War is history not to be recounted, preserved only in a few cracked photographs of strangers. My mother has given me no childhood memories; Father is secretive about the wife and son he had before the War. They do not recognize that past. They begin their history only as far back as the postwar recovery hospitals and resettlement cities. I find out about things indirectly, discovering the older half-brother when Father told me I need not say the blessing for the first born the morning before Passover. Although my mother's first, counting from Father,

72

the real count, I am second born. But counting from either side, I am born in stillness. I overhear incomplete pieces of conversation, try to match the jagged ends to stories Jonesey occasionally requests from his father, fill spaces with books taken from an unlocked yet clearly off-limits glass cabinet. Among them all, I have constructed perfectly clear visions.

I can see my mother in the cold deadliness of sunless dawns, standing at *Appel*, while Herr Doktor Mengele walks along the lines, jabbing an antiseptic riding crop in shapeless chests, pointing a no deposit no return direction for those that stagger from his thrust. I torture myself with dreams of my mother bidden to do whore's service and Father forced to choose between feeding wife or child with final crusts. But because I don't know them as they were before their transformation into who they are, I see my mother as a child woman, being possessed by Father who, after her days at Bergen-Belsen, might have recalled the uncertain safety of her own father. And I see him as shrugging off from around his neck and shoulder the death that had sat there through the Russian spring and winter. So for me mother remains a victim, a body on the waves, the upturned black earth under sharp plows, the transparent, wet breath of bulls, floating helplessly on the wind.

Yet there were times when she was strong enough to stand alone. Father was away when she invited Serena for the weekend, a fellow survivor who had scrounged for potato peelings with her, behind the tar paper covered kitchen shed and shared with her the flat taste, the dryness, the life. But also Serena who had grown sleek on compensation money shrewdly invested and was coming to visit with neither husband nor child but a "Villy," as my mother imitated her friend's accent, "a young man, a mere boy."

I thought she meant a friend for me. I watched her prepare for their arrival, pushing a mop around, sandals on her feet, a swirling long skirt around her waist, an old kerchief tied turbanlike on her long hair. I followed her into the bedroom when she offered to let me see "your mother become beautiful." Her hair loose, in a wide-sleeved hostess gown, she narrated her quick, decisive, precise movements. "No lipstick, just the tiniest bit of eyeshadow, my love, and they all think you're looking right into their soul."

Willy turned out to have wavy brown hair and a camel's hair coat a bit too long for him, perhaps inherited from Serena's previous young man. He was quick to light Serena's cigarettes but followed my mother's movements with his eyes. Serena didn't seem to mind, delighting in his alertness. "See my Villy," she laughed to my mother, twisting a gold bracelet dangling with charms, "he's the son I never had." And laughed and laughed. Stupid me, with my baseball cards and Superman comics and Hardy Boys Mysteries, and crocheted horse on the wall next to my bed, wondered why she couldn't have any children of her own and if Willy were adopted. They slept together in my room, which seemed reasonable to me since I got to sleep in my mother's room. During dinner I pretended that Serena and Willy were stepparents to my mother and me, the two of us brother and sister abandoned by a mean father.

After dinner my mother insisted they go out, excited by her Friday night liberty. "You're the man of the house," she laughed at Willy, "Can you handle two attractive women at the same time?" Offering each of them an arm, Willy could, and they left for nightclub, bar, or restaurant. What I remember most about Willy is how tight his pants were and how well he spoke English, a real American, where Father had to work constantly at his pronounciation, ironing out those foreign twists of expression. He knew the difficulties of selling slipcovers to Gentiles. "Who wants to buy from a greener," he would say and struggle with a special dictionary. "You won't have to be ashamed of me," he insisted, "in a little while I will talk like a native."

I went to sleep that night praying for Father to come home though I was fairly sure he would not be arriving Friday night. But I fell asleep, hoping anyway, waiting for the sound of shoeless feet on carpet, coat sleeve against the wall, swallowed thud of falling shoes, final squeak of body against the cushions of the couch, for of course, I would be in his bed.

After one of those returns, there were shouts and the sound of smashed dishes. Father stopped going away and my mother began to light candles Friday night and Father waved shiny scissors near my mother, snipping threateningly. That was the last time she stood up to him, holding his hand back, but that was no help to me because the scissors did swallow my hair and hers eventually disappeared too, under a kerchief that aged her. I waited and waited for her voice to rise, but it never did. She was silent, I was shorn, and scraggly; bearded Father was always home. And it was quiet, very quiet, after that time when Father came home and found me all alone in the house.

But I wanted to talk about departures, not homecomings. The front door of our house moves reluctantly, protesting whether it is opening or closing. I found Father oiling those hinges one day and to my surprise, accepting without complaint my carefully reasoned arguments for leaving. I told him I had a job as a tea boy in a kosher hotel and needed to live nearby, in Long Beach, for the summer. He simply nodded. The smell of oil filled the air.

"Is there a *shul* nearby too?"

"On the premises."

"And for *Shabbat*?"

"I have to serve late Friday night and Saturday afternoon. It's within walking distance."

"Well," he said, "it is too far from home, I suppose."

Puzzled, almost disappointed, how is one to measure the significance of a step if not by the volume of anger from those protesting the move. I asked my mother what was going on.

"Landau sold to a big company. They want your father but it would be on Seventh Avenue in Manhattan."

"He doesn't feel like traveling?"

She smiled, briefly. "He likes being closer to home."

"Well," I said, not conscious of the smears of family history, "he would be near the diamond center with all the people from *shul*."

I went to call Jonesey, to tell him of my unopposed exodus. When I left, the door swung closed behind me without a sound.

10.

Mind you, this coming forth into freedom was a little like the adventures of the ten year old who ran away from home but had to return after circling the block because he was not allowed to cross the street by himself. I dared move from Brooklyn into Far Rockaway, but crossing the borough boundaries into Queens did not mean that I was beyond the keen eyesight and bloodhound scent of the Orthodox Secret Service. Let that yammie fly off my head, let me enter a candy store that had shuttered for Passover, dare chew on a stick of gum that does not carry the K or u designation of the Rabbinical Council, and I've had it. Somehow, somewhere, where I least expect it, a member of the OSS network will notice and pass the word to the other faithful. From that moment on, you're damaged goods, my good fellow. You will be bypassed in synagogue even though a Levite is needed at the Scroll and you're the only Levite in sight. The bolder girls on Eastern Parkway will look at you knowingly but even they will refuse to return your wishes for a Good Sabbath, and your Father's neighbor, provided he has not unilaterally denounced you from the pulpit, will have a friendly chat with your Father after prayers in an attempt to straighten you out.

So there I am on Beach 44th Street, Far Rockaway, free, free, free at last, separated from Brooklyn and the guardians of the faith by double carfare and tolls, but there is a synagogue down the block, a sprinkling of *yarmukahs* on the beach, Father's buddy Mr. Hartstein on Thirty-sixth Street would be glad to look in on me, my mother is committed to bountiful visits, and Dov, the once and future Rabbi is ready to help me devote all my attention to all six hundred and thirteen precepts of religion. Some running away!

Our summer home away from home consisted of two rooms on a three floor walk-up. The bathroom was in the hall but the other rooms on the floor were not rented. The larger first room of our apartment split into a kitchen and a sort of alcove with a cot and dresser. The other room was under the slope of the roof and only partitioned from the first. There would be no secrets in rooms 5 and 5A. The sea air peeled the walls and sapped the paint from its original white, but Jonesey stood with an armful of *Playboy* magazines, ready to decorate.

"You take the kitchen, I'm not the domestic type. I'll take the other room, from now on officially known as the boom-boom room. If your pal ever gets here, he has a choice between your side and one of the other apartments on the floor." He held his armful of paper kindlings toward me. "Something for a cold night?"

"That's all right. I want you to keep them all, just like home."

"These are all new, man. I left the old ones to my brother-in-law. His Polaroid is busted."

From the other side of the partition, above the sound of stapling, he announced, "We're going to agree on one rule, Jase. Whoever's got a broad, has the place to himself. Deal?"

"Sure," I said, resigning myself to enforced walks outside while Jonesey manages inside. Not that I would need the rule or its modifications, but I remembered not to let it go by completely without a question. The rumor was that the Army hated to draft English and Philosophy majors. They asked too many questions, interfering with the chain of command. "Charge? Why charge? What is the meaning of charge? What is its reality? What is its antithesis? What is its etymology? When was it first used? Is its long, drawn-out beat more effective than say the two beats of 'forward?'" So, just to keep in shape, I questioned Jonesey.

"What's the idea behind the rule, Jonesey?"

"The eleventh commandment. Cunt is king and thou shalt not waste it."

"Cunt," I reasonably pointed out, "can't be king. Queen maybe. Or princess. But not king."

After a moment's pause, he said, "Can we agree it's sacred?"

77

"O.K., for argument's sake."

"Then come over here."

First I unpacked my suitcase and my JUDY BOND ON STRIKE shopping bag. Then I found a place in the dresser drawer for my special blue velvet bag that held the magic t'filin, the two boxes with the leather straps that I was supposed to wear every morning during prayers. Before closing the drawer I checked carefully inside the bag. In one of the stories I learned as a child, a doubtful father hides a twenty dollar bill inside the bag and discovers the boy's negligence when the son writes home for extra cash. The bag was clear and I went to Jonesey's section to debate further the rules and regulations of our new house of worship.

Jonesey met me at the doorway. "Close your eyes and give me your hand."

He dragged my palm quickly across the closest centerfold, a glossy, full-breasted girl standing in a boy's locker room, naked but for a sweatsock dangling strategically between her legs, so that I left a light smear behind.

"This is the beginning of your religious experience. You're getting laid this summer even if it kills me. Or you."

"A fate worse than death."

"Cute," he said, "very cute. Charm their panties off with wit. Tickle them with some Commentaries. Give them two fingers of Tales of Wonder-Working Rabbis. Girls will just lap up that kind of stuff."

"True," I told him, "the old Rabbis were no slouches. The sage Samuel, in an argument with Rav, claims that sexual intercourse can be achieved without injury to the hymen. How does that grab you?"

"Right where it should. How did it grab the old guys?"

"They all bowed to Shmuel's greater knowledge in such matters." He whistled with admiration. "Any pictures?"

"No pictures, Jonesey. You've cornered the market on pictures."

He bowed to the glistening skin on the walls and continued to sway in mock prayer. "Bless us, Father in heaven, during this new moon. Give us the flow of monthly happiness. Give us health, give us wealth, gives us wet pussy, and now we say amen."

I went to finish unpacking. He followed and watched me

78

hang a teflon pan on the wall near the sink and put silverware in a drawer. "I was counting on you and your mother to provide the domestic comforts. You didn't disappoint me. Thanks, fella, I owe you one."

"It's a dairy pan, Jonesey. Don't broil lamb chops on it, all right?"

He stared at me. "Listen, Rabbi, there is a question I meant to ask in school but was always afraid I'd get booted for it. Now listen carefully. If meat makes a dairy pan unclean, what does bacon do to it? Now don't rush your answer, take the full sixty seconds. The issues are the following: Does the pan become *tref* because bacon is meat, does it become *tref* because bacon is always *tref*, and if both, which first and why?"

"It all depends," I said, "on who asks the question and whether it's my mother's pan or not."

"I thought it depended on whether the owner of the pan ever found out about it or not," Jonesey said, and went back to his side.

I think of Jonesey as trapped in one of those amusement park games called the "Moon Walk" or "Moon Base." It consists of a gigantic plastic balloon that surrounds an empty plastic surface curved to make standing difficult. The idea is to jump and bounce, to ricochet without being hurt, to have the illusion of moon gravity flight. For as long as I have known him, Jonesey had been bouncing, the eternal spaceman, cushioned always by an excess of parental love. Because Jonesey could not harm himself, no matter how hard he tried. His parents, survivors both, absorbed the pain of all his pratfalls. Nothing sprang back at him. For the Kellermans there was nothing else after the war but love. No beliefs, no morals, no religion. That Jonesey went to a *yeshiva* was an accident. He played stickball with the boys on the block so he went to their school. He could have just as easily attended Colby's Academy or a fat camp in the Catskills. When Jonesey's father came to school, in response to insistent letters from Rabbi Koenig, we sneaked out of class to watch. There sat Yossie's father, blotting Rabbi Koenig's anger with a totally accepting smile and always agreeing nods of the head. Why was he the only one who understood how harmless our little games were? He did not seem devastated by news that his boy was caught in the cloak room reading dirty magazines or smoking or using words not properly part of a *yeshiva* boy's vocabulary. Yossie would march into the office. Through the glass door we would see but not hear his father become magnificently angry: smash his fist at the ceiling, clench it under Jonesey's nose, stomp, ask heaven for forgiveness with open arms. And afterwards, serious faced, yank Jonesey from school early and drive him home. The next day Jonesey would be back in class, seriously unrepentant.

"There is no Jewish mark on them," Rabbi Winkler complained in *shul,* "no *yiddishe pintele.*" And that must have been the line that brought the smile to Sander Kellerman's face. An epitaph for survivors, certainly. Calmly, Jonesey's father disqualified himself from further priestly benedictions on the holidays, though his voice was deep and warm and his tune that of the old country. I think this bountiful acceptance has fixed Jonesey's character, education and moral sense at the high school level. He remains in search of some act that would at least surprise his parents into displeasure. How fortunate for my own development to have had constant disapproval against which I could test myself.

But that was why I needed Dov out there in that summer place. With only Jonesey there, I wanted to push against Jonesey, always against rules. But between Jonesey the naysayer and Dov, the joyful dancing bear of acceptance, there is Jason, the reasonable searcher, the thoughtful mediator, the golden mean. With Dov absent, I am forced into the role of the apologist. I shrink from Jonesey's extreme but there is no one to repel me from Dov's total surrender to religion. How can the Defender of the Faith stand there bareheaded, with dollar bills in the pockets of his Sabbath suit? In a dream I sit in *yeshiva* bent over the Talmud. Asked to explain a passage, I rise, gesture with the thumb, speak, stop as Rabbi Baumel's face shows horror. I run through my comments, note nothing blasphemous, realize at last that I had not put my *yarmukah* on my head and had been speaking Sacred Words uncovered. I fumble desperately but cannot find my *kappele* in any of my pockets. Thus unarmed, Jonesey forces me to battle. Where was Dov, preserver of my youthful faith?

With a knock on the door but without waiting for an invitation, our landlady entered. She had asked us to call her Barbara, refusing the Mrs. Feuerstein we had offered her. She seemed to be about forty. Her early summer tan had not yet reached the leathery stage and she wore her shorts conscious of the way she moved. Her hair, worn high and tied off, fell downward in a little round burst, like the ends of leaves in a batch of celery.

"Are you boys settling in?"

Jonesey smiled. "We're on the ball here, Barbara."

"Listen," she said, her voice a little throaty, a bit affected, "I expect you to behave yourself here, you understand?" But she touched her hair, adjusted her shoulders, tugged at her shorts. "I took a chance, you know, renting to young men. We usually take only families, you know."

Jonesey walked close to her and smiled. "You can treat us like family, Mrs. Feuerstein."

"Call me Barbara," she said, "Mr. Feuerstein hates it when people think I'm old." She hesitated. "You *will* be good boys, won't you?" And then the joke must have hit her because she suddenly smiled very brightly and said, "Or mamma will spank."

With that, she left. From the back, the shape of her bikini panties was clearly outlined against her shorts, the golden mean between ass and pants. In spite of myself, I stared and felt my heart bounce. I swallowed and noticed Jonesey looking at me. "And the best thing is," he said, "she's got legs like a young girl, not a varicose vein in sight. And she says she's had her two kids natural, whatever that means, without a mark on her. Anywhere. Make sure you knock when you come in at nights."

I can offer no other explanation for having delivered myself up to Jonesey's summer guidance. It had to be the lure of flesh. I swallowed the taste and wanted more. I was a debutante and had to get out, formally or not. I have no other way of understanding why even as I began my daily schedule of taking the train to the red stones of Bobst Library, for a careful study of the books on the Comprehensive List, from Beowulf to Beckett. I also began an intense consideration of other possibilities, most particularly the offerings of the

81

SLURP girl on the boardwalk. I can only offer images by way of defense: the line of the woman's panties, the flash of Rachel's lips, the sight of girls at Bobst with seamless bras under summer blouses, and the SLURP girl curled on the counter, next to the waffle iron, knees whitening, licking ice cream from a cone.

And one more thing. Newly established, first time in Far Rockaway, a bow to the Orthodox. Beach 52, Friday mornings from 6 to 7 and all afternoons from 2 to 5 will be a closed beach for the Orthodox bathers. Only women allowed, no mixed sunning or swimming. As for the Friday morning hour (our landlady informs us, eyes wide), under a canvas hut, naked men rush into the sea and immerse themselves three times in ritual purification.

"The Atlantic is but a wading pool for the Believers," Jonesey laughed.

I was not surprised. Next door to SLURP, also of recent creation, Hebrew National Hot Dogs and Hamburgers, the servers with *yarmukahs,* and SLURP, sporting a multicolored K for Kosher, closes Friday nights and Saturdays. As for the SLURP girl, rumor has it, I inform Jonesey, that she is a *Bais Yaakov* girl, orthodox, religious, Jewish, untouchable.

"When she turns around, her apron doesn't reach all the way and you can see she wears a bathing suit underneath," Jonesey observes. Can she be the deep blue sea for a lapsed believer like me?

11.

"Room 5, telephone, room 5!"

Landlady Barbara's voice called me down one evening. I knew the call on the pay phone downstairs was for me because if it had been for Jonesey, she would have called him "Joseph," the name on the lease. I picked up the dangling shell and said hello, watching Mr. Feuerstein, stripped to the waist, his chest puckering at the breast as he hunched over and dealt pinochle to Hank, the black handyman and Dr. Fein, a retired gynocologist who wore gold rimmed sunglasses. At another card table on the porch Barbara Feuerstein was playing canasta, her nails the color of her brick shorts. There was a slight wind and little power left in the setting sun but Feuerstein would do no more even on rainy days than put a sleeveless undershirt on, and his wife wore shorts, she claimed, until November. Summer was their season; they closed the place down for the winter.

"How are you, Jason?" my mother said, "did I call after supper?"

"Sure, Mom. Jonesey is just doing the dishes." She laughed. "Did you do the cooking?"

"Meal Mart did. Don't forget to tell *Abba*. We're keeping the faith out here."

She did not say anything. Whatever it was that she allowed herself to think, she never said it to me about Father. They must have taught loyalty in the old days. I can recall only one instance when she contradicted Father after the move to Crown Heights and the transformation of the Koles. I was still in P.S. 12 and attending Sunday School after classes on Tuesday nights, at Rabbi Itzkowitz's house. Rabbi Itzkowitz was in a wheel chair, a little man, shrunken I think by his

83

disappointed wait for the Messiah as much as by his illness. But he had a wonderful voice that could whisper the sound and feel of robes at the Temple; gold and silver thread, blue, purple and scarlet yarn, fine linen, skins of rams dyed red, or the words for cubits, bushels, shekels, and other forgotten measures. He could swell above the noise of the power drills of Con Edison outside when he needed to roll the mighty names of generations, the begetters and the begotten. *Cain who begot Enoch to whom was born Irad who begot Mehujael who fathered Methusael who begot Lamech, these the generations of the accursed Cain the Wanderer.* I loved those sounds. I still do, although the modern litany of lost generations, the roll call of Auschwitz, Dachau, Maidenek, and Buchenwald, Sobibor, Treblinka, and Birkenau, camps of no begetting, have the same effect on me as the drumbeat of Biblical generations. Auden claims that poets revel in the sounds of those begetters. I hope only that my shiver at the sounds of the misbegotten would hone me into a sensitive teacher of poetry.

In any case, after I returned from Rabbi Itzkowitz one Tuesday evening, Father asked me about my lesson that day. I stood there, newly shorn, already being measured by my careful tailor of a Father for my new role in *yeshiva* and would not answer him. I was surprised by the question as well as troubled by the answer. I had learned about the story of Abraham's near-sacrifice of Isaac and had been frightened by the father's willingness to offer up his long awaited son. I had come home fearful, my neck tensing to the touch of the knife. After much urging, I confessed. Father put a hand on my shoulder (His mother's father was named Menachem, which means "comforter." Though not his name, Father was not yet weaned from kindness.) "Abraham knew it would be all right. A child's father always knows."

My mother said nothing then, but later, when he was away from home, told me quietly, "A mother is the only one who knows for sure," and laughed. I did not understand her meaning but sensed her feelings, and for a little while, was convinced of the powerlessness of fathers. But that is the only direct contradiction of Father that I recall.

"I called to tell you that Dov's father called. He doesn't

think Dov will be joining you. He is thinking of taking examinations."

"During the summer?"

"I'm only a messenger."

But I had long suspected Dov would not be making my withdrawal from 99 and $^{44}/_{100}$ percent religion any easier. I asked about my other dear departed friend. "Any mail?"

"Yes," she said, "something for you in a plain brown envelope."

"Come on, Mom."

"Actually," she said, "it's a letter with a Florida postmark."

"Bring it tomorrow."

"Tomorrow?" she said, teasing, "are you out of food already? I didn't think you would need me until Wednesday at least."

Her lightness was out of character and delightful. "All right, Mom, maybe I better come in for it right now. I've got time."

"If you'll settle for my postal service, I'll bring it out tomorrow."

I remembered the payment I had offered her for her help in convincing Father to let me go for the summer. "Come in the afternoon. The sun is great."

"Wait for me," she sang, "you won't be disappointed."

Upstairs Jonesey was brushing his teeth. "Who was it?" he asked frothily.

"My mother. I got a letter from Rachel."

He continued with his teeth, putting the brush all the way in to get the bristles on the inside of his teeth.

"Has Sheila written you?"

"All in good time," he said, "not to worry." He showed his teeth. "What do you think?"

"Beautiful. Where are you going?"

"Checking out the Boardwalk. Coming?"

"Have you met someone?"

"The good Lord will provide," he said. "I took some dimes from you, for the games at Fascination." In the doorway he winked. "If the landlady wants something, give it to her. Just lock the door." And he left.

In anticipation of having to leave the library earlier the next day and visit with my mother, I tried reading. I was still in the middle of the first segment of the six part comprehensives. Much lonely reading in the period. With the exception of Chaucer's pilgrims, stories of single heroes: the seafarer, the wanderer, Beowulf the rescuer, Pearl in the Garden, the death of Arthur. Old words, old deaths. I tried the furrows of Piers Plowman. The Middle English, looking strange but sounding familiar, was like the discussions in Hungarian between my parents; meanings I could sense but not understand, more words about more deaths. But the delight of spirit struggling beneath the burden of laws was perceptible.

Jonesey took off from work the next day. He had been going in most mornings, having heard that sun bathing during early hours is dangerous. The warning did not faze him but he was sure all the girls would have read about it and would be staying away. "No use hunting in the off season," he shrugged. But he stayed home that morning. "If your old lady shows up early with all the goodies, I want to be here."

I was also back early from the library but by one my mother had still not come. "Relax," Jonesey said, "maybe she's waiting for the day's mail."

"Expecting a good-bye note from Sheila?"

"To your address?"

When the phone rang I took the steps downward three at a time, meeting Mrs. Feuerstein's "Room 5!" in person. "How did you know it was for you?" she asked, surprised to see me, unaware of her preference for Jonesey's name.

"I'm the popular one," I told her and took the phone from her hand, eagerly. But Dov was not at the other end and my mother wasn't calling. It was certainly not Rachel, absentee tenant of my thoughts. The call was from the manager of the Grand Paradise, one of the kosher hotels in Long Beach where I had my name listed. I was needed for an early evening wedding, had to show by two-thirty for set-ups. He had called me late, I figured he needed me and got twenty-five dollars instead of the customary twenty, plus time and a half if it went after nine.

Jonesey watched me change into black chinos and white shirt.

"Funny outfit for the beach."

"Listen," I said, "my mother should be here."

"Hasn't she seen you in a bathing suit?"

I managed to get his attention finally by putting my bow-tie on. "A wedding?"

"Yeah. I'm a late replacement for the groom. Tell my mother I'm sorry I couldn't wait."

"Sure," he said. "What if she wants to go to the beach?"

"Let her," I told him. "She's old enough."

But I kept putting off the time to leave, needing the sustenance of Rachel's letter while serving at the Grand Paradise. The hotel was not just kosher but *glatt kosher*, ritually squeaky clean, and would have separate seating for men and women. Sometimes, if the people were insistent, the manager would hire waitresses to serve the ladies behind the partition but he hated doing it because it meant paying union wages. I did not look forward to serving the women. We had to wear the special velvet *yarmukahs* supplied by the caterer. We looked foreign in them and were treated with disdain by the guests, many of whom suspected us to be Gentiles and made remarks about us freely in Yiddish.

When I finally heard my mother's steps in the hall I realized I was not wearing my cap. I had time to jump for it but I held back. I was not at home; she was visiting me at my place. Even temporary quarters are legal castles.

Then my mother popped into the room. Like toast, like corn, like a cap on a bottle, she took a quick hop over the threshold and was a burst of color and sound in the room. The color was in the sharp green of her shift and matching kerchief that made her look stylish and vigorous, the sound in unlikely chatter and noisy movement. She began moving around the room, touching my neatly covered bed, patting the row of cans on the shelf above the sink, smoothing the paper on the wall on which Jonesey and I kept a running account of needs and costs. She paused to peck me on the cheek and place an elegantly wrapped little package on the table, talking without stop in a slightly feverish, high voice. She continued to clutch a shoulder bag against her side.

"I'm sorry I'm late, I hope you were not concerned, but it took me so long to prepare I lost all sense of time. I was actually going to wear a bathing suit but the only suit I had I

87

just couldn't wear, it was so old, I bought it when your father and I planned a vacation that we didn't quite manage." She turned to explain to Jonesey. "Jason was still a child. It was a long time ago. We were going to rent a cabin in the mountains. But the air here is just wonderful."

"Sit down, Mrs. Kole," Jonesey said, unexpectedly considerate, "we cleaned all morning for you."

My mother's smile was too bright, too eager. The train ride must have confused her or the open beaches. I felt vaguely embarrassed for her though there was no reason to be. She looked cool and elegant; it was only her voice that was unsure.

"Listen Mom, I have to leave," I said, but she would not let me finish. "I knew I would keep you from the sun. It's best in the afternoon, isn't it?"

She was looking right at me and must have seen my uniform, must have noticed the missing skull-cap, but said nothing. She had always valued my dignity and I wanted desperately to have her retain hers.

"I have a wedding to go to at the Grand Paradise. I'm really sorry, Mom."

"I was wondering why you looked so dressed up," she smiled, but I saw she finally understood I would not be going to the beach with her. The disappointment, hurting her, also restored her. She had learned her restraint well over the years. "Oh," she said, "it's just as well I didn't bring a bathing suit." Her voice calmed now, she relaxed completely, smiled. "I brought something for the body and something for the soul."

She reached into her shoulder bag and took out an envelope.

"Hey," said Jonesey, "what a thin little slice of bread for the body. Growing boys starve to death on diets like that, Mrs. Kole."

I simply took the envelope from her hand, inexplicably pleased by the slanted flow of my name on the paper.

"And for the soul," my mother laughed toward Jonesey, "in that little box on the table, the only thing I could find after wasting the morning with my own vanity, are Jason's favorite chocolates."

"Chocolate covered cherries," Jonesey said, surprising me

again and conscious of his effect. "Believe me, Mrs. Kole, they're my favorites too."

"I feel like a guest," my mother said, "a guest should bring a gift, not groceries, don't you think?"

"You're my housewarming present, Mom, you didn't have to bring anything." For the moment I could forget about Rachel's letter, realizing that my mother and I had reached a new level of complicity with our shared secret of my bareheadedness and her acknowledgement of the existence of that mysterious bathing suit. There was a third connection too. I did not consider how willing a go-between she was. It had seemed so natural to give Rachel my permanent rather than my summer address. I did not even rip Rachel's letter open, testing my powers of self-restraint but also intent on attending my mother completely for the moment.

"I'm really late for work, Mom," I said. "I tried calling to tell you not to come. A two hour ride for nothing."

But she was fine. Her sense of herself, as always when out of the house, was intact.

"It's all right, dear, it wasn't a waste. I got to see you and Yossie, I learned the route, I can come back next time."

"And thanks for this," I said, lifting the letter.

"Oh," she said, "that reminds me. There is another message. Your father wants you to call him. He'll be home after work."

"Anything special?"

"I think," she said, "he knew I would reassure myself that you are healthy. He probably would want to know whether you are also wealthy and wise."

"Well," I said, "tell him I'm off to work. As far as being wise, Jonesey said he would teach me some things."

She smiled, not unaware, I think, of the teachings of Jonesey.

"I think he is concerned that Dov would not be coming here." And to alleviate the slur on Jonesey, she turned to him and said, "I'll tell your father how well you're looking." And she stood.

"I'll drop you at the station," I offered.

"No," she said. "I'd like to go down to the boardwalk and walk around a little. I love the air."

"I'll walk you," Jonesey said.

"That's very sweet of you, Yossi, but please don't bother." She kissed me on the cheek and said, "We miss you at home. Don't forget to call," and left. I realized that I had been holding the letter clutched in my hand and had done nothing more than bend my neck to her kiss.

"That's some put together old lady you've got there," Jonesey said. "Want me to wait for you tonight? I want to go see what the high school twat is doing on Flatbush Avenue."

"I'll be working late," I said, and ran down to the car, to read my letter in peace, seeing Jonesey slowing unwrapping my gift of chocolate cherries.

With equal care, I unraveled Rachel's letter.

Dear Jason—I hope our letters don't cross. We got an earlier flight so we'll be in Mexico City by the time you get this. If you've written, your letter is sitting propped against my mirror, tempting my father's curiosity and my mother's concern. They expect an aura of sanctity in spite of anything I tell them. Sheila is very eager, her vegetarian diet at my house has sharpened her taste for meat, I'm afraid. I was looking forward to your letters, especially as you reached the love sonnets and the early Donne in your summer's reading. Write, please, but save them so you can read them to me after the summer. Think of us (you and me) together. Enjoy. I'll write.

She signed it "Love, R." What a regal signature, I thought, what a queenly scrawl, and resigned myself to a summer without either Dov or Rachel. Summer being her season, I wondered if she would have anything left over for my fall harvest. Then I went to work, wore my velvet cap, was assigned to the men's section and responded casually to questions in Yiddish by the dancing men, one of whom asked me where in Hungary my father came from, recognizing the slant of my vowels. I didn't know, I told him, I was born here.

12.

"I'll drive," Jonesey said when I got back to our place. He thought I had come rushing back, eager for the trip, but the wedding had taken place earlier than I expected. I had forgotten that Tuesday was considered a day of luck and the ceremony would take place in daylight. The setting sun, a pagan witness, cheered on the religious proceedings.

"Just take the car," I said, feeling crushed by time, the centuries of my summer reading as well as the weeks of my summer wait.

"Trust me," he said, "the night's on me."

I wanted to change, smelling on myself the evening's meal but he wouldn't let me. "You're dressed just right for the occasion. Even your little bow tie is perfect."

But I threw the bow tie on the bed anyway. No occasion seemed perfect for that.

He drove firmly, intent on the road and alert to the sounds of the car. The night was pleasant. We kept the windows open so that the wind ruffled our hair and made it difficult to listen to the ball game on the radio.

"Still the Yankees?"

"Can't catch anything else."

"Bring it in. I think I can get someone to fix it for you so you can pick up a winner."

Although the usual group of girls milled in front of Erasmus and a tougher bunch sat on the steps of the church opposite, Jonesey did not stop, passing by as he had the girls along earlier parts of Flatbush Avenue who were trying to hitch to the same corner. I didn't complain. Jonesey didn't say anything either. He turned right at Empire Boulevard, past Wetson's. I involuntarily sniffed for the baking bread at Bond's around the corner. Soon we were near my house.

"I just saw my mother today," I finally said.

"This won't be a family affair," he said.

He turned left into Brooklyn Avenue and slowed down so that we had to stop for a light when we reached Eastern Parkway.

"What's the idea? Meeting a Lubavitcher girl?"

"Look," he commanded, and jabbed with his head.

On the service road of Eastern Parkway a black girl was getting into a dark Cadillac with white seats. As the car pulled out, from across the Avenue another car slipped into the spot, cut its lights and waited.

The light changed and Jonesey streaked out, across the wide Parkway, made the first left, then another into New York Avenue and screeching, another left into the service road of Eastern Parkway, not stopping until he was parked on the near side of Brooklyn Avenue. Across, in front of us, the previous car still waited.

"One car," Jonesey gloated, "no waiting."

"What the hell," I said.

"You can't be that thick. The girl is working this spot. I've been noticing her for a few weeks. We're next."

"Are you crazy," I said. "For all you know, she's got diseases coming out of her ears."

"If she had, the union would be down here, picketing. Listen, she's okay. Frankie from work was here. He said he ran his finger inside her with alcohol and she didn't jump. If she had the clap she would have yelled."

"She should have yelled anyway," I whispered, "raw skin is raw skin. I think Frankie was paying for an ear job."

"Why are you whispering?" Jonesey asked.

The Caddy stopped on Brooklyn Avenue and let the girl out. She was tall and carried a shoulder bag. Her skirt was very short. I couldn't make her face out. She walked over to the waiting car, bent down, spoke for a few minutes, then got in. The car drove off. "This is it," Jonesey said, suddenly whispering. "Ready or not."

As soon as the light changed, he rolled the car into the parking spot across the street and stopped. Reaching into his shirt pocket, he flipped a piece of foil paper at me. "Here."

"I don't want it," I said. "I don't want anything to do with this."

"Hey," he said, "relax. I may be picking the tab up for this but we're at separate tables here."

I had counted barely ten minutes between the first car and the second. "Where do they take her?"

"Anywhere where it's dark. There's a willow in front of the church on Brooklyn that will make it as cozy as a four-poster."

The details intrigued me. I used them to postpone the decision.

"How much do you think she'll want?"

Jonesey grinned. "We can bargain for a rate. A Jewish deal."

"I'm not doing it," I said. "Anyway, the car's too small."

He opened his side, got out and got into the back. "Look. She's on a tight schedule. You drive. Maybe you'll change your mind."

I had automatically slid over to the driver's seat. "I'm getting out of here." He gripped my shoulder. "Here she comes."

"Looking for a date?" the girl suddenly said, leaning into the open front window. Her blouse fell away and I could see she wore nothing beneath it. A purple blouse, I noticed, from a crepe material that was nearly transparent. Her patent leather bag gleamed. She must have seen Jonesey in the back and began straightening up. "Sorry, fellows, no doubleheaders," she said.

Jonesey slid to her side. "It's only me. Come on in." But she stood there, hesitant. "Twenty bucks," Jonesey said, "but I gotta see it first." She must have decided. I felt cold. She moved to Jonesey's side and before getting in, lifted her skirt quickly to show she had nothing on underneath it. I looked around, fearful of a circling patrol car.

"Drive," she said, "stay on the Parkway."

I moved out, saw her sit back against the rear, pull her skirt up and extend one leg along the seat, bending the other at the knee. I went by Kingston Avenue, passing the Lubavitcher Synagogue, moved toward Albany, passing Jonesey's house along the way. "No kissing, no feeling," I heard her say, "you're on your own."

"Just make room," Jonesey panted, familiar with the contours of the back seat. In the rear view mirror, spying, I saw the bucking of Jonesey's head and the girl's dark face, the nose flat, back against the seat, just staring. I tried not to hear anything, strained for Phil Rizutto's voice on the Yankee broadcast. Jonesey gasped. There was the sound of shifting. The girl, smelling of Right Guard, tapped me on the shoulder. "How about you, honey?"

"He's waiting to fall in love first," Jonesey laughed. "What's your name?"

"Call me Iris," she said.

"Iris," Jonesey said, "do you blow?"

"You pay your money and you get your laundry," she said.

I pulled up on the corner of Brooklyn and Eastern Parkway. She jabbed at my shoulder. "Circle around. Fuzz." During that final loop, she lit a cigarette, never having removed her bag. "This your regular spot for a while?" Jonesey asked.

"Until it's time to move," she said. We were back on the corner. There was another car waiting. "I'll be back," Jonesey said as she was getting out. "The doctor's in, any time," she said, and leaving, "get a bigger car." Then she got out, smoothed her skirt down, flipped away her cigarette, took a deep breath and moved to the next car. The light changed and I turned left into Eastern Parkway, away from them.

"She must clear two, two-fifty a night," Jonesey said after a little while.

"That was fucking disgusting," I said.

"Sure it was," he said placidly. "What's wrong with that?"

"Everything," I said.

His voice was almost gentle. "You protect yourself too much. It's a fuck. That's all. It's feeling your strength. Feelings are always a little disgusting. Even good ones."

It was not the time to start a discussion with him. I suppose he had a point. I had been taught modesty. I believed too much in dignity. For what the body yearns, the soul spurns. Reflection quiets instant desires. I conceive too clearly of my departing disgust. I distrust anger too much, allow too much power to my imagination. For the moment, sex lives, devours. Peace, now, peace, now, peace, now. The rhythm of the chant stilled my thoughts. We got back to a dark house, card players asleep, SLURP shuttered, Jonesey spent. Only the ocean continued to grind away. If a man entice a virgin, I remembered before sleep, he shall pay dowry as to a wife, with fifty shekels considered the dowry of a virgin. But some commentaries think he must make an offer of marriage. The ruling comes in the middle of a section on compensations. The spirit of restitution lay heavily on Beach 44th Street, in Rockaway.

13.

I had to be reminded by another call from my mother that I owed Father a call. That wasn't the main reason for her calling, she said. She just wanted to know how we were. "It's very quiet in the house without you."

"I'm getting a lot of work done out here," I said by way of explanation, pained by the tone of her voice.

"I know," she said, and waited. Compelled by her silence, I apologized again for having left for work, urged her to visit whenever she liked. "The sand is so fine it sifts through cloth."

"You have nice color," she said. I told her that she too looked wonderful. "Well," she said, "the sun reaches the back porch late in the afternoon for a little while but by the time your father comes home from work the chairs are cool enough to sit on."

She didn't know what Father wanted. She wasn't quite sure of what she wanted. She just held on to the phone. I stood barefoot in the hall, sand underfoot, and ignored my landlady's silent disapproval. "You know," my mother said, her voice lower, somehow intimate, "I was thinking. In the camps we used to save beets. Before selections we used to rub it on our faces to give them some color, so we would look healthy. Did I ever tell you this?"

But she had not; she must have known that. She never told.

"Well," she said, "your silly mother always seemed to have color, I have skin like my father, and I'm ashamed to say that I worried only about looking pretty and would pinch my cheeks until they hurt. Not that there were any mirrors, of course."

"It was a long time ago," I said, my throat tight. "You were young"

She laughed, lightly. Her voice was normal. "I thought you should know."

I tried to keep her on a little longer but she said her show was coming on. "Your father would laugh. I think you do too." I assured her that soap operas were in the best tradition of the English novel, that Dickens wrote serials in the daily papers. "Thank you, dear," she said, "but it's all right, I feel much better."

The next morning, before the evening of the call to Father, I put my *t'filin* on and leafed slowly through the prayer book I kept inside the velvet bag. Jonesey had gone to work; I needed to explain what I was doing only to myself. Better to do the ritual than not to do it at all, I thought, conscious of being in the half-way house of Modern Orthodoxy. Other Jews wore their phylacteries six days a week and rested on the Sabbath. I wore it the one day when I would be dealing with Father. The first question in heaven is not whether you have performed the ritual but whether you have lived honorably and faithfully. For one day I would be ready for questions from both lower and higher authorities.

Wearing my skullcap, I visited the girl at SLURP, ordered my daily vanilla cone. Though I preferred chocolate, I avoided it as I did the girl's dark and smokey skin. She smiled when she saw the back of my head. "Don't forget to take it off before you go into the water," she said, acknowledging its rare presence.

"It's waterproof," I said. "Do you go to Brooklyn?"

Made garrulous by my *yarmukah* (she had previously only served, not spoken) she said, "In the evening, just for a few courses. I work as a Kelly Girl during the day but this pays more for the summer. What *yeshiva* did you go to? I thought you went to public school."

That is the Brooklyn equivalent of English school ties. At seventy I will be sitting on the porch of the Sea Breeze Hotel, rocking in the sun, when a talkative widow of sixty-seven will set her chair rocking to the rhythm of mine and leaning over, ask, "Were you a *yeshiva* boy?" And I will nod and ask, "*Bais Yaakov* girl?" calculating my possibilities. Like the stripe of metal on the forehead of the High Priest, the identification of high school years denotes the man.

I assured her that my formative years were spent in *avodah*, worship, and other good works. "I served."

"I serve," she laughed, and turned to a customer. I fell asleep on the beach and dreamt my mother was staggering under a load of letters while I waited in the car, somehow unable to move to help, so that she barely managed to reach the door before dumping the pile of envelopes through the open rear window. "You need either a bigger car or a smaller handwriting," she said. I woke up burned and dry on one side, puddled wet on the other where my face rested against my arm.

Father, it turned out, was filled with instructions rather than questions. He knew I would be busy working because between Shevuot and the seventeenth day of Tammuz when new Lamentations begin, there are scarcely two months. The rush of summer weddings is thus not the Jewish assimilation of June brides or the Orthodox acceptance of the biological urges of the season. Rather, it is a rare, joyous period, appropriate for celebrations. Bar Mitzvahs become particularly lavish, weddings magnificent, the Seven Days of Feasting following the wedding elaborate, the expense of coming in from the mountains to attend "affairs" enormous, inconvenient, necessary.

But on the seventeenth day of the fourth month, fasting and sadness. The walls of Jerusalem are breached, the daily sacrifices at the Temple are halted, Chaldeans advance upon the Holy of Holies. Three weeks of suspense follow though the cause is lost. Men stop shaving and cutting their hair. The Modern Orthodox Jew who had permitted himself an occasional movie now stays away. During the final nine days leading to the Fast of the Ninth of Av, no meat is eaten and no baths taken. Then on the first of the next month the ram's horn blasts each day. The month of penitence begins, summer ends. Suggesting that time passes in Rockaway unmarked by special days, Father reminded me of the approaching days of commemoration. Noting the *Yahrzeits* for wars ancient and modern, including days of remembrance for the expulsion of Jews from Spain, pogroms in Russia and burnings in concentration camps, he wondered if I marked special occasions for the current war. Finally, not inquiring, merely reminding, he quoted the Talmud regarding the study of Torah, namely, one day away from learning constitutes two days' distance since the Torah itself travels in the opposite direction.

In order, respectfully, I said there were red letter days at Rockaway that separated the sacred days and the profane, that the anti-war movement was usually quiet during the summer but that I did remember it with summer registration at Rabbi Baumel's *yeshiva* and, finally, that movement in all directions was slower during the summer.

"That slowing," he said, "is what is preventing Berish from sharing your house of learning. Without him you have no third for Grace."

Speaking with Father was difficult. We were too formal for anger, too rehearsed for irony, too unfamiliar for love. Almost mildly he said, "Do you remember to have Rabbi Baumel give you a receipt for the tuition?"

"Sure. He offered to put it under contributions."

"No," Father said. "Your mother would like to speak to you."

" 'Love peace, pursue peace,' " I said but my mother was already on the phone.

"You have a few letters," she said, "I don't know when I can come out there. Do you want me to open them?"

But no, I couldn't have her do that. "You might not be old enough to read them," I joked but her voice was tired, not amused.

"Nothing from Florida," she said "but something from the Board of Education says it's urgent."

I decided I could be there in an hour and be able to leave before Father was back from Evening Services. She seemed to brighten when I said I would come in. "I bought that coffee cake. We had *milchig* for supper, so we can all have some." But I told her I did not want to meet Father. She said nothing.

Getting there I found the house quiet and lit only by memorial candles. "What now?" I asked, surprised. "For my parents," she said, "this is the day when the transport arrived." On the table where the candles were burning I could see my letters, one a clearly foreign envelope. I also noticed lines on my mother's face and an unusual dullness to her skin.

99

She was wearing a kerchief but unlike at the time of her visit, it was tied under her chin, not rakishly behind her head. She pointed at the hotel envelope. "I didn't realize. Is that from the same girl?"

I nodded. She looked at me. "Is this something special?"

"I don't know," I said. "Maybe."

She kissed me shyly, quickly, a sisterly touch. "I'm glad. Is she pretty?"

"Her hair is short," I said.

She pointed at a package in aluminum foil on the kitchen counter.

"I cut the coffee cake for you. Don't forget to take it." She smiled briefly. "You know, that first day, after they stripped us and shaved us and dressed us and put us into the blocks, I remember seeing those bunks to the ceiling, with faces looking at us. Do you know what was the first thing I thought of?" She gave a low, vibrant, inappropriate laugh. "I remember seeing those faces and thinking, my god, they've put us in with men, are we to have no privacy at all?" She was looking at me. "I'm saying this only to tell you that hair grows back. Do you understand me? Those weren't men in there. They were women. Without hair, starving, they looked like just creatures, male creatures."

I wanted to tell her that she seemed to have lost weight, that she should go to the beach more often, that I loved her. She had clasped her hands together, holding the fist of one in the palm of the other. I touched the knot. I wasn't sure she was aware of it. "Can you imagine how stupid I must have been," she said, "I feel embarrassed every time I think of it, as if I had spilled something on my dress in company."

"It's okay, Mom," I said, "you don't have to tell me."

"I thought you should know," she said, calmly, the memory gone, "hair does grow back. Don't forget the cake."

Caught between Father's impending arrival and my mother's retreat toward memories of death, I stayed until he returned from synagogue but left without sitting down to the table with them. She seemed fine, teasing Father, as I left, for not removing his hat.

Parked in front of the house on Beach 44th Street, the windows to our room dark, I looked at my letters by the light of the Lancer. Two letters from NYU, the weekly circular from the Lubavitcher Rabbi, an envelope from the New York City Board of Education marked URGENT, and the even more urgent letter from Rachel. I opened hers first.

On a postcard inside the envelope, in tiny letters, Rachel had written this:

Mexicans use three whistles at the bullfights, high for skill, low for clumsy, high/low/long for American girls with short skirts who leave before all seven killings are done. I am forced into chaperoning the "Prime of Miss Sheila Brody." We're on our way to Guadalajara. There is a church there being built by hand since 1900 and an equal number of med students from the US here for intensive summer Spanish. Seems strange being a pen pal with silence. Love me? R.

The postcard showed yellow sand, a black bull with banderillas horning out of his back, a pink and black butterfly of a matador, splotches of color that suggested a whistling crowd. I had sent her the call of a swain, had received the bull in return.

That was the first time I had a sense that my summer had started slipping away from me. I was like that rabbit in the riddle who thought he was moving deeper and deeper into the forest but, having passed the midpoint line, he was actually on his way out from among the trees. I had grown up without the pain of uncertainty, having been protected in school by daily ritual and at home by my mother's concern. She must have prayed for me while I was in the cradle, asking that I be protected from suffering and be content to rest in the shade; that I may flourish, but flourish while rooted in one perpetual place. And now I was unprepared for twinges of doubt. I was suddenly vulnerable to my mother's past, beset by Father's furies, tortured by Rachel's faithlessness. Just once I opened myself to possibilities and found I could not cope. I had been trained for nothing all these years but being a surveyor of writing, a reader between the lines, a man filled with disputations.

Crumpling Rachel's card, I turned to my other notices: NYU reminded me to register in the fall and prepare for the days of the Comprehensives. The Lubavitcher warned that as long as the sanctity of the Sabbath was being violated, the coming of the Messiah would be delayed. There was also a veiled reference to Jewish participation in the anti-war movement. The parable told of two battling Gentiles, who, upon seeing a Jew approach, cease their own enmity and join in pummeling the Jew. Finally, the Board of Education was pleased to inform me that in early December I would be interviewed for a position in Day High School English, said opening to commence January 30, 1969, for one semester as a leave replacement. The possibility of subsequent appointment to be contingent upon review and availability. Respond now or forever be dropped from our eligibility lists.

Thus was my attention forcefully focused on the future: Father had me pointed through the next three weeks, until the Ninth of Av, Jonesey tied me to a lease, until the end of summer, the Board of Ed. to January, and stretching beyond and beyond and beyond, the spread table of endless *yeshiva* years, a feast for the soul, forever until the end. Willy-nilly, I would be a good, forward looking American. But how quaint of the women to remind me of the past: my mother with her history and Rachel, daughter of elderly parents, of our incomplete chronicle.

Upstairs in the apartment, assuming Jonesey was still away, I got into bed and was startled to hear his voice from the other side of the partition. "Lock the door."

"You're back early," I told him, finding myself still awake after a while. He did not answer and I squirmed to find a comfortable spot. After more quiet, his voice rose, strangely contemplative, the bravado washed out for once.

"I don't know, Jase, all these books in praise of older women. She comes in here without knocking and says, 'I'd like to inspect your room, you know you can't say no to a landlady.' When she put the latch on the door behind herself, I knew what was coming, only I didn't. She comes into my side and I feel kind of silly with the broads on the wall but she doesn't even look up. She just says, 'Hurry up, will you, it's almost dinner time,' and gets out of her shorts and top so quickly I swear to you I can't tell you the color of her panties. I jump in after her and I start touching and you know, kissing, not just because I like it but hey man, I'm no fucking slob, wham bang and thank you ma'am. But the goddam bitch keeps her mouth tight so I almost break my teeth against her and says, 'Just fuck, kid, none of this kissy, kissy stuff,' and grabs my cock and starts pulling me in, not even a stroke, for god's sake. It's a good thing Charlie down there has a head of his own and jumps right through the hoop like a good doggie. I swear, Jase, a couple of pumps, and I was down and out. I could hardly even feel her around me. She was dressed and out of here in ten minutes, tops."

He took a deep breath and was quiet. "Poor Mr. Feuerstein. I think." Then much later. "I don't find somebody quick, she's gonna eat me alive."

I never said anything. He didn't seem to want congratulations but sympathy seemed out of order.

14.

Mindful of his determination, from then on I always checked our window before coming upstairs, to make sure that the light was on. But one night I found the door resisting the casual shove of my shoulder. "Jonesey," I yelled, "come on," but by then I could smell the burning hay odor in the hall.

"Keep your pants on," Jonesey said, unlocking the door, "and make sure your zipper is closed. We've got company." Through the tobacco haze of his side of the room, I could see a girl crosslegged on his bed. Her man's shirt was open-necked and loose, its tails tied across her belly. She seemed so light haired that at first I thought she had no eyebrows or lashes. She smiled, not quite focusing, and greeted me with a circular movement of her palm, as if she were wiping a window. I stayed near the entrance, gripping Jonesey's arm.

"Are you crazy? She's not even sixteen."

"You're still wearing your yammie," he grinned at me, "did you wear it to NYU?"

I whipped it off. Still grinning, Jonesey rubbed his arm. "Relax, babe. She's a Barnard girl. Get it? A college broad. It's kosher. Go talk to her. She loves to talk."

That was Jonesey's Joy, his antidote to our landlady and long trips to the service road on Eastern Parkway. When she got off the bed, swaying a little, and offered her hand, I shook it gently, empty of all desire, recognizing in her another victim. Even as we shook hands, Jonesey stroked the wide and gentle ass inside her designer jeans, as solicitous as he had been with Sheila. Joy was aware of it, and though embarrassed, stood it. Blind hand, blind ass. Standing, she seemed more forlorn than she had been on the bed, not as tall as she would have liked. With a nervous hand she tried to push her soft, slippery curls of hair away from her eyes.

"You're reading for comps," she said, trying to make small talk, politeness inbred. "Are you done with Donne?" And she giggled, made foolish by Jonesey and his smoke.

"Join the party," Jonesey said, putting one arm around her waist. She seemed lost in his curve, stood with him wrapped around her like an overcoat too loose but necessary for winter. I imagined her trying to say something to me with her eyes. I knew she had lines of poetry committed to heart, but the rest of her fitted itself to Jonesey.

She had met him in the water, throwing a ball to friends and hitting him instead. The throw was deliberate. She was capable of one aggressive step, just sufficient for beginnings, then she had the capacity only for surrender. Her skin, she once showed me, bruised easily from white to blue and purple, but she felt no pain and yearned for the touch of something sharp and piercing, if nothing else, for the turning of the skin's color to the impersonal burning of the sun.

Without waiting for my answer, Jonesey walked over to the dresser and unfolded the small tin foil that held a chunk of hashish, a brown and green lump he had been saving for "a special occasion." With the edge of a nail clipper he carefully shaved off a bit of the stuff and mixed it with tobacco from cigarettes he had already stored in a shell. Then, carefully—in matters of the hand he can be extremely gentle—he poured the mixture into the hollowed papers of Marlboros. Ready, he offered one to me. "I've kept the filter on; nothing to be scared about."

Joy reached out for one and lost her balance so that I had to catch her and help her to the bed. We stayed like that for a minute, Jonesey offering, Joy waiting, Jason hesitant.

"I don't know," I said.

"It's good," Joy urged, "it's really good."

"The best Lebanese stuff," Jonesey said. "Come on, relax."

But I was not afraid of relaxing. I was afraid I would think too clearly, feel too strongly all the scratches and hurts I was trying to paper over. I was willing to let go. I was kicking and pushing to let go. I wanted to be more than a swinger on birches but the sap clung, would not release. I reached and took the cigarette from Jonesey's hand. Then the three of us squatted on Jonesey's big bed and, shell ashtray in the middle, sent straight smoke up, carefully maintaining a little tower of ash on each cigarette.

"Coming alive," I remember Jonesey singing just as I started to feel my head slowly being squeezed together, equal pressure on all sides toward the padding of fuzzy cotton in the middle.

"I guess I feel it," I admitted, "I never thought it would do anything for me."

"Don't swallow it," Jonesey cautioned, "draw it easy, inhale."

As always with mechanical detail, he was the careful workman. But I could see even as I started feeling dizzy and leaned back for support, that Joy was way ahead of all of us. I felt like a leaf, like a dead cloud. I might have spoken out loud because Joy turned to Jonesey, letting him feel her weight, and started quoting Shelley, quickly, taking shallow breaths: *A wave to pant beneath thy power, share the impulse of thy strength, only less free than Thou, Oh, uncontrollable!* And she started kissing his face, eyes and ears. I wanted to get off the bed but there was no need yet. Jonesey wanted things in his own time and his own way, because he set her up, straightened her out, laughing, and said, "It's okay, babe, relax, there is more, let's not forget we're with company here," and lit another cigarette.

I tried to concentrate on one thing, on somehow anchoring myself to the bed. I imagined attaching a cord to all four wooden posts and being held securely and tightly. I tried to watch one freckle on Jonesey's face but his red hair was an easier target. I thought of Father's sing-song warning:

> Roite Ferd
> Roite Hund
> Roite man
> Keinmal gut

His care at keeping Yiddish out of speech, his dislike of all redheads, all of them *kohanim,* he said, the priests always quick-tempered. I had a sense that if I started writing at that moment, a message to Rachel or Dov, my handwriting would pour and fill the spaces of letters already created, the characters round and fat and spacious, spreading completely across the page. I tried to concentrate on some physical act, some ordinary function that usually goes on beneath our awareness and confirms our existence, whispering to us not to worry, just go on, things are whirring, turning, dripping and spinning inside, a factory going at full speed, a cough, a sneeze, a fart, no big deal, no reassuring great voice. I tried to concentrate on just one single thing and fell to watching Jonesey, finally ready, politely but skillfully begin to unbutton Joy's shirt. Existence confirmed, it was time for me to go.

"Got a letter to mail, folks," I managed to get out and carefully got off the bed, already turning away. In my ears I could hearing a rushing, a call of trumpets. With drunken care I felt my way downstairs, feeling the lightness but determined to weigh myself down with caution. Oh, what a constitutional limitation a lifetime in disputation imposes on a young man wanting to fly! Because I could have been a dancing *Chassid* I think, earlocks flowing, if I had only been taught in ecstasy. I could have lived on that special spirit that enters the Believer on Friday Eve and keeps him joyful until it departs at Sabbath's end. But of the six hundred and thirteen commandments, only two hundred and forty eight urge you to do, do, do, live, love, produce. That left three hundred and sixty five prohibitions, a THOU SHALT NOT for every day of the year. Circumvention of the forbidden took up all my energies. I had none left for obedience and other such passions.

By the time I hit the street, I was calm though my insides were churning. I seemed to have summoned forth more of my quiet inside workings than was necessary. I moved toward the boardwalk, seeking the cooling of the sea air. I could feel the lightness wearing off; I could feel the spirit departing. I tried to return to the scene upstairs but found myself distracted by the demands of my stomach, stumbled under the boardwalk in a race with the upward rushing inside me and had time only to brace my forehead against a rail when the stream swept up from inside me and I spewed into the sand.

Fearing the bitterness of the aftertaste, missing the balancing comfort of my mother's hand against my forehead, I was surprised to feel cleansed, my taste almost sweet, swallowing willingly. Ever the fastidious young man, I scraped sand over

107

my leavings, a cat in cleanliness, and determined at the same time to treat it like afterbirth, beginning one more time fresh. I moved away from the spot, a bit deeper into the darkness, removed my shoes, tried to dream in the cool, dark smell of the erect columns and dimly reflecting sand. But I should have known how ineffective of late my prayers had been getting. I was not to be spared the primal scene back upstairs in Room Five.

I heard a sound that was different from the occasional scrape of feet above or the noise of bump cars in one of the arcades. I saw two shapes move in among the trunks of the columns from the beachside and watched them spread a blanket no more than ten or twelve feet from me. The girl leaned against the column that cut the center of the blanket from my sight, and flicked off her sandals. She had sharply etched hips, slight breasts, a cutting edge to her. Then the two of them embraced, lay down on the blanket so that I could see only their legs and heads, their middle neatly scissored by the column's censoring bulk. His head suddenly lifted, disappeared along with his legs. I imagined he was kneeling. Her legs remained outstretched, slightly apart, white. His head leaned forward, kissed, slid out of sight again. I heard a sound. Her arms lifted above her head, her feet arched, she flung cloth to the side. Certainly naked by now, she pulled his head down, pushed it further, away. There was no use leaning forward, I could not see any more anyway with the column in the way, the tree keeping me from the forest. I could hear her sound, drawn out, saw her legs surround his. I could see his head and shoulder urged forward. I could see his bathing shorts around his knees being pushed downward by her bent leg, freeing his hands. His head slid forward, back, forward, back, he anchored himself with his arms on either side of her head and thrust. Her head slammed from side to side. He collapsed on top of her face, hid against her shoulder, I could hear their sound. I saw them roll, twisting the blanket, so that her face was looking down into his. I heard them laugh. "I can't this way," I heard her say, saw him keep her on top, couldn't see their legs any longer either, because of the blanket. I heard their sounds.

Then suddenly it was over for them. They were standing. She leaned against him and put her panties on. I had no memories of her taking them off. They were gone. Done too quickly, I thought. I would have stayed in much longer. Would some curious child, searching for coins spilled accidentally from purses find a strain of hair or a more obscene rubber tube? But I would not be the one to clean up after them, I thought, and went back to the house. The time of all deeds, I hoped, was done.

Upstairs it was dark. Smoke and odor lingered. "You alone?" I whispered.

"Yeah," came Jonesey's voice from the other side, heavy. "How was the show?"

But he was only talking about his own bit of acting. "I didn't stay for the finish."

"Well," he said, drawling, "it's far from over. She's staying for the summer."

I undressed quickly, got into bed, felt wide awake yet moved by the sights. The spirit moves in and out in many ways.

"That was Shelley she was reciting," I said to him.

"Oh," his voice was already asleep. "I was wondering. You bring the best out in them, you really do."

Much later I was still awake, though I had grown tired of awareness and would have willingly surrendered to sleep. None of the remedies had worked. I had even recited the Night Prayer I remembered Dov never failing to say before sleep, invoking protection against evil spirits and evil thoughts. *Michael to my right, Gabriel to my left, Ariel before me, Raphael behind, and above me stands guard the Spirit of God.* But that did not help either. I was attacked by a weakness from below where no angel ever stands. And so I was awake, lying back on arms folded under my head, when Jonesey walked into the kitchen for a drink and saw me awake by the light of the opening refrigerator.

He finished his orange juice, stretched, his body at peace. Then he said, hardly disturbing the quiet, "You should stay next time. What the hell. It's summer."

I fell asleep finally but was troubled by old dreams of cars, of steering wheels coming loose, of Rachel in a convertible, her hair grown long, flowing, Sheila driving madly, chained to the wheel.

15.

Though there was no letter for me, my mother came out to visit one day the following week. I had called the night before, anxiously, dreading Rachel's silence.

"I'm sorry, sweetheart, there is nothing," she said, "but I'm sure there will be something tomorrow," reassuring me as if she were sister to my brother, comforting me without knowing precisely what the pain was like. Then the day she was supposed to come there was a letter for Jonesey from Sheila, brought upstairs coyly by our landlady.

"I suppose the perfume faded with the long journey," she said. But Jonesey was at work and the comment was wasted on me. "I'll give it to Joseph," I told her and she left, reluctantly, trying to get a look inside his room. But when Jonesey showed, he shrugged at the letter, began to take off his work clothes and change into a bathing suit.

"Aren't you going to see what she says?"

"Bullshit, probably."

"Maybe she found some future doctor she can love." Jonesey fingered a polo shirt Joy had left behind one night.

"The Lord taketh but the Lord also giveth." He finally opened the envelope, read the letter, laughed, flipped it toward me.

"Want it?"

"Does she say anything about Rachel?"

"Only that they are both beautifully tanned. All over."

Not ashamed when fearful, I read through the letter. It was mostly about the wonders of Mexico and the excitement Sheila was generating being still light skinned though deeply tanned. It seems all the proper Mexican girls had to be home

110

by nine or with a chaperone, making American girls much in demand. I added creases to Jonesey's crumpling.

"I knew that girl had possibilities from the first sight of her ass," Jonesey said. "I'll bet she comes back cracked open."

"Even while she is observing the Nine Days of Dairy," I said.

"One sin at a time," Jonesey said, "it's more fun that way."

We had once tried to imagine the greatest number of transgressions and Orthodox Jew could commit with one single act. Limiting ourselves to the normal elasticity and dexterity of a human being and the possession of the average number of limbs and other equipment, we figured that it would be approximately twelve sins, most of which would have been punished in the old days by execution. Jonesey's grand violation worked out to eating a ham and cheese sandwich in a car on a Yom Kippur that falls on a Sabbath, while not wearing a skullcap and making love to your sister but withdrawing and coming on the seat. Eating is one, ham is two, ham and cheese according to him is three, riding in a car four, the Day of Atonement being equal to seven Sabbaths falling on a Sabbath makes it eight and nine, a double whammy, bareheaded is ten, incest eleven, technical onanism twelve. Dov, joining the discussion in a moment of weakness, reduced the list to one, arguing that each greater sin cancels the previous lesser one. I had imagined an endless number of pleasures done concurrently and being charged for each separately, the sin being excessive enjoyment, clearly forbidden by both early and late scholars.

In any case, having considered the range of pleasures and possibilities herself, when my mother came later in the afternoon she brought with herself a bounty in an attempt to fill the void in the mailbox. Staggering under the weight of a suitcase—she had been unwilling to struggle with a shopping bag—she came into the room excited by potential offerings. She unloaded from the suitcase flat cans of sardines in tomato sauce, an entire Isaac Gellis hard salami, two ropes of kosher kilbassi (available, I knew, in only one butcher store in Boro Park), and in plastic containers, cole slaw, potato salad, chopped liver and noodle pudding. There were also cakes. A large chunk of checkerboard chocolate cake, frozen blintzes

111

and a coffee cake seemingly poured into chocolate. An excess of sweetness in which to lose the taste for the stuff altogether. Somehow I sensed through the heaviness of all these gifts the sharp, elegant taste of Rachel's teas.

"It will all keep," my mother said gayly, "just freeze what you can't eat right away." She watched me. "Will this keep you for a while?"

Jonesey watched, overwhelmed, already laying claim to the sardines. "The only thing, Mrs. Kole, with the nine days coming up, your poor son here will not be able to enjoy the kilbassi."

"I forgot," my mother said, her face serious, but this was another offering, I think, another secret to be shared between us, because she had not forgotten to stay out of the water during the three weeks, though she wore her bathing suit and an absorbent terry cloth robe over it.

"We won't tell if you won't," Jonesey said. "We'll even save some for you if you get sick of cream cheese sandwiches."

As my mother stood there, next to the laden table, I thought of how curiously empty of smell that suitcase was, as if the richness of the contents could not touch her, as if somehow she was growing tighter and smaller, saving herself but becoming harder and thus repelling tastes and odors of things around her. Such wealth didn't belong around her, not lately. She had become fit for poetry just as poetry was going out of vogue.

She came with me to the beach and rested on the blanket. Her unwillingness to lie back kept me restless too. I thought I would be able to relax because greedy Jonesey, though clearly tempted by the idea of joining us on the beach, could not resist sampling the delivery and had stayed behind. But my mother sat, knees drawn up, and stared into the Atlantic.

"Are there other people you're friendly with here?"

"You mean girls," I said, knowing she was thinking of Rachel.

"All right."

"A few. Jonesey found some girl. People visit. We meet. Whenever I go to work at one of the hotels, I practice opening lines, just in case."

"Your father gets home very late from work since he has started in Manhattan. I'm not used to it."

I could not tell whether she was telling me I could visit during early evenings without meeting Father or whether she was confiding in me her loneliness. "How does he like it?"

"He has to work directly with the models." She smiled. "He complains. The designer helps them off and on with clothes but they come to your father for little repairs, flaps that need tucking, hems, waistlines, buttons. He is very good at it. There are few master tailors nowadays. Models know it."

I speculate that before the War, before that tear in time, Father sewed slowly and with dignity. Single dresses, over-coats one of a kind, silken *kapotes*, vests of two materials that were lined with a third. Always careful to observe the strictures against mixing wool and linen, he helped smooth their wearers into the completed pieces. No rushing piece-worker, Father remembered his forgotten skills and became a master tailor again, sewing back together those flapping ends of time, for himself at least. Doctors and tailors make whole, scholars separate, mothers put soothing unguents on seams.

"What does he say? A blessing of thanks or a prayer for deliverance?"

"He says the girls are too skinny." I squinted at her.

"I've been meaning to ask you. Have you been losing weight?"

"I'll fatten myself on the chocolate cake I brought."

"If Jonesey leaves any."

But somehow, despite the sun's brilliance and the dancing lights on the water and a multicolored beach ball that was kept floating in air by people uniting just for that purpose so that the flashing ball stayed aloft across five or six blocks of beach, like the bouncing dot under a cheerful Mitch Miller sing-along tune, in spite of the attempts of the entire beach to keep things light and afloat, we managed to be inert and somber. Looking beyond the water, shielding herself from the massaging heat of the sun, she said in that wondering tone of voice I was beginning to dread, "I love the water, you know. I loved it without knowing what water was like,—just the idea of looking as far as you can see without seeing. I could not imagine it because where we lived there wasn't even a river but I waited for it very badly." She laughed. "Are there characters in books like me?"

"In many poems, Mom."

She nodded. "Then at the *laager* I had this fantasy that a great big flood, an ocean, would put the fires out and cover everything and I could be happy. But from Auschwitz they moved us to Bergen-Belsen which wasn't an extermination camp and I didn't see the ocean until we came here."

I was never quite sure whether my parents had met in Europe or here in the United States, whether they had come together, the idea of a child carried with them, or whether they had followed separate paths for their meeting in the glen. "We?" I asked, "you mean *Abba* and you?"

"All of us," she said. "The difference was that by then I already knew what to expect because in forty-three, if you can imagine, my father remarried and took us all on a holiday near Balaton-Füred. We were very close. From a certain angle you could look as far as you wanted and not see the other shore. So I wasn't completely surprised." And she waved a vague hand. "I had some idea of what to expect."

I could make no sense of what she said. I wished I had a joke to tell her or some incident at work I could describe that would amuse her but I could not think of anything. It would have helped to have Joy there and have my mother watch what we said to each other because it might have reassured her that I was still capable of generating affection if not long-distance love. But Joy did not show until the next afternoon, when I lay out there again, alone this time, charged by Jonesey to send her to the house if she showed.

"But make sure," he said, "that you talk to her first. Talk all you want. It's good for her. By the time she finishes talking to you, she is hot, she is burning, but she knows you're a shining knight pining away so she comes running upstairs to me, to have all those feelings fucked away so her mind can clear and she can just sit in the sun and tan without thinking."

So I was being a knight under the signpost out there, waiting like Gawain, not searching like Galahad, the tempted one, not the innocent one. I remember learning that there are three gates that guard the temptation to utter an evil word: the tongue that can refuse to move, the teeth that might not part, the lips that can deny their opening. But nothing guards against other temptations and circumcision has brought the flesh closer to the touch. A man can be known by the thoughts he has before sleeping. I woke from dreaming when Joy stepped between me and the sun.

"Jonesey coming?"

I stood to talk to her. She had pulled her hair back and tied it behind her but as always, tendrils escaped all around her face, giving her a slightly fuzzy look, a lack of hard edges, as if she breathed with her entire body and had no protection. She was defenseless on the inside too, she had once told me (*I hear* the words of the Hebrews as they accept the Torah, the genetic pre-disposition of Jews for psychiatric work), explaining she was built wrong for childbearing, an upside down triangle, narrow near the bottom, too wide in the shoulder.

"He's staying upstairs."

"Did he say anything?"

"Only that he was staying upstairs," I said, a stolid dependable messenger.

"Did he tell you to tell me that he was staying upstairs?"

"Yeah."

"What a baby," she said. She reached up and wiped some sand off the side of my face. "I'd go up if I didn't think he would be hiding behind the door so he can jump out and scare me."

"People have been known to be amused by such entertainments," I said, stumbling over the awkwardness of the sentence, feeling stupid. Joy tilted her head to look at me. I could sense her about to do her usual one aggressive step. Instead, she stepped back and said, "Would you write to me after the summer, Jason?"

"Sure," I said, "I'm a great little letter writer."

"People have been known to be amused by such entertainment," she mocked, then stepping close, kissed me quickly on the lips, her own lips a little wet, as if she had thought of the kiss early enough to have licked her lips in anticipation. When she stayed close, for the moment there was the temptation to kiss back and taste the taste of her but the gates held firm, my tongue didn't move, my teeth clenched, my lips

115

wouldn't part. My own vulnerability made me reluctant to exploit hers. So I did nothing, stood slack, though the messenger of a man may be considered the incarnation of the man himself, and she just walked toward the ocean, in a deliberate attempt to postpone the inevitability of her visit upstairs to Room Five. I watched her stand in the water for a few minutes, the ebb and flow washing over her feet. My mother stood like that also the day before, though for a longer time, and had turned away much more slowly than Joy. She, after just a few minutes, shrugged, turned and walked firmly back toward the street, cutting under the gloom of the boardwalk and emerging into the sunlight of Beach 44th Street on the other side. I walked as firmly toward the SLURP girl.

By then I had been the interested reader of the womanless periods in American Literature, had stepped easily through familiar Hawthorne and understood his yearning not to have to tell, to remain uninterrupted by clamoring strangers and unwelcome messages, to see only the onrushing avalanche when the temptation to hear and know proved stronger than the guard of silence.

I had two letters waiting for me when I had come back from the library, neither of them expected to the Far Rockaway address. Dov had written and so had Rachel.

Dov had written in Hebrew, insisting with it not on distance, though neither of us were very fluent, but on memories, because we had learned the language together and had practiced by exchanging letters even while we lived just blocks apart. He rambled in his letter, he made errors, he was saying good-bye before leaving, but his love came through. Rachel's letters were strung in precise lines, her words were lucid, there might have been a brush of affection, but though I searched every crevice between lines and letters, I could not find a single wisp of love, not even left behind by nostalgia. She seemed to have swept the letter clear, a thorough housekeeper, a careful designer. I think I would have made a good partner to a detective, not the leg man but the researcher, the guy in the office who can sense immediately whether there was just cause for suspicion.

Rachel had written on the back of a postcard:

116

The Pyramid of the Sun has a stunning view from the top and is said to have made it easier for the human sacrifices. The standard joke is that since they were rolled down the hill afterwards, it was at least easier going than coming.

And on notebook paper enclosed with the postcard:

Sheila insisted we go to the one kosher restaurant in Mexico city. I find names like Mordecai Rodriquez and Moshe Pinada hilarious. Jewishness does not lie low, in spite of it all. My hair has lost its ragged edges but when it is grasped firmly from the bottom the uneven parts bristle. We saw the moon landing with Spanish sub-titles.

And though she signed it "Love, Rachel," a full statement, it was clear that the act of writing the word had helped strip it of meaning. The secret, spoken, goes up in a thin, sharp line and dissipates, losing its edge. Only the kept silence cuts.

Dov's letter was as complicated as its foreign language. The Holy Tongue has always given me trouble, both its sounds and its content. He had passed his examinations, he wrote, but had asked for the formal ordination to be postponed though the *Rosh Hayeshivah*, Rabbi Mendel Mendelowitz, was eager to bestow the honor. But Dov did not want to go find a Rabbinate, he wanted to go to Israel and study with a certain Yemenite scholar and familiarize himself with the variant *dinim* of the Sephardic Jews. He felt himself unfinished, not yet ready, waiting. I could understand that. He felt I could. He was sorry we were to see, know, so little about each other. He remembered days when we had sneaked cigarettes from under Father's prayer shawl and had smoked them under a shared umbrella on the way to *yeshiva*. Our steamy, spotted glasses, short, serious, intense puffs. He hoped Father was capable of forgetting and I of remembering. Finally, anxiously, the letters stumbling, erased, corrected, he suggested I think about the difficulties with the name "Rachel." If I were getting serious about her, I should at least find out if she and my mother had the same Hebrew name, and if they did, do they have additional names that were different and by which they would be willingly called. Otherwise there would be serious difficulties. The Code clearly

117

states, "A scrupulous person should not wed a woman whose name is the same as that of his mother." Although it was a matter of custom rather than absolute Law, only very few authorities granted dispensation, and only if alternate names were available. Otherwise the Rachels cancel each other. He hoped he wasn't interfering, no doubt I had thought of this already, he hoped I was happy, would I come to see him off at the airport. He signed with a flowing script, as if finally relieved of obligations, "Dov Ber Laufer," giving the weight of potential rabbinical authority to his cautioning words.

Jonesey's "little Jew" had become a big Jew, I thought, and put Dov's letter in a cigar box with Rachel's. Wrong timing, Rabbi, I laughed, a needless warning, his letter made unnecessary by hers. And who thinks of his mother by her first name? Better if he had reviewed with me the laws against being alone with women, same volume in the Code, later chapter. Even before my mother came to visit and even before Joy stood on tiptoes to kiss me, I knew I would be heading for the SLURP girl's counter as Jacob and Moses moved toward the sheepherders' well.

16.

I didn't need its urging and the SLURP girl didn't ask for an excuse but the sudden evening rain made it convenient for me to seek shelter inside her boardwalk hut. The big, fat drops splattered on the boardwalk in large splotches that soon united for a smooth, shiny cover. In a few seconds, both the beach and boardwalk were empty.

"How nice," she said, rubbing her arms to clear them from the goose pimples the quick wind had raised, "a rider on the storm, seeking refuge."

"I'm not a freeloader," I said, "I'm dying for a waffle."

"Vanilla." She turned to pour the prepared batter into the squares of the waffle iron. The skimpy apron could not cling to the fabric of her yellow bathing suit. She had long legs. I could hear hear thighs brush together. Because I had said nothing, she turned back. "Not vanilla?"

Her name was Miri, from Miriam, but I think of her only as the SLURP girl, can see clearly that one tooth that turned slightly inward and seemed a bit sharper than the rest. A Boro-Park girl, she had told me that her equivalent of Eastern Parkway was Thirteenth Avenue on Friday nights, Fourteenth on Saturday afternoons but that neither, unfortunately, had benches like the Crown Heights Promenade did.

"What the hell," I said, "I feel wicked without my skullcap, make it chocolate."

"I knew it," she said, "I always thought you were a chocolate person." Waiting for the waffle to bake, she leaped on crossed arms on the counter, between the coke fountain and the root-beer barrel.

"Anything else?"

I shook my head no, not yet ready to articulate my desires.

"I'm not popular when it rains," she said. "People run next door for something warm. I told my boss we should be serving coffee." I watched her tiny Star of David hanging between her breasts. I could see the down covering their curve vibrating to her breathing. "Listen," I said, "how do you get home from here?"

"My father meets me at the train station exactly one hour and a half after I close here. He even pays a token to be able to see me get off and yell at the conductor if I'm late."

"Too bad," I said, "I could drive you. I could drop you off at an earlier stop so you can arrive by train."

"How nice to have had a *yeshiva* education," she laughed, turning to the pop of the waffle iron. I did not watch her draw the ice cream from the snout of the gleaming machine but turned to look at the rain instead which had changed into a thinner, more steady spray. I turned back when I heard the clatter of plastic utensils. She was looking at me, head slightly tilted. Her skin had a darkness that had preceded the tanning work of the sun.

"I never see you on the beach," I said. "How do you tan?"

"In the morning the sun shines right in here. I just close my eyes and bask. I can serve blind, just by touch."

"If too many people want coke and not enough waffles you'd be more tanned on one side."

"I straighten it all out on the roof, *Shabbat* afternoons," she said. "How is it?"

I carved off a chunk of waffle with the serrated edge of the spoon making sure there was ice cream on it, and lifted it to her mouth. She took it, held the spoon with her teeth so that I had to tug to get it away. "Keep it in there too long," I said, "and you melt the spoon."

"I could close early," she said. "When it rains like this I'm done for the day."

"You can introduce me to your father."

"Does your high school graduation picture show your *yarmukah*?"

"If you hold the page up to the light and look from the back."

I moved behind the counter, like stepping behind a pulpit, made ready to dispense soft and hard ice cream, drinks, other sweets, but scowled to discourage any potential customers, while she hung her apron on a hook (the reaching lifted and tightened her ass), then went to the bathroom, to change. She emerged transformed, in a long denim skirt, blouse and shoes, hair loose and demure, eyes downcast. "Wow, you change into religion as fast as I do, and all I have to do is whip my *yammie* back on!"

She shrugged, put her yellow bathing suit into a paper bag, under the counter. "It's no use taking it home," she said, "I'll abandon it after the summer."

"Sure," I said, "styles change anyway."

She closed up the register, folding the bills into another paper bag, leaving the silver. I remembered I had not paid for the waffle and insisted on giving her the money. I got a nickle and a quarter in change, had the grace not to check, let her tickle my palm for a moment, touching her for the first time.

Before I touched her a second time in the parking lot of still another hotel in Long Beach—Miri reassuring me that Cross Bay Boulevard would get us home in plenty of time—we walked past my house and saw the beach chairs, fans and TV sets from the street in a pile on the porch. Card games were in progress, one of the lights was burning, there seemed to be a light on in the room on the third floor. "That's where we live." I waved upward, the rain by now a fine mist on our faces. "Everyone has heard about your friend," she said.

Parked in a private corner to which she guided me confidently, we began kissing, the car no more fogged up than all the others, empty cars in the lot that had warm air trapped in them by the rain. We were both sweating. I opened her blouse, unclicked her bra, slid it down awkwardly so that it trapped her arms and she had to stop kissing me to help. I licked my tongue between her unsunned breasts, startled at their natural darkness. "Let's go to the back," she whispered, and I hesitated, remembering the history of that seat, but I had always been scrupulous about keeping it clean and the stains were only in my memory. Bare-breasted, she clambered over. I got out, got in through the rear door, leaned forward to open the front windows slightly for some air. The rain seemed to have stopped. The lights in the lot were on but little illumination reached our corner. The SLURP girl had chosen well. "Too much air," she whispered, fearing that our foggy protection would fade away but I knew we were breathing hard enough to generate additional haze. Amazed at myself, I sat back and lifted my legs to shuck my pants off completely. Leaving skirt on, she bent at the knees and whisked her panties off, reached inside my underwear, tugging. I was all over her by then, sweat making us both slippery. She wanted to kiss, sucking and licking my tongue while her hands were busy elsewhere. One hand on her ass, the other between her legs, I risked one finger, two, passed my Eastern Parkway limit of three, churned with both hands finally, the seat screeching, mystified at the total absence of smell, closing my eyes to try to sense it. I tried to reach down to get rid of my shorts but she took both hands and placed them on her breasts, holding on to my wrists insistently until I continued her movements, then put her hands flat on top of mine, moving them along. When I moved down again, with both hands, again holding her from either end, she squirmed so that her wetness was all around her, and I too was drenched with her from below the waist. Naked finally and though cramped, managing a comfortable position, feeling so hard that I could feel capillaries expanding to their limit, her hand sliding up, I moved downward, was about to enter, but her eyes snapped open and she twisted away, only not away but around, offering me the deep groove of the end of her spine and back, whispering, "Go on, go on, that was close," and raising herself to meet me so that I could do nothing but fall and come, feeling her ass along my entire length, grabbing her around the shoulders and feeling her shiver a bit and breathe long and deep.

We stayed like that for a while. I wondered how to deal with the oil gluing my stomach to her back, feeling myself contract, disappear, the air cool on my own back and ass. She twisted her neck so she could kiss my face and said, "Stay like that for a while, it really feels nice."

"It couldn't have been very good for you," I said, "what happened?"

She lay back on the seat, squirming a bit so that I bent toward her again, but then stopping as she shook her head. "We have to go soon," she said. "It's a good thing nothing happened. I almost forgot myself that time."

"You're a virgin," I said.

"Of course. What did you think?"

"Then why?"

She shrugged and we got dressed. She combed her hair, opening the windows wide as I drove so that the breeze could dry it. Under the elevated on New Utrecht Avenue, waiting for the warning rattle of the train, she said, anxiously, "It was all right, wasn't it, it isn't bad for guys that way, is it?"

"No," I said, "it's almost the same."

"Anyway," she said, "I'll never know boys like you after I'm married, especially since you really aren't religious, are you?"

"I guess not," I said, "don't worry." Then we heard the rumble of the train and she ran, barefooted, carrying her shoes. "We're closed *Tishebav*," she yelled back, then was up the stairs and into the station. Crossing the Marine Parkway Bridge, as I stopped to pay the toll, there was the inappropriate smell of evergreens though there was only the sparsest grass outside where the gulls screamed on the grabage strewn beach.

17.

The kosher hamburger emporium was shuttered for the nine days leading to the Fast Day of the month of Av, observing the days of dairy, and SLURP itself closed by noon of the eighth day, so I certainly did not need Father's Early Warning System of phone calls to remind me of the day's approach.

I tried to be away in the evenings, on the boardwalk, on the rides or pitching nickles for prizes. The Ski Slide and Himalaya seemed foolish after a while and I was losing too many dimes into the slots at Fascination Bingo. The approaching fast day had brought a halt to weddings and the closed hamburger place had increased the dairy business at SLURP so that I could barely get a wave in reply to hellos and had to pay my way to stand at Miri's counter. I was also reading more, finding myself getting up late in the mornings, often too late to go to NYU, and thus forced to supplement my daily quota with evening studies. Jonesey was not home, having discovered that Joy's parents were avid cardplayers, never returning to their bungalow before midnight. I stayed upstairs, in the mood for the pain of the books I was reading, but distracted by my landlady's frequent requests that we defrost the refrigerator and by Father's calls.

He would call and ask about what I thought of Dov and how pleased his parents were. In his voice I could sense a bit of puzzlement why the lure of Dov's success could not draw me home and dissolve my ox stubborness. "Good for him," I told him, "if I really like being away from home, I'll consider moving to Israel myself." He told me that the next fast day commemorated not only the destruction of both Temples but also of the razing of Jerusalem and the abolishment of the kingdom. "Anything to keep me from going to Israel, right?"

124

He was not amused. I told him that neither of the Temples was actually destroyed on the ninth, the first was on the 7th of Av, the second on the 10th. He asked me if we were keeping kosher. "I'm a regular housewife," I told him. "We've used up all the meat from the freezer and now I can defrost it." He reminded me that I need not put my phylacteries on until the afternoon of the fast day. "Did you know," I asked him, "that Russia entered World War I on *Tishoh b'Ov*? And that Jews were evacuated from the provinces on the same day a year later?"

"In Hungary," he said formally, "communications were difficult. We never knew where other Jews were or what they were doing."

"It's also the date of the expulsion from Spain."

"That I know," he said, "news from the past reaches us much more easily."

It got so that I would refuse to go to the phone, but Father got through anyway, on the tail end of calls I would make to my mother.

There was the sound of lamentations in her voice too. She was apologizing for too many things. She was sorry she could not bring us anything, that she couldn't visit, that it rained too many days, that there were no letters for me. "Relax, Mom, it's not your fault," I said, "there is nothing you have to do."

But she would not be comforted. "Would you like to come in for *Tishoh b'Ov*?"

"That's all I'd need," I said, "but listen. Write me a letter so the postman won't think I'm weird waiting for him."

"All right," she said, brightening, "I do have very nice handwriting and I really don't get a chance to write. Did I ever tell you my penmanship in school used to be so good that my teacher would walk around showing my notebook to the class?"

"No, you never told me." I felt impatient, needing comfort myself, unaware that her wheel had begun to spin backwards and would stop when it met itself on its turn.

"All right," she said, "but your father wants to speak to you."

And Father would manage to distract me again from everything except resentment. His voice on the phone made it

125

actually easier to argue with him, irritating me with its careful pronounciation and precise diction, the rehearsal in them obvious. Nothing impressed him, that bothered me most of all—not my work toward the degree, not the scholarship, not the offer from the Board of Education, not even my departure. It was all *shtuss,* nonsense, stupidity, unimportant. I hoped that my anger would touch him at least but I think he had become inured to anger over the years and could easily ignore *chutzpah* too, treating it like he would the pranks of an irresponsible child, acceptance a father's easy lot, particularly during this period of mourning. Like overnight knots, I was combed out of his beard.

Expected woes multiplying, I came back from *shul* having been unable to ignore the sad siren tune of the *Kinos,* to find the door locked. The Eve of the Fast had driven Joy's parents from cards, J&J to the sanctuary of Room Five. I could hear Joy telling Jonesey to open the door but Jonesey, thickly, yelled, "The line is busy," and would not let me in. So when I finally got back in from a boardwalk early dark and deserted, carrying a slick-covered mystery I had been reading under the porchlight, I argued with Jonesey, pointing out the accumulated dirt in his room, the ripped sheets, the refrigerator that had not been defrosted.

"Ask your mother nicely," he said, "maybe she'll do it."

But by the time I was back from NYU the following day, following my schedule despite the Day, the place was clean, swept, dishes washed, Jonesey's bed and mine made, all drawers neatly tucked in and even the ragged edges of some of his pinups neatly pasted to the wall. Joy's smell lingered but my mailbox was empty and the next day a new girl was in SLURP, a sunny, smiling girl, who had no idea what had happened to Miri though she told me her last name was Lieberman and that she did live in Boro-Park.

"What the hell is the matter with Crown Heights," I said, and left. I dreamt that night that my mother was standing near my bed with a bag of groceries, not moving, just watching.

"When did you get here?" I asked, surprised to see her there that late.

"Early," she said, "I wanted to see you sleeping."

"Why didn't you wake me?"

"I didn't want to wake up the others," she whispered. That was when I noticed that in the other bed slept Jonesey and that Dov was sleeping on the other side, behind the partition. So that's how we would have divided the place up, I thought, noticing how neat everything was.

"Were you cleaning or something?"

"No. Just watching. Jonesey sleeps with his arms thrown wide, he is very confident. Your curl up on your stomach."

"And Dov?"

"I think he's up."

"You shouldn't have come when we weren't expecting you," I told her. Touching my face, she said, "I had a dream about you, I had to."

"What a weird dream about my mother last night," I told Jonesey, who just rolled his eyes with disgust. But I remembered the dream and also a story she had once told me, a rare gift I am surprised I had forgotten, about waking up once as a small child and seeing her mother standing there watching her quietly. It was so still and motionless that she said nothing, at least remembered saying nothing. There was just her mother's quiet, stolid, silent stare. Going through her mother's papers, after she had died, my mother found the photograph of a child looking seriously into the camera and was not shocked to discover that it was a sister who had died young, a child whose name had never been mentioned.

18.

During the week that followed, natural laws seemed suspended. Days of 100 degree heat vaporized the metal and cement that connect glass to granite and the entire city seemed to float off the ground, heat waves radiating downward and exerting an upward force. The nights crackled as if they were dry forests. TV screens shrank towards the center as power dissipated. The Mayor took to walking through Harlem. In Williamsburg, normally dark clothed Chassidim appeared on the streets wearing only white shirts and broad striped fringed garments on top, their black jackets abandoned for once. People who ventured outside moved slowly and carefully, feeling the reluctance of sinews and bone to remain firm. As the weekend approached, a certain frenzy began to build. Though by the calendar it was mid-summer, other rhythms had begun to inform us that the time of fall responsibility was approaching. On the beach, bathers charged into the ocean, more careless than usual about scattering sand and splashing water. They dove more wildly. There was an angry edge to the friendly races and water fights and no one was tolerant of the inadvertant collisions. Through a cloudy haze, the sun burned. The trailing sign on a small plane—PRESTONE ANTI-FREEZE—let loose and floated out to sea. The throng roared, jeered, would have welcomed the fiery crash of plane and pilot. More people wore red bathing suits. At Brighton Beach Bay 3, the unofficial Jewish beach, Israeli immigrants smacked viciously at small black balls with wooden paddles and refused to apologize when their missiles struck spectators. The thin line between Bays 2 and 3 narrowed, then disappeared as a Puerton Rican family, radio loudly tuned to a Spanish station, encroached. Carefully the family sat, backs to Bay 3, lowering the volume after the first few minutes.

On Saturday, in synagogue, dressed in hat, suit and tie, Father and fellow congregants compare summer heat in Hungary, Galicia, and Lithuania, recall legendary burnings, agree that the airconditioning in the *shul* had been a good investment. In Far Rockaway, the white sun blinds and the wooden boardwalk smolders. The night is thick and heavy. The sand has been ablaze since sunrise and now, even in the dark, it singes.

In the evening, with little respite from heat, Dov called, his voice unfamiliar. Would I see him off at the airport in the morning?

"I hardly recognized your voice, Berish," I told him, adding affectionately his middle name by way of apology. "How come it's so hoarse?"

"It's finally changing," he laughed. "Late maturity. Look, Yanki, it's a charter flight. I have to check in by twelve."

Next to me Jonesey and Joy waited. "Say hello for me," Jonesey said, "tell him it's great one of us made it into the majors."

"Yossel says hello."

"'Deliver us . . . from hidden foes,'" Dov quoted the Prayer for the Traveler. "Has he changed?"

"Of course not," I said carefully, "everything is just the same."

Joy was tugging at my arm, demanding to talk to a Rabbi. I shielded the phone from her with my body. "Your parents don't mind you're leaving?"

Dov laughed, another unfamiliar sound. "My father wants me to carry on personally in the fight against mixed swimming facilities in Jerusalem."

"All right," I said, "I'll try to be there early. It'll be great seeing you," and made a note to wear my skullcap for the farewell visit.

"They give them a course in deeper voices so they can sound more impressive from the pulpit," Jonesey explained to Joy. She laughed, linking one arm through his, the other through mine. I could feel the pressure of her unbound

129

breast. Its looseness tightening me, we went to the board-walk. SLURP, with the new girl behind the counter, was actually opening up, the Sabbath day just passing one of the longest of the year.

With Sunday morning came lawlessness. The resistance to authority was so massive that police could do nothing. On their way to beaches, people vaulted turnstiles and ran red lights. Crossing the toll bridge into Rockaway they cheated exact change machines. At Yankee Stadium it was Jacket Day for children fourteen years old or under, but midgets, hunched-over high school kids, even short adults with smooth faces demanded and received the free jacket with the insignia. Closer to Beach 44th Street, cars parked on both sides and curled around corners, disregarding NO PARK-ING and ONE WAY restrictions. Traffic cops on motor-bikes were mocked as "fuzzy-buzzy," their directions ignored. Life guards could not enforce NO BODY SURFING, NO BARBECUING, NO LOITERING, DANGER—ROCKS regulations. Their whistles were constant, piercing, ineffective.

It was anarchy, it was urban bacchanalia, it was summer-fest, it was sun festival. It was a spontaneous linking in emotion, a mass denial of approaching autumn. It was a united forgetting of the world.

I thought to separate myself from it all by leaving early for the airport, but somehow lost my way, then was caught in traffic when the drawbridge was raised on the Belt Parkway. By then it was the dead calm of the day. Had I been the lead car in the waiting caravan, I might have leaped the splitting bridge, gunning the motor like a gangster in a chase film. As it was, I was too far back in the line for heroics. I could only sit and wait for the bridge to realign itself with the highway. Behind me, beyond the curve of the road, the drawbridge was not visible, so horns began to blast, an insistent prayer for release or rain. I strained but could not see the ship passing under the bridge. By the time the road opened, it was too late to catch Dov, but I continued to the airport anyway, deter-mined to fulfill the commitment to see him off. Finding the airport emptied of his flight and avoiding his parents, I turned back to Rockaway but on an impulse, exited on Flatbush Avenue and drove home, hoping to surprise my mother. "I thought she went to visit you," a puzzled and perhaps suspicious Father told me. I sat down to wait, expecting her any minute, sorry she had taken the trip to the sea for nothing.

And truly her trip was for nothing. While I was waiting on the road, my mother was making herself ready, emptying herself completely of memories the way a sleeper prepares for dreams by emptying himself of the waking day. Hollow, she let herself fill with the energy of the day and took the trains to Far Rockaway, taking additional courage from the daring of the cowboys who rode the bucking platform between cars. Finding our door closed, she persuaded our landlady to let her in. Inside, after leaning a letter she had brought from Rachel against the mirror, she changed into her white, one-piece bathing suit, took one of the towels familiar to her from home, and walked out to find a narrow space on the sand. She left behind her clasp pocketbook and her kerchief, carried her clothes with her. While I was at the airport waving farewell, she seeded the garbage cans in the area with items of her clothing, each bit into a different bin. Her mind bare but her body gathering the necessary strength, she lay on the towel for a while, then, as Father and I sat at the kitchen table and waited, with the beach at its loudest and most confused, with lifeguards waving their arms like mad conductors, she made her resolve and walked into the water. Slowly it rose. Unnoticed from the high perches, she moved further and further out, in a determined Australian crawl, soon an invisible dot in the blind spot where the lines of sight of adjoining lifeguards converge. When she stoped, she sank. Stoning, burning, strangling, beheading: these forms of death are available for land-dwellers. My mother was destined to keep her appointment with water, even through the fierce fires of her time in concentration camp. Only in the time of the ancient Temple could fire and water meet. A woman accused of infidelity was brought to the Priest who would give her to drink a cup of bitter waters. If guilty, she died by the fire in that water. If innocent, the water helped her bear children.

131

My mother, if ever found, will have only the minutest taste of the sea in her. Her death in water would not have been by water.

The scenario is mine and for me it does well. I live by it and I mourn by it, as does Father whose face has lost flesh as if he has not stopped fasting since the Ninth of Av. As for official versions, there are many. Police are skeptical of young suicides where problems are not discernible. My mother fits more easily their profile for runaways.

"I know of a man," a sympathetic Detective Meisner tells me, "who got out of the car to wipe snow from windows. With lights on, motor running, his wife waited but he was never seen again. His time to run had arrived."

Does the notion that she left the beach, hitched a ride in the first available car, and was somewhere else now, beginning anew, comfort me? What does it do to Father? I see Adam and Eve, standing irresolute over Abel's body. The bite of the fruit, a small nibble, had not prepared them for the knowledge of death. Informed finally about life, they did not know how to handle its end. But at least their recognition of death was confirmed, so that when the ravens arrived and one died to be interred by the other, Adam and Eve also knew how to deal with the aftermath of death. I knew nothing. I was unprepared and unlettered in death.

"Suicides," another kindly comforter reassures me, "always leave letters."

What, other than her good-bye note, was Rachel's letter, propped against my mirror? And yet my mother could not have read the letter, could not have known that Rachel was returning with her hair and love grown back. Although, I suppose, she could have been caught up in the spirit of that illicit day and steamed open the letter with the same aplomb that enabled passing mothers to lift a ripe banana or nectarine from the open air fruitstands and lovingly peel it for their baby-carriaged children. And having read about the return of a Rachel, decided the time had come for the departure of another, though such exactitude is not part of her character and has never bound her before.

When I returned later to the place in Rockaway, the missing person report had already been filed and nothing had been heard. Rachel was coming home and I drove out to end my stay on the beach. Father was along, trying to encounter my mother's presence by retracing her steps. Entering the room, his hand rose to touch a *mezuzah*, automatically adjusting to a mere two fingers in anticipation of just a tiny scroll. Though his fingers did not find anything, he completed the movement anyway, touching fingers to lips. Inside, brushing at his dark suit as if he had been attacked by the motes of dust and avoiding Jonesey's side of the place, he looked around. "Are you sure she didn't say anything or bring anything?" He had been asking the same question since the first day of her departure, suspicion never far from sorrow in his voice. As I had since the first time he had asked, I told him she had said nothing, brought nothing, left nothing, not telling him about Rachel's letter. That letter was my business; not even the police knew about it.

"Why do you ask?" I finally demanded, "don't you believe me?"

His face contracting under his wide brimmed hat, Father shook his head. "If only I had sent something with her. An agent of *mitzvah* is always protected during his mission." Then he helped me move most of my things downstairs to the car.

III

. . . beckon me with thine eyes which are sweeter than wine
and show me thy teeth which are sweeter than milk . . .

(Talmud)

19.

Three angels come to visit Abraham. Why three? we ask. We learn that the creatures, exhausted by daily attendance at the Throne, are restricted to one task at a time. Thus, Eeeny comes to inform Sarah that she would be bearing a child in her old age, Meeny comes to destroy Sodom and Gomorrah, and the aristocratic Miney-Moe to rescue the family of Lot, a job he bungles terribly, losing Lady Lot to salt and Sir Lot to the incestuous minstrations of his daughters, for which he is banished to the rear of the choir for the next chorus of Hallelujahs. Eeeny, Meenie and Miney-Moe catch the tiger by different toes, in other words. Maddened by my summer readings, I can't help but interpret this as but an obvious example of assembly line division of labor and list *Genesis* alongside other great prose works of the Industrial Revolution. And list myself as kin to Eeny, Meenie and Miney-Moe, semi-observant, semi-rebellious, restricted somehow to one love at a time. Only Father seems to have escaped the piece worker mentality. When he sews those samples for the models, he makes the skirt or suit entirely by himself, working with the whole cloth directly from the designer's sketches. If the dress pleases the buyers, out it goes to the factories, each part parceled out to a different worker. The sleeves, the collar, the pockets, the button-holes, the zipper, the buttons, the lining, the slits, each loving thread Father had personally stitched is given out to speedsters at the machines. How often does the paster-on of pockets walk to the end of the line to see the finished product? Father sees it all through, beginning to end. I wait somewhere in the middle of the sequence, my expertise limited, my line of sight obscured, my hands constantly emptied of one item before they can pick up another. How I can admire Rachel's presence of mind that enabled her, even as she was acknowledging her need to return to me, to get a partial refund for their shortened hotel stay, arrange Sheila's separate flight home, and stop for a brief visit at her parents' house.

She arrived early and waited calmly at the baggage claim while I rushed toward her along the narrow, circular paths of Kennedy Airport.

By the time I reached American Airlines, the conveyor belt was moving through its loops with a single, blue-grey American Tourister its only passenger. I should have seen Rachel right away but looked for the same courdoroy pants and tailored shirt she had worn leaving and didn't recognize her in patch-pocket shorts and ribbed sweater.

Not having forgotten how embarrassed I would get when caught unprepared, she didn't call out when she saw me. Instead she began to take long strides toward me and I finally recognized that energetic walk of hers, the kick of the legs that was a bit too vigorous for grace. When she saw that I saw her, she waved, still greeting me without words. No Sheila there for distraction, I noticed that her hair, parted in the middle and pulled away from her face, had grown longer and moved evenly. Other than carrying a shoulder bag of plaited straw and a small leather case she might have picked up in Mexico, she seemed unaffected by her summer travels. Well met, finally, she dropped her case, let slip the bag next to it and hugged me, standing slightly on raised toes so that all need for bending on my part was eliminated. Standing there I was aware of the whisper of her breath and touch of her hand on the back of my neck. I felt the pain in that feeling, was stung by the thrust of her hip, bruised by the pressure of her arms. No wonder I had protected myself so carefully all these years, I thought. A sweet and subtle poison, Hawthorne would have said, this smooth and slick and fluidy Rachel, seeping in to fill the shape my mother had voided.

"I've been meaning to ask you," I said, kissing her, "how come you don't have a mustache like other dark girls?"

"I wash in milk, can't you tell?"

"You look the way I remembered."

"You've grown," she said, noticing the change in me. But

she was wrong. I had been shrinking most of the summer as parts of me had left for areas unknown. I was not sure whether it would have been more appropriate for me to recite, on behalf of both my mother and Dov, "The Prayer for the Traveler" or "Blessed be the Judge of Truth," the acknowledgement of divine justice. Determined to celebrate life, I stayed close to her, feeling her breathe, against the warmth of those womanly breasts whose growth she had noticed at ten, sitting in the bathtub and touching herself on the left, near the heart, with a hand slippery with soap.

With one finger I traced the length and width of her mobile and generous mouth. "Let's save this for the car," I said, but before I could take my hand away, she caught the tip of the finger in a kiss.

"Have you heard anything?" she asked in the car, holding my hand.

"Strong tide, open bay, too many middle-aged runaways. Husbands, wives, fathers, mothers, everybody is on the run. I've even heard of a grandmother who ran away from her daughter's house and back to an old age home where she had secretly married someone."

"Well," she said, "as long as you haven't heard anything."

She leaned over and kissed me, firmly and cleanly. "I came back to tell you that I love you."

"But you've told me that before," I said, wonderingly, never at loss for a question.

"Oh," she said, "I must have forgotten." And she rested lightly against my arm as I drove. "It'll be all right," she said once, "I just know it."

That afternoon we made love for the first time. I spent the night, too, but I did call Father around ten to tell him I would be staying at Jonesey's, in Far Rockaway, having gone there to retrieve some forgotten things and found time passing. "Will you be all right?" I asked him. "I just hate it when the phone rings," he answered.

But this was after we had already made love and I didn't ask him any more questions. It had been the new sheets, I think. We had walked into the dusty apartment, opened curtains and windows, flushed the toilet to clear it of a rusty ring of disuse, let the taps run to cool in the bathroom and kitchen.

139

In the bedroom the bed had been stripped, Rachel a thorough housekeeper, laying bare the green and gold floral pattern of the mattress. I hadn't planned on anything. Rachel asked me to help her with the linen, dumping sheet, cover and pillow cases, a matching set of diagonal chartreuse stripes, on the empty mattress. She did the fitted sheets, I the two pillow cases, pulling them inside out the way I remembered my mother doing it at home. The cover we did together. We worked smoothly, Rachel apparently familiar with the inside-out method too. Done, we stood there, the room filling with a clean, fresh smell, the linen releasing the spring that had been stored in them. Then Rachel began to take her clothes off, first shucking the sweater over her head together with the T shirt underneath it in one motion, then her bra, turning from me and bending to unhook it. Her shorts next, then her bikini panties, the material so thin that it seemed colorless, the elastic so gentle that it left no mark. Doing everything as if she were alone, she took a flat case from the second drawer of her gold and white dresser and walked into the bathroom, leaving me with the barest flash of that startlingly light patch of skin within the slanted outlines of a narrow bathing suit.

By the time she came out of the bathroom and paused to let me see her again, smiling a little at the theatre in her pose, I was already under the cover, unclothed, my undershorts neatly tucked inside the fold of my pants. Then she was next to me. The room was decorated by slanting rays though the air was cool, the linen moved reluctantly, unwilling to crease, and with the inevitability of endless arrivals and departures, we made love, her willingness making my inexperience no hindrance. And all the while, during the gradual timing of our bodies, Rachel's eyes never left my face, so that even when I paused elsewhere it was only for a moment. Her eyes forced me up, a serious, steady look that at another time might have stopped me but this time I moved beyond fear and beyond doubt and simply tried to move together with her.

Her eyes never wavered, perhaps for a moment, near the end, when she grimaced, her neck twisting, and her eyes closed while she got in touch with her own feelings. Then, for a while, we rested, but I stayed the night, for the first time, and remember dreaming through endless naps the color red.

All this was quite proper; I should make that clear. The laws for mourning are explicit. They simply do not apply unless the evidence of death is so positive that the surviving spouse may remarry. Mourning begins at the time of discovery. Should a body reappear later, mourning fills the blood, little time capsules of sorrow releasing of their own volition. But we will accept no circumstantial evidence. Even when there are witnesses to a disappearance into the sea, into a water having no end, absolute proof of death is necessary. In my mother's case, a double doubt of death, double doubts always liberating. Perhaps she didn't go into the water. And if she did, perhaps she did not go too far into it.

This was how I allowed myself to make love, properly refusing to accept the strictures to the mourner against such activity. But when I consider the possibilities, when I reject technicalities, all I can think is that she drowned. What else could have happened? No one goes running away from home, son, husband, wearing only a bathing suit. And what does it mean that among the thousands she must have passed on the beach, no one saw her? Why is that surprising when witnesses tried to recall her by matching their own images of what a middle aged woman looks like to the way my mother looked? And when no photographs exist of the way she looked with her hair loose and in a bathing suit? My god, Father himself would not have known her, so how could strangers, looking at a photograph of her in long sleeved dress and tucked wig?

But there was no body and if you are a man of the Law, that ends all other considerations. There are no other eventualities. There is only the Law. And the Law protects those that observe it. Ask Father. Faithful to detail, he manages to forget.

It's easy. Try it. Concentrate on being like Father. This is the way of forgetfulness, this is the blessing of observance.

Wake with sticky eyes but keep hands from relieving the itch. Must not touch the body with the hands made unclean by sleep. Hands at side, eyes open, say *Modeh Ani*. I thank Thee King for having returned to me the soul you held overnight in your safekeeping.

A prayer while still unclean? Relax. The Name is not mentioned. You speak to Thee, you speak to King, you avoid the name Adonai.

But do not think. Just remember what you've been taught. Play the rehearsed response. Remembering is easier than forgetting. Lean out of the bed and prepare to wash your hands. Next to your bed is the cup and basin you had prepared the night before. Follow the rules. Pick the cup up with your right hand, give it to your left, let the left pour cleansing water on the right, then let the right purify the left. Do this three times.

As you begin to dress (first making sure you do not take steps without the night *yarmukah* securely on your head), be careful you are never completely naked. Remove pajama top first then put on undershirt before removing the bottom. Just pay attention. Concentrate. Forgetting is better than remembering.

Right sock goes on before left.

Right shoe goes on before left.

Tie the laces of the left shoe first. Don't wear loafers, simplicity is the enemy. Ceremony goes before thought. Father's shoes have many eyelets, his frazzled laces demand careful threading.

The morning service does not cease at the bathroom door. The strength of the morning erection can now be utilized to point the streaming piss into the bowl without the need for directing hands. Because an unmarried man does not hold his penis during urination. The first graffiti in the Law, "If you shake it more than once, you're playing with yourself." And though there is no prayer before, there is a blessing to be recited after, a hymn to the leaders, pipes and gutters of the body, may they let the liquids pour unimpeded, may the waters be everflowing.

What next? You have dressed and brushed your teeth (unless of course it is the Sabbath in which case you could not use the brush for fear of tearing out bristles or the tube of paste because the squeezing alters its state) and so you are ready for morning prayer. No eating or drinking. Nourish the soul before stuffing the body. Now pay attention. Take the little wooden boxes with the leather straps you have had since your thirteenth birthday and, in the correct sequence, put it on your arm, let it be a reminder on your forehead, wind the straps toward the heart or away, twist is across the hand, snake it arond the finger. Touch. Kiss. Pray.

You're a lefty? I did not forget you. Instead of the left, put the phylactery on your right arm. The weak hand strengthened, the unclean sanctified. With marriage comes the large prayer shawl, a flap of wings, a veil under which to hide.

Prepared for prayer, pray. Solitary prayer is acceptable; with the quorum it is more effective. Faster at home, the familiar words rushing off the page to meet your voice half-way. After prayer, prepare to eat. Wash. Bless. Eat. Thank. Leave. Don't forget the *mezuzah* on the lips of the house. Touch it. Kiss the finger made holy by that touch.

Afternoon prayer. Evening prayer. Evening. Before sleep, say the prayer that lets dreams fall. Having said it, be still. No more than three additional words may be uttered. The soul makes ready to rise and write in the great book upstairs the deeds of the day. Sleep. Remember, a man can be known by the thoughts he has before he sleeps. Unbridled by soul, dream. Upon waking, begin again. Everything is the same. There is no body. There is only the Law. Father's way to forgetfulness. While I, having failed before at following Father's lead, fail also at his forgetting, though Rachel was a capable and eager deliverer of sleep.

Except, of course, during those first few days when we could not stop screwing, even when it became painful to continue. But I felt the way I did when I was fourteen and seemed to be in a permanent state of erection, when the rhythm of the Nostrand Bus was enough to send me sweating and I dreaded the summer when I could not disguise myself with a jacket or a sweater. Although I had never worn a *gartel*, that thick black strand of silk around the middle that many of the Orthodox put around their waist before prayer, in an attempt to separate the earthly part of the body from the casing for the soul, I felt as if I had always worn it and had suddenly removed it so that all the denizens of that upper part of me were suddenly released downward and had only one place where they could emerge. I screwed mindlessly and thoughtlessly, I dozed through dreamless naps, I abandoned the sophistication of my lips and hands and let the blind head have its way until I ached.

But when we finally calmed down, or because we did, I started remembering again and became unsure. Should I have been thanking her or should I be apologetic for having monopolized her so? In my uncertainty, I became shy and would put shorts on again even for a brief trip to the bathroom. Yet we had been long familiar with each other's bodies. If I had been a body on a gurney, she would have been able to identify me by the patterns of my beauty marks and a circular discoloration of the skin near my spine, while I, having noted carefully the weight of her breasts, would have been able to recognize her in a taste test while blindfolded. But not knowing whether to be grateful or guilty, concerned again whether I should be maintaining the vigil with Father, aware also that he was doubting my explanation that I was with Jonesey, using Jonesey's *t'filin* for morning prayers, I rushed into my shorts and began to close my eyes while making love.

"Relax," Rachel finally said, "you suffer too much from pleasure."

"I don't feel guilty," I told her. "I'm just surprised when I lose control like this."

"Don't think of this as losing a virtue. Think of it as bringing a lapsed Jew like me into the fold."

"Well," I admitted, "I guess I can't help thinking about what comes next."

Rachel laughed. "Stop worrying. Planning is too much in your blood."

But I suffered from more than a lack of planning. I also had the problem of over-extended supply lines. I had moved with Rachel into no man's land, having violated both prescribed and unacknowledged boundaries, and had placed myself beyond the protection of air cover. I had ignored the history of behavior; I had made myself subject to an absence of laws. Not knowing what was expected of me, I was at a loss. Do I avoid or accept the responsibility? Making ready to go home for the weekend, to share the Sabbath with Father, I stood in front of the metal plated door, picked at the rotting wood of the side panels, exchanged kisses.

"I hate going," I finally told her.

"Rest will do us both good," she laughed.

"I mean for the weekend."

"Me too."

"I'll call you."

"Good."

Hesitant still, I said by way of leaving, "I love you."

"You sound as if you were packing for a trip. Don't forget to write."

I kissed her. Squeezing the ends of her hair I discovered that bed and sleep had uncurled their springiness, had softened her all over. I got home in time to intercept Jonesey's call. He wanted to borrow the car to take Sheila to the Catskills for the rock concert at Woodstock. "That's over and done with," I told him, mystified, "except for the garbage and the traffic."

"She just wants to see the place," he said. "Are you just back from Rachel?"

"What about Joy?" I asked him, ever conscious of responsibilities.

"Ask her," he said, "I don't think she's busy. You know I wouldn't stand in your way."

"All right," I told him, "but check the transmission, I feel it hesitate between second and third."

"I'll bet you do," he laughed.

I wondered how inventive Sheila would be in explaining her whereabouts for the coming few days to her parents. And whether Joy would be sorry for her short summer. And how much safer green pastures might have been for me than the seashore.

20.

Even Rachel's presence could not dispel the uneasiness of approaching *Rosh Hashanah*. Not in Crown Heights. Summer not yet done, *Elul*, the month of preparations, begins. In streets still empty, the morning call of the ram's horn demanding repentance, reminding of obligations, can be heard. Attendance at the Loew's on Nostrand Avenue drops perceptibly on Saturday nights; even the romantic and lush *Romeo and Juliet* plays to empty houses. The Kosher Pizza Shop on Kingston begins to close earlier, its bright lighting suddenly unappealing. The Sabbath-observant-car-rental-and-driving-school suffers too. Anything catering to leisure or amusement falls on hard times. It is not a frivolous time of year. The evening news empathizes. Egypt is restless, Ho Chi Minh suddenly dead. Although a drop in monthly call-up is anticipated, the withdrawal from Viet Nam moves slowly and the fate of Israel, government sources say, is intricately tied to Viet Nam's. Not needing encouragements toward sobriety, I found myself to be a very serious young man at this time of the year, marking the shortest distance between Father's house and Rachel's and hauling myself earnestly back and forth between them.

Before making the right turn into Empire Boulevard I would stop by the precinct house on the corner and get waved directly upstairs to Detective Meisner. My Lancer had become familiar. The cops came to accept it as their own and did not ticket it if I parked it illegally.

Whenever he saw me, Detective Meisner would say, "Still looking," even smile at me. But despite his violet striped suspenders and thick mustache which suggested an interest in crimes of passion, he cared more for the technology of detec-

tion than the psychology of guilt. He prayed to the computer, sacrificed to the lie detector, was brought to near
arousal by print-outs of statistics and voice patterns. He was
eager to solve more challenging cases than my mother's disappearance. A green-sneakered rapist was loose in the area and
stone throwers had somehow eluded the patrol car permanently stationed outside the Lubavitcher Rebbie's residence.
Worse, a load of caskets was stolen from Ortiz's Funeral
Parlor right across the street and Meisner had a feeling the
three cases were related. I left him to his dreams of flickering
lights and headed toward Rachel, passing along the way the
drawn white blinds of Rabbi Baumel's learning parlor. The
yeshiva, shuttered until after the Fall Holidays, gave me an
Indian summer of freedom while the Rabbi and I waited out
the results of the Draft Lottery Bill being debated in Congress.

The only other landmark before Rachel's building was the
bulletin board outside the entrance to Prospect Park, with its
listing of daily events. I would check it hurriedly, fearing the
day it would announce the opening of the Wollman Rink for
ice skating, knowing that such an official acknowledgement
of water freezing over would be an undeniable sign that it was
time for searches to end and mourning to begin.

Not that I was eager for the additional responsibilities that
mourning would have brought. I think I was obscurely relieved at the uncluttered way my mother had arranged her
disposition. It was as if she had decided to relieve me of the
special set of ceremonies, the awkward procedures, the unre-
hearsed formulas of mourning which would have forced me
back into the Orthodox camp. Because the pious take over at
transitions. At birth, puberty, and death, biological turnings
beyond human control, the Orthodox move in. Other Jews,
busy with everyday details, relinquish control during special
circumstances. The Observant become the officiating priests.
They perform the circumcision, arrange the redemption,
confirm manhood, conduct the burial service. Watch the uncomfortable settling of skullcaps on unfamiliar heads outside
funeral parlors. Watch the man in charge move with aplomb,
his *yarmukah* firm in grooved lines in his skull. We are
birthed, manned, and interned to mysterious tunes only a
select few can hear.

147

My mother, by disappearing, preserved me in my movement away from religion. She allowed me to mourn in my own way instead of forcing me to follow chapters in the *Code* beginning with "The Rending of the Garments." No formally torn collar in an old suit for me, no whispered formulas of comfort, no prohibitions against bathing, shaving, and cohabiting. And not sentenced to the daily synagogue, to wait for ten just men to appear three times a day so that they may help speed my *kaddish* on its way. Instead, I was left on my own, my mourning limitless, my time for it endless.

And I made sure it would be a private thing, having learned my lesson well from those semi-detached houses in my neighborhood. Whatever the memories (night after night I dreamt that my mother was trying to teach me to whistle, telling me to purse my lips as if in a kiss), I was as imperviously nonchalant on the outside as the Crown Heights houses. Nothing disturbs the faces of these residential streets. Trellissed porches keep the streets out; if there are secrets, they go on behind recessed windows and wooden shades painted a light, metallic white, the color of rejection, not absorption. On late summer afternoons neither sound nor light escapes from within those brick houses along Montgomery Street, with their red front steps and black enameled railings If they had their own deaths inside, their outside gave nothing out. I remember looking carefully at adult faces the day after Jonesey had explained the actual procedures involved in the concept "fuck." I was searching for any indication that they had done it. Nothing showed. Surely there would be a sign, a secret look, a button that said "Yes," a badge like the side curls and beards of the Orthodox. That everyone fucked but no one revealed was a notion difficult to accept. Even later, while I was a busboy in honeymoon hotels *(glatt kosher)*, and knowingly took part in pools on the time of morning descent by the happy couples (I won consistently by betting on early hours if the two struck me as being a pair of self-conscious young marrieds, late hours for those the second time around), I still looked for the giveaway, the telltale sign, not of tenderness but of transforming carnality. But there was nothing on the faces. And my neighborhood admitted no changes either. Fall could scatter leaves and summer make the asphalt ooze but the houses confessed to no alterations. The house next door to us was taken over by a Christian family that did extensive interior remodeling but left the tiny mezuzah on the front doorpost untouched under layers of old paint. On a weekday the Lubavitcher Synagogue looks like a private home and I knew that during the Festival of Booths, the *sukkoth* on the upper porches would be uniformly prefabricated, presenting a calm front. Only storefronts reflected the changes. Schwartz's grocery became Munez's and displayed enormous bunches of green bananas and an Israeli took over the penny candy store, introducing Hebrew newspapers on his magazine rack.

But the new year was coming and preparations were going on in my area. Rachel's parents were coming up, a yearly pilgrimage to New York, the Holy City, to renew acquaintanceships at their old Temple. My comprehensives would fall soon after the final days of *Sukkoth* and I also had to help Father make his household ready for new beginnings. We went together for early morning Supplication and shopped for honey and apples, a somber search for sweetness. And we bought the seats for the High Holy Days at the *shul.*

Chaim, the Rabbi's second son, destined for the business world, waited at one of the back tables, furthest from the Reader's Lectern. In front of him was a spiral notebook into which he had drawn a seating plan for the entire synagogue and filled it with peel-back labels. Next to it he had a looseleaf binder with heavy pages, one per member, in which he kept a running account of donations at the Scroll during the year. On Saturdays, with writing forbidden, ingenious Chaim slipped pieces of paper into cleverly constructed pockets, each sliver equal to a dollar. At Sabbath's end he would make the proper notations, in indelible ink.

"*Harav* Kole," he said, ignoring me. I was merely an adjunct on Father's page. "You are paid up as usual." Then, looking down at his records, he asked Father how many seats he wanted for the High Holy Days.

"Three," Father said clearly, without hesitation. "Two here and one in the wives' section."

Ignoring my stare, he paid. Moving quickly, afraid perhaps that Father would change his mind, Chaim put the money into a green index file box then wrote "Kole" on three labels, two adjoining, the third for the area marked off for the women. "Next to Mrs. Hartstein," he said, "as usual." Father said nothing.

We watched Chaim peel the labels off and paste two of them side by side on the back of the appropriate seats. Usually we sat on plain wooden benches and leaned against the wall. These seats were more comfortable, round backed, low chairs that seemed to have been ripped in pairs from some old movie house. When he peeled off the third label and walked toward the section behind the curtain that was now pulled over, bunched to one side on its thin wire, I decided it was time for me to leave. To my surprise Father walked out with me. "It looks like a big crowd for *Rosh Hashanah*," I said.

He nodded. "The three-day-a-year Jews always fill the *shul* up," he said.

"They come like ghosts," I told him, wanting to hurt. "Then they go back to where they came from."

He stood squinting into the sun where two tiny planes, like gnats, were spilling their white exhaust in crisscrossing lines, the earliest parts of the lines already dissolving, fuzzing out into nothingness.

Rachel was preparing for the holidays too, her clock radio surprisingly tuned to an all-news station while she was setting up a sleeping spot for herself in the front room. I watched her shove three jumbo pillows end-to-end and drape blankets over them, creating a firm rectangle she covered with sheets. She would be her own guest in the living room while her parents slept in the bedroom.

"If you had made it look that inviting the first time I was here I might have stayed all night. Now I think of all those months we've wasted."

She stepped back to examine her handiwork. "A ready girl almost sent you running. A prepared bed would have scared you into another country. Think of the three months you spent getting used to yourself."

Before I could answer, she lifted a hand to stop me. There were news bulletins about fighting in the Mid-East. Israel was in the Sinai, Egyptian planes were in the midst of engagements, Golda Meier was thinking of postponing her trip to the U.S.

"Your friend in any danger?"

"Only from eyestrain and matchmakers. He hasn't been drafted."

I had called Dov's father when the fighting in Israel first began. Dov was all right, he reassured me, protected by his task. It seems Dov had made a commitment to study around the clock, a Torah for Peace Vigil. He was safe in Safed provided the Syrians stayed out of it. Was I learning too, Mr. Laufer asked.

"For peace and security," I told him, "just like Dov."

Rachel had piled some of my things in one corner. Mostly books, since I was reading for the Comps whenever I could, and always left the house carrying books in case Father asked where I was going. But I could also see the large-eared orange mug of unbreakable plastic that held my razor of initiation, the can of Barbasol I had learned to prefer to the Palmolive, and a semi-tough Tek toothbrush bought especially for overnight stays. Rachel noticed me watching. "Clearing out the past year's sins." But she smiled saying it.

I wasn't concerned. The albums I had occasionally left at Rachel's—a Simon and Garfunkle, a lush Moody Blues, the Beatles' *Abbey Road* and *Sergeant Pepper*—were still intimately combined with her records. Still, I would not have minded even more mingling of possessions, her books snuggling against mine on her shelves, our clothes warm in her closet, our laundry intertwined, a single toothbrush even, provided we could agree on soft, medium, or hard. The circles on her wall calendar that marked family birthdays, exhibitions at the Coliseum, and concerts at the Fillmore East had been joined by more circles: my birth date, the date of the Comps, upcoming revivals at the Elgin and the Regency. I welcomed the tiny links. Having given in to Rachel when she had come back, I was ready to get in all the way, all strings freely attached.

She lifted one of the many cardboard boxes she had brought home from Waldbaum's and covered with cloth for use as scatter tables and hid my things under it.

"Out of sight, out of mind."

"The day my parents fly back to Lauderdale, they'll reappear."

"Why not leave them in all their glory? Didn't you say you tell them everything?"

"But not that I show them everything. We're considerate about showing. We show each other the kinds of courtesies people usually save only for strangers."

"You politely give them directions or the time of day?"

"I spare their eyes and let them use their imagination. Which they can control very nicely."

She was kneeling on the pillows, bouncing, testing their firmness. Not one to waste an opportunity, I kicked off my sandals and ran to kiss the back of her neck, brushing her hair out of the way. I was careful to restrain myself. I was learning to reserve courtesies for loved ones. Though still early in our second beginning, I had catalogued the sensitivity of her neck. Knowledgable about tension, I learned that if the rigidity left her neck, it would flow immediately into my body. I knew that if she relaxed a bit, she was signaling that I was welcome to leap. She did more. Laughing, she let herself fall on the makeshift bed. "I should find out how comfortable this is," she said. I stroked the rough cloth of her shorts, a gentle quester between her legs, expecting to be interrupted with her caution. But she urged me on. "It's OK," she whispered, "I expected you to come over," and because I was moving very slowly and very carefully, working my hands into her warmth, she said, "It's such a waste, come inside, quickly." But I had time, I knew I had time this time, and continued to touch her softly, even as the pillows pulled apart and we slipped into the spaces between them, went on touching her with a sudden understanding of sensation. It was the fire within the hail, that liquid warmth, the destruction that rained on Sodom and Gomorrah transformed into pleasure. Oh, the wicked are punished as they have sinned. "I'm a tailor's son," I whispered back, "I can't resist touch and textures."

Helping her straighten up later, I could not resist kissing a breast through her shirt, leaving a wet imprint on the madras cloth. "What did you do before me?" she asked.

"Haven't you read Portnoy?"

"Oh," she said, "and I thought you were saving it for me."

"Renewed, I'm like new," I told her.

"I told my mother to read it too. She wrote me that she was glad she had a daughter."

152

"The definitive novel about a Jewish girl is still waiting to be written."

"Down to intimate details of self-amusement?"

"Right."

"I guess that lets out Marjorie Morningstar," she said.

"Am I going to meet your parents?"

"If you want to. You don't have to."

"Then I might as well," I told her, not forgetting that tiny pile of my belongings in the corner. "I wouldn't want them to spend their retirement pay for nothing."

Rachel shrugged. "What an honorable man. You'll get along. They're still upset that your letter stayed on my dresser in Florida so long."

"Not to mention those you didn't write."

"For every letter I didn't write," she said, "I thought of you ten times."

But there had been times when she didn't, I knew that. Walking through the bull ring, after the fight, through the excessively yellow sand that had been scattered over the spilled blood, past the rest of the congealing blood that had been shoveled into a wheelbarrow, she stumbled and almost fell. Sheila gave a little shriek, could only hug herself but two Mexican boys who had been following the American girls, grabbed Rachel under either arm, saving her from falling. And one the boys, bold, brushed against her breast and continued to hold her arm, smiling at the feel of it against the bristles of his hand.

"Good thoughts evaporate in the hot sun," I told her.

"Don't waste your time on tropical novels while you're studying for your comprehensives," she said. "Stick with all those sensitive young men. It's the boy in you I like messing around with."

"I thought it was the joys of *Yiddish*," I said, and made ready to go, knowing I was in for it with this girl, nothing ever easy for the *yeshiva* boy. I had been willing to give her all of me, retaining just one part. She was willing to lend bits and pieces but not all of her. What a regular swain I would have to be, I thought, hoping those years of mute courting on Eastern Parkway would not have been in vain. Because apparently getting into her bed was not the same as signing on the dotted line below her name on the lease. Scrupulous person that I

153

was, I was ready to make full payment but she wasn't acting as if I were her debtor.

We arranged to meet in Prospect Park, on the other side of the lake, where the Flatbush and Boro Park Jews gathered on Rosh Hashanah for the symbolic casting away of sins into the water. Usually scheduled for the first day of the two day holiday, the Sabbath on the first day forced its postponement to the second for that year.

"I'll be wearing a blue yammie," I said, "so you'll know me."

"I'll be wearing parents, one on each side, and a dress. Will you know me?"

"Even in the dark," I said. "Should I bring along extra bread crumbs for you?"

"We'll have our own supply, probably left-over *challah*. I don't think I need any help with this holiday."

I had thought only that having helped with her sinning I would contribute to her means of repentance. She didn't seem ready for more joviality. I got out, leaving behind one of the Lawrence novels I had to finish. More bread upon the waters.

At home I came upon Father busy in the doorway. "Oiling hinges?" I asked, thinking their quiet would help my late night arrivals.

Father didn't answer and I noticed his mouth was full of tiny nails. He always held straight pins that way when he was doing cuffs and pockets at the sewing machine, practically spitting the pins into his hands. On the tray part of the ladder I noticed the wooden husks of the *mezuzahs*, the doorway talismans, and on the sidepost the empty spot where one had been. "Are we converting?" I asked.

He removed the nails slowly, mastering their points and his anger. "I'm checking them," he said, "you never know, with age a letter is erased or there's rain damage. I should have looked earlier."

The ladder was blocking the entrance so I sat and waited and watched Father reset the sacred burglar alarm of our household, carefully examining the prayer on the parchment for the tiniest flaw.

21.

If September was made ragged by mandatory *shul* attendance on two days of New Year, eight additional Days of Repentance of which the last is *Yom Kippur*, an all-day job, followed by nine days of Tabarnacles, it was also made whole and full by constant formal dinners. Two meat meals a day called for a well-stocked larder, and Father and I spared neither bird, beast, or fish. We bought our food for the New Year, spreading the wealth down Kingston Avenue at the Meal Mart and Sinai for ready-made delicacies. Anything a good housewife would make: chopped liver, *tzimmes,* breaded veal cutlet, chicken soup with thin or thick noodles, with matzoh balls, with barley, roasted stuffed chicken, homemade, the thread still inside, even a fish-head for Father, a staring carp, the traditional reminder of the watchful, unblinking, heavenly Eye. We provided for everything that needed to go on the table. I prepared the candles, burning off the wicks so that they may be lit easily at lighting time, Father blessed them all, not a candle missing, not one unlit. He even bought two kinds of *challah*, one scattered with poppy seeds, the other heavy with raisins. But while well prepared for meals with Father, I was worrying about the meal at Rachel's house, the welcoming dinner she was making to which old friend Gondo was unaccountably invited.

"He wants to see a really traditional meal. His parents don't even care about this," Rachel explained. "Besides, he's an old friend, almost a brother. Last year his mother asked him what special meal he wanted for Passover dinner and he told them lobster, as a joke, and would you believe she had them, Maine monsters, bib and all?"

"Since when are you in the business of reclaiming lost

souls?" I complained, unhappy about her elaborate preparations, not seeing my place anywhere, my mother's absence emptying me, Rachel, thinned for the summer, not filling me, feeling like the prescribed empty mourning vessel. "He can come eat at my house for tradition."

"He wants to see tradition, not Hungary," she told me. "What time are we meeting in the Park Sunday?"

"I'm walking," I told her defiantly, "it's *Rosh Hashanah*."

"We are too," she said, surprising me.

"How come?"

"I keep on trying to tell you we take the High Holy Days seriously. You're just not listening."

"Oh, how serious can you three-day-a-year-Jews be? You don't know Holy Days until you have to wear sneakers on *Yom Kippur*."

But certainly she had made it clear that hers was not the place to sneak to for illicit sustenance if the fast became too much for me. And by the way people were shopping, it seemed that Crown Heights would be stripped of food by *Rosh Hashanah* Eve. The run on honey was so great that Berel Altman, the druggist's son, managed to sell the high-priced, genuine bee's honey packaged as a virility aid that had been under the counter for two years. And a Shlomo Weiss bakery truck, arriving posthaste from Williamsburg only three hours before sundown, was mobbed, late shoppers grabbing *challas* right off the bearded deliveryman's tray. All perishables were sold. All stores were closed. Detective Meisner exchanged with Detective Smith, trading *Rosh Hashannah* for Christmas. A hush descended on Crown Heights. Because the two days fell on Saturday and Sunday, Lindsay had no need to suspend alternate side of the street parking regulations. Otherwise he too would have observed the Days of Awe.

Though the cupboards of commerce were bare, food was unavoidable. In the synagogue, freshly whitewashed, it was the odor of cooking seeping down from the Rabbi's apartment upstairs that dominated, contrasting oddly with the swaying, white-robed men. During the following day, the smells dissipated by the cold stove of Sabbath, we sat so long in *shul* that my stomach growled, audibly. "You should not have had the cold milk," Father whispered, hearing the noise. "It was all you let me have," I whispered back, wondering where Gondo slept, imagining him suddenly developing religion, and unable to drive, staying over at Rachel's place.

Before the Reading of the Scroll the Portions were sold off as usual on holidays. The men at our table, seeing Father was not bidding for the *haftorah,* or final portion, though that is known as the piece most effective in delighting the soul of one lost without proof of death, decided they would not chip in and buy it for him but began to joke instead about the bids being offered, comparing them to costs and commodities on the open market in the old days. The princely *cohan's* portion went for the price of two plump hens, the *haftorah* for three goose livers, the privilege of opening and closing the curtains of the Ark for a ten kilo bag of potatoes.

"*Gül Baba* potatoes," said Mr. Laufer, a new presence in *shul* at Dov's long distance insistence, I think, while his mother stayed at their regular synagogue so as not to remind us of my mother.

"The *Rozsa* brand was even better," Father said, "although that did depend on the year."

"Idaho, Washington, New York," Bernie Altman said, his prayer shawl with its silver trim on his head, "all junk. Black rot everywhere. By the time you finish carving, you can plant a candle in them." In addition to being a druggist he was also a notary public and spoke a half-dozen languages, all with a Hungarian accent.

"What do these *Amerikaners* know from potatoes?" Dov's father said. "A new potato, fried in fat, in the middle of winter, from your own pantry! I survived a year in the Ukraine just thinking about it. If the Pasha went to the trouble of bringing it to Hungary all the way from Turkey, I thought, the least I can do is come back and taste it once more."

I looked away, toward the women's section, absentmindedly waiting for my mother to beckon, adjust her white silk kerchief, and ask me how I was managing. "Lots of fun," I would say, "except for the self-flagellation," and she would urge me to be gentle, then whisper that as usual, Mrs. Hartstein had been the first one there and had been standing

157

throughout the prayers, although this day she had noticed her leaning more than usual against the edge of the table, the after effects of her heart attack unmistakable.

But though the curtain moved often, there was no one looking for me. At the table the talk of food had not ended. It was about wartime provisions now, how badly the Hungarian army had been fed, how miserably clothed for the Russian winter. All of the men around the table had been in forced labor gangs during the war, dragged toward the Eastern front by the Hungarians while their women and children were shipped in the other direction. But the Hungarian Jews were taken late, Eichmann had to come in personally to negotiate, and by the time the Hungarian transports arrived to the camps there were plenty of accommodations, the Polish women being long gone, going up in rich smoke while the Hungarians were still marrying and having children in Forty-two. To this day they have not fully learned to accept each other, maintaining separate *shuls* and butcher stores. The Poles resenting the Hunks for living, the Hungarians the Pollacks for being *kapos* or overseers in the blocks. And so, during the pause between the morning prayer and the afternoon, while the all-seeing eye watched and the all-hearing ear listened and the incessant scribe wrote up decisions, the men around the table in Father's *shul* were inevitably back at their point of departure, at the beginning of their time, arriving there at weddings, funerals and prayer meetings, during lunch breaks and casual Sabbath walks.

I heard my stomach rumbling. I was angry for wanting to listen so badly. I imagined Gondo wiping greasy fingers after eating his meal at Rachel's and rinsing his mouth from my cup. I remembered my mother involuntarily buying that extra jar of oil, just another bag of sugar, laying aside a heavy shawl, just in case they would come in handy for emergencies. Yet she never insisted I eat for the sake of starvelings around the world, never reproached me for causing her pain and making her return from the camps worthless, though I knew of mothers who did. If nothing else, these people around my table had a dignity, even talking about potatoes, that they were not aware of. Grubby Bernie Altman, Berel's dad, and his cut-rate and closeout cosmetics and blabbing mouth about the afflictions in the neighborhood, he had it.

And Mr. Laufer, owner of vineyards in pre-war Munkàcs, whose wife was the appointed wig-maker for the wives of the other Munkàcsi survivors, he had the confidence of mastery, having managed to resist eating the flesh of a forbidden horse even at the risk of starvation. Dignity lit him up. And my own tailor father, his fingers scarred by a million pinpricks and his hands calloused from lifting the coal-heated, heavy, pressing irons by their broken wooden handles, he had dignity, a central calm I knew I was destined never to manage to disturb; that only my mother had succeeded in doing.

They had come back, they had survived, nothing else could shake them. Their secret society admitted no one else. Even after that day when Father decreed us religious and changed everything else, the one thing they did not change was that whatever friends the two of them had, they had all graduated from the same summer camps and would invoke the name, the date and number of days there instead of passwords and secret handshakes.

In the afternoon, eating lunch late, I stayed home while Father returned to synagogue for Psalms. Heavy in the belly and sleepy, I stayed awake, honoring my mother's peculiar insistence that he who sleeps on this afternoon sleeps away his good fortune.

"You mean the way Benjamin Franklin said it?" I would joke, "That opportunity knocks only once? Knock, knock, God here, I'm making a final decision, anything to say in your defense? And I answer with a snore?"

"Do it for me," she would say, "in case I want something from you."

So I stayed awake and read chapters of *Second Skin,* a reading out of love since the book wasn't on my list, and thought of poor helpless Skipper, falling into another evil dream but knowing I was treating myself kindly again, lapsing into pity, thinking Rachel out of touch, Dov out of reach, my mother's wishes unfulfilled.

When the phone started ringing, I thought it might be Rachel but remembered she was serious about the day. It could only be Jonesey. Already practiced in deceit though I had been at it only a short time, I let the phone ring six times, as if it were a wrong number running its course, then picked it up after the end of the ring so that either Levin listening upstairs would have to think that the ringing had stopped of its own accord.

"Well," came Jonesey's voice, "*there* is a breach of *Rosh Hashanah* etiquette. Since when do you answer the phone on the Days of Awe?"

"Starting now, I guess," I admitted, startled into the realization that this was the first breach I had committed since sundown. "What is it, Jonesey?"

"Don't whisper," he said, "no one is listening. Doing anything?"

"Reading."

"Were you done late?"

"Late enough. What's with all these questions? Shopping for a *shul*?"

He wanted to know if I could be meeting Rachel the next day and where. He could walk with me until the Crown Heights side of the lake, past the Botanical Gardens, to the flesh exchange triangle where the three great religions from Crown Heights, Boro-Park, and Flatbush meet. He was not interested in discarding old sins, rather in committing new ones. "I'm meeting Sheila. I told her not to wear panties."

"Don't tell me about it," I told him, "please."

"I wasn't going to," he said, sounding injured. "not over the phone, anyway. This story needs hands for the telling."

Having violated the strictures of *Rosh Hashanah*, I realized that of my fantasized list of transgressions I lacked only the eating of forbidden foods, incest, and the various combinations thereof of all the others. I determined to remain in synagogue all day on Yom Kippur, avoiding all opportunities at sinning.

22.

On the New Year it is written and on the Day of Judgment it is sealed. What shall end and what begin. Will Benjie Wertheimer's father relinquish control of Lily Knitwear on Rogers Avenue to his son trained only in the use of different sets of phylacteries and will Menashe Schwartz, graduate of Brooklyn Law, have the opportunity to plead a case for a client not related to his family? Shall Rav Weintraub, Torah reader extraordinaire, lend his voice to future services at the *shul* or shall he ship out of town for the holidays, to Middletown or Monroe, and conduct services at a thousand bucks a throw? Should my schoolmate Itchie Roth accept the offer of a dowry in the rag business with Rifkah Popover's father, to suffer endless *shmate* jokes although it is true in rags there is gold, or should he continue to sit fiercely in *kollel*, learning for all he's worth, until a better offer came along? And what should be done, dear god, with Sander Silver, sitting there in the corner without friends although as a young man he already owned three of the charter coaches to Liberty, New York? What will it come to, this brooding passion for Rabbi Winkler's younger daughter, already notorious for bypassing Eastern Parkway for the illicit benches at Lincoln Terrace Park? Who shall live and who shall die, who shall miss and who achieve, who to reach and who to cease? Will Avery Asher Eidelberger choose to do his residency as proctologist or ophthomologist, both rackets since people, he insists, don't know their eyes from their assholes and will Karl Kasriel Feldman finally convince his father's partner that leather bikinis would be in this year, that it's the latest *goyish* craze and a good investment? Will Moishie Klein's pimples disappear so that he can go on the road with the number three accounting firm in the city and will Mottel Michael Saltzman's dream of million dollar policies and the elimination of death benefits be fulfilled? Who by water, who by flames, who by hunger, who by thirst? Who would buy Mr. Laufer's religious articles, who would be the first to sell to blacks when they crossed that invisible line of Eastern Parkway, who would Sammy Saffran be replacing in his meteoric rise from bank teller to vice president in a business traditionally under-represented by Jews, who could know if the Mets would go all the way this year and if *Sukkoth* would be rainy? Who else would go into business with his father, who would be converted to observance by love, who would be the first one in the graduating class to die? Above all, who shall roam and who shall rest, who for wealth and who for dearth, who to heights and who to depths?

Thus we prayed through the second day of the new year. And in the afternoon, the jury still out on further troop reductions, my chances in the draft lottery, my grade on the Comps, an offer from the Board of Ed, my conversation with Rachel's parents, I headed to the waters of Brooklyn, to make libations, scatter crumbs, purify myself of secular thoughts, and to meet, of course, at the gathering of the lake, every person I had ever known.

Accompanied by Jonesey (who was in a double-knit, double-breasted), both of us in *yarmukahs,* we cut through the Botanical Gardens where police lines were already set up near the Japanese Rock Garden in anticipation of the Lubavitcher contingent's appearance later in the afternoon. It would be a day of gorging for the fish and the geese; there would not be a dry bit of *challah* left anywhere in Crown Heights.

"What does her old man do?" Jonesey suddenly asked. "Hasn't your father asked you yet?"

"He wouldn't ask."

"Sheila says they have money."

I looked at him curiously. "Has the holiday affected you?"

"I'm practicing domestic things. Sheila wanted to know what I was going to be when I grew up. Got time to listen?"

We were walking steadily toward the far end of Prospect Park, cutting across many of the fields where I remembered playing ring-a-livio Saturday afternoons before we had begun our devotions to Eastern Parkway one summer. "Just don't talk to me about careers," I told him, "in *shul,* if you're not in business, law or medicine, they want to know what went wrong. And why I'm not married. I told Altman after he announced that Berel would be a full partner when he was done with pharmacy school, that he makes a living off other people's problems. Lawyers pray for the same accidents doctors do. What's wrong with being a professional, he asks me. I told him I'm the only one at the table who hopes his customers are healthy instead of sick."

"A real noble you are, Jake," Jonesey said. "I'm amazed you haven't enlisted."

"My body is destined for science not fertilizer," I told him. "What's with you and Sheila anyway?"

Uncharacteristically neat, his hair brushed, his nails scrubbed, walking almost daintily so as not to stain his polished shoes, Jonesey said, "I'm not promising anything but she's got me by the balls. It's a good thing she doesn't know it."

We stopped for a minute under the cool shade of a tunnel, lowering our voices automatically to keep them from booming in the echo. "Is this Sheila we're talking about?"

"Listen. You know that Pic-a-Shirt near the college? I picked her up after she went to register for the fall, she insists I meet her, and kisses me hello so that the yammie boys from *Bra* to *Bro* who are registering at the same time can see she's graduated from the ranks and plays feelies with a *shaygetz* in broad daylight. But all right, you know me, cunt is cunt, whatever turns her on. She wants to go shopping, she says, do I have the car? Jason is using it, I tell her. She laughs. It's an old joke. I begin to feel comfortable and horny but she wants to go shopping and between the two of you you could write a book about the thousand and one ways to come close but no cigar."

"Hey," I said, surprised, "you mean nothing happened up at Woodstock?"

"I know I kiss and tell, man," he said, "but I don't tell stories. Did I say anything happened?"

I shrugged. "You sent me that cartoon."

"I didn't say it was with Sheila, did I?"

I didn't argue. If not Sheila, who? The whore on the Parkway? But it was fine with me. I was all for regeneration of virginity. Damaged cloth made whole, a good piece out of bits of material, a tear invisibly mended. Another master tailor.

The air was light with the smell of green. We had walked beyond where Puerto Rican families had been barbecuing and playing baseball. I wondered how official this meeting with Rachel's parents would be. Would I have to ask her father for a position in the business? Would he expect to know what my mother's hometown in Hungary was? Would he be wearing a *yarmukah?* Should I be? Does anyone on *Rosh Hashanah* die of indecision and of waiting?

"Finish your story," I said, "you're holding up the National Book Awards."

"Just wait. Anyway. Inside the place she says, 'I'm buying, let's get matching shirts and dungarees.' The guy knows her, she's a regular, he has a rack of dungarees named after her even though she has to sneak pants out of her house in a paper bag and change into them. She takes three pairs, a couple of tops, hands me a few without asking me for my size. All right, I figure, the chick is into shoplifting, I'm nobody's conscience, I'm even turned on a little and grab her ass, she enjoys that in public. But it turns out I'm wrong. She calls out to one of the fags behind the counter, 'Harry, honey, we'll be a while,' showing him the pile of stuff we're holding. I'm starting to get the picture when we get inside the changing booth. It turns out not to be one of those up and down cubicles but the length of the entire store, with half of the store carpeting sticking through. Are you with me so far?"

"Too much introduction, not enough action."

"Not to worry. Action news follows. She locks the door, puts the stuff on the floor and says, 'I need an opinion.' 'Sure,' I tell her, 'the walls are thin, we'll give everyone an opinion.' She starts taking her pants off, turning her back to me. I turn my back to her and take my pants off too, figuring it's another Sheila blueball special. Instead we bump asses and next thing I know, we're on the carpeted edge of the floor, fucking away for dear life without making any noise but knowing that the goddam floor is filled with pins from shirts and pants, I mean we were humping away naked from the waist down but looking like we could go to a fancy restaurant from the waist up. But I'm nervous about the pins and needles and not concentrating hard enough and it turns out she's dropped her cherry somewhere along the way because she had no problems, before or after. Well, I wasn't going to wait until they started banging away at the door so I worked at it as fast as I could, feeling the breeze from under the door on my ass and trying to stuff Sheila's noises back in her throat. And when I'm finally done, and I have to tell you, I wasn't paying any attention if Sheila was still on the train or getting off at the same station I was, when I'm all done I'm for pulling my pants back on and getting the hell out. And Sheila says, 'Relax, we brought enough stuff in here,' and locks her legs behind me so I would have to fight her to go. Get this? I care for nothing like getting in and there I am trying to find the ticket for getting out."

"People drill holes into changing booths all the time," I observed, remembering the tiny pricks of light inevitable in camp showers and beach club cabanas.

"Don't I know it," Jonesey said, "for all I knew, the fags were selling tickets."

"But all right," I said, "so what's the point?"

"You did ask why Sheila, didn't you? I'm trying to tell you. She's got nerve. I mean real guts. Just as if we were in a motel, she gets down to skin and pulls me down on her tits. I swear to God, Jase, I came like a champ while some guy outside tried to match a shirt and suit to this tie someone gave him for a present."

"That's it?" I said, "this is what you couldn't describe over the phone?"

"The gentleman and scholar gets laid and he turns into a big *knocker*. I'm trying to explain something to you. I'm trying to tell you what it is about her. That after all this, she goes back home wearing a neat little skirt and sits down to eat *glatt kosher* meat and waits six hours before eating dairy and says a blessing for waking and walking and rainbows and albinos. And I feel like I've known her or someone like her all my life. I know that if she went to *mikvah* she would get a kick out of seeing how the competition was built. Am I getting through?"

"It sounds like true love," I said, "you've just described yourself."

He laughed but was more flushed than usual, as if being

serious was an exertion he found too difficult. "Well," he said, "I just wanted to explain. I get a kick out of hearing her curse in *Yiddish*. And she took my bet on the Mets. So I guess that house plan party you dragged me to that time worked out."

And he punched me lightly, full of friendship and camaraderie, but I wasn't going to make his tender feelings easier for him to handle by understanding them. He had laughed at me for too long, and had thought too little of even the simplest emotions. Let feelings be as hard for him as doing has been for me, I thought.

"Hey, Yossel," I told him, "it's really touching, this thing of yours for Rachel's religious friend. I can just see you getting your own car and making a down payment on a diamond. Listen, I'll get Mottel Saltzman to insure the stone for you and I'm sure your father knows someone who knows someone at the Diamond Exchange. What do you say? Should I get the ball rolling?"

"You prick," he said, full of good feeling in spite of me, "if I ever need one I'll get a kit and build one."

I had arranged to meet Rachel beyond the Boro Park tip of the lake, near the equestrian gate on Coney Island Avenue. Jonesey and I followed the riding path there, carefully staying on the grass to avoid the dust of the walk. Sheila had prevailed on Jonesey to come all the way up Fort Hamilton Parkway where she would meet him near the cemetery, to come without a car and to wear a *yarmukah*. "I wanted to compromise," he said, "wear a yammie and drive, but she said I'd get caught and banned from Thirteenth Avenue."

"Don't get tempted by the lush grass inside the cemetery," I told him, wanting to give him some advice on relationships with religious girls.

"Sometimes," he said "she stands there behind the fence, reading the names off the tombstones. It's not as if they were relatives, just strangers with unfamiliar names. She reads the names and dates. And sometimes, on hot days, it's the only place in Brooklyn where you can smell freshly cut grass."

"A poem to Greenwood Cemetery, by Yossel Kellerman," I said.

"It's Joy's influence," he laughed, "she taught me to appreciate the finer things in life."

We had arrived near the gate, having managed to avoid the buzz near the lake. "By now," Jonesey said, ready to move on, "we should have met the entire Eastern Parkway crowd."

"Everyone's moving to Boro Park," I said, "only the Lubavitcher are going to stick it out in Crown Heights."

"As long as the Rebbie can continue to arrange marriages for them. Hey," he was grinning, "remember Malkie Rabinowitz? If they hadn't married her off so quickly I think she would have converted Dov. I used to think he was queer until he got the hots for her."

"You're going to be late," I said, "don't lose your yammie, they'll run you out of Boro Park."

And the Jews gather for the casting away. In swampy Canarsie, an area only recently inducted into the society of Jewish neighborhoods, they trudge to the abandoned water works on Flatlands and spill their crumbs into a meandering brook that seeps out of the reservoir. In Williamsburg, those Chassidic sects that go to *tashlich* on the New Year, go to the East River, careful not to encounter rival factions. The men sway at the river's edge, sprinkling their bread. A few fishermen watch curiously. The water is oily and filled with mutations that refuse to nibble either at Jewish loaves or fishermen's bait, sustaining themselves instead on raw sewage and rotting wood. The Brighton and Sheepshead Bay crowd have the ocean enviably close by and go tramping across the sand in holiday shoes, surprising late season sunbathers. And between Boro Park and Crown Heights lie two places of worship—the casual and unpredictable turns of the lake in Prospect Park and the carefully landscaped, fenced-in sanctuary in the Brooklyn Botanical Gardens.

It is the opening of the fall season, the first reunion after the summer dispersions. The historians and statisticians are at work. It has been noted if arrivals had ridden or walked, if they had come hatted or bareheaded, single or paired, most important, if with wife or child in tow. Check the yes box on the last two items and your draft exemption will be forwarded in the mail. Better to marry than to burn, even better to father. If not for hire or sire, turn into a *yeshiva* boy and test some Rabbi's ire. Or be a school boy or teach a school boy. Final options come to self-mutilation (as in the Old World), or Canada. But *tashlich* is the happy hour. Great moments in the lifetime of Brooklyn's Jews have taken place here.

Heshie Pearl, whose mother liked to tell my mother (the two of them neighbors in *shul*), that her boy was destined by his good looks for a career in law, was officially introduced to the girl of his dreams, his *zuvig*, his draft exemption, his Fayge Tennenbaum, page 47 of the Central High School for Yeshiva Girls yearbook, nowhere else but right on the shores of the Brooklyn Botanical Brook, *tashlich* day 1968. And Mickey Wiener, my poker partner in *yeshiva*, was on the verge of enlisting or getting engaged until discovering the Baumel Draft Board Repelling Compound during the tides of *tashlich*. And it happened during *tashlich*, years ago, that Dov Laufer, preserver of Israel's sanctity, future leader of an Orthodox congregation somewhere in Iowa, henceforth known as Rabbi Laufer, was struck from the blind side by the spirit. He was watching a mad group of Lubavitcher *Chassidim* following the Rebbie to the shore, the men directly behind him linking their arms to keep the mass from trampling the Rabbi who walked slowly and calmly, apparently oblivious to the turbulence behind him. Though properly awed Jason Kole stood near Rabbi Dov, the angel bypassed him and landed with a soft thunk on the Laufer boy, sending him forever in quest of the Rabbi's serene center and the followers' agitated devotion. And it was to *tashlich* that Lindsay came, and at *tashlich* that fall fashions made their first apppearances and during *tashlich* that intermarriage between Boro Park maidens and Crown Heights *bochurim* is managed, mixing the nations, refreshing the gene bank, re-establishing Hand Job Haddie's winter reputation. So when I sing of *tashlich*, I sing of the blessed on a holy day. I sing of the names in the young Jewish Who's Who in Brooklyn. I sing the song of reunions. No need for us to print in high school yearbooks the names and addresses of the graduates and to pinpoint some future date for a get-together. We have instead the yearly *Tashlich* Convention, playing for your pleasure at two convenient locations.

For the more serious, those of you with crumbs in your

pockets, the place to go to is the Botanical Gardens. You will find older people here, including parents, and prayer books that are functional rather than silver gilted for display. There will be more material here for the matchmakers. The boys wear hats, looking spiffy in dark suits and modest ties. A bit of fluffy hair peeps from under their hats, advertising their progressive attitude toward religion. The girls are all *kallahmaids*, canopy ready, in long sleeved dresses and sensible shoes. They empty their pockets of crumbs, then wander in pairs along the narrow paths that surround the lake. Call this place the Eastern Parkway of *tashlich*.

The Lincoln Terrace of the *tashlich* scene is Prospect Park. Couples show up here, holding hands. Guys are more rowdy, often resorting to bumping into girls. There is much giggling. Many of the kids have been counselors or division heads in co-ed camps and there is much storytelling. Off to one side, a group of Ph. D. candidates. In a clearing near the Greek temple, the newly married. A sudden sensation as Big T. Mandel appears, in uniform, on a three day pass from Fort Dix. How did the *shmuck* get drafted? He claims he enlisted, worried that the Selective Service System was on to the *yeshivas*. The rumor is he had gotten his girl friend pregnant. Closer to the paths we can see baby carriages. Give Moishie Klein, the *shul*'s star accountant, a little deduction and an iron bound exemption, both in one shot.

The day is simply too short. Dov and I used to return late, shoes and suit dusty, run directly to *shul* where Father waited grimly but managed to contain himself, not wishing to contaminate the entire year by displaying anger on the day that may typify the coming twelve months.

23.

Rachel and her parents were late, perhaps as unsure about our meeting as I was. I stayed close to the gate, away from the paths, not in the mood to renew old friendships, looking toward Parkside Avenue from where Rachel would arrive. To my left, away from the road, was a thicket of red-berried bushes over which the branches of a willow hung, an intimate curtain, much like the ones that used to hide necking couples we would surprise during those ring-o-livio days in the Botanical Gardens. Jonesey called them movies, bargains at the price. When I had first taken up my post near the gate there had been the sound of laughter from that direction but there had been no special rhythm to it so I had ignored it. Only when I heard rustling from the same spot did I turn to look, seeing a man emerge backwards: shiny black robe, hand holding a dark, beaver pelt hat, finally a close cut head, with a velvet *yarmukah*. The birds sing for everyone, I thought, hope he's got enough crumbs, and waited, shamelessly curious about the bird in the bush.

The girl emerged stooping, one hand held by her partner, the other brushing at the limber branches of the weeping willow. By the particularly deep blackness of the color and the careful combing I could tell that she was wearing the kind of fashionable wig favored by married religious ladies. At least they're married, I thought, watching unabashedly, filing the scene for Jonesey's amusement. But then she straightened up and although I didn't know it at first, seeing her recognize me I realized I had been miraculously reunited, bless *tashlich*, with the elusive Miri Lieberman, alias the SLURP girl of my Rockaway summer.

"*Gut yontiff*, Miri," I said, "still trying to convince the boss to sell hot coffee on rainy days?"

But if I had thought to rattle her, I was to be disappointed. She had the confidence of the newly wed about her, looking as puffed with important secrets and private information as the proudest honeymooners I had ever served at the hotel. Her hair stylishly combed into the wig, her outfit a neat, lime-green suit, high heeled and nylon stockinged elsewhere, she remained calm and not unhappy with the opportunity to display to a new husband her attractiveness to old lovers.

"*Gut yontiff*," she said. "I lost my ring under the tree but Mechel found it." Smiling she held her hand out. "It's a carat and a half, almost flawless, with two baguettes, right Mechel?"

"Then you must be the almost flawless Mechel," I said, remembering clearly the smooth tan of Miri's throat and neck and back, unaccountably angered that there was hardly a square inch of her showing now. Next to her the man actually growled. *Yeshiva* boys, trained in subtleties, are always on the lookout for irony or sarcasm.

"This is Mechel," she agreed. "Aren't you going to wish us *mazel tov*?"

"A whirlwind courtship is the only way," I said, shaking his hand. "Congratulations."

"With God's help, may it be you next," he said in *Yiddish*, giving the standard formula. Next to him Miri stood, lit, pleased, picking particles of leaves off the side of her linen suit. She knew she was safe. There was nothing for me to say. I might have been briefly acquainted with parts of her but he had full knowledge. "I guess she won't be back at the board-walk next year," I told him.

"Mechel's father owns a bungalow colony near White Lake," Miri said, dimpling. "Did you ever hear of Steinberg's?"

"Near the Bobover camp," Mechel said, glowering still, his eyes keeping Miri a full arm's length away, his silk capote, fit for a bridegroom, gleaming, the covered buttons straining slightly out of the material. The happy expand, no question about it. Like the foot of Titus, swollen by news of his emperorship, Mechel filled the space before me.

"Are you a Bobover *chassid*?"

"Puppa," he said, naming a Williamsburg sect.

"Well," I said, "go scatter while the fish are still biting."

Mechel Steinberg, caftaned lover of Miri, hoarder of her secret waters, replaced his hat, neatly tucking his *yarmukah* underneath it. "We go on *Sukkoth*," he said.

"Good idea. Much opportunity for sinning in between."

"My wife wanted to come and see what the *shkotzim* do on *Rosh Hashanah*," he said stiffly, obviously choosing his words carefully.

The little wife, her snaggle tooth gleaming like gold in her mouth, cooly nodded. "I've always been curious. It's like a party here, isn't it?"

"Yeah," I admitted, looking pointedly at her skirt, "for some."

Thickening Mechel, restrained by the public's eye, would not take her hand but nudged her with a silky elbow. "*Nu*, Mir."

Already moving backwards, she said, "Mechel, you know, this is Jason, I didn't even introduce you." And Mechel, grinning, unable to resist the sign of possession, rested casually against her. "The Torah Vodaath boy who liked vanilla ice cream," he said.

Was there a sheet with a hole between them? I wondered. Does Miri like it from the back and how well does she use all that she has learned? Above all, what had I become in her telling? Clearly not a hero, probably not even a forgotten suitor, possibly nothing more than the quick change artist with the *yarmukah* who ate much vanilla ice cream. Though at least that one time it was sprinkled with her chocolate.

"Listen," I said, "if she can remember that, it had to be a boring summer. One week in the bungalow colony and you'll hardly remember Rockaway."

They left, walking toward where the crowd around the lake seemed thickest, slumming among the lapsed Jews of Brooklyn. "The religious Jews," Dov had written to me in a New Year's card, "are like the canaries the miners used to take with them into the shaft. At the barest whiff of gas, the birds turned their feet up and died. That's what they are for. They're sensitive to the slightest breath of anti-semitism because they walk around looking so obviously Jewish. When the trend is to mock the guys with the hats and beards, start packing, the gas is not too far behind."

At day's end, belatedly, I would send him my wishes for the new year.

Dear Dov, (I would write) I've spotted a new trend among the canaries. The young marrieds like to grab a quick feel in the bush on *tashlich*. What is the interpretation? What is the significance? Could the Messiah be on the way? Keep me in mind during prayers. Write soon.

And would date it "New Year's Day, 5730," though writing it in the evening which already belongs to the following day. It was also the Chinese year of the moon. And for Jonesey, the year of the Mets, as the winter before had been the season of the Jets.

24.

Rachel's father had the largest hands I have ever seen. If not for the cracked and seamed skin, marks of his years as manufacturer of venetian blinds and shades, those hands could have served as the ones that All State uses to keep its insured safe. When we shook, my hand disappeared in his. I felt like a child.

"How does it feel to be a guest at your daughter's?" I asked him. "Do you feel at home?"

"What he really wants to know," Rachel said, "is if you could notice signs of his absence in the apartment. Tell him you started reading the book he deliberately left behind, Mom."

Very chic she looked, my girl, splendid in finery befitting a future designer of ladies' outerwear. Quite proper for the ceremonies near the waters but very stylish too, with her suede jumper, buttoned way down, and a little drawstring that kept her snug and clipped at the waist. Most of the other people were handling over-the-knee-minis with determined aplomb but Rachel was prescient, longer skirts were inevitable. Father said the same thing. Under the faintly purple suede, a lavender, long-sleeved blouse, and jauntily, a beret on her head.

"Jason," her mother said, "isn't that a funny name for a Jewish boy? Especially a rabbi?"

"Did you tell her I was a rabbi?" I asked Rachel, fidgeting in my misleading *yarmukah* even though everyone was capped, Rachel in her beret, her father in an old fashioned, wide-brimmed hat that was pinched in the front, making him look like an old New England church with its steeple, and even Dora Ramsess with a tiny pillbox on her head, including a little crippled veil. "It's a temporary vocation, I think. I'm not a rabbi."

"Dora, Dora," her father's voice, as deep as the echoes in the Prospect Park underpasses, boomed, "names don't matter. Who would name their children nowadays Dora or David? Those young rabbis we have down in Florida who walk their poodles on the Sabbath aren't even called rabbis but doctors. One name is as good as the other."

"He's not a rabbi," Rachel said. "Gondo was joking. He wouldn't know a rabbi from a rabbit." But because she was enjoying herself, crisp in the early autumn air, surrounded by people who loved her and clothed in something she loved herself, she added, "Not that Jason wouldn't be a perfectly good name for a rabbi."

"My Hebrew name is Yaakov," I surrendered, "that's like Jacob, so the initial is the same as with Jason. With Hungarians matching the initials between the Hebrew and English names is the best you can hope for."

"I don't trust initials," Rachel's father said, standing close to his wife so that Rachel, as if needing connections, moved closer to me. "It made me nervous about Johnson, you know. All those perfect initials. Lynda Bird and Lucy Bird and Lady Bird. Too much self-awareness, too much consciousness, I said, didn't I Dora?"

"Lucy *Baines*," Dora said.

"Yes. But I still didn't vote for Goldwater."

He was looking at me entirely full of kindness, clearly approving his daughter's choice. Solemn with the bushiness of his eyebrows and mustache, his voice concerned, he asked, "Have you been to the lake yet?"

I was thinking how unlike books the reality of people was but how much more real book reality sometimes seemed. I had fully expected Dave and Dora to conform to those older American Jews whose European ancestry was merely a whiff and whose *yiddishkeit* but a shadow in the heart and a twist (as lemon, in a drink, lightly) in their speech patterns. I had come to accept the existence of two groups of Jews in New York City. Post-war Europeans and pre-war Malamudians, with the late arrivals never taking the six edged star off their sleeves. Where did these two fit, with their eagerness for the waters, their retirement to Florida while the princess, the daughter, was still unmarried, and their fondness for each other which placed the center of their existence precisely into that center spot of the bed where Rachel said she always tried to crawl? If it was their long years together before Rachel was born that had made them focus on each other rather than on the warmth emanating from their child, why had Father not managed as well? Why couldn't my parents have treated me with benign neglect, allowing me to learn by watching rather than by being press-ganged into service? Rachel seeed not to have suffered from an absence of love and I envied the casual affection among them. But there was never anything casual in my house. We cared or ignored, observed or defied. Nothing in-between, like the prayer book in Dora's hands or Rachel's special outfit for the holidays. Having chucked my yammie I was determined to chuck it all and had brought no prayers or crumbs along for *tashlich*. Father had a Hungarian version of "Love it or Leave it." I had learned my lessons well.

"I waited for you," I told them, looking at Rachel. "Did you bring me extra crumbs?"

"No pockets on this jumper," Rachel said, holding her hands out, shaking her hair, which looked thick and sleek, moving evenly from side to side, all those rough edges from our first meeting completely gone.

"I had plenty in my pocketbook," Dora complained, "but Rachel made me leave it behind. She said it would look conspicuous. How could a grey pocketbook look conspicuous with a grey dress?"

But I realized she had kept her mother from looking out of place in the midst of the religious crowd around the lake. Well, the four of us certainly dressed as if we belonged. "Great outfit," I told Rachel, "another class project?"

"My High Holy Days' ensemble," she said. "Daddy's tradition. A new dress for New Year's and for Passover. He sent me a check and specified it to be spent on clothes. A fresh start, each year, head to toe."

"Very becoming, Rach, but only married people wear hats here."

"It all stays on together or comes off together," she whispered. I looked to see if they had heard but David was busy reassuring Dora that he was well provided with cracker crumbs in both pockets and would not miss her pocketbook.

They had tuned us out quickly. I wondered what to do with Rachel. Should I take her hand? Her arm? Walk with a handkerchief between us? Let her hold Dora's hand while I abandoned mine to David's? While her parents were still distracted, I pecked Rachel quickly on the cheek, moving away before she could return it.

"It's all right," she said, "it wouldn't shock them."

"It's not that," I explained. "Too much passion here sets the tone for the rest of the year. And it's the same as an engagement proclamation. You take my hand at your own risk."

She put her arm elegantly through mine. "We'll send out not-engaged announcements." But there was the slightest bit of hesitation in her defiant gesture.

"All right, all right," her father was saying, "let's go and send our sins on a long voyage to the sea."

And so we went, murmuring. Rachel's mother never opened her prayer book, having apparently brought it along as an accessory instead of her pocketbook. But we all sprinkled some crumbs, even waited for fish bubbles to break the surface, but the fish, either stuffed or overwhelmed by the sanctity of it all, stayed away.

Afterwards, David Ramsess took a deep breath and surprisingly serious, proclaimed, "I am a new man for next year. I feel clean and light. Take a deep breath, Dora, it's not often that New York air is like this but when it is, it's rare, it's a treat. In Ft. Lauderdale where we are," he said to me, "I can feel the weight of the air when we breathe."

"Would you like to start something new?" I asked Rachel.

"We can try things we haven't before," she laughed and pressed my arm against her breast.

For people known as the ancients and the originals, for these Jews of tradition and old books, we certainly have a penchant for celebrating beginnings. Not enough to have one new year's feast, we have three, the next one after *Rosh Hashanah* none other than the coming *Sukkoth*. In less than two weeks, another celebration of opening, of starting up anew. The roadways to the Temple are hard and dry. The pilgrim brings his fruit and grapes for the sacrifice. The old year has been gathered in, the new year's seeds wait the arrival of rain so that planting may begin. The roads leading out of Jerusalem are awash for the departing pilgrim. Greening had begun. And not enough to have two celebrations of the new year in *Tishri*, the seventh month, but there is still another waiting in the wings. On the fourteenth day of *Nisan*, the first month, a night of swollen moon, a spring festival, there is a rousing welcome to firsts: first lamb, first grain, first deliverance. *Begin, begin, begin*, goes the urge of the people of the book. *Remember, remember, remember*, goes the song of the prayers. What perfect Americans we Jews could be, always optimistic, always forward looking, stripped naked in swaddling clothes three times a year. If only we could forget, if only the baggage on the back and the fear in the heart and the numbers on the arm weren't along to remind us of the past.

Prayers done, sins like stones cast away, we walked together down Parkside Avenue, past the tennis courts and past New Caledonian Hospital where Rachel was born. It was twilight. I knew I would be home late and would be telling Father that I had been to another *shul* for evening services. The day had calmed down. We spoke more softly. The brilliance of the holiday outfits had dimmed somewhat and faces across the street became indistinct, finally passing beyond recognition. Though I had expected to meet schoolmates, *shul*mates and neighborhood acquaintances, I had met only Mickey Wiener, looking up to see his eyebrows lift at the sight of Rachel's arm in mine. I had waved to him with a free hand, a wave that held no invitation, and Rachel had waved playfully from the other side. Not knowing her and restrained by me, Mickey kept his distance, no doubt exasparated at the *Yeshiva*'s extended recess that would keep him from asking questions until October.

Walking down Parkside I somehow found myself alone with Rachel's father. Rachel and her mother had drifted ahead and though their outlines were getting fuzzy, they maintained their separateness, Rachel kicking with the vigorous walk her father had settled on her, her mother taking short, ladylike steps, the nylons of her legs no doubt whispering together in that old-fashioned measure of proper deportment. The softness of the evening even absorbed the knock of Rachel's boots against the sidewalk so that the two of them seemed to float there ahead of us, ghostlike.

"Teaching," David Ramsess said, "is it worth waiting for?"

"I hope so," I told him. "Besides, I have to wait."

His eyes were on the shapes in front of us. "You know you will never teach what you are studying."

"It doesn't matter," I said. "All that is for me. It's in the blood, this learning. Only for me it's Twain and Tolstoy, not just the Talmud."

"True. And the benefits, of course, are there. Dora was a schoolteacher you know. Her pension is very nice."

"Rachel didn't say."

He stopped and looked at me. "I retired too early," he said, quietly but fiercely. "The day I closed the business I could set the heaviest wooden venetian blind into the window and still hold the other with my left hand. But Dora was ready to retire and I had an excellent offer. Now I tan in the sun. Even the cracks in my hands are filled in."

He held out those hands but in the growing darkness the deepest grooves could not show. If I had not shaken them I would have thought his palms smooth as soft cloth.

"But what happens?" he continued. "Shades come back in. In Boro Park they buy the fanciest ones, all patterns, shot through with silk and gold threads, squared edges, scalloped edges, inlaid stock, a different design in each window, in each room. A boom time for shades."

"What about the venetian blinds?"

"They should be called Japanese blinds," he said, smiling faintly. "They came from the Orient before the Venetians latched on to them in the sixteen-hundreds. Did you know that?"

"No," I admitted, noticing that up ahead Dora had come to an uncertain stop and was looking back toward us.

"Well," he said, "I was cutting back on them anyway, I could tell shades were going to be the thing." He paused. "They're perfect for churches or synagogues. Venetian blinds, I mean. Did you ever see them? Outside sunlight, inside, slanting in through blinds, part of the holy hush. The first record of it in this country was in a church, did you know that?"

179

"No, Mr. Ramsess," I said, not at all irked. "Where?"

"St. Peter's Church, Philadelphia, Pa. seventeen sixty one," he said promptly. "Let's walk."

But almost immediately he stopped again. "My own daughter has drapes instead of blinds. But nothing is better than blinds. Slant it upward and they keep the light out but let the breeze in. It doesn't occur to people to slant it upward."

"She loves colors and materials," I said in Rachel's defense. "It's her career."

"She's a good girl," he said. "A lovely girl. She came to us so late, I hardly could feel she was mine." He peered at me, his voice intense. "Is there something you'd like to ask?"

Surprised, I could only say, "The name, Ramsess, I've never seen it."

Disappointed in me, he drew back, shrugged. "Better ask Dora. It's Spanish, somewhere in Spain, my father claimed there was once a title and a crest. It doesn't matter. Is that all?"

"I guess so," I said, feeling the pain of his disappointment. "I'm sorry."

We began walking again, came up to Rachel and her mother who had turned back toward us. "What are you two having such a serious discussion about?" Dora asked brightly.

"I was inviting the young man to join us when we go to that favorite Italian restaurant of yours," her husband said.

"David!" Dora was genuinely shocked. "Rabbis eat only kosher."

"I'm not a rabbi," I said. Rachel was grinning.

"Well," Dora said, "Orthodox people then. Don't tempt him, David, not right after *tashlich*, all right?" And to me she said, "You know, to this day, we have two sets of dishes."

"Rachel told me."

"Maybe a nice kosher restaurant, then," she said anxiously, "Rachel, darling, isn't there one in Brooklyn? We'd love to have you."

"It's all right, Mom," Rachel said, "I'll cook him a kosher Chinese dinner next week, okay?"

Having reached Ocean Avenue, we parted. I shook hands with Dave and Dora, extended a hand to Rachel who took it, smiling, but returned also, quickly, the tiny kiss I had given her earlier. Then they went down Ocean, to the right, toward the Italian restaurant on Quentin Road Dora adored, and I went left, following the curve of the Avenue into Empire Boulevard, walking into the Crown Heights dark. I walked past the closed Botanical Gardens, the greenness of its trees swallowed by the night. All the other people on the route were returning from *tashlich* too and I walked just fast enough so that I passed no one and was not passed either. My black skull cap, I knew, was invisible in the dark. Not that anyone was looking.

I thought that perhaps I had come to an understanding of sorts with Rachel's father although I was not sure what exactly it was. Though the Boulevard was filled with people, there was none of the excitement of earlier in the day. Returns are tiring. There was no laughter. It was as if I were being reminded that though *Rosh Hashanah* was over, we were barely into the Days of Repentance, not yet done with the time of the year when my mother's presence in the house seemed most definite.

25.

Early Sunday morning, nearly at dawn when God's attribute of mercy is predominant, Father and I walked to the butcher on Nostrand for *kapporahs*, the scapegoat sacrifice that is performed the day before *Yom Kippur*.

"Choose a white," Father instructed me as we stood inside the butcher store, waiting our turn. "The whiter the better. Then look carefully at the comb. If it's all the same to you, make sure it is not twisted or pinched. It should almost glow."

I searched among the roosters within their flat cages and tiny compartments.

"How about this one?" Father asked, jabbing at one that was crouching, head to one side, peering warily.

"No," I said, unwilling to choose one that seemed so conscious of its fate. "How about that angry one? Can you reach it?"

Father pulled back. "It's a red. Angry is all right, but it's a red one. Don't you learn anything in that *yeshiva* of yours?"

My rooster was trying to get at its neighbor through the wire netting. "I know what the Code says. But there is an older tradition that suggests red. For all we know, the Black Prince even prefers pale company."

Father stared at me. "An older tradition? The truth?" I nodded. He shrugged. "All right, as long as it's written. Maybe a red does drive Him off, who knows, especially with a comb like the one on his head." He turned to look toward the other cages. "For myself, though, I will stay with a white. And for your mother, a white hen, of course. But I'm satisfied. For yourself you chose well."

Fleischman's little used back room stank of the hens and

roosters. The wire cages were piled atop one another, most of the fowl screeching and scratching but a few squatting as if resigned to their role. The feet of many were already marked with twisted paper, a color code only Fleischman understood, indicating that someone had already selected the rooster or hen and pronounced the *kapporah* passage over it. Those bits of colored paper marked them for death. *This instead of me, this is an offering on my account, this is in expiation for me, this rooster,* said three times, wailing chickens waved in the air over the head, then lowered to the floor for lightly placed feet on their necks. Sympathetic magic this. Take this thou beast, accept this thou stone, thou piece of wood, thou dish broken in the midst of festivities, take that sinner, violator, transgressor, let it be thou, not I, your death, not mine, your departure, my long and happy life. Even as we were choosing our own proxies, at a table in the corner a young boy, not yet thirteen, was gripping a screeching bird by the legs while his father helped him lift it and swing it around his head. The boy was flushed with excitement; his father had to restrain him from stomping on the rooster's neck. The bird, frightened, refused to lay its head neatly on the ground and, curving upward in protest, pecked at the boy's hand who released him. Loose, shrill, the rooster ran and flopped madly across the room, father and son chasing, the other fowl splitting the air with cries, until Father, having moved calmly into the doorway, grasped the desperate bird between two hands, and stroking, calmed it before coaxing the boy into accepting it.

"And who can blame it," he told me, "why go other than kicking and screaming?"

"I've heard of quieter marches," I muttered, but the spirit was upon Father. His suit covered with the soft underfeathers of the rooster he had captured, he reached to check the red I had selected, holding it by the wings firmly and turning it to see if someone had already chosen it. Twisting, the rooster tried to reach him with its beak. "May you peck the devil's eye the same way, *yokkele*," he laughed, enjoying himself.

"Superstition," I said, "it should have been banned in Babylon when they first tried it."

Hearing it, he didn't get angry, savoring his good humor. "And why not? It comforts. Wave it around your head, here, take it, it's yours, you've chosen. Wave it and tell me how you feel. Take that, I always say, let it be on your head."

I held the struggling, smelly fowl, convinced it would shit on my hand or head and be justified doing it, but recited along with Father, "Sons of Adam" and the rest, even unto the stepping on the head, thinking, *thee instead of me, fowl, myrtle branch, crumb, woman, sins cast in sea, a kapporah all,* while the rooster, suddenly silent, watched me quietly with its blinking eyes. And Father, determined, paid a puzzled Fleischman for three, our two roosters and a spotless white hen he selected with great care, managing to find one that had somehow kept from soiling itself and had none of the dirty yellow underfeathers of the other whites.

Outside he said, "This girl, this *tzatzke* of yours," lurching again into *yiddish* though he was usually careful about avoiding it while speaking English, "have you helped take care of her *kapporos?*"

"Her family uses money," I told him stiffly, "then they give it away."

"A fastidious family," he said, "are they perhaps from an actual city in Poland, not from the countryside?"

"They're Americans," I told him, "her grandparents also, I think."

"Oh, well, of course, if they're Americans," he said, "that makes all the difference. That's the truth. Why not money?"

The day after *Yom Kippur* I helped Father build the booth or *sukkah* on the back porch. I held the rusty screws while he placated unruly cross bars and aligned them; rolled the sticks of bamboo across the roof beam so that only a little space showed; decorated the canvas walls with the elaborate paper stars my mother had made over the years. That was most painful, the sight of those decorations. The shiny papers of many colors cut in patterns and folded into one another, the paper chains, the tiny jars of oil, wine and honey, the bird shaped hanging containers for apples and eggs, the Christmas tinsel and balls converted here for the Tabernacle trinkets, every one of them selected by my mother, made by her, neatly packed by her from year to year.

But I managed. I ate with Father in the booth, agreeing that yes, it was a blessing it didn't rain, a comfort that it wasn't

184

too cold, a wonder how tough a rooster could be. And I blessed the *Esrog* and the *Lulav*, sniffing the citron and shaking the palm leaf branch as prescribed, attended services every day even as I was gasping through Faulkner and Joyce, rushing to reach the 1950's, at which point the history of English Literature becomes the living present instead of ancient past as far as my Comprehensives were concerned, even beat the willow branch with fury on the Seventh Day, the little Day of Repentance, whipping the son of a bitch until there wasn't a green shred left on the stem. And I walked out of the synagogue on the Eighth Day, along with everyone else who did not need to recite the prayer for the dead. I cracked a bit only then, full up with breast-beating, and managed to call Rachel so that *Simchat Torah* night, when Crown Heights began to celebrate the Scrolls, when Eastern Parkway was blocked off to traffic entirely on the service road between Brooklyn and Kingston, when the Lubavitcher synagogue was filled to the ceiling with Chassidim dancing to the Rebbie's waves of the hand, when visitors came from Russia to participate and the *tashlich* scene was replayed but this time in encouraging darkness, on that night of paeans to Jewish joyfulness, when Chassidim are stained purple by gallon jugs of malaga, on that night I rushed to Rachel's apartment and was comforted.

But about *Yom Kippur* that year I want to say that the air conditioning broke down and the tiny vials of smelling salts that were often used for nothing more than startling awake Reb Weintraub and Altman the druggist who would cat nap during the all day prayers, on the *Yom Kippur* of my mother's absence, the salts were used in earnest. Mrs. Hartstein, perhaps because my mother's cool stare was not there to prop her up, collapsed and had to be revived and the vials moved briskly around the *shul*, disappearing for a few seconds under the prayer shawl hooded heads of nearly everyone in the room.

When I heard that Mrs. Hartstein had fallen, I felt a taste in my mouth other than just the staleness of fasting. I decided to stand for the rest of the day, rising as a joke perhaps but turning it into a vigil. I became an all day statue, an honor guard for the unknown soldier.

Because the *shul* was nothing more than the downstairs of a two family house no different from ours, with the living and dining rooms the men's section, and the kitchen and dinette areas, separated by the opaque but light curtain, the women's section, Father and I were actually sitting approximately where the dining room table was at home. Though my map is not exact, when I stood I was not standing all that far from the high backed, red velvet covered chair where in my corresponding house my mother used to sit. So when I stood it was almost like standing in attendance on her, a faithful pageboy ready to pour the wine for the lady of the house, abandoning her only when Father forced me to go outside during *Yizkor*, the prayer for the dead.

Of course, standing worshippers are not an uncommon sight on *Yom Kippur* and Father said nothing. But from that day on, each time I was in *shul* with Father I felt as if I were a ghostly attendant in my mother's shadow home. And so, when it came time for the recitation of the Mourner's *Kaddish* by the reader and he would be joined by the people observing anniversary remembrances and by Reb Berger, the sexton, who was paid to recite for those who could not be there, I would stand up with them. I would say nothing, at first even lounged, casual in my symbolic commemoration of the dead. But after a while I began to stand ramrod straight, an exclamation point Father could not help but notice.

Saying nothing, I stood, listening to *kaddish* and knowing that one day soon, in spite of everything, Father would sigh and stand too, next to me.

Evening services ending the *Yom Kippur* fast that year broke all existing speed records. With the final *amen* people simply bolted for home. For the first time that I could remember, fewer than ten men remained behind on the street in front of the *shul* to offer a blessing to the moon and show God that they were aware of judgments still pending.

26.

On the third day of my Comprehensive Exams, a Thursday, there were no deaths reported in Vietnam for a twenty-four hour period.

Then the qualifications. No *American* deaths. No American *combat* deaths. No *reports* of.

By then, since Tuesday, for three hours in the morning and three in the afternoon, I had been writing about the life and death of characters from Beowulf to early Bellow, each answer in the present or habitual tense, the method by which the English language makes the existence of created characters eternal. Led by the questions, I grudgingly acknowledged that Huck Finn just might have been a bit unsure about his masculinity, that waters and houses were important for American writers, fields and churches for the British, that Lawrence was a social critic as a lover and Sir Thomas Browne a purveyor of local color.

During lunch break, on the third day, I met Jim Lang, the Melville man, the golden girls on either side of him. He was sunburned, his hair, even his eyebrows bleached of color. But his eyes were bloodshot, strained from the nights of group study with Miss Gordon and Miss Goldman.

"Mr. Kole," he greeted me, mimicking the Seminar Professor we had taken, "my dear Mr. Kole, on your Jewish writers, as you know, I am not very keen. But on your Jewish girls!" He kissed the tips of his fingers and rolled his eyes. "If only your Jewish writers would allow themselves to be inspired by your Jewish women!"

"Then what would your *goyim* do, Jimmy?" I asked him. "Dark skinned women have rescued you from reading nothing but he-man novels. Without my Jewish girls, you'd have nothing but your Melville in the boat and the rest of his pals in the wilderness. Jewish girls have made love and sex possible in the American novel."

"Not to mention in NYU," he laughed, casting mock amorous glances toward his study partners. "Are you managing to quote critics?"

I showed him my green knapsack. Onto its folds I had scrawled the names of a dozen or so respectable critics. "An old *yeshiva* remedy," I explained. "Have you got anything?"

"Only Miss Goldman's deerskin ass," he said. "I peek at her answers while I nibble at her ear. She is both brilliant and generous."

But it was a glorious day anyway, even with two Jewish girl establishing their liberalism with a WASP like Lang, what with no American combat deaths reported in Viet Nam and with what seemed finally to look like the light at the end of the tunnel leading to the doctorate. In celebration, I met Rachel outside Berkey's on 13th Street and went to eat and to a movie. Tuna fish for me, my observant stomach unable to cope with Rachel's roast beef sandwich. We walked into *Easy Rider,* lines not as long as when it had first opened, and watched the cease fire being violated over and over as Dennis Hopper was shot tumbling from his bike.

"There is no fall in this city," I said, shivering outside the movie, "just early winter and late winter."

"We could get a drink," Rachel said, "there's a place near here the FIT kids go to."

Wrapped in a blazing scarf, Rachel leaned firmly into the wind that rippled the britches above her boots. She seemed to have been struck upright by the same film that had pushed me deep into the seat. I moved closer to her.

"I've got a better idea."

"Oh, oh," she laughed, "my place or yours?"

"Yours, Rach, the cats would bother us in mine."

We began to hurry toward the warmth of the train station, managing to match strides and retain contact through the rush. Just before the stairs Rachel broke away and ran into a liquor store, returning with a bottle and stuffing it into the knapsack on my back. "A sparkling red," she said, "almost as sweet as your *kiddush* wine but more bubbly."

"A Friday night spritzer a day early."

Her apartment was stuffy with the smell of radiators burning off their summer dust. "It's a good thing you don't really
have cats."

"Once you've had a roommate, cats make poor substi-
tutes."

I opened windows while she unwrapped herself from
within her scarf. I came back to her, took the bottle from her
hands, touched her cheeks which were red and cold, stayed
away from the nipples hardened by the wind. When I kissed
her, she said, "Before the wine?"

"And after," pushing from my mind Dennis Hopper spinning off his bike, Dov Laufer swaying to the rhythm of
bombs. "Why not?"

"I don't know," she said, giving my face tiny kisses like
bites and slipping her hands inside my shirt, making me
shiver. "I thought your studies would have drained you and
left me nothing."

"You fill me up," I told her, "endlessly. Besides, the
scholar, by law, has daily connubial obligations. You can
look it up."

And as we stumbled inside, to the bedroom and the bed we
had reclaimed from her parents, I thought, *Duties to a wife,
no one else,* but then forgot all about it.

With the holidays over, I went back to *yeshiva,* keeping the
fires on the home front burning three times a week, during
the morning, evading War Orders with Holy Orders. On the
same Mondays, Tuesdays, and Thursdays Rachel was at
F.I.T., concentrating on her graduation year projects in Cos-
tume and Design. Baumel Institute cancelling Fashion Institute, those mornings were out. But I was in Tuesday and
Friday afternoons, when Rachel was not working at Berkey's
and there again after my NYU classes the other nights. Friday
nights were Father's, sometimes afternoons too as the cleaning and shopping chores for the Sabbath became mine, just as
the cooking and laundry evolved into being his. Saturday
nights, ever earlier, were Rachel's. On Sundays we rested,
sometimes together, sometimes separately.

With the holidays out of the way and relative quiet on
ancient battlefronts until Chanukah, the Festival of Lights,
there was a noticeable increase in weddings. I could not work

some of the ritzier palaces that were becoming fashionable among the orthodox because I was not a union member, but even without the Aperion Manor, Menorah Temple, The Statler Hilton, The White Shul, and the Grand Paradise, there were smaller, externally less imposing places, like the various Young Israels, the Sea Breeze, even out-of-town emporiums in Monsey and Spring Valley, that would hire me to serve. In white gloves and thin waiter's vest, shiny silk *yarmukah* stamped on the inside with the name of the participants and the date of the occasion, I would be a swift and efficient workman, eating my fill of the smorgasbord entrees so that I would have strength to serve the meal after the *chupah*.

On some nights then, I was away. But when it became too many nights of Harry and Judy, Robert and Shelly, Isaac and Helen, Bernard and Michelle, I told Rachel to come and join me. From the catering hall, already in uniform, I would call to describe that evening's style. "Gowns, Rachel, last year's." Or, "Modern orthodox. Midi-skirts, elaborate hair." Or, "The bride's mother is wearing hot pants."

Dressed appropriately, her hair now long and pliant, easily manipulated, Rachel would come to join me at the hors d'oeuvres, demure or flashy, as the occasion demanded. Her favorite was the cold table. There, frustrated artists of the school of catering carved roosters and ducks out of chopped liver, adding pimentoed olives for eyes, formed glaced fruit stars and sunbursts, shaped flowering branches of the Trees of Knowledge and Life out of stalks of green celery and tiny buds of rose red radishes, planted neat rows of salami, turkey roll and bologna, squeezed a tunnel of white chopped meat into caves of dark meat, creating brilliantly suggestive wedding symbols. While in the center of this table, separated from the dishes by a miniature rock garden that came complete with tiny Japanese trees, was the triple tiered punch bowl, spraying a thin liquid from the mouths of twelve lions, the colors of the flow changing with the flashing of the spotlights on the bride's podium.

I would have prepped Rachel by then, armed her against the challenge of any relatives of the bride or groom, by giving her all the pertinent information I had gleaned from the imprints on the skullcaps, the matchboxes, and the Grace after the Wedding Meal prayerbooks, all in the color of the brides-maids' gowns.

Though I encouraged her to try the hot table—chicken fricasse, Swedish meatballs, chow mein, sliced corned beef, southern fried wings—Rachel would merely pick at a sliver of white fish, try a shaved piece of *challah*, crunch on a piece of celery she broke off carefully, without disturbing the pattern of the trees.

I would put my jacket over the tight black vest and, modish in my waiter's bow tie, mingle among the guests. When I would find Rachel at the cold table, I would tap her on the shoulder and we would go into the hallway where we could hold hands, hug, kiss, in general, look like the couple either on its honeymoon or destined to be the next one to rent the catering hall.

"Get me a job in the cloak room," she said, "and we can be together between courses, huddling on the floor with mink jackets for beds."

"Next time they call me from the Sea Breeze, we'll apply as a team. How does the food rate?"

She shrugged. "Nothing special. But the guy who does the layouts is an artist. God, melon ball petals and pineapple chunk trees! Baked herring racing for the gold medal in cucumber lanes. It's just fantastic. He must take hours."

"He graduated from *yeshiva* with me. Instead of going to Brooklyn College like everyone else, he went to a Kosher Cooking School. Graduated with honors in marination and marzipan."

Sidetracked by the introduction of sweets, she asked what dessert was.

"Honeyed carrots and fried pineapples sprinkled with brown sugar," I informed her. "The plates are beautiful. This guy Elly is the best. Roast beef with pink centers, amber carrots, green broccoli, beige pineapples, I swear, you can enter the plates in an Easter bonnet contest."

"You can make jokes but I can really feel for the guy, arranging all those things only to have people grab at it without even noticing."

"If you'd come ready to eat you'd have more sympathy for the eaters."

191

"I came to be with you, not to eat alone."

That was easily enough managed, but only until about half-way through the *chupah*. Then she had to leave because I was on full duty, rolling the laden tables into the back of the room during the ceremony. Soon after that, the meal begins and the beginning, while the happily couple just blessed is having a brief encounter in a private room, the two of them sometimes alone for the very first time since they met, that beginning part is the most hectic. There seems to be a restlessness among the guests, a kind of incompletion, a waiting, none of which is satisfied by the fruit cup, the salad, the pickles and the breads on the table. While the usual quintet (at least one accordionist) plays warm-up tunes, gently gauging preferences for old show tunes or Chassidic *nigunim*, the waiters are kept hopping for side orders, usually the bottle of scotch on the next table. But then the newlyweds and the soup appear and things cool down for the waiters as they heat up for the band.

Sometimes the bride's parents were reluctant to let the band play into overtime and on those nights I would finish early enough to stop at Rachel's before heading home. But usually the band played on while the departing guests lined up on either side of the head table where the bride and groom sat with a carton at their feet under the table. One by one the guests greet the Mr. or the Mrs. and along with good wishes, hand over envelopes of cash, checks or savings bonds, taking in return commemorative matchboxes and *yarmukahs*, doggie bags from the Viennese table, and, the more enterprising ones, the flower centerpieces from the tables. Early the following morning, having blessed their union in bed, the bride and groom squat in the middle of the living room floor and slowly empty that carton. Then they count their blessings all over again, one more time distinguishing between "your side" and "my side," keeping a list of donors for the sake of later reference by their parents when the time comes to dig deep in reciprocation. Father would place an agreed upon amount into the gift envelope without sealing it. My mother would then slip inside an extra five dollars, investing in my future. For all I knew, Father too would add a five, his own hedge against inflation in case I married very late.

So, if the music to give gifts by played on, I would finish

192

late and go directly home, knowing Rachel preferred that I didn't appear at all rather than drag out of her warm bed at three in the morning so that I would be present and accounted for at Father's morning inquiry.

Not that she ever said anything. She would not even protest my Friday night loyalty to Father's Sabbath home. "As long as you do it out of love, how can I complain? Though you do suffer too much for love. But I've told you that," she said, and used Friday nights for herself, visiting with Andreas and Cindy whose arrangement seemed quite domesticated, going out with Lizzie, her Berkey co-worker who seemed to be working out her own arrangements with Gondo, but staying away from Jeri who had started bar hopping, a female city-fucker, working her way up and down Second Avenue single spots.

I missed those Friday night rushes to her house. Their memory was often enough to excite me though in those early days our love-making had been only inventive substitution. But there was no need any longer for those desperate hikes in the Friday night dark. Instead, I prepared explanations for overnight absences that I offered Father periodically. I would say that I would be out of town, waitering in Monsey, that I was attending a convention of Hawthorne buffs in Salem, that I was visiting Jonesey, but spend the weekday night with Rachel, going to *yeshiva* from her house in the morning. Never presuming, I might add, always waiting to be asked or soliciting her interest first. It was like the utterance of a blessing, such an asking, as before eating, drinking, or sighting a wonder of nature. The old habits go on working. Before taking a shower or combing my hair I involuntarily remove a phantom skull cap from my head and with an unconscious gesture, smooth the hair down where a non-existent bobby pin had raised a furrow.

"This is working out so well," Rachel said, "because our bodies are the same temperature."

"Or because we warm up and cool off at the same rate."

"Well, we know about the first part. You haven't given us a chance to find out about the second."

We were in her apartment again (where else), an early evening, under her old fashioned heavy quilt that rose like dough all around us. The radiators were keening softly. We had been lying quietly, side by side, holding hands, but to confirm her statement, I moved on top of her, sliding low enough so that it was my belly against the warmth of her thighs and hair, and put both arms around her, pressing my face against one breast and shoulder. I linked my arms under her and squeezed fiercely, trying to return to her the strength she was giving me, trying to show her that we were connected at various other points of our bodies, not merely at the crotch. When she gasped, I slid higher up, determined to keep myself soft and peaceful down below, and slowly and carefully kissed her eyelids, her cheekbones, her upper lip, her chin, casting the sign of the cross over her without either of us noticing. "I just thought I'd tell you," I said, "in case later I forgot."

"These literary gestures," she said, "you can say you love me without violating the spirit of the muse."

"I was just breaking my love up into smaller pieces so that they would last longer. Like a little kid smears chocolate on his fingers so he can suck it off later."

"It's still the same amount of chocolate," she said, thoughtfully.

"Wrong, Rachel, it's constantly replenishable." With a careful finger I moved between her legs, folding her back and apart until her natural generosity asserted itself and she began to flood. Sliding into her, trembling with control, I said, "You're wet from my fingers, I'm hard from your touch, it doesn't matter what happens scientifically."

But she was right, of course. At least to the extent that amounts do diminish, by erosion or by use, unless more is added. I remember a riddle about the snail struggling to reach the top of a well. Each day he crawls up three feet but slips back one. How long, the question goes, does it take him to climb out of a fifteen foot well? Not 7 and a half days, at two feet per day, but merely seven, since he reaches the rim on that seventh day and so will not slide back. But before reaching the rim, he falls backward each day, must struggle three feet to achieve two, would sink out of sight altogether if he merely rested one day and refused to climb. Could the two of us keep from sliding back if all we did was try to step slowly and carefully on even ground? A smooth path calls for a flat plain, but you can't avoid the definition of flat as fizzed out, on the fritz, no spritz in the bubbly. I wanted more than the

194

comfortable mood we had fallen into. I was afraid that love and affection, like the peripatetic Torah, would recede if left unsought. Just because Rachel did not require it did not mean that my inbred sense of responsibility had atrophied. I made my commitment even if she did not acknowledge it. Rachel was quite content to leave things just as they were.

But my old *yeshiva* habits would not allow me to accept endless continuation. There had to be a conclusion. It is with the greatest reluctance that the contending Rabbinical schools throw their hands up and say *taykuh*. *The return of Elijah at the time of the Messiah will crack all unsolvable nuts* is a rare admission of defeat. Usually there is contention, and much furor, but eventually, even if it waits for the decisions of Maimonedes, there is resolution. I could not settle for seamless days with Rachel. I gave her gifts of books, snipped styles out of magazines, requested her help in shopping for clothes, proofread her essays, tutored her in *yiddish*. I had no school ring to offer and no fraternity pin but tried to mark her in other ways with my presence, offering to speak to Father about a position for her with the designer at Gamble's Fashions, nee 3L Clothiers, nee Landau and Sons.

"I'm not ready," she said, "don't do it, Jason," but her face expanded, she blushed, excitement rose from her like heat waves from a stove. I was determined to bring it up to Father. I felt the need to woo her, to court her continuously, because I could sense that there was still a reserve somewhere, a part of her she was keeping for herself, a private spot within her I could never insist on. I could imagine Jonesey, the old Jonesey, asking me what I wanted when I was already getting everything I had imagined just a few months ago. But she possessed something else, I understood that; she was a person beyond my *yeshiva bochur* perceptions.

Eventually, there would be judgment, decision, finality. Maimonedes making a determination among the rabbis, the Draft Board about inductions, the police about my mother, the Board of Education about jobs, Rachel about me. All converge, even parallel lines eventually bending toward each other, before final dispersions.

IV

This is the law of the burnt-offering, of the meal-offering, and of the sin-offering, and of the guilt-offering, and of the consecration-offering, and of the sacrifice of peace-offerings.

(Leviticus 7:37)

27.

On Oscar Wilde's birthdate the Baltimore Orioles lost to the New York Mets the final game of the 1969 World Series, repeating the pattern of other Baltimore/New York encounters that year. On the same day, a team of parachutists in red, white, and blue jump suits, floated down into the midst of a Central Park anti-war rally, demonstrating, papers said, pro-war sentiments. Professor Leahy, in the Edwardians and georgians Seminar I was auditing, was willing to cancel class for Moratorium Day observances but was dissuaded by a man in rimless eyeglasses who threatened to sue for a refund of his ninety-four dollars per credit tuition. Rachel and I went to a peace march up Fifth Avenue that ended in a candle light procession in front of St. Patrick's Cathedral. The crowd was so large that we had to forego candles and clutch each other for safety. We both shouted and whispered "Peace Now." Most of the store windows had no price tags on the merchandize and clothes.

On Ezra Pound's birthdate (fighting diminished by the monsoon season), I came home to find Father in the dining room, intent on the tiny Sony on the sideboard. I had been away so often during early evenings that I didn't know he had become a serious fan of Uncle Cronkite. Teddy Kennedy's picture was on the screen, behind Cronkite's left shoulder. The Massachusetts Supreme Court would not unseal the Chappaquidik file.

"Now we'll have to wait for John-John before another Kennedy will be president," I said. "And he'll have to wait his turn after David Eisenhower, that Howdy-Doody look-alike."

"This business with the girl," Father said, holding on to the high back of his chair, "she was alive for quite a while. Air gets trapped near the top of the car."

"Not enough, *Abba*," I said, wondering at his interest.

"No," he agreed, sounding like a man still believing in his own faith, "but with an old fashioned car there would have been more. Especially with the windows closed."

I said nothing. He knew as well as I did that my mother did not drive. Yet I had also badgered Detective Meisner to check all reports of accidents. Could anyone know for certain what people like my mother knew or did before the war? But it seemed Father was interested in another Rachel.

"Assuming something was available," he said, "what size is this special friend of yours?"

Surprised, I said, "If what was available?"

"A dress," he said, "samples. The models don't care for them because they're just put together to look good for the show. If I fix one up, what is her size?"

"I don't know."

"You've had enough opportunity to look. Bigger than your mother?"

I nodded. "What about around the shoulder and waist?" he asked. I tried to speak without using my hands.

"She's a tall girl."

He squinted, measuring, "About a ten? Does that seem right? Bigger than your mother, you said, right?"

"What size is she?"

We shared the tense. "A perfect eight. I can bring things home without needing her there." He nodded. "We'll say size ten then unless you find out different. Set the table."

William Cullen Bryant's birthday came at the end of the monsoon season. The "lull" was over. There were new attacks. Withdrawals slowed slightly but there was no increase in call-ups. The new head of the Selective Service System promised changes. The next day Solzhenitzin was kicked out of the Russian Writers' Union. During the next two weeks the death toll rose steadily, total casualty figures reaching 300,000 Americans. Lieutenant William Calley was indicted along with Staff Sargeant David Mitchell, both of Charlie Company, First Battalion, 20th Infantry, 11th Infantry Brigade, Americal Division, for the massacre of 109 men, women and children in the hamlet of My Lai, village of

Songmy. And Conrad and Bean were described as joyfully romping on the moon. Director Tarr said that the first Draft Lottery since World War II would be held on December 1. My Board of Ed. interview was for the third of December, Joseph Conrad's birthdate. Forced to wait for everything else, I pursued Rachel vigorously, even asking her if she wanted me to arrange things for Friday night.

"Your Friday nights," she said, "aren't any more important to me than other nights of the week. I'll see you whenever you like."

"I would *like* all the time. I just can't all the time."

"That's what I said," she said, "whenever you can."

"Who are you passionate about seeing?"

"My design teacher, of course, I do have to pay a lab fee so he's obligated to be there."

"How about your parents? Are they inseparable?"

"Not those two. They've been married so long they can spend the day apart and think they've been together all day."

"That's why," I said carefully, "I wouldn't want to get married. Who wants to stay apart all day?"

She laughed. "Not me. I'm with you all the way." I was on my way to classes and still waiting for an answer about Friday night. "It's too bad though about this disdain for marriage. I could probably get a discount at one of the halls."

"When you find one with a comfortable cloak room that would also let me make the designs for the cold table, let me know. You'll be late for class."

I was unsatisfied but I left. Once at NYU, I called from a booth. "I forgot to ask. What size are you?"

"A fitting?"

"No marriage jokes, Rachel. Father wants to know."

She was quiet for a few minutes. "Were we really talking about marriage?"

"Sure," I said, fearing my dime would run out, "we're trying to decide whether I was asking you or you were asking me."

"Jason," she said, "let me ask you something. After class tonight, would you come straight here and stay without calling your father to explain?"

"Are you asking me to do it?"

"I'm asking if you would."

201

"I would if you wanted me to."

"All right, Jason," she said, her voice calm, "let's wait to talk about this some other time."

The next night, feelings between us tender, I called Rachel from the Sea Breeze. I was serving a *Sheva Berachot,* a post-wedding celebration that goes on nightly for a week, named after the seven blessings of the ceremony. I often worked alone, getting paid for being both busboy and waiter. As usual, this was a party for a rotating number of friends and relatives during which many speeches would be made, but few jokes.

I called Rachel during the Talmudic *bon mots* from the kitchen. I had been banished there until the speechmaking was done, the clatter of silver and dishes dangerous to the subtlety of fine points. The rhetorical opening of the bride's father had been, "How is a pre-war identification card similar to nitro-glycerine pills?" I waited to see the beginning of the unraveling—the similarity had to do with the extent to which both were essential to life and hence licensed to be carried about on the Sabbath—then dialed Rachel, a bit intrigued, I have to admit, how the Sabbath laws would eventually be connected to the blessed event of marriage. Was there some position available for Sabbath use that was not permissible during week days? Was the Slurp girl's inclination for back rubs so tainted with the ordinariness of the work week that she could not prevail on her carat and a half Mechel to lean on her on the Sabbath?

On the phone I recognized Gondo's voice and he mine, the familiarity mysterious since we had never spoken on the phone. "Rachel is out," he said, "she went to get some things."

"Gondo," I said, swearing to disbelieve from then on any statements made by women about former dates and lovers, "I never had a chance to ask you about your traditional dinner with Rachel and her parents."

"It was the best, man. You should have been there. I'm making sure my parents get into it. You're converting us all. Next year in Jerusalem, right?"

"You're mixing your holidays up but it doesn't matter. Tell Rachel I called."

Taking pity on my tight voice, he said, "Listen, Lizzie is

202

here, they went out to get some Chinese food and wine. Why don't you come over?"

"Still seeing her?"

"Sometimes," he said, "she's a good kid."

"Rachel likes her."

"She's a good kid too. Are you coming over to join these wonderful kids? They're getting a gallon jug."

I would be done too late, I told him, meaning that I would try to leave too late to see him there. "Just say hello."

"Will do. No love and kisses?"

"Gondo," I said heavily, "fuck off, will you?"

"Lighten up, Rabbi," he said, laughing, "I approve, I really do. There is nothing like some old time religion. It brings a glow to her cheeks and a song to her lips. Your brand of it, anyway. Lizzie is into religion too, you know. You're talking to a believer. I wouldn't kid you."

"I know, Gondo, you're a wonderful kid too. Just say hello, okay?"

"No sweat," he said cheerily, "we'll see you then."

Even for a friend, I thought, he is much too familiar, and went back in through the swinging doors to clear the tables.

I was done that night sooner than expected. The radio had reported a slight chance of snow. I didn't care since Jonesey's stewardship of my car included equipping it with snow tires at the first smell of winter. The guests, perhaps less adequately prepared, hurried through the final blessings, and by eleven the   shaped arrangement of tables was empty, ready for my closing minstrations. The shape was, of course, that of a *chet*, the first letter of the word *chai*, or life. Nothing is ever left to chance at religious ceremonies except my pressing desire to leave this one early. Still, it was well after twelve when I stood in the short hall of Rachel's building and found the infrequently locked front door unyielding this time, slowing my arrival. Outside the thin snow had fallen, offering no difficulties to travel but obliterating the yellow center line of Ocean Avenue, making that street seem wider and more silent than usual, the tracks of my car wheels the only marks on the smoothness of the snow. I gave the three short buzzes of my call.

She rang back, a short blast I chose to interepret as an

awareness of the lateness of the hour rather than irritation with my presence. I hoped to find her in bed, reading, her knees tucked under her long cotton nightgown, the emerald color soft and faded with years of washing. Not having a key meant that my arrival inevitably had to move her out of her comfortable position. But no matter. Barefoot though the apartment was cooling, Rachel let me in. "Staying or visiting?" she asked.

The smell of wine was in the front room. Her bedroom door was slightly ajar, a small lamp's light slanting through.

"Staying," I said, "I've lost my taste for cold sheets."

I took off my long coat, the mock fur collar stained with the remnants of the few flakes of snow that had touched it while I had run from the car to the building, gave her my gloves, pushed out of my ankle boots without unzipping them, standing all the while just inside her door, waiting for her to invite me further in. "It's snowing but it won't stick," I said, by way of explanation. "Do I smell of roast beef?"

She sniffed at me, her face and hair dark. "No, you smell lemony."

"That was the dessert," I said, "sponge cake with lemon icing, the Sea Breeze cheapo special. If you kiss me hard enough, you'll be able to taste it."

She kissed me, her fingers light but warm on my face. "You're wearing your *yarmukah*," she said, "is this an official visit?"

"An official staying."

"In that case, keep it on."

But I took everything off, undressing in a warm tiredness that recognized desire without insisting on it. I wanted to retain the calm of that feeling, to show Rachel that I was capable of voluntary love, not only of the uncontrollable spurt of sex. Although I slept more comfortably on my right side, turned toward Rachel (developing the habit easily), I had to settle for the left side of the bed because Rachel had burrowed back into the shape she had left on the side closest to her reading lamp. Leaving the light on, its shine scattered by the dull pewter of its base, she turned toward me, leaving the magazine she had been reading on the floor next to the bed. I leaned over her to see its cover. "News of the world late at night?"

"The fashion magazine," she said. I could see the glossy cover of the French monthly Father brought home from work periodically, scornful of the designer who would make variations of the styles inside. Skirts were getting longer still, blouses less severe, there were bare breasts showing in this one. "The designer's *Playboy?*"

"I think of it as homework."

I kissed the back of her neck. "So do I." She shrugged me off, wriggling away. "Let's see if we can just hug and be nice for a while."

"For as long as you like."

"I'll settle for as long as we can."

We lay like that for a while, knees and foreheads touching, arms around each other. Close up, shadowed, her skin seemed more full, not as taut as usual. In bed, the generosity of the rest of her extended to her face. Her eyes, also dark, absorbed. Her voice, though still sure, was softer. I hardly recognized her.

"We're too close, Rachel. I can't see anything."

"Even with the light on?"

"It's in my eyes."

"Close them."

"I'll fall asleep."

"I'll make sure you won't."

"Can we kiss?"

"We sure can. But we won't."

"Can we talk?"

"Sure."

Her hair, wispy in the front, tickled my face. Unwilling to let go, I tried to blow at it. She returned the breath.

"You smell of wine."

"Cheap stuff lingers."

"Did Gondo?"

"Gone with Lizzie by eleven."

"At eleven I was discovering that nitroglycerine pills may be carried on the Sabbath in the hatband or pinned to the shirt."

"What?"

"Life threatening situations supersede the Sabbath strictures. A story they told at the wedding tonight. You mean you don't see the connections?"

"Be serious."

"I always am," I said, "How about you?"

"All right," she said. "Sheila called. She says she is ready for the big move."

"I thought she had already made it. With Jonesey."

She smiled. "Not that. Those moves you can make without moving. I'm talking about a change of scenery."

I interrupted her by shifting, pulling my arms out from under her and flexing my fingers. "Can we please change places? I miss my spot. And the view is strange."

"No," she said, surprisingly, "You'll wear a groove into the mattress and my parents would ask questions."

I sat up and looked down at her. "I've been meaning to ask you. Where did your girl friend sleep anyway when you were sharing the apartment?"

"Cindy? On a cot. That's why she went off with Andreas. She likes cuddling. That's what I wanted to talk to you about."

I slipped under the covers, not touching her but feeling her warmth. "So talk." Out of sight, under those covers, I knew that her long nightgown had worked its way up to her thighs, leaving her bare. I wondered whether she had worn panties to bed and whether she had anticipated my coming over by slipping in her diaphragm. And I wondered why there is no benediction to be said before sex when there is a prior blessing for everything else, and why no grace in thanks afterward. True, holy thoughts are prescribed and lewd laughter forbidden but the loophole seemed great and inexplicable.

"Sheila," Rachel said, "took a Psych course with a guru professor who is into liberation. He suggested she liberate herself from her parents' house in Boro Park."

"And come here?" I said, "to you?"

She shook her head. "No. To him. He has a *pad* in Brooklyn Heights where she could stay until she gets settled."

"I'll bet," I said, "with a cot or two for cuddling."

"Actually, it's a sort of mini-commune, Sheila said, for other kids in his classes who want to be free from parents, religion, you know, restrictions." She looked right at me. "What do you think?"

"I think they're going to get him on moral turpitude. He actually gets them to move in?"

She nodded. "What did you tell her?" I asked. Rachel shrugged, not an easy movement lying down. "I told her not to do it."

"Not to move in or not to move out?"

"In," she said, sparing with words as with touch. I waited, looking away from her at the collage of photographs on the wall, noticing Gondo in too many of the pictures, Jason in too few. "That's what I wanted to talk to you about."

"Listen," I said, angry, "tell her to go to hell and stay put at home."

"That's what I thought you'd say."

It was my turn to shrug, easier for me since I was sitting up, out from under her cover, goose pimples beginning to form on my arms.

"It's not what you think, Rachel. You can't imagine what religious parents will do. If she moves in with the guru, they'll sue the city, the college, the teacher, even you, for encouraging her. And if that doesn't work, they'll consider her dead and gone, scatter ashes on their head, sit *shiva*, put her out of their mind once the mourning period is over. That's under the best of circumstances. She moves in with you, a Jewish girl even if slightly soiled, then the real trouble starts. They'd figure she is a sinner but retrieveable. There's no telling what they'll do. They'll hire deprogrammers, they'll hire Lubavitcher hit squads that would set up shop right on Ocean Avenue in front of the house. They'll park in a big yellow truck, put 'My Yiddishe Mamma' on the loudspeaker, and pray around the clock until you feel so guilty you kick her out. Are you prepared for a siege? Your Nabisco crackers are not only not kosher, they wouldn't even last a week."

She was grinning. "She wouldn't move in till next week. I'll have time to stock up."

"Is she really moving in?"

"She was ready to go off and join the commune. I figured she'd be better off here."

"What about Jonesey?"

"He'd prefer she move in here."

"Tell him to marry her."

"All this talk of marriage in the middle of winter. Whatever happened to waiting for spring blossoms?"

"But Rachel, Sheila, of all people. You'll have to get another set of dishes."

"That's all right. Some of my best friends are religious."

Since we were obviously no longer talking about Sheila, I felt at a disadvantage. For negotiations I would have preferred to be pacing or at least sitting opposite Rachel at a baize covered conference table, its size and shape carefully agreed upon by our representatives. In bed, absurd on one elbow, I had little dignity, while Rachel, primly patting the quilt rising on either side of her, her back straight against the backboard, had nothing but presence. Arguments are made for twin beds. Queen sized mattresses force people into unnecessary reconciliations.

I got out of bed and began pulling shorts and pants on. "What are you doing?" Rachel asked.

"Making room."

"I didn't say it was settled."

"Then what are you saying?"

"That you can stay here."

I wasn't sure I heard her. "Did you say can or can't?"

"Could. I said you could."

I was beginning to feel the cold in the room, had to decide about either putting my shirt on or getting back under the covers.

"Well, I'm here."

"No," she said, "I mean *stay.* As an alternative to Sheila. Or cats."

"Just like that? I bring over my typewriter, my laundry, and not leave?"

"Only to go back home for your teddy bear and your sea shell collection."

I started to pull my zipper down and got it stuck, had to sit on the edge of the bed to tug at it. Pieceworkers do shoddy work. Time makes all the difference in the world. Zippers Father puts in are plastic tipped and fold into each other like butter without ever catching. Loosening it, I slid it up rather than down, but sat on the bed next to her, on the outside of the covers, back against the headboard, pillows with their frothy edges between us.

"It's not that easy, you know. Have you thought about the names on the mailbox? Am I supposed to buy you seats in *shul* for the High Holy Days? Do I assume the burden of your exotic teas?"

The cover was pulled up to her chin and the swell of the material hid the lines of her body. The empty space between us cut. She turned away from me and pulled the beaded chain of her lamp into darkness. The bedroom window faced the courtyard and helped hem us into darkness.

"Do whatever you like."

"I'd like to introduce you to Father."

"As what?"

"I don't know."

"I wish," she said, speaking slowly and clearly, "that you'd goddam stop calling him Father as if his whole name consisted of nothing but capital letters. Can't you call him anything else? What did your mother call him?"

"Rabbi Kole."

"You're hopeless," she said. "I wish I had double blankets."

I put both feet on the rug and waited a moment. My feet were not yet cold because under her bed Rachel had spread a multicolored rug made of old rags and remnants, spun into oval braids that stood away from the polishd boards underneath, keeping the cold distant. But just a few more steps sent me to the floor, and once the cold of those shiny boards entered my feet, I knew I was on my way home, another incomplete night with Rachel.

28.

Entering the kitchen, I took my shoes off for quiet and stood in stockinged feet, shod like a mourner, when I encountered Father, driven by sleepy thirst. Who else but Father, the man with the dry throat and cold bed, to be walking squinteyed in search of seltzer. When I heard his slurred steps on the plastic runner, I realized I had not put my *yarmukah* back on and that it was, in any case, too late. The eyes of a man who could thread a sewing needle with white thread in a single swoop would not fail to notice that the falling snow had settled on my hair, not my cap. We met that way in the kitchen, illicit midnight drinkers, Father in his bathrobe, slippers, and wrinkled sleeping cap even more fully dressed than I. He nodded, said nothing. Taking one of the upturned glasses from the wire rack on the dairy side of the sink, he opened the refrigerator and tapped inside until he found the seltzer bottle, squeezed, drank, returned the glass upside down on the rack. Even by the light of the fridge lamp he seemed not to notice my bare head.

I always thought of him as thin in his daily dark clothes but in robe and striped pajams he seemed quite substantial, not at all a body at loss in nightclothes. His beard and hair were not ruffled and there seemed to be a vague crease in the legs of his pajamas. Only his *yarmukah*, wrinkled with use, seemed uncared for. Otherwise, he looked as if a careful wife had been pressing and laundering for him daily.

"You'll catch a cold," he said, looking at my feet but no doubt meaning my head.

"The floors are warm," I said, "they lose heat slowly."

He nodded. "Can't complain about the landlord, that's for sure."

"No," I agreed and made ready to turn. "Listen," he said,

"in case I don't see you in the morning, there is a package for you." And he waved toward the living room table. "A sample," he said, "a tweed dirdnl."

"A what?"

He waved his hand. "She'll know."

"Thanks," I said, forced into formality, "I'm sure she'll like it."

"If not," he said, "I'll let it out." He closed the door of the refrigerator decisively. In the darkness it was easier to remember another version of him, a smooth-haired and smooth-chinned Father, between beards, pleasing my mother. We used to meet in those days too, both of us wanderers in dark houses. He would be dressed, about to leave on another trip, leaving while it was still dark, and we would meet like that in the kitchen, parched, blind, our kinship undeniable. "Take good care of your mother," he would say, unusually talkative for the early hour. *I love you and I'm sorry your hair is getting thin*, I always wanted to say in those days, never quite getting around to saying it. "Sure, *Abba*," I would answer and walk back to the other end of the house while the nightlamp in its plastic husk filled the kitchen with the fake warmth of red.

But that Father was not present and the shape in the darkness seemed to be waiting still. I had rehearsed anger sufficiently to be able to do the job in the dark, even without crib notes, but I was beginning to feel the cold and the counter-balancing warmth of his present on the living room table. I turned to go again, thinking of the warm bed I had voluntarily relinguished, denying my kinship with Father's unwarmed twin bed.

"Since we're here already and up," Father said, "I have a bit of news."

As always, I thought of my mother but there was no drama in his presentation and he did lack the cruelty that would postpone news like that. "Local or international?" I asked him.

"Both," he said. He might have smiled but his back was to the kitchen window and thus completely in the shadow of even the vague light from the alley. "The Debreciner Rabbi," he continued, giving Rabbi Winkler the name of his Hungarian place of birth, "is moving to Boro Park."

"What do you mean moving? You mean moving the *shul*

too? The entire franchise? Doesn't he need somebody's permission?"

"He is not on salary," Father said. "We told him he can go. The druggist was thinking of moving too. Now he will."

"How do you get news like this in the middle of the week?"

"Evening prayers. I was home from work early and I went. They always have trouble with a quorum in the evenings."

"I'm looking forward to the big announcement on Saturday."

"By *Shabbat* there is no one who would not know."

A bus rumbled by outside, not stopping across the street. It occurred to me that each Friday afternoon Father twisted the bulb in the refrigerator loose in its socket, assuming another of my mother's jobs, so that the opening and closing of the door would not affect the light in violation of Sabbath laws. I began to feel uncomfortable in socks and uncovered head, too bare in front of him. Why couldn't the news have kept? Why were we sharing it as if it were a secret? I would have liked a cold drink but decided not to risk it.

"So," I said, "when is he going?"

That seemed to have been the right question to ask. Father answered immediately. I was hoping for no answer, just a gradual petering out of talk so that we could go back to sleep.

"Before *Pesach*," Father said, "so that he won't have to do special cleaning again."

"Well, why not," I said, yawning, genuinely surprised that we were not shivering. The ever-burning pilot lights must have been adding extra warmth to the kitchen. "Everyone else is moving to Boro Park too, why not Rabbi Winkler?"

"Not the Lubavitcher," Father said fiercely, moving closer. "They're not running and neither are we."

I think he believed that he would come home one day and find my mother in the kitchen, one foot on the stepstool, peeling potatoes into a plastic bag in the sink. He could hardly move while he believed that, could he? I stepped back and to the side, leaving room for him if he wanted to leave. When he didn't, hesitantly I said, "About Rachel, since we're here, would you like to meet her?"

I could not make his face out but I heard his silence.

"Officially?" he asked.

"No," I said quickly, "just to meet someone I've been with more often than you for the last few months."

"Then no," he said, decisively, "not if it is not necessary."

Then, "Give her the skirt. See if it fits. If not, tell me. I'm putting a factory sewing machine in the basement."

My room was cold. I fell asleep on my stomach and slept with one arm stretched out, as if trying to keep in touch with Rachel's ass. I dreamt I was standing in front of a brownstone with high windows that seemed inadequately guarded by short, round-bellied iron rails. At a curtainless second story window there was a vague shape I knew to be Sheila, and I was urging her to jump, somehow convinced she would land safely, either because the sidewalk was soft or because the net would arrive in time. I work with my right hand still reaching out, and could not loosen the stiffness in my shoulder all day long, catching myself whirling the arm in vain attempts, a tired pitcher's windup without a delivery at the end of the arc.

This was obviously the time for the rally of Jewish friends and relatives. Like a convention of John Smiths gathering to give fame to their anonymous name by sheer accumulation of numbers (at Smithtown, sucking Smith Brothers' cherry drops, many blacksmiths and out-of-work silversmiths, an occasional stray Goldschmidt), we should have been surrounded by offers of help. So where the hell where the uncles and aunts from as far away as Arizona, and where were my snotty nosed cousins who would keep me up to date on the progress of the Knicks even during personal crises, and where were the big bosomed grand-aunts from forgotten parts of Brooklyn, from East Flatbush and Bushwick and New Lots, where they have lived since after the war and remained despite the changing neighborhood, never venturing out at night and guarding themselves with window bars and police locks? Where was my maternal uncle with his magnificently stinking Corona that he would smoke only out in company? Where were the *landsman,* the angels who helped refugees come over and enjoyed nothing more than basking in gratitude, not at all ashamed of reaching only the lower levels of Maimonedes' eight steps of generosity? Why no rich relative by marriage, a friend with a contact, an intimate of the Lubavitcher Rebbie or some other wonder-working Rabbi?

Why no pots of chicken soup, no groundswell of sympathy, no attempt to assemble a *Bet Din*, a court to deal with the disappearance of wives or the appearance of tempting lovers?

No help. Ours a family poor in resources, orphans in a race poor in land but supposedly rich in people. No dribblings of five dollar checks on my birthdays from people familiar only on greeting cards for the holidays. My mother, bereft of family and separated too long from her campmate Serena, had persistently refused to attend memorial gatherings of survivors. Father, rumored to have cousins in Israel, was isolated from them by the palisades of religion. The only son of an only son, his mates in synagogue were only minor companions of the pauses during prayer, his membership in the Burial Society an act of responsibility not friendship. This is how we are left to each other, Father and I, an abbott and a monk working our individual little patches of garden amid vows of silence.

29

Talk to me Father. (I am sitting at the small table in the dinette area, my feet on the cast iron base hidden under the sweeping folds of the brown and red flowered tablecloth, watching Father awkwardly grip an aluminum pot, the dairy washcloth around his hand.) Tell me if you can remember the courting days: smiling at her, taking her arm in public for the first time, bending down to kiss her under the arch of a stone gate, you know, the beginning. Teach me what you know. When you decided you wanted her, did you ask? With what words? Or did she ask? Or say yes? Or were no words exchanged? Come on, this is your Jason, the remembrance. You can even call me Yaakov if you like. Just describe what it was like loving her once upon a time. Did you ever stand weak-kneed in front of her? Did you miss the comforting presence of intermediaries, matchmakers, go-betweens or were you so experienced, so accomplished, so old, that you could commit yourself all over again without really thinking? How about a hint, Pop? (A clear plastic covers the Sabbath table. On it is a double-bowled salt cellar with a curving swan's neck at its center, salt in both bowls and no matching pepper, a clear lucite napkin holder and a silk backed little prayer book, a remnant from a wedding. Father and I stand next to each other in the doorway, about to leave for services, and unaccountably turn to look back at the table in unison.) Just give me a tiny clue. How do you feel being noticed on the train, on the street, anywhere you go, by the shine of your black cap and white cropped skull?

Is it a vise, squeezing, like a band around the finger, a hoop around the barrel heart, so that even in distant motels on the road, away from the City of God, when you clicked the light on, having been forced into darkness by love, did you feel you were doing wrong and that God's lightning would crawl down the wires and freeze your transgressing finger on the switch? Or had you already come to terms with everything by the time you were my age, taking wife, siring child, learning the sewing machine's craft, determined only to be master at what you were doing rather than waiting to find what you could master? I've grown up bereft of advice, stupid about adulthood. I'm all empty ears. I want to hear things I cannot read. (Because I am taller than he is I have to bend awkwardly to fit under Father's prayer shawl. Our heads together, we follow the benediction of the priests in Father's *Prayers for the Holidays*, the prayer book pushed away from both of us so we can see it more easily. Under the canopy of the black striped shawl I can smell my own morning breath. We are covered up to avoid looking at the extended arms of the priests. A look at the W of their joined hands carries with it the penalty of weakening sight, then blindness. Dare I, an unmarried boy, without a protective shawl of his own, take chances? I hide under Father's, leaning my height on the pine of the long wooden table. I would talk to him under the intimacy of that coverlet but these are prayers to be said and Father hates interruptions.)

Tell me something, Father. In a year when less than 20 percent of all college graduates have turned to their fathers for advice about sex, I ask you questions about love. Friday night love; the married man's secrets. In exchange, my own Friday night secrets. I could tell you about the ten block Jewish area, the Orthodox ghetto, beyond which you can whisk the yammie off your head and the money out of your pocket, and hand in front of face only as a reflex, walk safely into a movie. The Friday night surge through the brightly lit lobby, the nestling in the dark belly of the theatre.

Listen well, Father, I expect much in return. While you and other good Jewish fathers sit with a glass of tea and read the *Jewish Press*, while you digest the Friday night meal and wait for the time clock to shut your lights off, while you acknowledge the appropriateness of a day of rest, your sons are busy. They go sneaking out of Crown Heights and Flatbush and Boro-Park (some claim to be refugees from Williamsburg), into cars parked out of sight on the other side of

Empire Boulevard and under the flaking El of New Utrecht, into train stations and unlit taxis, to bars and ball games and Friday night dates. And by one o'clock they are all back, every last one, back in skull caps and neckties, their breaths freshened by Binaca, their hands scrubbed of pool hall chalk by liquid Rokeach soap. Back from Channel 14 on Twelfth Avenue, back from Spot and Cue on Utica, back from the Flatbush Avenue Rialto and Kenmore, back (if they were more lucky than good) from the type of non-religious girls you dread, who use bacon instead of beef fries and are only visitors to the front steps of Temples on a few special days of the year. Back they are to bed, back to rise the next morning and, dressed in Sabbath finery, to accompany their well-rested fathers to morning services. Then, in the afternoon, second meal behind them, we begin again. What tans we have gotten, Father, sitting in the bleachers at Yankee Stadium with our shirts off on long summer afternoons. And how the white on white patterns of Sabbath shirts chafe freshly sunburned skin.

But not to fear, old man. You're the only one who knows. Secrets are well kept and reputations safe. Superboys are alive and well in Crown Heights as long as you reveal no identities. We enter Sabbath homes with disguises in place, having cleaned up more than once in the generously open lobby of Crown Heights Yeshiva.

And now, your turn. I want more than permissions. I want answers. If my father and my teacher are both laden with burdens I must relieve the weight on my teacher's back first. What a burden that knowledge is for me. But go ahead and teach me, Father. I would risk the double weight of your words. Let us learn. If an unidentified body is found between two cities, the nearer city is responsible for the burial and the expiation ceremony. The question is, Father, from where is the distance measured? Is it measured from the mouth of the body or is it measured from its navel? In other words, does my responsibility begin when words emerge from my lips or has my body already announced my intentions, confirming by way of that central depression my connection to Adam and Eve? From where do I reach? (As for measuring from the feet, I remember walking home from synagogue on Yom Kippur Eve, two steps in front of my parents, eager for bed.

Walking toward us, single file because of the wide hedges of Crown Street, two well-dressed boys without any headcovering. Clearly fellow Jews, equally obvious they are from the Brooklyn Jewish Center, that haven of semi-Jews, admittance by ticket only, three elevators, no waiting. As they pass, they smile. One says, "Who won the game?" I am mystified until I realize they were commenting on my sneakers. The wearing of leather forbidden, I was stepping smartly in my ankle high Pro Keds. Father, befitting his age, wore rubber summer shoes with perforated vamps, was exempt from derision. Sin is measured from the feet.)

But my father talks to me in sleep, my father speaks to me with silence. He is a Nazirite with information, a miser with meaning. His words mean little, his gestures reveal some things, his silences are everything. He seems to suggest that it is better to marry than to burn but implies at the same time that marriage might be a burning.

But even if Father would not, others were willing to talk. Bobby Seale would not stop, and so Judge Hoffman ordered him bound and gagged once more, reducing the Chicago Eight to Seven and a Half. And Agnew wouldn't stop either, oiling his tongue in anticipation of the Moratorium March on Washington, a weekend of peace rallies Nixon promised to observe by watching football games. Jonesey was busy making his own little speeches, urging a new domesticity on Sheila. And Rachel was willing, agreeing to meet outside. "A long way to go," I told her, "to wind up where we met months ago."

We were sitting in the car, in front of her house, the car hiding a fire hydrant. Parking spaces were harder and harder to find in Flatbush, another up and coming neighborhood. Ocean Avenue was particularly well policed for parking violations and, being in a different precinct, I could not count on being recognized by cops from the old neighborhood. Every few minutes I would shut the motor off, then start it again as the cold became insistent. Rachel leaned against the door, away from me. Our feet were separated by the hump of the transmission and, wearing gloves, we couldn't feel the weight of each other's hands. I had left class a few minutes early and timed my drive down Ocean Parkway and Foster Avenue to coincide with her emergence from the D station on Foster. But there was no parking spot available. "Let's go somewhere," she suggested. "Someplace to eat. A kosher place, if you like."

"I'll risk non-kosher," I said bravely, my heart not in it.

"That's all right," she said, patting my arm extending across the back of the plastic-sheeted seat, "when you have that first meal, it will be for punishment, not hunger. You'll order something really hot and spicy that will burn your guts out and cause you so much pain that you won't feel guilty doing it."

"Like what?"

"There is this taco stand in the West Village where even the dessert can bring tears to your eyes."

"As long as it's out of the neighborhood," I said.

Rachel shook her head. She had taken her stylish little tam off, with its fuzzy pom-pom, and her hair swirled, ends neatly curving under and up, a glossy, smooth slide. "I once flew back here from Montana when I was about twelve. I kept on looking out of the window expecting to see the lines between the states. They're not there, you know. Not even between Boro-Park and Crown Heights."

I turned the motor on again, felt the rush of warm air against my feet. "What were you doing in Montana?"

"We had inherited land there," she said, surprisingly, "my father's brother. We went there to sell it."

I knew of no one who had ever inherited, much less owned land. The war had taken care of death duties though Jonesey swears that throughout Europe great wealth is buried, jewelry, gold coin, silver candlesticks, snow white linen, hidden as the war approached, never recovered. But to own land, in America, and to sell that land, that was new but then Rachel was never from my old neighborhood.

"No wonder you shop at Bloomingdale's," I told her. "The only other person I know who can afford it is Father's designer. He says it's the only place to get these darling little hundred dollar cashmere pull-overs."

"It's true," she said, challenging. "There is no other place for them."

I pushed the drive button, felt the transmission kick.

219

"Where are we going?"

"I thought I'd show you Sea Gate, show you all the romantic spots and change your mood. Unless you're too hungry."

"I'm fine. But let me drive."

I had relinquished the wheel often enough in the past not to mind doing it once more. With a practiced ease, I got out and walked to get in on the other side. I got in to see her staring intently forward, rectangular glasses in place. Without looking at me, she said, "They're practically glass but the license says corrective lenses." But she wouldn't turn to me full face and as she drove she leaned forward, bringing her hair forward too, concealing even more of the glasses. I did not press it. Vulnerabilities are matters of perception, not of fact. Rachel was near sighted about nothing, far sighted only at appropriate distances.

"Do you know the way?"

"The garden spot beyond the Coney Island slums," she said.

"Just drive through the gate when you get there. They know the car."

She drove intently, keeping both hands on the wheel and crossing them over on turns, the way people are taught in Drivers' Ed. All the advantages of the non-*yeshiva* education. At a red light she unzipped her parka completely and unbuttoned her blouse's collar. A faint smell, lighter than the warm smell of the car, floated. She was wearing narrow pants tucked into high boots, blouse pinched into pants, high collar, so that she would have been impervious to my touch even if I had not restricted myself.

"With both of my hands busy, I thought there would be places where your hands would like to be, doing things I know they like to do," Rachel said, looking straight ahead.

"That FIT ensemble is like a chastity belt."

"Then do it with words."

"I've tried. They don't work with you."

"You haven't tried the right words."

Hands restless, I had nothing to say. This is the way Father should meet her, I thought to myself, from the side rather than head on.

Once past the guard (the car waved through) I offered to

take over, drive us to my secret shade myself. "I can follow directions," Rachel said.

"I'm not sure I can give them to you," I told her, "I just know how to get there, not the names of the streets."

Somehow we found the dead-end street anyway. Even from the car we could see the bay open its arms toward the Verrazano Bridge and Staten Island. With the heat off, the clear night disappeared as the windshield began to fog up. We began to kiss, awkwardly, our positions reversed, my head back against the seat, her glasses forgotten, interfering. Anticipating the creeping cold, I worked my hands into her waistband and under and up her blouse, holding her warm back and belly, palms open and fingers still. It was very exciting but no good. There seemed to be little sense in grasping her so desparately in the scraggy wilderness of a dead end street in Sea Gate. No matter how willing a fish, I was an inept fisherman. Finally Rachel moved. "You're letting cold air in," she whispered and I carefully withdrew, returning to smoothe her blouse back into the pants. "It used to be so exciting," she said.

"Us?"

"No," she said, "I'm talking about being sixteen, about the time before apartments, when there was no place to come back to. Before you got lucky."

"Then let Sheila move in. The sooner the better. It will revive us. Jonesey has had nothing but good things to say about the comforts of the back seat."

She wrote "Jason," in flowing script, on the inside of the windshield. "Your problem is that you're never sure whether you're proposing or propositioning."

"And you," I said, "you're convinced a proposition is the only sign of true love."

"The skirt your father sent me," she said obscurely, "fits perfectly. Thank him for me."

"Sure. He thought it would."

She added "and Rachel" to my name on the windshield. We were completely fogged in, even the back windows milky. "And a heart around the names," I told her. She drew the heart, the two halves curving neatly, an expert hand guiding the lines.

221

"Were you coming over Saturday?"

"Not without asking first."

"I'm not going to be home."

"Off to Mexico?"

"Not that far and not with Sheila. To Washington, with Lizzie and Gondo. We're marching for peace."

I tried to dissuade her. The sale of Mace had risen to 8 million dollars that year, triple what it was before the '68 convention. There would be National Guardsmen. The White House was already ringed by buses lined end to end. Roads would be closed. There was a run on gas masks. It was expected to be the coldest day of the year. Gondo might leave Lizzie behind. Rachel smiled crookedly. "*Yeshiva* skepticism. We're not staying overnight."

"What kind of car does he have?"

"Who needs a car when the girl has an apartment?" Rachel laughed.

"There will be a march here too, from the Kennedy Memorial at Grand Army Plaza back south on Flatbush Avenue. I was planning on going."

"On Saturday?"

"It'll be after *shul* anyway."

"Your contingent from *yeshiva* coming along?"

"I was elected their representative."

"Well," she said, "it's right you should. That's why I'm going to the march on Washington. As your representative."

When we arrived back in front of her apartment house, she said, "Look for a spot."

When I hesitated, she smiled. "I have no designs on your virtue. I'm getting my period. I just want you to keep me company while I'm eating."

On my third or fourth circle around the block, a yellow Volkswagen pulled out, but a Pontiac that had been searching in front of me tried to back into the spot, ramming cars fore and aft. I double parked the Lancer and waited for him to give up. "It must drive him crazy knowing you're behind him."

"I've been practicing waiting," I told her. "Think of it as a victory for the little guy."

Upstairs, Rachel headed for the kitchen, not even bothering with lights. I followed, the dry smell of the radiators familiar and welcome.

"I haven't eaten since a chef's salad for lunch."

By the light of the open refrigerator I watched her eat crackers and American cheese, with olives, pickles, and sharp red peppers, her fingers flying. Inside the refrigerator were wrapped packages of turkey, tongue, brisket, corned beef, pastrami and both soft and hard salami. Preparations for the trip to Washington, she explained. "Kosher stuff?" I asked. "On the road I'm always Jewish," she said, "it's only in the city that you'd don't have to think about it all the time."

Hesitant, I asked, "Is it definite that Sheila's moving in with you?"

"Only as far as Jonesey is concerned."

"In that case," I said, speaking carefully, not unaware of the length of her legs and the peculiar shadows in the kitchen, "why not consider other offers?"

One finger in the narrow necked bottle of Spanish olives, she paused. "A counter offer to my offer?"

"My Father," I said, fully conscious of the possessive, "doesn't think we're very serious."

"Oh," she said, "have you told him we're messing around on a semi-regular basis?"

"If I had, he'd consider our relationship even less serious. Truth is, we started wrong as far as he's concerned. We met on our own. If we were worth anything, some intermediary would have invested time and energy in introducing us. As it is, what can he think? You and I are seconds, a slightly damaged top and bottom trying to become a suit."

She stood up and put both arms around my neck. I could feel her breasts alive against me. I leaned against the doorpost for support. Her mouth barely below mine, she breathed deliberately, testing me with the spicy cave. Then she circled my closed lips with many soft, quick, tiny kisses. Once again surprised, I stood there, courted instead of courting, in need of a swain's manual.

"That," she said, still holding on, "is a very serious kiss. It's a declaration of war. Think of yourself as the defense minister, holding on desperately. Your father, whom I don't know, is prime minister, an honorary post, for life. Your mother, whom I never met, the minister without portfolio. Dov, far off somewhere, for all I know a figment of your imagination, Health, Education and Welfare, or better yet, the Minister of Justice, sacred as well as secular. And Jonesey, the one member of your administration I've met, he is the Minister in Charge of the Interior, specifically Sheila's. All of which is by way of saying how serious you are, my love, in defending against my seriousness. And that," she stood flat-footed, slightly lower, more distant, "is the last I'm going to say on the subject."

"You're mixing governments," I muttered.

"Did it ever occur to you," she said, stepping back, "that every time we have a really good screw you won't leave it alone?"

"What's your explanation now?"

She sighed. "You act the same way when we haven't had a good one."

While it was true that I had not been officially invited up or in since my last unannounced appearance, it was also true that I had not come knocking on her door either, with or without my *yarmukah*. When I said nothing, she took my hand and tugged me toward the bedroom.

"Come with me."

"You said you were getting your period."

"It's on the way but not here. I'm just tender all over." She touched her breasts with both hands in a protective gesture. "You'd have to be very gentle." When I still hesitated, she looked at me wonderingly. "It isn't that, is it? I'm not about to trick you into violating a taboo."

"No, that's not it," I said, though my hands, remembering their resting place, jerked, and I touched one palm against my pants leg. "I don't want to hurt you."

She took my hand again, still drawing me. "There are other places, other ways, aren't you the expert?" But that wasn't true. I was a master only at avoidance. It was Rachel who knew everything and I was not about to follow her to her bed for only innocent and carefree pleasures. She was my teacher and I wanted her to demand her due, to follow her, as the Talmud says, honor bound to the teacher even at the cost of abandoning a burdened Father. And so I left, but kissed her before I did, the warmth rising from her mouth rooting me outside her door long after she was back inside. What could I do, though, other than leave? I wanted to follow precepts but Rachel was satisfied merely in avoiding transgression.

The next day the drawing of the Draft Lottery was confirmed for December 1, and Jonesey called, eager for definitive word on Sheila's chances.

"Don't count on it, Jonesey," I told him.

"I've been trying to get into Rachel's place for a year and I'll get there yet," he laughed, revealing his early attempt at betrayal.

I spent Saturday morning in *shul,* the afternoon marching, and the evening anxiously switching channels for news stories on the Moratorium in Washington, not relaxing until Rachel called Sunday. And just to prove that I was still afloat, an unattached electron, an iron shaving on a plastic page waiting for a magnetic pencil to tug me in place, I received a letter from Dov on Saturday, a letter I had to wait until Sabbath's end to open, Father eager to hear about the one friend who made good. Writing to me as if we were still *yeshiva* boys, ritually rocking at the study bench, Dov gleefully announced his participation in the great Jerusalem controversy. The public pool, mixed bathing for men and women, was being built as planned in the Holy City and Dov was marching, sitting-in, protesting, praying at the Wailing Wall. Father was pleased. Dov was in a country where religion and spirit were as one. He said he had seen signs up in the synagogue hallway that there would be sympathy protests in the United States. Dov was sending posters.

With Rachel safe, even if distant, I ignored Dov's letter and began to check the mail for word on my Comprehensives.

30.

In the two weeks before Draft Lottery there was little learning harvested in the Yeshiva of Torah Gatherers. Under normal circumstances, attendance was infrequent during the long stretch between the end of *Sukkoth* and the beginning of *Chanukah,* the Festival of Lights. Not provided with holidays, we would make our own. World Series Day, opening of basketball season, ticker tape in honor of the Mets, Samuel Taylor Coleridge's birthday, James Boswell's, Emily Dickinson's, George Eliot's. Architects, accountants, computer technicians having their own heroes and celebrations, it was difficult getting a poker game together. But before the Lottery, attendance was remarkable. We gathered for encouragement and to speculate about the good life if we drew a high draft number. The Knicks were on a winning streak; we all wanted to hop on for the ride. Safe in our hideaway, we fantasized about high stakes gambling.

Rabbi Baumel seemed distracted, forgetting from day to day the pages of our studies and finding excuses to rise in the midst of lectures to leave the room. His brother-in-law, the purist in Yiddish, also concerned, lapsed into English, saying "explanatzien" and "memorizieren," and "redemptieren," growing Yiddish inflectives on English roots, if anyone cared to hear my analysis. No one did. During the pauses provided by Rabbi Baumel's departures and the breaks between periods, we surrounded Rabbi Baumel's mad nephew and threw questions at his drooling face. "What do you say, Irv ben Moshe, who'll be exempt?" Irv Baumel had correctly predicted the results of the three way race involving Lindsay, had picked the Mets to go all the way and had put a man on the moon a year before the Apollo shot and so was not to be taken lightly though each of those statements at the time seemed merely to confirm his madness. Hiding his wet face in wind chapped hands, a handkerchief twisted around his neck for either warmth or decoration, Irv nodded arythmically, delighted by our interest. "A congressman's son will go first," he said, grinning, "they have to show they're patriotic, no exceptions."

Back in our seats, my bench near Mickey Wiener's, I was full of questions. What would Rabbi Baumel do? Would *yeshivas* become extinct? Could they diversify? Could Baumel branch out into religious articles? Was there a Grand Rabbi of Bookies where he could lay off some of the bets on the lottery?

"Don't worry about Baumel," Mickey said. "He's negotiating a Burger King franchise."

"They go for fifty grand, plus," Sammy Schneider, our praticing accountant, added from next to Mickey. The two of them were learning partners on the few days when they were there together.

"You're both crazy," I told them. "A religious person can't have anything to do with non-kosher stuff."

"Listen," Mickey said, "you don't know crap. At Whitehead Cafeteria there are big doings. The place is sold and guess who's coming in?"

"A branch of Baumel's Yeshiva, right on the Brooklyn campus, in full violation of recruitment laws."

But Mickey was shaking his head. "Coming into Whitehead is a quick order hamburger place."

"So?"

"A *kosher* fast food place," Mickey said. "They'll call it Kosher King and give away crowns with the star of David on them. You have no idea what this means. I'm not kidding. Glatt kosher meat. French fries heated in oil under rabbinical supervision. Bakery goods from Williamsburg and non-dairy creamers in the coffee. Baumel will close this place down and never miss it. He'll make a mint."

"Impossible," I said, but Sammy was nodding. "One of our clients is doing the ads. I think they'll have trouble with the name though."

Arnie Moskowitz, computer technician, on a rare visit, came over, tugging a knitted vest over his young pot belly. "How about a couple of quick hands, guys?"

"We'll be working behind the counter, Arnie," I told him, "with chef's hats on."

"Irving making predictions?" he wanted to know.

"No," I said, "Mickey and Sammy. Predictions and tax returns. Baumel will become the ritual supervisor at McDonald's."

"There *is* a Kosher King in Coney Island," Arnie said, "right on Surf Avenue, near the go carts. An old Wetson's, I think."

"That's where Baumel moonlights," Mickey said, "he supervises *kashruth* and handles the french fries."

"It's the biggest hang-out place in the city," Arnie said, "nothing but religious girls, dressed in stockings and dresses, just waiting to be introduced."

Mickey was nodding, his whole body rocking with eagerness. "That's what Brooklyn is gonna be like. Sinks for washing before meals, little plastic sheets with Grace After Meals printed on them. Eyes meet over the blessing. You bite into opposite halves of a kosher hamburger. If they call it hamburger. They'll probably call them meat burgers. It'll be tremendous. They'll be coming from all boroughs. The kosher pick-up place. When I'm finally in the market!"

I refused to accept the ease of such transformations. Didn't the demons of butchered meat need to be exorcised before the ritual slaughterers move in? Doesn't the odor of unclear linger? Could Baumel don an apron over his jacket and tails and forget his role as nurturer of rabbis and protector of cowards? There had to be a transition of some kind, an outer manifestation of inner change, a sign of the struggle. Didn't I carry the imprint of Rachel's kisses? Hadn't the yammie left a circle of fire on my hair? Could I erase circumcision? It was all nonsense, I decided, we were maddened by the approach of the lottery.

"I can just see it," I told Mickey, "Baumel a silent partner in Kosher King and the rest of us counterboys on work/study fellowships."

"I did see him in Coney Island," Arnie said.

"Probably negotiating for chicken parts, for our tests," Mickey laughed.

"No tests," Sammy Schneider said, ever the expert in money matters. "We're just gonna draw lots. Winner gets to

228

be Rabbi and gets all the tax deferments for clergy. Loser becomes chaplain in Saigon. The rest of us continue to pay tuition until we reach twenty-six, get maried, or die."

Ever hopeful that there would be alternatives, I invested heavily in New York State Lottery tickets and ventured two dollars on a Daily Double wager at Aqueduct that Gondo went to bet. "Freedom Flyer," the horse, liberated me from the money, finishing last, but my odds for winning were improving with each loss. The papers speculated that those born on the first one hundred days drawn were sure to be drafted, the second hundred were possibles, the last hundred certainly safe.

"Does your father mind that I'm sitting this war out?"

"We don't have a tradition," Rachel said. "He was too young for the first, just right for the second, too old for Korea. We do our duty but we don't train for it. No one wants to be a gold star mother. Not with this war, anyway."

Trotting home during lunchtime to check the mail, I found a letter from NYU. I ripped it open by savaging the cellophane at the little window of the envelope. "We are pleased to inform you," I read. So I had passed. Containing myself, a bit disturbed even that my losing streak was ending too soon and that the Lottery was becoming a greater risk, I read through the note, searching for a personal slant, a remark from one of the readers perhaps about the excellence of the answers. There was nothing, just the form. Substitute "regret" for "pleased" and it was the same letter. That's where the magic lies, I thought, in the control of the format. I write personal letters, emotional pleas, applications, requests, comments, essays. In return I receive prefabricated lines. It makes sense. The disorder of emotion can be handled only by regulation. The Marines shave your head. So does the *yeshiva.* Other authorities send form letters. The Board of Ed. requests my presence on the third. The Graduate School of Arts and Sciences is pleased. Your local draft board is thoughtfully concerned. The Holocaust Survivors Club regrets to inform you that your mother, nèe Braunstein, is missing in post war action. All efforts will be made to locate and repatriate POW's and MIA's. The return of our loved ones would be a non-negotiable demand of any peace treaty. We hope you understand. "Braunstein" is the only word written in. "Jason Kole" is the only name written in. The rest of the text is of a solid consistency, waiting for the day when individual names will be typed in matching color, the form and the person one and inseparable, the uniformity no longer spoiled by the odd colored ink of the names.

"If I luck into a high enough number, I can go for the doctorate full time," I told Rachel, calling her from Mini and Mac's phonebooth and pretending to be a customer of Berkey's, in search of misplaced negatives. "I'll drop Baumel's and grab the Board of Ed job."

"Listen," Rachel said, her voice professional, "have you checked the envelope? Sometimes the strips stick together and sometimes they fall in with the prints. Would you double-check, please?"

"I've looked and looked, miss, I'll look again tonight."

"Wait," she said, her voice back to familiar, "Gondo wants to know about this DD place of yours. Could he get in if he gets screwed in the lottery?"

"Oh, the calling has come to him?"

"He says the student deferments will be gone."

"No way," I told her, "though the 2S is certainly not as safe as a cyst. Does your friend have a cyst, Rachel?"

"If the *yeshiva* doesn't work out, maybe he'll grow one," she laughed. "How many nickels do you have lined up?"

"I won a quick hand of five card draw. How about kids? Why don't you tell him to grow a kid instead?"

"Lizzie," I heard her say, "Jason has big plans for you."

"Lizzie," I said, "is that still on?"

"Yes," she said, reassuring me, "but he's doing it for the fun of it, not the deferment."

"Hey," I said, "that's all right. If Lizzie will take care of his fun, I'll handle his deferment. We'll figure something out. Tell me. Does he use his trigger finger for plucking his guitar?"

"He's a lefty," Rachel said obscurely, "as far as the guitar is concerned but otherwise a righty. And thank you, sir, for developing at Berkey's Photo."

"Thank you, too," I said, "for developing."

"Jason," she said, her voice beginning to rise early for the question, "can you ask your father for some remnants, you know, pieces they would be throwing away? Odds and ends are fine."

"Another class project?"

"What else? Total consumption. Making torn pieces whole, throwaways functonal, the afflicted healthy. The age of Aquarius is over, the decade of ecology is here."

"Yours?"

"No. The new FIT brochure."

"I'll ask Father."

Only I wasn't seeing that much of him either those days. No matter how early I would leave in the mornings, he would be away before me. I would wake to see the streetlamp's purple filter from Montgomery and turn back toward sleep, not even bothering to check the radio alarm clock, but suddenly become aware of his soft murmuring from the kitchen. He would eat his toast and drink his coffee rich with milk, the milk heated so that a skin forms and clings to his spoon. Then he would leave for work, to say the *sh'ma* later, perhaps during coffee break, in broad daylight. And at night he would be sleeping, the house once again dark. Not seeing him, I could pretend he and my mother were managing well in my absence, as always. Which doesn't alter the fact that I was living there, returning even if I was out late with Rachel. And I was calling it "home" in conversation and never spending too many hours away from it, checking in at lunch time after leaving Baumel's and in the evenings after returning from NYU. Though I was avoiding Father quite successfully, I still kept in touch with his presence, through the phone messages he left for me on a little wire notebook hanging on the wall, the letters he neatly arranged on the formica counter top under the phone, the breakfast he set for himself for those early morning departures. The brown and red flowered dairy tablecloth, the burnt orange place mat on top of that, cup in saucer, butter knife leaning against plate, paper napkin, weekday saltshaker, and on the stove the enamel pot for warming the milk. All that was Father, along with his prayer shawl and phylacteries bag, similarly prepared on the other side of the table.

That was what I was coming home for, to touch, sniff,

confirm familiarity. How could I resist? How could my mother? Was it impossible that she would return too, for another helping, much the way I kept on dipping back in? Obviously she was staying away much longer than I was or could have, but could she do without a return altogether? Just before *Rosh Hashanah* a young wife had disappeared. A newlywed, a Lubavitcher, she was doing holiday shopping on Kingston Avenue, was seen laden with bags and dragging a shopping cart, even had an order for *challah* outstanding at Fayvel's on the corner of Montgomery, then suddenly she was gone. Foul play was suspected; no religious wife leaves the holiday table unattended, people said, not willingly. For the two days of the New Year the police detail in front of the sloping lawn of 777 Eastern Parkway was increased. People looked darkly across the Parkway at the encroaching black neighborhood. In *shul* Rabbi Winkler spoke eloquently of souls summoned willy-nilly to be witnesses in heaven.

Two days after the holiday, she turned up. She had not wanted to marry her husband, she explained to police (my Detective Meisner handling her?), she had had a cold, it had been a day too beautiful to be spent inside a synagogue in prayer. She had gone to her parents' house but found it busy with preparations. On an impulse, she turned and went to the Port Authority where she took a bus (still laden with her *Rosh Hashanah* victuals) to the bungalow colony where she used to spend summers as a child. She had spent four days there, eating gefilte fish and cake in the deserted bungalow. Eventually lonely, she had come home, she said. Longer marriages perhaps demand longer absences. At what point do absences become permanent? I had not yet found out. Had my mother? And could one return, from short trips or long, unmarked? Crown Heights preserves; the areas beyond Orthodox borders spoils. Beyond the protective limits of the area the good are lost, the perfect damaged. Father has been invited to join the *Eruv* Committee. The plan is to encircle Crown Heights—Bedford Avenue on the west, Eastern Parkway on the north, Albany Avenue to the east, Empire Boulevard to the south—with thin wire on slender poles, a ring of safety that would enable the Jews within to carry on the Sabbath, the invisible wires symbolically rendering the area they surround private domain within which the orthodox Jew could carry a handkerchief or push a baby carriage on the Sabbath.

The Lubavitcher Rebbie was said to have suggested the plan, hoping to entice Jews to remain in Crown Heights. In telling me this, Father, hesitant, said he had been approached by someone in *shul* about a *shiduch,* a match.

I looked at him, startled. "For you," he said quickly, not letting me ask the question. I thought of people in *shul* with daughters. "A stranger," Father said, "I'm not mentioning names but it's not someone you know."

"So what's the offer?" I asked, laughing. "Do they still think I'm *shiduch* material?"

Father allowed himself a brief smile. "They don't, that's why they mentioned it."

I waited. "It's a *modern* girl," Father finally said. "College and everything. She wants a *modern* boy. She is also working. Not for her father, I mean."

"Oh," I said, "that's it. They're offering me a *kalyeke,* right? A girl gone wrong, is that it? What did she do? Date a boy without a *yarmukah*? Wear her sleeves too short?"

"I said I would mention it," Father said, already turning away.

"Tell them I'm already dating a *modern* girl," I told him.

This was on the Sunday before the Monday of the Lottery.

31.

I never used to go courting in the middle of the night. When I was still spending the nights with Rachel, my fingers would twitch in sleep, feeling the fabric of dream cloth, and I would find myself entangled in her. We would wake just enough. She would hurry me inside her, impatient with preliminaries, both of us behaving as if we had been traveling together far enough while asleep not to need further preparations when we met awake. Now that my nights were as chaste as Father's, I discovered that our voices could substitute for our presence. I would call her late at night and our words would slide into each other with the ease of long practice, scarcely recalling the awkwardness of our first conversation, somehow avoiding the conflicts of our present estrangement. I called her the night before the Lottery Drawing, Sunday already into Monday morning, another imperceptible melting.

"Can't sleep," I told her, "too excited. Not even nervous. Expectant."

"You are. You're being reborn. Have you thought what you'd do if you caught a low number?"

"Nothing would change."

"In that case," she said, "I'll root for a late number. You'd never move in as long as you're a potential rabbi."

On the other hand, I thought, she might never marry me unless it was an act of mercy to a soldier in uniform. But this was not the time for it. "I don't think Father realizes that this might be the end of my rabbinical career."

"If I know him," she said, "he's got a sewing machine set aside for you, just in case. But I don't know him. So how do venetian blinds strike you?"

But it wasn't the time for that either. Days of Judgment are to be met alone and purified. But when Rachel suggested a lottery party at her house, I agreed.

In *yeshiva* the next day, an air of festivity. We went around shaking hands, wishing each other best of luck. Mickey dug a worn sexton's cap out of a drawer and declared himself the Crown Heights version of Miss Liberty. Arnie Moskowitz, unaccountably present though lately he had been making Wednesday his day of appearance, organized a pool. Incapable of shaking poker rules, he announced that the pot would be split high and low, shared by the recipients of the highest and lowest numbers. We each contributed a buck. "How about getting Baumel to chip in?" Cantrowitz asked.

"This is costing him enough as it is," Mickey cackled.

"As long as it's not fixed," Arnie said, "I'm okay. I'll always take my chances with the cards."

Rabbi Baumel's cousin did not give his morning lecture, and Baumel's nephew announced at eleven that the Rabbi would not be lecturing either. We nodded, knowingly, began to leave, already sensing the loosening of authority. Only Cantrowitz was cautious. "Jesus, one of us gets a low number and Baumel has him by the balls forever."

Released early, I started toward the house. Passing the precinct along the way I gave in and went upstairs, willing to take one more chance on a day of fortune. Detective Meisner was wearing a sweater in the dank room. His violet suspenders, sapped of color by winter, were atop the sweater. I noticed for the first time that the walls of the squad room seemed to have been painted by the same guy who had done my first *yeshiva;* cool compositions of olive green and off-white, the olive green man-high from the baseboards, the rest like an aging egg. In *yeshiva* the green protected the walls from smearing childish hands. What was the point here?

"Kid," Meisner said, "what's doing?"

"That's what I came to ask you."

He waved one hand, palm up. "No news is good news."

"I'll bet you say that to everyone."

He went to stand in front of the windows that looked out on Empire Boulevard, turning his back to me without rancor.

I saw that the suspenders split into two branches at each end and went into the pants where he must have sewn buttons to accommodate them. "Are you married?" he asked. I said no. "Girlfriend?" I nodded. "Serious?" I raised my shoulders. Turning, he saw the gesture. "You don't have to say any more. I'm up to my ears in lovers. We get a dozen stabbings a night. One yesterday where a guy knifes his girlfriend because she slept with her own husband. Can you believe it? And the same thing with husbands and wives, and parents and children, and cats and dogs. Go talk love." He rubbed his face, pretending he'd been working all night long but he was smooth shaven, his sideburns clipped so close that a thin, white line separated the hair and the cheeks. "Want my advice? Look for your mother on your own. Circulate among Jews. Go to the Bronx, try Rego Park, try Coney Island, hang around bingo games in synagogues. She could turn up, you know, she's a survivor. But it's all over for us here. We've become a neighborhood 'in transition.' We're into wife beatings and drunk driving and muggings. We gotta protect the Jewish auxiliaries from the black auxiliaries and the Lubav patrols from the Baptists." He looked at me. "You got a classification?"

"Four D," I said, "student of divinity."

"Smart kid," he said. "Stay in the neighborhood. With them moving in, there is a bigger pool to draw on. My kid wants to enlist in the Air Force." He snapped his suspenders, the right side flicking a second ahead of the left. "Everybody's got problems, right?"

Who could argue? I went home, the house shaded from the cold sunlight, and turned the thermostat back on. Too early still for mail, I sat on the living room couch carefully, trying not leave too deep a depression in the springy material. When the phone rang I remembered the end of a ring as I had first walked in. Having just left Meisner, I was relaxed. The call could have been only from someone I didn't know.

"Mister Kole?" a voice asked.

"Sorry," I answered, "he won't be home till after five. Can I take a message?" I actually looked forward to leaving him a note, some formal but courteous indication that we were still inhabiting the same household. There was a pause at the other end, then the woman said, "It doesn't matter. Tell him to just keep his regular appointment at the Board of Ed."

Forced into it, I admitted to being a Mister Kole as well and asked for the information. The woman was hesitant, asked me if I was sure who I was. It was the only time I thought that attaching "junior" to the name could have been helpful.

Finally convinced, she told me she was calling from South Shore Senior High.

"I know it," I reassured her, "that new, round building."

"Could you be here by 1:30," she said, "with your diploma? Mr. Berliner, our principal, would like to interview you today."

I promised to be there, puzzled by the call. Teachers are usually assigned, catch as catch can, good neighborhood or bad. I knew no one at South Shore, could not have been requested or traded for a man to be named later. I had already thought what I would wear for the Wednesday interview and had prepared the outfit, in some things unavoidably Father's son. I changed into a pale blue striped white shirt and wore my Sabbath suit, a dark blue double-breasted outfit. Hair combed, shoe polished, necktie a smooth sheen of solid blue, I was as squeaky clean and shiny as I had been on the Day of Atonement. If I had worn rubber sneakers instead of shoes I could have passed for a man in search of forgiveness.

Ready, the day even more full than anticipated, I got into the car and could not start it. The driveway was lit up by the sun and the hood of the car warm to the touch despite the cold but the Lancer would not turn over. I pumped until the smell of the flooded carburetor penetrated the car even through closed windows then gave up. It was time for friends, no matter how old and lost, I thought, and called Jonesey at Hirsch's.

"Hey, man," he said, picking up the phone, "I meant to call you to wish you luck. If you can't have a cyst, you might as well have the good wishes."

I asked him if he had a car on the lot he could let me have and, once again in payment, asked him if he wanted to listen to the drawing at Rachel's place.

"With Sheila?" he asked cautiously.

"Sure," I said, "we'll have a real reunion and she can look around and see how cramped the space is."

Surprisingly, he laughed. "Don't sweat it. Wait outside."

He picked me up in a gleaming, emerald Sedan de Ville. I

got in and let the weight of the door slam it with a heavy sound. "They see me in this," I said, "and they'll expect *me* to pay *them*."

But Jonesey was making preparations to get out. "Registration's in the glove compartment. I filled it up."

"You're not leaving," I said. "I can't drive trucks."

He got out carefully, as if afraid his overalls would smear the kid glove interior. "I'll try to get your bomb started."

I perched in the driver's seat, squinting to line up my sight with the Caddy medallion on the tip of the hood. Jonesey watched me from outside the open window. "Be careful," he said, "it's all power, especially the windows."

"I can't believe Hirsch let you take it off the lot."

"Didn't have to ask him."

I finally stopped trying to measure the distance from the wheel to the tip of the hood. "How come?"

"Private stock," he grinned, "check out the registration."

" 'Herman Brody,' " I read. "So?"

"Daddy Brody," Jonesey said, both proud and embarrassed, "as in Sheila Brody?"

"She's sending you business?" I asked, still not fully understanding, not yet admitting the change in him.

"It's more like me giving him the business."

I wanted to know more but he slapped the hood of the car, much the way the western hero sends the horse of the second banana out of danger, and walked toward the squatting Lancer. I floated in Sheila's daddy's car to South Shore.

The generations, the sages claim, are getting weaker. Late rabbis can thus never modify or overrule early lawmakers. Old sins and hurts remain, new ones simply accumulate. Fathers, by definition, are always right; sons must wait to rule over ever-decreasing territory. It is all a question of authority. I should have known it was all a matter of higher authority.

You have twenty minutes in which to consider the questions below. You may not make notes.

a) Your class persists in ignoring your entrance into the room, chatting and moving about. What would you do?

b) You have assigned a book for outside readings. You re-

238

ceive a call from the school librarian who informs you that students would never read the book you have selected. She urges you to choose another, one she suggests would work. What would you do?

"I would give them the benefit of the doubt and assume they hadn't noticed me. I would put my bag on the table with a thud and begin writing on the board."

"Your bag?" asked Mrs. Karpov, the Chairman of the English Department, also known as the Department of Language Skills and Arts.

"Bookbag."

"Oh," she said, "of course," reaching up to adjust an unlikely jade velvet band around her graying bun. "And what if that didn't work?"

Should I have said that I would bring a briefcase next time, the one with the stiff bottom that makes a louder, more resounding sound? "Well, next time," I said, looking away from her to Principal (your *pal*) Berliner, a small, dark man with the thinnest and neatest mustache I had ever seen, "I might not have the problem. I would have ended the previous class with a question, set up some kind of an expectation, which they would be eager to have resolved."

The principal gave me a thin smile. "And if that didn't work?"

"Ring a small bell," I offered. "Catch their attention."

"And if that didn't work?"

The third person had not asked anything yet and I turned toward him, hoping that he would be more sympathetic, being closer to me in age and wearing a white shirt with an open collar, an informal version of my Sabbath uniform. He had been introduced as "Mr. Klein, a member of our department." He seemed somehow familiar but I accepted him as an impartial observer, part of the peace keeping force, though I did not fail to notice that all three had Jewish names and did not forget that Brooklyn College had produced more than half the teachers in the City's public school system.

"I would speak to the leaders outside of class, divide and conquer or punish, no reason to reprimand the whole class for the actions of the few." I remembered the story of the Hebrew advance scouts to the land of Canaan, their despair mortally infecting the rest of the nation so that in punishment for doubting the word of God, none of that generation ever reaches the Promised Land.

"And if that didn't work," I continued, leaping to intercept, "I would make the ring leaders my assistants, give them special responsibilities. Make them obligated."

But Karpov was not satisfied and Berliner was also shaking his head. "And what if that didn't work either," she insisted. "What then?"

No help was coming from Klein. I was either being perceived as Orthodox and was suffering from the disdain of these non-observant torturers, their ire aroused by the numerous *Yeshivas* listed on my resumè, or (noticing on a folding chair within reach of Klein's left hand, a black hat) they were Orthodox and they were punishing me for my transgressions, as indicated by my bare head and lack of questions about kosher eating facilities and special accommodations for Sabbath observers.

I could only shrug. "I hope it wouldn't come to that."

"It often does," Mr. Berliner said, dryly. He and Mrs. Karpov bent over yellow lined pads and scribbled notes. Klein was not writing and looked at me with what seemed a reassuring cast to his face. In one of the legendary tests for the rabbinate the candidate is handed a volume of the Talmud. One of the three examiners pierces the pages with a pin. The volume is opened to the random page the pin had merely dented rather than penetrated. The candidate is asked to recite the contents of the page and cite the controversies and commentaries. In another exam, the candidate determines the *kashruth*, the ritual cleanliness of a chicken, with freshly scrubbed hands deep in the fowl's gizzard. Why couldn't I, a student of literature, recognize the symbolic importance of such questioning? Why couldn't I respond to what these people were rèally asking me? I tried my best, sitting up straight and answering forcefully, refusing finally to be dominated by the sun shining in my eyes, by the three of them sitting behind the low table, by the excessive neatness of the principal's office, with its rectangular and square furniture that made Klein's shapeless hat the only object not constructed of straight lines.

I pushed my own folding chair further back so that I could

see the legs of the interviewers and concentrate on contact with the parts below the division line. The use of that table as a desk, meant to bring students closer to the principal, helped me to put them at a distance. Berliner's flat gray suit ended where matching nylon socks began, a pattern of vertical lines on the socks making his ankles seem narrower. His black shoes came to vicious little points, the kind Jonesey used to call Puerto Rican sharp, perfect for spearing cockroaches in corners. They were also old fashioned, laced high with many weak eyelets. Mrs. Karpov's unisex loafers, dark brown and sensible, were betrayed somehow by tongues of lighter leather and by nervous knees surreptitiously rubbing each other. Even Klein's feet, though hidden by the leg of the table, revealed hidden passion by the openness of his knees falling to either side of the table, the feet angled wide, like the open arms of a romantic. I answered the second question in a louder voice, aggressively reassuring that I would be sure to take the librarian's expert view into consideration. Then I shook hands, left to right, clockwise, and in alphabetical order. "You'll hear from us in a week," Berliner said.

The secretary stopped me outside and offered me a chocolate chip cookie from a paper plate. I declined but couldn't walk away from the insurance and payroll forms she insisted I complete. Assuming it was standard procedure to keep all candidates hopeful, I filled the forms out quickly, not taking my usual care with the neatness of the lettering and the use of the comma between my last name and first. No one came out of the principal's office while I worked on the forms.

I was near the paneled door leading out to Flatlands when I turned, hearing Klein calling, briefcase in one hand and hat in the other, hurrying after me. I stopped to wait but he motioned me outside. Once the door was closed behind us he put his hat on and reached out to shake my hand. Puzzled, I shook.

"*Nu,*" he said, "what do you think of our *rosh ha yeshiva?*"

I stared at him. He clapped me on the back. "Relax, he had to make it look good in front of Karpov. You think we wouldn't hire an old Torah Vodaath boy? How many *yeshiva* guys do you think apply these days, *tzaddik?* Mrs. Zeiger's husband works at the Board of Ed. He told her, she told

Berliner, he asked me, I called Rabbi Winkler, he said you were Dov Laufer's *chavruse*. That was it."

"It was a long time ago," I said weakly, "I've had other study partners since."

He set down his briefcase and after pushing his hat more tightly on his head (the hat slightly back so that a little whip of hair showed in the front, the dead give-away of a fellow quester on Eastern Parkway), buttoned his black, wool coat, smoothing the velvet slashes on the collars. "He has *smicha*, right?"

"Dov? Sure. He's post-doc-ing in Israel."

Klein smiled. "He's getting married too?" I laughed, suddenly aware that he was watching me carefully. "Do you need a ride?" I asked him. He shook his head. "Inside they don't want you to wear anything, it's a different sort of neighborhood even though Canarsie is Jewish. They send their kids to *yeshivas* not public school. But hats are O.K. Berliner sometimes wears an ivy league cap or one of those crushed ones, like Moynahan at the U.N."

I realized finally that he was edging to see my *yarmukah*, wondering when I would take it out of my pocket and confirm my secret identity. Panicking, I remembered I was using Herman Brody's car and unless Sheila's father had a yammie tucked away in a pickle jar for such emergencies, I was caught flat. When is an ID card like nitroglycerin pills? When safety depends on them both.

"Listen, Klein," I said, "what was the answer to those questions? I wanted to say *taykuh*, wait for the arrival of the Messiah."

A bit mollified but still waiting for me to be dotted, he said, rubbing his chin and unconsciously sing-songing in the manner of old *yeshiva* days, "He wanted you to say that you would go to the Dean of Students or the Principal. Understand? Back up the ranks, to the source, the Torah from Sinai, *lehavdil*."

The final word meant "to separate," an apology for the analogy linking the sacred and the secular. That was it, I thought, the boundary line, the thin wire between the Sabbath land and the weekday ground, between permitted territory and forbidden, between Klein and Kole. "Well," I said, standing straight, keeping my arms to the side, "I would've never said it."

Impatient with me, he said, "He just wants to be told he's boss, that's all."

I nodded, waiting. "For Fridays," he said, "we can leave early, especially when *Shabbat* is by four-ten."

His face was turning red, cold or anger. I noticed that strands of hair were escaping from behind his ears and realized that he had maintained his *payes,* his side curls, folding them from before to behind his ears. It must have been easier for him when he was getting baldie haircuts. Black hair like his left a helmet of dark haze, no matter how closely the barber's electric shaver cropped it. While I, lighter everywhere, shone. Dropping one glove, I leaned forward after it, giving him an unobstructed view of the back of my head, denying him the comfort of thinking I had somehow maneuvered one of those tiny *yarmukahs,* dimes we used to call them, on the back of my head.

"Kole," he said, his voice different, "I remember you. You used to play basketball, right?"

"Klein, Klein," I said, "you were a senior. You used to stop the game when someone's yammie fell down, right?"

He nodded, eyes watery, wind or pain. I stuck my hand out, genuinely sorry for his mourning but feeling light. "Thanks." Then I left, feeling his eyes in the back of my head but resisting the impulse to pretend to feel in my pockets for that elusive bit of round cloth. Driving homeward I watched the setting sun light up my rearview mirror, making the receding streets behind me glow.

32.

Representative Alexander Pirnie, ranking member of the House Armed Services subcommittee on the draft, requested the privilege of drawing the first of the 366 sticky papers out of a cylindrical glass bowl. Earlier in the day CBS had announced that Mark Rudd had been indicted. His high school graduation picture, the one stapled to his application form to Columbia, showed him to be truculently thick jawed, an acceptable foreshadowing of his present bushy beardedness. Obviously a radical, the facing photos suggested, a predilection from birth, predating the Viet-Nam conflict. After the dates would be drawn, the letters of the alphabet would be selected, to determine the order of call-ups within each day. "Some," the commentator whispered, "would be chosen, others spared."

"Another chance," Rachel said, "for you to be one of the chosen people."

"I wish I had been born in a leap year," Gondo said, gloomy. "I can feel it coming, I just know it."

Rachel hugged him from behind, wrapping just his head into her arms. "It wouldn't be worth it, sweetie. You'd only have a birthday every few years and Lizzie could be arrested for transporting you across state lines. Anyway, they've got a little piece of paper for leap year babies too. They're drawing 366."

"Yeah, Gondo," I told him, ignoring her show of affection, "worst comes to worse, you can be my learning partner at seminary."

"I think I'd rather be a baby," he said, "or have one." He looked around. "Could I adopt one?"

Sheila and Jonesey, holding hands and silent since they had

walked in, looked at each other. He was full up with news, I could tell, but I was not going to ask. Each time Sheila looked around I imagined her measuring the place, figuring what she would have to displace in order to move in, so I wasn't asking her questions either. Anyway, his ass was safe because he had a safe ass and we were at Rachel's to discover how safe Gondo and I would be. His news could wait.

Because the TV stations were going to make only spot announcements, we were going to listen to the broadcast on the radio. Rachel unplugged her kitchen Panasonic and brought it into the living room. We squatted on throw pillows, the radio on the carpet, in our center. Gondo salaamed. Expectation and nervousness were making him high. When he had shaken hands with Jonesey he had slid his hand thumb against thumb, anticipating a test of strength, recognizing a fellow spirit. But that was the old Jonesey. Gondo need not have bothered. Not knowing of the alterations, aware only of that open-faced look and challenging slant of the back, Gondo worked at topping Jonesey. He lugged the jug of Gallo red in and poured into Rachel's hand-painted coffee mugs, pushing them into our hands. My throat was dry and I felt cold, would have preferred coffee or even Rachel's specialized teas. Mug in one hand, pale-skinned, buttoned-shirt Lizzie in the other, Gondo tried loudly to keep the draft away.

He tucked Lizzie's tailored shirt under her bra straps; he rolled his eyes toward Shelia. Jonesey and Sheila, held hands and smiled benignly, Sheila sitting with her knees tucked under herself, gray midi cushioning her ass from her legs, Jonesey very upright, determined to overcome an embarrassment none of us were privy to. What a lady she was and Jonesey, what a gentleman! The two of them could have been sold as matching procelain figurines, kept clean from dust on a special shelf in a china closet, chipped somewhere, of course, a deliberate blemish, that would enable such carved images to be kept in Orthodox households without violating the Second Commandment. Who could tell, looking at them, that the butter in Jonesey's mouth had often enough melted between her legs?

I had opened the door for them, acting as host, and accepted Sheila's peck on the cheek. "I didn't know we were such good friends," I muttered. "It's just that I have so much love left over," she had assured me, smiling Jonesey's secret smile. While we were still in the doorway Jonesey flicked a thumb toward the thin finger of the *mezuzah* encrusted with layers of paint on the doorpost. "Leave some loving for that." To me he said, "I can't wait till your old man catches sight of that. It must be a hundred years old."

"*If* he catches sight of it," I said.

"What's so special about the *mezuzah*?" Sheila asked. There was a fullness to her I hadn't noticed before but then what other than her ass had I ever noticed about her?

"Nothing," Jonesey said. "Jason's old man is a *mezuzah* hunter. Every time disaster strikes, he checks them out. If he finds a missing letter, he's got his answer. It was the parchment that did it, right, Jase?"

I shrugged. "My father changes them every time there is a burglary in the neighborhood," Sheila said.

"Well," said Jonesey, "of course, if it's to protect the family jewels, it's all right."

Sheila, in response, pursed her lips and the two of them kissed, a loud smack. Amazingly, Jonesey's hands never moved from his sides.

Rachel set stoneware plates on the carpet, their starburst designs covered by Tam-Tam crackers, potato chips and cheese doodles. I felt compelled to try to help, not quite sure whether I was number one guest, co-host, or just one of the gang. Her hair was up, pinned by a bone clasp, leaving the back of her neck bare. Gondo patted Lizzie's shirt pocket, just above the bump of a nipple. "If it's good news, I've brought some stuff to celebrate." Lizze blushed quickly but her skin swallowed color so well that she was pale again almost instantly. "It's in my bag," she said, "as if you didn't know it."

"It's like the Kennedy election," Rachel said, "it's the first one I remember watching."

Before anyone could say anything about the last Kennedy scenes he remembered, I put the radio on. The sound from Selective Service System headquarters at 1724 F Street in Washington, D.C. was hollow, the voice of the announcer hushed. "It's a little like church," Lizzie said, meekly. "They

246

should have gotten Cousin Brucie to do it," Gondo said, "or Mel Allen." Rachel sat down next to me and let one hand rest against the side of my leg. Possession, like love, is indicated with little gestures. Father would let his hand hover near my mother's elbow while they crossed the street. Gondo's casual ripple across Lizzie's breast had pinned her next to him. I wondered where they were headed. How far would a Jewish boy like Gondo go?

"September fourteen," the radio said.

"That's me," Sheila giggled.

The next four numbers were April 24, December 30, February 14 and October 18. None of us was touched. "So much for the top five," Gondo said, sobered. He poured from the jug. Before David Eisenhower landed call number thirty, Henry David Thoreau, pacifist hermit drew the 15th lot. When October 12th was called out, number 72, Jonesey said, "Well, they got Columbus." But they hadn't gotten any of us. "After the first hundred," Lizzie said, her voice a prayer, "it's much safer, right?" Rachel's hand was holding my arm. Jonesey looked like he would make another announcement about the wonderful kink in his ass but managed to restrain himself. "Come on," Gondo said, urging the roll call with a clenched fist, "anything but November." I wanted to open a window but didn't dare move. A change in position was a change in luck and I had been doing fine where I was.

Melville went number 111. American Lit. was not being dealt with kindly but Hawthorne was still safe. How long would I keep? No longer pure for matches arranged in Father's synagogue, I was still acceptable as an offering to Uncle Sam. Damage is relative. Jonesey's cyst disqualified him from the army but did not void him from the priesthood. He could still be a *cohen* and spread his hands in blessing. But if he had scabs, scurvy or crushed stones, if his nose lacked a ridge, if his eyebrows hung too low, if the whites of his eyes encroached upon his pupils, he would be banned from performing the priestly Benediction, but would be embraced without hesitation by his friendly, local Draft Board. The blind, of course, and the lame, the maimed, the crookbacked and the dwarf are exempt from both.

At 180, ten times *chai*, or life, Rachel's lips grazed my face, the warmth of her breath startling with its familiarity. "A few more," she whispered, "and your body comes into my safekeeping."

"Look what you did with my virtue."

"Would you like it back?" she asked, touching my thigh.

"Who needs used merchandize?"

At 200 we were clapping each other on the back, even Jonesey letting go of Sheila's hand. At 221 Gondo's number came up and at 231 Jonesey's. Hawthorne and the entire nation went #279. By then I had been marked down for number 259. It was over. On a night filled with numbers I would be designated class of 1969A, special non-com category. I was officially a person who would not and had not. Hardly a witness, I was the ultimate bystander. Somehow I had managed to live through the entire decade on second-hand experiences. The national events were brought to me courtesy of television, ABC, NBC, CBS affiliates from Dallas and Memphis and L.A. and Chicago, even from the moon; pooled resources, no competition, no waiting. The local events had come by word of mouth. Not having done much, I tried to know people who had. I was a careful court stenographer. I heard an eyewitness account of LaFayette Park, was once introduced to the brother of a Viet Vet, had played soccer in a Brooklyn College gym class with a bearded fellow in SDS who everybody knew was a member of the Weathermen. Jim Lang, the Melville man, has told me of dropping acid in a Denver commune. I also count among my acquaintances Rachel's friend Jeri who was in the process of screwing her way back down First Avenue bars, moving against traffic. And sitting alone in Far Rockaway during the summer I heard tell of doings off in Mexico, in the Zona Roja, (a version of Greenwich Village although it translates closer to the red light district), where two American girls avoid other tourists in college sweatshirts but are helplessly drawn to a boy in shades dressed in the uniform of Billy Shears, the leader of Sergeant Pepper's Lonely Hearts Band. And is not my permanent seat on Eastern Parkway, my *pisgah,* my observation post, confirmed, down to the installation of a small metal name plate, by the fact that I am the intimate of people who have survived both Bergen-Belsen and a Ukrainian death march?

248

So. The results are officially in. I would be a non-participant, raised to the highest rank of inactivity granted to a civilian during war-time. A drop-out from rabbi school and a graduate of the decade marked by an asterisk, no one ever to accuse me of being a Jewish do-gooder, I was designated finally as a irreligious non-doer and as an unmarked but wounded draftee of the marital wars. Right, Rach?

After we chopped Gondo's dark brown chunk of hashish with a brown handled knife (meat or dairy?) and mixed the corkscrew shreds with the tobacco of Shelia's Larks, rolling awkwardly stiff new smokes that burned much too slowly, after Jonesey and Sheila added to our joy by confirming what his loud lip smacking had long suggested, that they were engaged to be engaged and Sheila would therefore not be moving in with Rachel, everyone went home. I stayed to help Rachel clean, sharing work without the need for articulating division of chores. After we washed the mugs and hung them upside down to dry on the plastic tongues of the draining trays and scraped the potato chip remnants from the crevices in the carpeting, the golden chips difficult to find in the amber folds, and after letter K had been selected to be called 17th, and thus 6 slots later than normal order, in other words, as my adolescence in the world of war seemed infinitely extended, Rachel and I faced each other.

"How did Jonesey get his hair to stay down?" she asked, pulling me against her amid the beads of her alcove.

"Sheila's magic touch," I answered, speaking as always when we were alone in her house a bit more softly, as if afraid of being overheard.

We stood there like that, resting against each other, our heads away from each other, necks touching. Once again I was conscious of how much warmer than I she always was. "You know, Rach," I said, my breath disturbing the shorter hairs on the back of her neck that had escaped from the polished bone of the clasp, "that job is mine if I want it, even without the *yammie*."

"He's not going to help you."

"Yes, he will. I would if I were him, just to prove I wasn't prejudiced against sinners."

"Generous."

"No, superior. It's a way of showing it."

When she said nothing, I said, "It starts at 12 thousand." She still said nothing, so I pulled back and looked at her. "What do you say?"

She smiled. "Half the rent is 80 dollars."

"Half a hall would cost more but they'll let you arrange the cold cuts."

"You were only liberated an hour ago," she said.

I nodded. "That's exactly it. And now it's my choice." In answer she began to trace my face, beginning with the line of the eyebrows, watching me carefully with a painter's half eye, as if trying to file it in case it would not be easily available in the future. "Jason," she said, "you have such a strong sense of obligation."

"It has nothing to do with that."

"Then you're much too religious still."

I pulled her hand away. "Religious?" Other than where I had grasped her hand we were not touching anywhere. As she had traced my face I wanted to touch her breasts, by way of memorizing permanently the way they were solidly of her, their entire circumference resting on her body, their womanliness so much a part of her entire self.

"Serious," she said, "heavy. Fully explained. All the limits clear. The right way and the wrong way. Final results. Always checking with higher authorities. When I start with a piece of material, it can become anything. I don't know what it's going to be. I don't want to know till it happens. Do you understand?"

"Sure," I told her, "it's called floating. Dancing in air. Avoiding decisions. You're talking to an expert, remember? Don't you know me by now?"

"We're not talking about you. We're talking about me. About what I want."

"You mean about what you don't want," I said, stepping away from her.

Rachel shook her head. "You grew up with too many ultimatums." She came after me and leaning close, kissed me quickly on the lips. As I tried pulling back she held the back of my neck and kept me close enough to lick my dry lips and quickly kiss them again. "That's a hello kiss," she said, "I learned it from you. I want you to stay. We can get another place together. But no guarantees for my Dad or yours to sign. Just you and me. Because I do love you. And you're good for me."

But she had not been good for me. She had spoiled me for all those nice religious girls in Crown Heights and had spoiled my wants and ruined my daily desires. Saturdays would never be the same again; there was a permanent tear in the insistent wires of the Sabbath boundary that would surround my neighborhood. With Rachel's help I had made it out of the vineyards of the Orthodox. But while the Lubavitcher would be keeping the land I left behind green and safe, ahead of me lay uncharted wilderness and reluctant guide. What were the perimeters of shacking up? What were the rights and what the responsibilities? Would she light Friday night candles and buy two sets of dishes to make my transition easier? Would she take separate vacations and retain visiting rights for Gondo and silence about early years? When we go visiting David and Dora do we get to sleep together or am I assigned to the living room couch while she gets the fluffy pink of her childhood room? And if she wanted to come to my house, would she sleep in my room while I would have to stay at the Laufers', like any Orthodox boy during his engagement, only my engagement would be permanent? But back with Dave and Dora, do I, as permanent lover, dare piss now into the center of the water in the toilet bowl or do I continue to spray the sides with a minimum of sound, the assertive splash a husband's perogative? Does she retain guardianship over conception or do I assume half the responsibilities? What will our place cards say at Jonesey's wedding and how will our names be listed in other people's alphabetized phonebooks? How do we sign New Year's cards? Do we send New Year's cards? Do we celebrate anniversaries? Is there a special counselor for live-in couples? If we split up, do we go to Sheila's guru for official separation decrees?

Maybe I was being persistent in my religion, if religion was definition, a way of doing things rather than things to do. Bernie Altman claims his father never goes anywhere without considering an escape route and a hiding place, sanctuaries in case of unexpected attack or knock on the door. Moving in was nothing but escape routes. And if all I was good for was considering all sides of a question and accepting none, weighing all precedents and choosing none, seeing all possible freedoms and taking none, how was I any good to anyone?

"I don't know, Rachel. I'm not so sure."

She moved from me to the corner of her front room and searched without looking among the links of the brass chain for the switch of the hanging lamp. "Remember," she said, clicking the room into darkness, "our deodorants are compatible and you're developing a taste for my teas."

"And you a taste for Talmudic reasoning," I said.

In the doorway we kissed with short, sharp pecks, eight or nine, tiny knocks on each other's awareness rather than any confirmation of love or desire. "Call me?"

"Of course," I said, "what else?"

33.

Father's fingertips beat a call on my door the next morning. Even in the dimness of the room there was sufficient light for me to realize this was no ordinary summons. Father should have been at work. There was too much light for him to be home still. I lay without moving, unwilling to get up. It was going to be the first morning of my refusal to Rabbi Baumel. Yet here was Father, waking me for morning prayer.

The knocking came again. He was doing it with his pointing and middle finger, a steady patter. "All right," I called out, wanting only to stop the manic rhythm. I stepped into jeans I had left on the swivel chair and went to open the door, checking for my *yammie* along the way. Because I had been walking around more and more often with my head bare, not slipping the skullcap on until I was in the front hall of the house, I have been forgetting to remove it once it was on, sometimes falling asleep with the bobby pin firmly clamping my hair to the knitted material. I opened the door to Father, feeling for the pin with my free hand. "Aren't you late for work?"

"I can't tell," he said, watching my arm at my head, "whether you have anything up there."

Finally locating the pin, I held it out. "I know it's not much but you're welcome to it."

But Father was not dressed for war. When in the midst of praying, silver trimmed prayer shawl like wings, black leather of phylacteries at forehead and biceps of one arm, like the unhealed marks from previous fights, he looks impervious, an attack bird, a kamikaze plane. But he was not wearing the cape of the avenger. He was dressed in civvies, a steel gray suit cheered by bold red checks, a white shirt with collars stiffly extended, a solid tie, wider than usual, carefully shined shoes with an oval design of tiny circles at the nose, on his head a charcoal gray hat, crown neatly pinched. I had not seen him dressed so festively since the summer, had a vague memory of the suit being pushed against the deep side wall of the closet, elbowed out of the way by quieter, more sedate outfits.

"I would like to wait for you," he said. "I would like you to come with me."

Courtly Father courting, I thought. I realized I would have to go through the charade of putting phylacteries on, dragging the velvet bag from the one deep drawer of my desk and winding the thongs tightly around my left arm (seven twists) and in the shape of   around my hand and middle finger. I could read peacefully while entwined. Father would not walk in on me, but once I was outside he was not above checking to see the marks the straps had left, so I would have to twist deep and hard.

"Where to?"

He raised one finger. "I will tell you. But later." I tried to make my bare shouldered shrug indicate my indifference. "Fine with me. I wasn't going to *yeshiva* anyway."

Father nodded. "The lottery has made you a Rockefeller."

"Number two-five-nine. I did better than Eisenhower," I said, pleased he had been listening to the results.

"Numbers are like that," he said obscurely, then smiled slightly. "A leap year number is even later than your number. But there are times when numbers are meaningless." He turned towards the kitchen. "Please hurry."

Neither he nor my mother bore the blue concentration camp numbers on their arms. The men in the work gangs were not tagged and my mother's transport somehow missed it, having arrived just as the indelible ink or the steel for the needles was in short supply. The Hungarian Jews were deported very late; Allied bombers were penetrating deep enough into Germany to buzz the slowly moving trains before pulling away, screaming.

While I was still bound in the straps of the *t'filin* (the leather, despite long disuse, was soft and limber, winding itself effortlessly around my left arm), the phone rang. Hoping to forestall difficulties in case it was Rachel, I went quickly into the kitchen to find Father leaning over the portable sewing machine that stood under the wall phone. "I will tell him," he was saying, smoothing the three-cornered crocheted cloth that covered the metal top of the machine, "he can't come to the phone. He is *davening*."

Forbidden to speak during prayer, I could only look questioningly.

"Someone named Mechel or Mickey. He won the low. You are the high."

He had a question in his voice, but I simply nodded and bent back to the tiny prayer book in my hand. Facing east, I swayed silently to the Eighteen Blessings. While still held to one spot and silence, I felt Father come close and touch the phylactery on my forehead with a roughened finger. "It is chipped," he muttered, "and peeling at the corners. Damaged. You must get them fixed. Give them in and use mine for a while."

And when we were ready to go, he inspected me again, finding the loose button on my coat. Though already wearing his own coat, he could not leave me hanging. From the racks inside the door of the sewing machine, he selected a roll of gray thread just the shade of the material, slipped a silver thimble on his finger, ripped a long length of thread off the spool with his teeth, in one smooth motion slid the thread through the eyehole of the needle, evened the lengths, tied them off, was ready, the entire procedure graceful and efficient. I moved to take my coat off, but he stopped me. "Once you're on the way out, you don't make trouble by coming back in. Here."

He unrolled more thread and snapped it off with his hands. Crumpling it, he handed it to me. "Chew. Even the little you know I don't want you to forget."

What could I do? Obediently I began to chew on the thread, an ancient protection against loss of learning, although I had read it grew out of fear of death, the sewing of the shroud cloth. Chewing on the thread maintains proof of life. It is touching a cat that makes a *yeshiva* boy forget his learning. But what could I do? I stood and watched his darting needle and thread, comet and tail, wriggling spermatoid, tighten the button to the coat, stood and chewed as he whirled a circle around the stalk, tied two knots, and done, ripped the thread away with a sure hands. "There," he finally said, "it will last longer than the coat. I'll check the other buttons later."

Always meticulous, he replaced everything, waited until I spit the ragged thread into the garbage can. "They send these things out to be done in China and Japan and they fall off with a strong wind. But Landau said it was still cheaper. Do I know? I sew." Securely buttoned against the cold, I was ready.

But for what? Other than the synagogue Friday night and Saturday morning, when Crown Heights streets are filled with other father-son pairs, the two of us did not go anywhere together. I avoided it because I was too aware of being a version of him: capped son, hatted father. Visible proof of the eternal generations. Moses received the Torah on Mount Sinai and handed it to Joshua; Joshua to the elders; elders to the prophets; prophets to the Men of the Great Assembly, and so on, all the way to Montgomery Street and Kingston Avenue where yammied boys drive their hatted daddies, identical beaks, similar stances, only the most minute difference in the diffidence of the *yarmukah* to the confidence of the hat, those little bits of cloth, knitted or sewn like the opened husk of bananas, solids, stripes, checks and embroidery, all like the short pants of adolescents doing service in their fathers' house.

What I am trying to say is that other than on errands of religious significance, to *shul* or kosher butcher, I tried avoiding Father's company in order to avoid wearing the badge of obedience. When he thus said, "Drive me to Boro Park, to Thirteenth Avenue," and hurried out of the house ahead of me, I knew I was in for it, a parade through the new center of Orthodoxy, with identification prominently displayed. I selected a coat with a high collar, turned it up, clipped my yammie low in the back, tried to pretend I was the driver not the son.

Sitting next to me in the Lancer, his knees together and his hat straddling them, Father said, "You should drive in here backwards so you can just roll straight out when you're leaving."

We had both been staring straight ahead, at the blank, brick wall of Ernie's Automotive while waiting for the car to warm up, our breaths visible in the cold air. When I didn't answer, he turned to me. "Well? Wouldn't it be easier?"

For a man, I thought, who still struggled with the jambs of the car, confusing window and door locks and slamming the door too hard or too soft when leaving it, he was very free with advice. "It's tough to back in at night."

He nodded. I made an illegal turn into Montgomery Street, twisting against the reverse direction of New York Avenue, and came around to Empire Boulevard. When we passed Baumel's Sanctuary for Sunshine Soldiers I sneaked a look at him but saw no reaction. He was looking straight ahead, brow wrinkled but mouth slightly open in a sort of smile or half hearted licking of lips in anticipation, erect in spite of the soft springs of the front seat, the tip of the black *yarmukah* he always wore under his hat just an inch or two from the dome of the car.

"We had the showing at work." Father said. "I have time now."

I answered reluctantly, hesitant about direct communication. Indirection had become a successful way of dealing with one another. I wanted no confidences. Not having to talk we could concentrate on careful observation and active imagination. The sense we had of each other by those methods, even if inaccurate, was preferable to any discovery that could be learned only through direct questioning. By not confronting each other we remained whole, retaining without harm our views of ourselves and of each other.

"How was it?"

"A complete success. The *faygele* designer was so happy he gave me a bottle of something and one of the models a pair of gloves. Landau has enough orders to keep his factory busy in Japan."

His smile surprised me. It lifted his chin and the insubstantial beard so that from the side he seemed transparent and vulnerable, as if the recognition of weakness in others was somehow debilitating. We stopped for the long light at Flatbush Avenue. Turning to look across me, he pointed at the Wetson's. "Is that where the murder was?"

"It's safer around here than you think," I said, thinking of

257

my own lone wanderings along the same route to Rachel's place, where Wetson's marked the area beyond the prying eyes of the Orthodox Secret Service.

He sat in the car with his knees still up and tense, gripping his hat with both hands. Having grown up in outdoor places (a suspicion based on the solid red of the back of his neck), Father is destined never to be completely at ease in a car.

"I wouldn't be afraid to live around here," I said, making the turn into Parkside, feeling the Lancer tug in its attempt to continue up Ocean, on its customary route toward Rachel.

"It's not a neighborhood for our kind," he said flatly, "and it will get worse."

"Are we going househunting in Boro Park?" I finally asked, curious about this expedition into a rival neighborhood, one that might establish its Sabbath boundaries before Crown Heights managed it.

"That's not what I wanted to talk to you about," he said but didn't continue. Fearful of revelation I ducked more deeply into the upturned collar of the coat, feeling the hair on the back of my neck curling against skull cap, but he said nothing else.

The tennis courts at Park Circle were empty, the nets removed from their steel posts, but there were cheerful green signs up, announcing the construction of winter domes for year round games. We made it halfway around the circle but were stopped again by another light. The bridle path leading across the grassy plaza was pitted, ruts frozen. In front of us were two signs: to Ocean Parkway, great white way of Flatbush, old Jews, old money, and to Fort Hamilton Parkway, gateway to Boro Park, up and coming center of religion, new home for the Bobover Yeshiva, formerly of Crown Heights. And to Father's right, Hirsch's American Station, specialists in foreign cars.

"That's where Jonesey works," I said, pointing.

Father rubbed at the window, clearing a spot. "Yossel?"

"Yeah."

"Well, a *mazel tov* on that," then added, formally, "with God's help let it happen to you."

I had forgotten about the efficiency of the Orthodox tom-toms. Events requiring ceremonies are broadcast instantly and what events among the observant do not require ceremony?

"Is that what you wanted to talk to me about?"

"Her father," he said carefully, "is from Kassa. Before the war he had a soda factory. *His* father was a learned man. Not a big *yichus* but not to be sneered at. A *bal batishe* family. For Kellerman it is a step up. Everybody in Crown Heights knows he hasn't *dichened* in years. In Boro Park they either don't know or it doesn't matter. But that wasn't what I wanted to talk to you about."

Would they say, if I married Rachel, that Reb Kole was rising too, exchanging the tailor's cross-legged squat for the stepladder of the shade hanger? I took the ramp leading to Fort Hamilton. As the Rollerdome on my left disappeared, we left Crown Heights behind.

"A whole discussion about the happy couple and we haven't mentioned either of them. Remind me to ask Dov's father about his prospects."

"As for them, her father is buying him a partnership in the garage which will now become a *Shomer Shabbat* establishment. The happy couple has been taken care of. With God's help."

I wondered if Sheila's father had also bought Jonesey a seat on the bench next to him, closest to the East Wall of the synagogue. And would Jonesey, when established, go stealing from his Sabbath observant home for a quick shot of Kentucky Fried Chicken? But we were entering Boro Park, coming up Thirteenth Avenue under the arch of the season's decorations strung from the facings of opposing buildings, green, red, white, non-denominational star in the center. The destiny of Boro Park, ascendant. My yammie, a circlet of heat, burned.

"Drive slowly and look around. I want you to see this. This is where Jews can be religious and not worry about it."

"The Lubavitcher Chamber of Commerce would be disappointed in you."

"This is not for me," he said, "I'm not moving. We came here for you."

At the speed of light time stops. At theoretical absolute

259

zero it freezes. In amber, insects lie preserved. The things of the modern world, entering Boro Park, are dipped into the translucent lamina of Orthodoxy. Weinstock's World Wide Travel Agency closes early Fridays, stays closed Saturdays, plans its itineraries carefully around holidays, demands strict adherence to dietary laws. Microwave ovens on jumbo jets breathlessly await rabbinical dispensation. On 47th, corner of Thirteenth, Calceterra Florists tears gladiolas out of hothouses, imports summer flowers from warm climates, makes the petals of roses curl open with hot lamps for the natural look, all for the sake of *Gut Shabbes, Gut Yomtov,* and *Mazal Tov* greeting cards. Stylish young ladies in long skirts stroll with baby carriages during their midday leisure. Modest Marmets, Perego peacocks, a graceful Silver Cross with plastic sidewindows for easy viewing of the babe, a red thread prominent in joints, for warding off the Evil Eye, supplied free of charge by Berman's Baby Boutique. The girls sparkle. Their red, healthy faces glow. They control the carriages with fur gloved fingers. They wear shiny rabbit at the throat and sleeve. Mexican women labored to grease their hair, cunning men concocted rain proof coloring, nimble fingered women (like Dov's mother) combed the wigs into Doris Day flips just so that these content young women could wear the *shaitels,* keeping their own hair from the covetous gaze of men, as the Law required. Modern science does nothing more than enable the ancient laws to survive. Time clocks separate Sabbath night and Sabbath day according to the wishes of the religious rather than the vagaries of seasons; plug-in hot plates ease the day's passing. Pilot lights burning eternally permit the lighting of stoves on holidays; steam heats the rain water gathered painstakingly for ritual baths. Double breasted and wide lapeled suits from Pierre Cardin and Botany and Three G's are grist in *Shatnes laboratories* where they are tested for the separation of wool and linen; Glauber's Jewelry stocks nothing but tie clips, brooches, and belt buckles, all bejeweled with the special Sabbath key. Synthetics make shoes on fast days wearable.

But I watch the young women. Marvel how chic they are. Their skirts have always been long but now the designers have come around with the midi and made their habit fashionable. How proudly they exhibit the child in the carriage and the child clinging to the coat, little boys in fur hats, side curls jangling, little girls in coats matching mommy's, chestnut hair only slightly at odds with mother's ash blond coif. The time of the entire day is at their disposal. Time to stroll and lunch. The kosher eateries are numerous. Once past the last non-kosher food stop—Vinnie's Pizzeria at 41st Street—a smorgasboard of acceptable emporiums await the ladies' pleasure. Three kosher pizza shops, no waiting, mozzeralla is by Miller with the K, tomato sauce by Manischewitz with the u, *felafel* in pita straight from Dizengoff in Tel Aviv. Weinberg's Glatt Kosher Deli. Carvel Ice Cream under Rabbinical Supervision (the Boro Park Slurp). Famous Dairy Restaurant, haven during the lean weeks before the Ninth of Av. Nosherai. Kosher Chinese Take-Out: ground beef in the Moo-Shoo-Beef, hamburgers renamed beefburgers. The girls sample with outstretched fingers, daintily licking the drippings. Boro Park—showcase of progress, exhibition hall of religion—the K and u brands glow on the foreheads of the stores, patent retired. The world of Moses and Mount Sinai, as modified by the commentaries, maintained in the style it has been accustomed to on Thirteenth Avenue. Here the tents have been set up. No world but this world; none Jews but these Jews. I may still eat my way down the Avenue but no other part of me belonged here.

I waited in the car, unwilling to expose the back of my head, while Father went inside Kova/Hats to cover his with a satin trimmed black homburg that made him look like a bridegroom being led to the canopy. "Park as close to Fiftieth Street as you can," he said after putting the many sided hatbox with the old hat inside into the back seat. I found a spot across the street from the bus stop where people waited sitting on the cement base for the fence surrounding *Eitz Chaim Elementary,* Boro Park branch. Within the high wire fence a young man with a neatly trimmed beard watched a group of ten year olds playing punchball. The *yarmukahed* batter hit a smasher to the hatted shortstop who grabbed the ball in wind-reddened hands and threw it to the skullcapped first basemen. There was an argument. Though he was not umpiring officially, the bearded teacher accepted the responsibility of judgment and called the batter out. I could have been one of the boys. Father would have accepted their teacher as his son.

"What now?"

"Come with me. I need you."

I looked across the street, down Thirteenth Avenue. The Grand Luncheonette, Tiv-Tov Hardware and Carpeting, Goldstein's Bakery, Semel's Food Center, an arts and flower store, Mazal Dry Goods, Eagle's Electronics, F&B Food-stores. None offered purchases that seemed to require my point of view, no matter how literary or sensitive.

"I'll wait in the car."

"Come with me."

Reaching across him to open the door, I brushed against his hands holding the new homburg. Still cold from his venture outside, his fingers were at odds with the fist. The wrinkles and dark brown spots ended where the fingers began. Those fingers were long and slim and supple, still capable of a virtuoso dance in support of a silvery needle. Outside the car he came over to stand next to me on the sidewalk. He looked me over professionally, turned my collar back down, smoothed my shoulders. "You haven't bought a decent coat since I've stopped buying them for you. There is a sale at Alexander's. They bring them in from Poland."

I shook his hand off. Nodding, he walked briskly across to the bus stop where he stopped for a moment to read the latest poster from the Jewish Defense League. "It started in Crown Heights, you know," he said to me.

"Just lead on," I told him, feeling the wind stirring my yammie.

We crossed Thirteenth Avenue and began to walk, past the Luncheonette, the carpet store, the bakery, stopping finally in front of the grocery. "What do they have here we can't get in Crown Heights?"

Father raised a finger. "No sarcasm. Keep your eyes open. We'll get a carriage. Behave like a customer."

Though narrow, the store stretched. With the glass of the doors fogged and the smell of fresh rolls in the air, the aisles were narrow, comfortable tunnels. "What are we buying?"

"Anything." He began to pile boxes into the cart. Educator cookies, Tam Tam crackers, Cheerios. In the next aisle sodas—bottles of *Mayim Chaim* or living water, a kosher brand—and plastic wrapped paper goods, napkins, toilet paper, paper towels, the bulk filling the cart. I simply followed behind him, pushing the cart and arranging the tumbling packages, wondering what possessed him, curious about the relevance of his homburg to the proceedings. Though I was hot I would not unbutton my coat and had once again flipped the collar up, like the accordion collar of an Elizabethan courtier. Seeing the cart was filled, Father moved behind it, next to me, and placed a hand on the metal handle, so that we rolled up to the single cashier like the many three generational Boro Park promenaders: father, son, grandchild, kosher products down the line. But there was unexpected excitement in Father's hand, an eagerness to move ahead, an anticipation in his posture as he leaned his weight against the shopping cart, keeping its revolving rear wheels pinned against the floor and moving straight forward.

A bald man in a big black skullcap, apron around his waist, was filling the bag of an elderly woman, sliding the store bag neatly into a nylon net bag. "I could have it delivered, Mrs. Schonbrun," he was saying. "Another bag would be nice," the woman said and with a shrug, the man, presumably Mr. Semel himself, folded another bag into her nylon net. I felt Father's hand on my arm, through the coat. "Look now," he was whispering, insistent, "take a good look. Don't say anything, just look."

What was I missing? I had been piling the contents of the cart on the smooth, well-worn countertop, observing the paper bag extortion. But Father's pressure increased until I had to yank my arm away, clenching my fist, furious. Looking at him I saw him staring at the cashier. Puzzled, I looked; looked back at him still mystified. The cashier, a middle-aged woman in a blue, buttoned sweater, the kerchief on her head there to keep strands from her eyes rather than to keep men's eyes from her hair, was ringing up the items and sliding them behind her for the packager. Perhaps she moved more slowly than I would have expected and seemed more withdrawn, a look turned inward, but I figured her for the owner's wife, not a professional checker, the numbers coming by way of her eyes rather than right off her fingertips, but there was nothing remarkable about her. Yet in my ear Father's warm breath. "Look carefully."

263

At the risk of impoliteness, I whispered back. "What is it?"
"Just take a good look."

Totaled up, the cashier looked at me only briefly. She offered her hand toward Father who decorously, gently, placed a ten dollar bill in her palm. She returned change, stretching across me to do it. Our purchases, packed in two bags, were just as automatically handed to me. What could I do but accept them? "*Nu*, Reb Yid," the owner said to Father, jovial, "a *simcha*?" Sure, I wanted to say, we're celebrating Draft Liberation Day, but delivery boys and beasts of burden speak only to God. Smiling, Father said good-bye and took one of the bags from me.

Inside the car, I turned to him. "What's this all about?"
"The woman."
"The woman?"
"Nobody. A Mrs. Abraham."

I stared at him. "A nobody," he said again, speaking slowly. "Someone nobody knows. She came into the store, she spoke Yiddish, they had *rachmonos* on her, they gave her a job. Now you understand?"

But I didn't. "What does this have to do with me?"
"Laufer called me up. 'There's a woman,' he said, 'a Jew.' I thought he was mad. 'Not a match,' he told me. '*A beispiel*,' an example. She is from nowhere. Just a name. Now you understand?' I'm smarter than you are. I understood right away. 'Laufer,' I told him, 'this is not Europe and it's not a D.P. camp. Nobody gets lost here.' But I had to come and see. So I came. I can see."

I might have whispered, "*Abba*," in disbelief.

"Don't say no," he said, angry, as far from me as possible against the door of the car. "I believe it, so can you. In America anything is possible. People like your mother can disappear without a trace because they are what they are. What do they have? A social security number? A library card? Not even a number on her arm. She can start again. She did it before. We all did. We died, then we lived. That woman walked off the street. So she spoke Yiddish. Anyone from Europe could speak Yiddish. She is who she says she is. And she is alive. Do you understand? A Jew can be anybody because we can hide anywhere. We can disappear into blue eyes and white skin and straight noses. They can kill us but

264

we don't kill ourselves. We survive. We're supposed to. We get lost. Then we're found. That's all there is to it." And he took a deep breath. "And that was what I wanted to talk to you about."

I imagined Father peeking into random stores and restaurants, following familiar shapes down Brooklyn streets, eavesdropping on conversations in Queens, ever on the lookout for runaways and amnesiacs, making the rounds of hospitals in the better neighborhoods, placing lost and found ads in the *Jewish Press*, trying to match the face inside him to the faces outside, never empty because filled with hope, never lost because always searching. I wished I had not grown up estranged from kissing him because with words I could offer no comfort.

"I don't believe it, *Abba*."

"You don't believe in anything," he said flatly, "that's why I brought you here." He looked away from me. "It doesn't matter. You can go to your *shiksa* or you can stay."

"It has nothing to do with her."

"It's the generations," he said, looking at me, his face harsh, the lines rigid. "It's like a pencil. Thinner and thinner down toward the end, thin at the point, so no matter how sturdy the wood is, pressed against the paper the point breaks." With his hands he made the gesture, balancing the hat on his knees at the same time. "Snap. It's finished."

We were home before dark. I went to my room and closed the door. He didn't call me when he made dinner for himself, used, I think, to my evening absences. At seven, driven from my room by the need to go to the bathroom, I found him in the kitchen, sitting at the table. Only the night light was on. He was wearing pajamas, the collar of the shirt spread out as if welcoming the sun. He was slowly peeling an apple with a short, brown handled *parev* knife, carving the skin in a smooth arc into a paper plate. I wanted to say that it was too early but I had been away too often and did not know if this was an unusual night or if he had been going to sleep at this hour for a while now.

Leaving, I think of my arrival. Ecstatic about the birth of a Jew, a future sage, above all, a male heir, Father raises me

265

high in the air, in his arms, into the rising warmth of the heated convalescence room, lifts me high to gleam in baldness amid the white and glass of the room, holds me up and decides to name me Yaakov. It is unspoken naming, not to be uttered until the circumcision, but unsaid it is still an unavoidable sentence. I am committed to the path of the flaming cloud by night and the smoky cloud of day. It is decided. Though his skullcap is slipped to one side and his tailor's measure still hangs around his neck (he was called from work, I was sudden, surprisingly painful to my mother), my life and name are carefully chosen. Yaakov the son of Mordecai. The name of my father's father, as Mordecai was the name of his father's father and Yaakov of his father, each second generation dead, making names available. I am named Yaakov *ben* Mordecai by Father who is Mordecai *ben* Yaakov. With my senseless baby head warm in his palm, Father consigns me to his forefathers.

Dreaming of being cold, dressed insufficiently or too lightly for winter, I woke that night to find that I had fallen asleep fully and was ready for travel. I imagined a small room and a tiny kitchen somewhere in Brooklyn, Bensonhurst maybe or Red Hook or Brooklyn Heights, in any case, a place out of Crown Heights and away from Boro Park, beyond the silvery wiring of the Sabbath boundaries, a neighborhood where the streets are a little wider and the houses a bit further apart. I had nothing to pack, nothing to take away. The house, as always, would be filled.

Leaving, I took my *yarmukah* off. Folding it neatly into a half moon, I put it on my desk, placing it carefully so that it could not be mistaken for an important but familiar item accidentally left behind. I stood for a minute in the kitchen, thinking how the white, triangular shade of the night lamp made it look light the thick glass container of the fat, twenty-four hour *yahrzeit* candles. Then I left, sliding the heavy latch off the door and wondering if it would be slipped back in behind me. As I walked down the steps I sensed behind me at the window a vague shape. Resisting the impulse to turn, I continued downward, my head naked to the air. The stairs, curving, quickly turned me from the window. Though almost facing it, I could not see it.

266

Epilogue

I couldn't find a spot anywhere along Ocean Avenue. Those who had come early in the evening were staying the night. I settled finally between two driveways on East 24th Street, the line of sidewalk too short even for the Lancer so that I was violating both lanes slightly. I had to squeeze out of the car as the door opened against a thin, winter-stripped tree, then hop over soft spots in the sparse grass around it. At least the car was safely at rest. Parking was permitted on both sides of the street Wednesdays.

Foster Avenue was quiet. Though still dark at my level, higher up the air was graying. A slight thaw was on the ground, an overnight warming, false spring before it was officially winter. I walked slowly toward Ocean, bareheaded and empty handed, not quite sure if I had locked the doors of the car. I was hesitant about waking Rachel. Though leaving him behind I had tried not to interrupt Father's sleep. Yet here I was, about to walk in on Rachel during that half-sleep that comes an hour before waking, when seconds seem more insistent than usual and the sleeper can smell the cold and feel the morning light with fingertips deep in the darkness of blankets.

With the entire neighborhood entranced, I walked quietly, unwilling to add unnecessarily to my accumulating list of disruptions. But the silence was denied anyway, by a tremendous whirring and humming, like the song of crackling power lines or the drone of TV sets tuned to flickering test patterns. I looked for telephone poles or open windows but there were none. Rather than build, the sound waxed and waned, moving yet stationary, like the flapping of gigantic sheets in the

267

wind. I had stopped near a slick spot, ice thawing back into puddle, and saw a movement in the shallow surface, like the flash of fins. Wonder of wonders, magic fish in flat New York waters? But that was impossible in Flatbush, so far from the domain of magic Rabbis. Alternative directions exhausted, I finally thought of looking upward.

The sky was filled with thousands upon thousands of tiny birds, quickened against the light. Squadrons of them moved steadily forward in ragged swatches that managed to coalesce into regular formations. The cawing was all around me. The birds shifted, twisted upon themselves in tight arcs, darted away, yet continued to align themselves eventually into familiar elongated wedges, V upon wide V, like the secretive hands of the *cohanim*, palms extended in holiday benediction under the protection of their prayer shawls. Late winter birds leaving or early summer returnees to abandoned nests, their shape and call rushed down to me in the funnel of the buildings. I stood and watched them spin, heard them scream, saw them separate and unite endlessly and move steadily forward at the same time.

New York skies are squares of light at the top of airshafts. The birds were out of sight quickly and in minutes had pulled their sound after themselves. The sudden stillness startled me into a determined trot toward Rachel. I was in the front hall of the building quickly out of breath but finding the front door unlocked and my rush unimpeded, I continued swift up the stairs though more gentle finally with the three short rings of my call.

When Rachel let me in, she stood sideways, shielding herself with the door, offering me a sharp edge of hip only partially softened by her nightgown. Closing the door behind me, she turned to face me, our positions reversed. "Come on in," I said to her. We looked at each other for a few minutes in that dim morning of her hallway until I saw her shifting her bare feet, impatient with my silence and the cold. Since she wasn't coming, I went to her. Without touching her I kissed her lips but she wouldn't open for me. Letting go, I stepped back. This time she came after me, smiled, stood on my shoes with both feet to avoid the cold floor. I had to hold her to help her balance. Letting me feel her warmth against my entire length, she said, "Moving in?" I held her by the arms. We saw each other clearly. "No," I said softly, "out," but holding her I knew I would at least be staying for the morning.